**Coming soon from Hudson Lin
and Carina Press**

Going Public

Also Available from Hudson Lin

Stepping Out in Faith
Inside Darkness
Three Months to Forever
Fly With Me
Lessons for a Lifetime

Between the Tension Series

Between the Push and Pull
Embracing the Tension

Coffee House Shorts

Take Me Home
Ipso Facto ILU
My Name on Her Lips

This book contains the following subjects that some readers may find difficult:

• Car accident involving bicyclist
• Mentions of sex trafficking

HARD SELL

Hudson Lin

carina
press

carina
press®

Recycling programs
for this product may
not exist in your area.

ISBN-13: 978-1-335-50015-1

Hard Sell

Copyright © 2021 by Hudson Lin

This edition published by arrangement with Harlequin Books S.A.

For questions and comments about the quality of this book, please contact us at CustomerService@Harlequin.com.

Carina Press
22 Adelaide St. West, 40th Floor
Toronto, Ontario M5H 4E3, Canada
www.CarinaPress.com

Printed in U.S.A.

To those who are tired of the grind.

HARD SELL

Chapter One

Gazing out from the conference room, Danny Ip contemplated the brightly colored walls, the plush couches tucked into corners, the Ping-Pong table next to shelves and shelves of snacks, and the casually dressed employees mingling around a hot breakfast in the kitchen. WesTec's offices resembled every other technology start-up Danny had seen.

As did the CEO. Gray-haired and dressed in jeans and a hoodie, Cyrus West held court with his team, building camaraderie, showing them he was one of the guys, despite clearly having twenty years on most of them. It was an executive-level skill as important, these days, as knowing how to run a company.

WesTec had come onto Danny's radar a few months ago as a promising start-up, and Danny desperately needed one of those. He'd been a mainstay on the finance industry's top forty under forty list for several years now, earning a name for himself by buying up failing companies, turning them around, and selling them at a profit. But if things didn't turn around for *him* really damn quickly, he wouldn't be making the list this year.

WesTec had potential. It was on the leading edge of the alternative data industry and its people had shown themselves to be innovative and bold. But it was struggling with an issue common to companies its size: after years of operating at a loss, how do they break even and start turning a profit? That's where Danny came in. His team had spent weeks poring over every piece of information they could find on WesTec, and all signs pointed to the start-up being a winner. Now Danny needed to close the deal.

Alternative data was nascent, and only a few companies had managed to establish a viable market share. WesTec was one of them. They created software that scraped information from public—and some not-so-public—sources, analyzed the data, and provided investment recommendations to their clients. Satellite photos of parking lots showed which stores were attracting more customers, leading to more sales and increased profits. Flight plans of private jets showed which cities CEOs were visiting and hinted at the inner workings of their companies.

Information was money in the finance world, and alternative data was the new dealer on the block. In a game that could pivot by the millisecond, stock market investors needed every edge they could get. WesTec could provide it.

Cyrus West was one of those charismatic leaders who

had just enough tech knowledge to talk to the IT guys and just enough business knowledge to talk to the MBAs, but mostly, he was a pretty face who wore cool graphic tees. From what Danny could tell, he'd gotten WesTec to where it was today largely out of sheer luck. But luck never lasted forever.

Cyrus broke away from the circle of employees surrounding him and waved to Danny through the glass walls of the meeting room. Danny didn't wave back.

He burst into the room like he was the star of a show. "Hey! I'm Cyrus." He offered a handshake and when Danny took it, Cyrus tried to pull Danny toward him in an attempted power move.

Too bad Danny had at least twenty pounds of muscle on Cyrus and wasn't about to be pushed around. "Daniel Ip. Jade Harbour Capital."

Cyrus dropped into a seat, waving vaguely at the table as if inviting Danny to do the same. He leaned back, the office chair creaking in protest, and clasped both hands behind his head. "Yeah, yeah, I've heard of you. You're kind of a big deal, aren't you?"

He didn't seem enthusiastic per se, more amused at Danny's presence. He looked relaxed, laid-back, no hint of the stress he should be feeling given the state of his company's finances. Word on the street was Cyrus was difficult to work with. Didn't seem like it to Danny, at least not yet. But who knew what kind of person lay beneath the easygoing, friendly persona? What you saw wasn't always what you got in finance.

"So, what can I do for you, Danny-boy? What brings you all the way from the big city to humble little Calgary?"

Danny let himself frown. If Cyrus wanted to play it casual, Danny could do casual. But no one—no one except his friends—was allowed to call him Danny. He pulled out the chair opposite Cyrus and made himself comfortable. Maintaining direct eye contact, he said, "It's Daniel." He paused to let the instruction sink in.

Cyrus stared back for a moment before lowering his hands and re-clasping them across his lap, elbows propped up on the armrests. "Right," he said, though he didn't look thrilled to be corrected. So much for easygoing and friendly.

Danny continued. "WesTec is doing interesting things in big data."

"Damn right we are." Cyrus nodded once, a hint of pride in the simple movement.

"You've got good market share and name recognition in the industry."

"Yep."

"Promising future."

"If I do say so myself." Cyrus's smile grew wider with each compliment Danny piled on.

"Jade Harbour likes working with the best of the best."

Cyrus spread his arms like he was presenting himself for Danny's consideration. "If you're looking for the best of the best, you've found him."

Danny highly doubted that. He nodded out toward the rest of the office. "You've got a fantastic space here. I wouldn't mind a look around if you've got the time."

Cyrus didn't jump at the suggestion, which didn't surprise Danny.

"I think you'll find a signed non-disclosure agreement in your inbox." Danny had signed it himself a week ago and WesTec's legal department had confirmed they'd received it. He wasn't new to this game—no meetings in the finance world were held without strict confidentiality agreements.

It took a few seconds before Cyrus's expression went from suspicious to pleasant. If that wasn't a mask falling into place, Danny didn't know what was. "Yeah, I guess I can spare a few. Come on, let me show you around." As if it had been his idea all along.

Danny followed Cyrus out of the meeting room and into the bullpen filled with standing desks, yoga ball chairs, and aromatherapy humidifiers shooting puffs of scented mist into the air. "This is where the analysts sit. They're my superstars, making the connections no one else can."

Most people didn't even notice Danny and Cyrus weaving through their section. Those who did looked up with curiosity before quickly turning their gaze back to their screens, shoulders hunched as if weighed down by their giant over-the-ear headphones.

"My innovation team is over here." Cyrus paused near the back of a group of desks arranged in a three-sided square, all facing a giant whiteboard. One person was scribbling away on it while other members of the team shouted out ideas at random.

Cyrus leaned in with a whisper. "All my good ideas come from here."

Danny resisted the urge to correct him—if this team came up with the ideas, then they weren't Cyrus's, were they?

Cyrus led the way toward the innards of the office, far from the windows framing the Calgary skyline and the mountains in the distance. "This part is pretty boring." He waved to some desks lined up in neat, compact rows. He didn't bother stopping but spoke as he breezed through. "My lawyers, my accountants, my IT guys—not my real tech guys, you know. Just the ones keeping the AC running in the server room and helping people reset passwords and all that."

"The server room. Let's check it out." It wasn't a request.

And Cyrus noticed. He let out a chuckle suggesting he was impressed. "Guess you do know what you're talking about."

Had Danny given the impression that he didn't? His track record had years of investing in technology companies; of course he knew how important the server room was. All the company's data was stored there, everything that made the company what it was. Hardware malfunctions and security breaches were very real risks that could end a firm in the blink of an eye.

Cyrus rapped his knuckles on some guy's desk. "Hey, need you to show Danny-boy here the server room." He pointed at Danny with his thumb.

The poor guy had probably been engrossed in whatever he was studying on his screen. He looked up at Cyrus, as if startled, and blinked in confusion.

"Server room?" Cyrus repeated, pointing down a long narrow hallway. "You know, where the servers are?"

"Yeah, yeah, of course. Sure." He jumped up and stuck his hand out at Danny. "Hey, I'm Jace."

"Nice to meet you, Jace. I'm Daniel. Sorry to interrupt you."

"Oh! No problem. I'm happy to help with whatever. You wanted to see the server room?"

"Yes, please." Jace nearly jogged down the hall like this was his once in a lifetime chance at stardom. He tapped a blank white card against a card reader. The lock disengaged and he pushed the door open.

"Here it is!" He sounded much too proud to be talking about a room full of computer equipment.

Inside was noticeably colder than the rest of the office. Environmental controls whirred, pumping cool air in between the rows upon rows of black metal racks. Multicolored cables ran in neat bundles overhead.

Cyrus hung back, arms folded, peering into the room as if seeing it for the first time.

"Can you walk me through the security measures?" Danny asked.

"Yeah, sure!" Jace held up the key card he'd used. "The only people who have access to the room are me and Kai."

"Kai?"

"Oh, Kai heads up our IT department. And see that?" Jace pointed to a camera mounted on the ceiling. "Takes a picture of anyone who steps foot in here. Any unauthorized entrance, and Kai and I will get notifications on our phones." He held up his cell phone.

"We also have dual firewalls, monthly patches for virus and malware definitions. We're doing vulnerability and penetration tests every six months. All staff get fake phishing emails to see if they click on stuff they're not supposed to…" Jace went on, but that was about the extent of Danny's knowledge of cybersecurity.

Jace walked him through each row of equipment, pointing out the backup power supply, the backup internet connection, the temperature monitor, and a sprinkler system in case anything caught fire. Guess the IT guys did more than keep the air conditioning running.

"Anything else I can show you?" Jace asked, eyes wide and eager.

"No, that's all." Danny gave him a grateful smile. "I wouldn't understand any more even if you did."

"You've had enough?" Cyrus was leaning against the doorframe, looking bored.

"Thanks for your time, Jace." Danny shook the guy's hand before motioning to Cyrus to lead them out.

Back in the conference room, Cyrus assumed his laid-back, casual attitude again. "So, what do you think? Impressive, eh?"

"Sure." The office was, and if Jace was any indication, WesTec's staff were too. Cyrus? Not so much.

"Well, now that you've had a look under the hood, let's talk about why you're really here." There was an edge to Cyrus's voice that hadn't been there earlier. The time for pleasantries was over.

Danny got right to the point. "You have cash flow problems."

Cyrus let out a single chuckle, as if he hadn't expected Danny to go straight in for the kill. "Hold your horses, I wouldn't call it a problem exactly. It's not easy doing what I do. Equipment is expensive. People are expensive. I want to give my clients the best and that ain't cheap." He broke out a placating smile. "Let's say I'm in the investment phase."

"And Jade Harbour would like to invest."

That usually had people sitting up straighter, giddy with the idea of millions of dollars flooding their bank accounts. But Cyrus sobered, like prey sensing the presence of a threat.

"Who says I'm looking for investors?"

"I did."

"Maybe I already have some lined up."

Possible, but highly unlikely. Jade Harbour had networks all over the place, and the information they fed back told Danny no one wanted the hassle of dealing with Cyrus West. If he had any other option, he wouldn't bother either.

They locked eyes and Danny settled into the extended silence. He would bet his newish Audi R8 these supposed investors were nothing but a figment of Cyrus's imagination.

Cyrus blinked first. It didn't take him long. His gaze shifted over Danny's shoulder as if distracted by what was going on outside. Then his eyes lit up and he jumped to his feet, waving at someone walking by.

What now?

He yanked open the door and dragged someone in by their elbow.

"Hey! Tobes, my man. Come in here."

Tobes was tall and slim. Dark brown oxfords polished to a shine. An off-the-shelf suit tailored to fit his frame. His hair was stylish, one of those short on the sides and long on the top designs so popular with young people these days. Danny could appreciate a well-dressed man. Then he took a second look at Tobes and the whole room flipped upside down.

"Danny?"

This wasn't Tobes. This was Toby. The awkward kid who followed Danny and Wei around all the time. The Lok family baby who so desperately wanted to be grown up.

Wei had been Danny's best friend since before he could remember. Growing up together, Toby had been as much Danny's kid brother as he was Wei's. As children, they'd been almost inseparable, but then Danny had gone off to university and business school and then straight into a demanding career in finance. By the time he'd stopped to catch his breath, Toby had grown up and moved across the country to Vancouver. Danny hadn't seen or spoken to Toby in almost a decade.

Except for one weekend seven years ago. The one fateful night Danny would never forget.

"Toby."

Toby broke out a smile that bordered on a cringe. "I go by Tobin now. You know, more professional." Except the way he shrugged reminded Danny exactly of the little boy from years past.

"Wait, you two know each other?"

Damn it. Danny had completely forgotten about Cyrus. Seeing Toby—no, Tobin—again was like getting tossed in a mixing bowl and coming out not knowing which way was up. Joy, nervousness, and embarrassment volleyed through

Danny so quickly, he could barely differentiate one from the other.

"Well, damn. It really is a small world, isn't it?" With both hands on Tobin's shoulders, Cyrus led him toward a chair and pushed him into it.

Tobin didn't resist. He threw Danny a sheepish look but directed his answer to Cyrus. "Danny's my brother's best friend." Not that it was any of Cyrus's business.

"Is that so?"

The smile he gave Danny over Tobin's head made him want to punch the guy's face in.

"You grew up together, eh?" Cyrus still had his hands on Tobin's shoulders, making it awkward for Tobin to look up at him. "That means he knows about you, right?"

Danny nearly jumped to his feet to get in Cyrus's face. What the hell was he trying to say?

"What? That I'm gay?" Tobin's voice held more than a hint of steel. "Yeah, he knows."

If Cyrus thought outing Tobin would give him the upper hand, he was sorely mistaken.

"Do you have a problem with us being gay?" Danny dared him to say yes.

Cyrus didn't miss Danny's carefully selected words. "You're gay too, eh? Wow. Lots of gays wandering around these parts. Times sure have changed."

They sure fucking had, and if Cyrus didn't take his paws off Tobin soon, Danny was going to remove them for him.

"Uh, I'm sorry." Tobin pushed out his chair and turned in the same motion, effectively dislodging Cyrus's touch. "Did you need me for something?"

"Oh, yeah, yeah, I did, Tobes. You were just the man I was looking for." Cyrus dropped into a seat again. The chair creaked under his weight. "You see, Danny-boy here wants to *invest* in my little company. What do you think about that?"

Tobin glanced from Cyrus to Danny and back. "Oh, um, well, I'd have to look at the numbers before I form an opinion. But I can definitely do that. Are you considering an external investor?"

"No."

Tobin was momentarily speechless at Cyrus's curt answer, but he rebounded quickly. Smart kid. "Okay, well, outside investment is always an option and I was going to look into that as a possible way forward. But if it's not something you're interested in, I can de-prioritize it."

From what Wei had told Danny, Tobin had gone into management consulting at a boutique firm, helping clients cut costs and generate revenue. If he was here, then WesTec must be in worse shape than Danny had suspected. People like Tobin were called in to help struggling companies avoid bankruptcy. Maybe Danny could use this to his advantage.

He let a satisfied smile slip through and reached for the preliminary term sheet his team had drawn up. He slid one copy across the table to Cyrus, and then his spare copy to Tobin for good measure. After all, Tobin needed a complete set of information if he wanted to help keep WesTec from dissolving. As far as Danny was concerned, selling to Jade Harbour was the best option they had.

"At Jade Harbour, we pride ourselves on providing a sup-

portive growth environment for our portfolio companies."
Danny could recite the spiel in his sleep. Hell, it was written on their website. "We take a collaborative approach to
working with founders and management teams. You came
up with the idea, it's your baby. We're here to help you
nurture the baby until it can stand on its own two feet."

Danny nodded to the package Cyrus had yet to touch.
"I think you'll find our offer quite generous."

Out of the corner of his eye, Danny caught Tobin flipping through the term sheet with a slight crease between
his brows. If Tobin was any good as a management consultant, he probably wouldn't be impressed by the numbers
he found. Calling this initial offer generous was, well, generous, but no one started a negotiation with the number
they were actually willing to pay.

Cyrus certainly didn't look impressed. He took one
glance at the deal summary page and pushed the package
away from him. "Aw, come on. You're pulling my leg,
aren't you, Danny-boy?"

"I don't know what you mean."

Tension reverberated between Danny and Cyrus, a silent
struggle for power that would have painted the room red
if it'd been visible. Tobin fidgeted in his seat as it dragged
on, but Danny had no intention of giving in to Cyrus's
bullying.

It was Tobin who broke the silence first. "Uh, well, unless there's anything else you need from me..."

Cyrus didn't respond. Neither did Danny.

"I believe the finance team is waiting for me...so I should

go." Tobin rose slowly, as if any sudden movement would ignite the pressure in the room.

"Uh, it was good to see you again, Danny. I'll, uh… catch up with you later?"

Danny blinked once, deliberately and calmly. He wasn't surrendering. He was declaring himself the victor. He stood and gathered his things before turning to Tobin. "It was good to see you again too. Walk me out?"

Tobin shot a look at Cyrus as if seeking his permission. But he caught himself a second later and straightened, rising to his full height.

Danny's chest expanded with pride.

"Yeah, sure. I can walk you out."

Neither said goodbye to Cyrus and he didn't try to stop them. Didn't even bother getting out of his chair.

Danny adjusted the watch on his wrist as he headed out. If only he didn't need a win so god damn badly. He would love to march back into the meeting room and rip up the offer right in front of Cyrus West's face. What smarmy remark would Cyrus have then?

Unfortunately, Danny did need a win and, even more unfortunately, WesTec was his best shot. Maybe his last shot. Jade Harbour's financial backers were starting to notice that his once stellar track record wasn't looking so stellar lately. His ass was on the line, which left Danny with very few options.

Outside, he stopped, still vibrating with adrenaline from the confrontation.

"That was pretty badass." Tobin looked back through the

doors they'd exited, as if Cyrus was going to come bursting through them at any minute.

Perhaps it was, but Danny saw no reason to take pride in it. His job was to close deals and sometimes the sellers needed a little encouragement.

Tobin turned to him, and suddenly WesTec and Cyrus West didn't matter anymore.

Was he dreaming? Was Tobin really standing in front of him? Chubby cheeks had given way to sculpted cheekbones. A bit of acne scarring on his skin made Tobin look even more adult. He held himself with such self-assurance; like he'd grown into too-big clothes that now fit him just right. He was striking. He would turn heads when walking down the street. Danny's body certainly made its interest known.

Danny took a step backward, needing the extra foot of distance between them. Seven years ago, he had succumbed to Tobin's appeal. There may be years and geography between them, but one thing hadn't changed. Tobin was undoubtedly special.

Did he remember that night as vividly as Danny did?

A shy smile tugged at Tobin's lips, as if he'd read Danny's mind, and Danny couldn't help but return it. It didn't matter what Tobin did or did not remember. They were... childhood friends, practically family, connected in a way Danny didn't have words for. It'd been too long since they were in touch. No matter their reasons for drifting apart.

"Are you free for dinner tonight?"

Tobin's smile exploded at Danny's invitation. "Yes! Yeah,

definitely, totally. Uh…" He patted his pockets. "Shit. I think I left my phone upstairs."

Danny reached into the inner pocket of his suit jacket and pulled out a business card. Always be prepared. "Here. Give me a call when you're done, and I'll send a car around."

Tobin took the card and ran a thumb over the embossed letters, as if committing them to memory. He clutched the card in his hand. "Oh, I, uh… I can meet you wherever."

"Don't worry about it. I'll send a car for you."

Tobin looked a little taken aback, almost as if he was going to put up a fuss. But then he chuckled and nodded. "Okay, sure. I guess I'll give you a call when I'm done." He held up the card in a wave as he walked backward toward the doors. "See you later."

Danny nodded and watched Tobin go. At the building's main entrance, Tobin stopped and glanced back at Danny as if checking to make sure he was real.

Danny felt exactly the same way.

Chapter Two

Danny turned the glass tumbler round and round on the bar top. The amber liquid glowed in the dim lighting. Jazz music played softly through the lounge's speakers and the hum of easy conversation filled in the gaps.

It was an impressive restaurant, at one of Calgary's upscale hotels. Leather seats, velvet walls. Clientele equipped with platinum credit cards. A replica of hundreds of other hotels around the world. How many had Danny been to? Too many to count.

Wei was always commenting on how exciting Danny's life was. Jetting off to new destinations on a weekly basis, fancy hotels and even fancier restaurants. Rubbing elbows with the rich and mega-rich. But after a while, even the most luxurious venues lost their appeal.

Danny had been feeling it recently, an apathy toward the

things that used to get him going. Tracking his quarterly performance numbers as they inched upward. Collecting enough airline loyalty points to graduate to the next level of perks. Sliding into the back of a fancy town car and watching the rest of the world stream by.

This was a life he'd only dreamed of as a kid with a single mom who worked more hours than not. He'd set his sights on it as a young man and did everything in his power to achieve it—some of which he wasn't overly proud of. But what good was any of it at the end of the day?

This question had started nagging him a couple years ago, initially no more than a wisp of doubt he easily brushed aside. But it'd grown more insistent in the past several months. Enough that he couldn't ignore it anymore. Enough that his work was suffering for it.

Joanna Chiang, his boss, had pulled him into her office last month to issue a warning. Get his head on straight or else he'd be looking for a new job. It'd been a wake-up call at the time, but now, with a month of perspective, the warning didn't feel so dire anymore.

What the hell was he thinking? Danny tossed back the rest of his drink and pushed the glass away. This was who he was. This was everything he'd wanted in life. Besides, Jade Harbour had been his professional home since he'd started his career and he owed it to Joanna to be at the top of his game.

He stood and stretched, rolling his shoulders to get the kinks out. Movement at the restaurant's entrance caught his attention.

Ah, Tobin. Still dressed in the suit from earlier, one hand in a pocket, the other held palm against stomach. He'd already spotted Danny and they gazed at each other from across the expanse of the restaurant like silly long-lost lovers.

There was something about seeing Tobin standing there, handsome and dapper, that stirred an age-old longing in Danny. Tobin was a beacon, drawing him in. It must be Tobin's association with the only home Danny had ever experienced; Danny was lonely, a little homesick, and Tobin had shown up at exactly the right time.

They walked toward each other, synchronized to some invisible rhythm. As they got closer, Tobin's eyes smoldered with makeup that hadn't been there during the day. Not tons, but enough for Danny to notice in an entirely unbrotherly way.

Danny sucked in a breath. That wasn't why they were here. They were old friends catching up on life. He was checking in on Tobin on Wei's behalf. They were essentially siblings. There was no reason to notice how sexy Tobin looked.

"We have your table ready, sir." A voice broke through Danny's thoughts. "If you'll follow me." The restaurant host led them to a cozy rounded booth near the back.

Danny slid into one side and Tobin slid into the other. Their knees banged under the table. Tobin cast Danny a shy smile and shifted his legs. "Sorry."

Danny fought the impulse to hook his ankles around Tobin's and draw them closer together. He cleared his throat and deliberately kept his feet tucked as far away from Tobin as space allowed.

"So, how have you been?" Tobin fingered the cloth napkin as if it was made of the finest material. His nails were well-manicured; a hint of a dark color around the edges suggested he'd only recently removed some nail polish.

Better now that you're here. Where the hell had that thought come from? But it was true. He was breathing a little easier now than before Tobin arrived. The weight he'd grown so used to carrying around didn't seem quite so heavy all of a sudden.

"Good. I'm fine."

Tobin shot his kohl-lined gaze in Danny's direction and it was all Danny could do to hold it. He'd spent years constructing a polished and imposing mask that stood up to the most discerning of folks in the one percent. But would it work on Tobin? After all, Tobin knew the person Danny had been before even the idea of the mask existed. Could Tobin see how tired he was? How bored he was?

If he did, he didn't bring it up. Thank god.

"How's Wei? Constance and the kids?"

Danny was pretty sure Tobin already knew. "They're good. Don't you keep in touch with them?"

Tobin gave a one shoulder shrug as if a full one wasn't worth the effort. "Not as much as they'd like."

"How much is that?"

Tobin tilted his head and rolled his eyes. "Mom calls me at *least* once a week to talk about everything and nothing. Wei messages me every other day with pictures of the twins. If I don't respond within a few hours, he'll call to make sure I'm still alive."

Danny had to laugh. It sounded so quintessentially Wei.

"Oh my god, and Dad? He calls to see if I have enough clothes to wear. As if I'm not more than capable of buying my own clothes."

From Tobin's outfit today, Danny had no concerns about the state of his closet. "They miss you."

Tobin rolled his eyes again, harder than the first time. "Yeah, I know. It's just…" He heaved a sigh. "It's a little much."

Perhaps. But that kind of attention sounded wonderful to Danny. He didn't have anyone calling him to chat about nothing or to see if he lacked any of life's necessities. Now that Wei was busy with a family, they only got to hang out when Danny went over to help with the twins.

"Why do you think I moved to the other side of the country?"

Danny had suspected as much. "So you're liking Vancouver?"

The slight hesitation in Tobin's response was surprising, but he recovered quickly. "Yeah, you know, it's good! It's not as cold as Toronto. People are more chill."

"But?"

Tobin grimaced like he was loath to answer. "No, but. You know, it's expensive. There's not much of a nightlife. The great outdoors is only fun for so long. And I don't have a car, so it's basically impossible to get anywhere. But I still like living there."

If he did, he wasn't doing a good job of convincing Danny. "What do you like about it? Besides the weather and the people?"

Tobin propped his chin in his hand and gazed off toward the ceiling in contemplation. If the question required this much thinking, Danny wasn't sure Tobin liked Vancouver at all.

"I like the freedom. Doing my own thing, on my own terms. I don't have to answer to anyone."

Danny stood corrected. In fact, he could see the difference between the Tobin sitting before him now and the younger Tobin, who had always struggled to break free of his family's well-intentioned smothering. He looked lighter, brighter, like he could breathe easier. It left a warm, glowing feeling in Danny. "I'm really glad to hear that."

Tobin's shoulders inched up in a mini-shrug, as if he were a little embarrassed to admit it. "And I love my job. I got promoted to project lead a little while ago, so I'm heading up my first project now."

"WesTec," Danny guessed.

"Yep!" Tobin sobered, as if only then remembering their encounter that morning. "WesTec."

"Congratulations."

"Thanks."

The waiter stopped by their table. "Hi there, ready to order?"

"Yes, steak, rare. With a Greek salad. And the 1992 French Bordeaux." Danny ordered without looking at the menu. All the menus in places like these were the same and Danny had long ago learned what was worth ordering.

Tobin, though, scrambled for the big leather-bound folio, quickly scanning its contents. "Um, I'll have the…" His eyes widened as he read the menu. "I'll have the burger."

"How would you like it done?"

Tobin blinked at the waiter for a moment before recovering. "Oh! Right, um…medium."

"And with fries or the house salad?"

"Fries. Definitely fries."

Danny smiled. Kid Tobin had loved fries too.

He watched Tobin as Tobin watched the waiter walk away. His gaze wandered around the dining room before returning to Danny. "You always eat in places like this?"

"Yes."

"Glamorous."

"A little."

"Only a little?"

Danny chuckled. "Okay, a lot. It's not like you've never been to upscale restaurants before."

Tobin took on a look of mock offense. "Not in a long time. And never on my own. Besides, upscale Chinese restaurants in the suburbs of Toronto are nothing compared to this."

That much was true. Tobin's family was firmly in the upper class. But despite living in one of the more opulent neighborhoods in the Greater Toronto Area, they were never ones to shell out cash when more affordable options were available. Hell, Danny still remembered the bootleg DVDs they watched in the family's home theatre suite.

It had been a world away from the one-bedroom apartment Danny had shared with his mom. The fridge was always empty, the air dusty. If his mom happened to be home, she'd usually be asleep from having pulled double shifts as a nurse. It was why Danny had spent so much time at the Lok house. Doing homework with Wei after school, eating dinner with the family, falling asleep on Wei's bedroom floor when his mom got caught up at work.

"We've come a long way," said Tobin.

At first Danny thought he was referring to Danny's

childhood as a charity case. But no. That's not what Tobin said. "We?"

"Yeah. We."

Was Tobin still talking about his hard-won freedom? Or something to do with his finances?

"You know I don't live off my parents' money, right? I haven't since I moved out for undergrad."

No, Danny hadn't known the details, but he wasn't surprised given Tobin's independent streak.

"I mean, not even tuition. I basically cut myself off from them the moment I wasn't living under their roof."

Now that was news. "Not even tuition? How did you get away with that?" Danny could not imagine Uncle Man and Auntie Grace being okay with Tobin fending for himself on the other side of the country.

Tobin gave a half shrug, like it was no big deal. "They tried to send me money. I donated it all to charity. Eventually, they stopped sending me money."

Danny was impressed. Tuition wasn't cheap, not to mention books, food, rent. He should know. He'd scraped together the funds for it all, mostly by himself. Plus a little help from the Loks. The mysterious fifty-dollar bills that "fell" into his bag whenever he was over. The red envelopes containing thousands of dollars right when tuition was due. The brand-new "hand-me-down" suits that were exactly Danny's size and yet fit no one else in the family.

They'd never said a word about it. Neither had Danny. He had taken what they had offered, and everyone had gone about their business as if it were all normal behavior.

Danny lowered his chin to his chest, staring at his hands

clasped on the table in front of him. Everyone thought he was a self-made man. That he'd pulled himself up by the bootstraps—if he could do it, coming from a single-parent home with barely enough income to survive, then anyone could. What people didn't know was that he'd had the Loks, and he wouldn't be nearly as successful if it hadn't been for them.

And here was Tobin, with all the resources in the world and parents who were generous to a fault, refusing to rely on the leg up. Determined to forge his own way in the world, based solely on his own skills and capabilities. Tobin put Danny's success to shame.

"Hey, you okay?" Tobin reached across the table and put his hands on top of Danny's. "I didn't mean to make myself sound like Mother Theresa or anything. I mean, I got lucky with scholarships and part-time jobs. Paid summer internships for the win!"

Danny forced a smile for Tobin's sake. He deserved to brag about himself, he'd worked hard. Instead of his little pity party, Danny should be congratulating him.

"That's fantastic. I'm really happy for you."

Tobin's smile was smug, and he had every right to be. "Well, you know. Little Toby always trying to prove he's one of the big boys."

Tobin held Danny's gaze long enough for Danny to suspect they weren't really talking about financial independence. Tobin dropped his chin and peeked up through thick black lashes, a smile rivaling the Mona Lisa's on his lips. Danny's mouth went dry and his gut clenched. No, they were definitely not talking about finances.

Seven years ago, they'd sat in a booth not unlike this one,

in a Banff hotel not far outside of Calgary. They'd been alone then too, with Wei and his bachelor party domineering the dance floor. Tobin had smiled exactly like that. Danny remembered the feeling of words whispered against the shell of his ear. Then the next thing he knew, they were naked in bed together and Danny had never felt so much at home.

The waiter returned. Danny focused on the elaborate steps for pouring a sample of wine, taking a sip to give his approval, and then filling up two glasses with the perfect amount of liquid.

He nearly drained his first glass in one gulp.

"You have a boyfriend." Gone was the expertly veiled flirtation. Tobin sounded resigned.

Danny nearly choked on his wine. "No." He didn't have time for a boyfriend. Hell, he barely had time for Wei.

"You never called."

The accusation slapped Danny in the face. *He* never called? He was the one who'd woken up the next morning to a cold bed and an empty room. The only evidence Tobin had even been there was a note scrawled on hotel stationery. *Thanks for last night.* "I didn't know you wanted me to call."

Tobin let out a huff. "Would you have if I'd asked you to?"

Yes hovered on the tip of Danny's tongue, but he caught himself. Would he have? Under the bright light of day, without the blurry euphoria of alcohol, would Danny have had the guts? At the time, he'd been on the cusp of making it. He'd already been singled out as an up-and-coming name to watch in the finance world. Wei had had to throw down an ultimatum to pull Danny away from work and to the bachelor weekend. Not to mention the whole mess of Tobin being Wei's little brother.

If he were honest, no, he probably wouldn't have.

"Yeah, that's what I thought."

The waiter returned again, this time with their food. Tobin grabbed the ketchup bottle and squirted a sea of red onto his fries, then began to eat them one at a time.

How had Tobin expected him to answer? Danny stabbed his steak and cut into it a little more aggressively than needed. The perfectly cooked piece of meat separated like butter under a hot knife.

It wasn't like they were strangers meeting in a bar, exchanging phone numbers in case a fling turned into something more. They knew each other. They had history. One could even call it baggage. What would Wei have said if he'd found out? If Auntie Grace or Uncle Man found out? There was more to it than whether Danny called or not. How did Tobin not understand?

"Sorry," Tobin mumbled as he used a fry to trace circles in the ketchup. "That wasn't fair."

And just like that, all his righteous indignation evaporated as if it had never existed. He never could stay angry with Tobin, not in any real way. "It's okay. I should have called. Even if it was to make sure you were okay."

Tobin nodded with a tight smile. "I was okay," he said unconvincingly before popping another fry into his mouth.

Almost all his fries were gone now, but he hadn't touched his burger.

"Is the patty cooked to your liking?" Danny nodded at Tobin's plate.

It took a second for the confusion to clear on Tobin's face and he looked at his burger as if only now remembering it was there. "Oh, yeah, I'm sure it's fine. I, uh…" He gave a half shrug. "Sometimes, I don't like mixing my food."

Right, the admission brought back memories of Uncle Man chiding Tobin at the dinner table. *Why are you eating one thing at a time? Eat it all together!* And then Auntie Grace would smack her husband on the arm and tell him to leave Tobin alone. *As long as he eats everything, it doesn't matter!*

Tobin still did that?

"Don't laugh." Tobin pointed a fry at Danny like he was wielding a weapon.

Danny held up both hands in surrender. "I'm not."

"You are. Inside. I can tell."

"I would have thought you'd outgrown that."

"I have, for the most part. But sometimes when…" Tobin took a deep breath and let it out in a huff.

"When what?"

Tobin gazed at Danny with that penetrating look and Danny got the profound sense he was being evaluated. Was he trustworthy enough for Tobin's secret? "Never mind. You don't have to answer."

A crease formed between Tobin's brows. "It's fine." He dropped his chin and poked at the burger bun. "I only do it when…when I'm upset."

Which in this case was because of Danny. Damn. The realization cut through him like a knife. "I'm sorry."

Tobin shook his head but didn't meet Danny's eyes. "It's okay. I get it. I'm just baby Toby, right?"

Yes, but no. He wasn't—the number of times they'd fucked

that night was evidence enough. But Danny couldn't ignore Wei and Auntie Grace and Uncle Man. They'd done so much for him. Tobin might not have been a baby to Danny anymore, but he'd always be the baby of the Lok family.

Danny took a bite of his steak, but the juicy tender meat didn't taste as good as it had a moment before. He still ate it and washed it down with a mouthful of wine.

"Anyway." Tobin shook his head as if the motion could disperse their complicated past. He ate his last fry before changing the subject. "I'm sorry about your mom."

Damn, the past was really catching up with him today. A pang of nostalgia burst in Danny's chest at the mention of his mom. The woman he loved and who loved him back, even though they barely knew each other. When Danny had started earning enough to support both of them, he had forced her to retire. That was the same year she'd gotten her diagnosis.

"She'd fought a long battle. She was ready to go." He'd been by her side, holding her hand, though it hadn't been clear who was comforting whom.

"I'm sorry I didn't go to the funeral. I wanted to, but Mom said I should stay at school."

Danny remembered Auntie Grace mentioning something about exam season and Danny had agreed there was little point in Tobin flying all the way back to Toronto for the intimate ceremony they'd planned. In the end, a lot of people Danny didn't know had shown up for the service. Apparently, his mom had touched more lives than he'd realized.

"I remember Auntie Helen would give us our flu shots every year," Tobin said with a wistful smile.

Danny found himself matching it; he remembered the flu shots too.

"She always gave us candy after."

"You always got to pick first."

"I *was* the baby. It's got to be good for something."

Danny's smile widened. Tobin's did too. And then they were staring into each other's eyes again.

Seven years.

A whole childhood.

So much that could have been and could never have been. Dreams Danny had written off as fanciful delusions resurfaced like a sharp pain in his chest. Sometimes he wanted so much, he could hardly breathe. But he already had so much. What right did he have to ask for more?

As it had done earlier when Cyrus pulled Tobin into their meeting, the whole room flipped upside down. This was merely dinner between old friends, he told himself. Nothing more. And yet, Danny could feel his carefully ordered life begin slipping through his fingers.

The waiter came around again, placing a small folder on the table. "Take your time. No rush."

They both reached for it. Tobin's hand landed on top of Danny's.

"I'll get this." Danny pulled the folder toward him, but Tobin grabbed his wrist with a surprising amount of strength.

"No." His voice was steely with determination. "I can pay my half." His eyes dared Danny to disagree.

Chapter Three

Tobin almost lost his nerve and let Danny pay for their overpriced dinner. But at the last second, Danny relented, loosening his grip on the folder.

"Okay. We'll split it."

Oh, thank the heavens above. He never bothered fighting over the check when he was with his family. There was no point—he'd always lose. But since he moved out, paying for himself had become one of those hills he would die on. He'd paid for himself as a poor student, and he could pay for himself now that he was earning a respectable adult salary. Besides, this was a work trip and Paradigm should be picking up the bill.

As Danny waved the waiter back and asked for the bill to be split, Tobin took a bite of his burger. Even cold, it was good. Still, he would have been happy with a combo meal from McDonald's.

The Danny sitting across from him was different from the one he'd grown up with. Not better or worse, just different in ways Tobin never would have expected. The custom tailored suit, the shiny gold watch, the authoritative and entitled way he held himself. It was going to take a bit of getting used to.

What *had* Tobin expected, though? He knew Danny was successful. It was kind of hard to ignore when he regularly sent Mom and Dad off on luxury cruises or got his hands on the not-yet-released hottest toys for Wei's kids. Hadn't he gotten Mom that limited edition Chloé handbag last Christmas? Sure, Tobin grew up wealthy and privileged, but these days Danny was next level.

Yet, there was still a little bit of the old Danny in there somewhere. Tobin could see it peeking through every now and then, but only because he knew what to look for. The older boy with the buzz cut, who looked like he could and would take on anyone in a fistfight. His silent intense stare that instilled fear in playground bullies had morphed into intimidation in the boardroom. Seeing Danny handle Cyrus that morning? Hot. Really hot.

Like, jerking off fantasy–level.

Everyone had said he'd grow out of his childhood crush on Danny. He'd thought maybe he would too. But then he'd turned nineteen, gotten drunk at Wei's bachelor party, and decided to test the theory. He hadn't grown out of it then, and it didn't look like he'd grown out of it since. If anything, those childhood daydreams had matured into adult-rated fantasies.

Tobin shifted and gave his chubby a mental note to calm the heck down. "Do you come to Calgary a lot?" He took another bite of his cold burger.

Having polished off his steak and salad with record speed, Danny leaned back against the plush padding of the booth. Tobin kept his eyes trained on his burger for fear of drooling over the image of carefully restrained power.

"I'm here more these days than I used to be. There are a number of promising technology start-ups in the city."

"Like WesTec."

"Like WesTec."

Awk-ward. Usually, Tobin didn't mind getting pulled into random last-minute meetings by clients. It gave him a scoop on the inner workings of the company he was trying to save, and the more information he had, the better able he was to do his job.

But he'd never expected to get dragged into a meeting room and confronted by Danny Ip. "You're trying to buy them out?"

"That's the idea."

"The offer you made was kind of shitty." Tobin didn't know tons about the private equity corner of the finance world; they were the cool kids in the yard. Tobin was over in the teacher's pet corner, vying for brownie points from the client in hopes it would result in more consulting work down the line. A client couldn't hire Paradigm for future consulting contracts if the client went belly-up.

But he knew enough about valuing companies to know

WesTec was worth more than what Jade Harbour was offering.

Danny smirked, looking amused and impressed. "It's an opening bid."

"So you plan on going higher?"

"That's how the negotiating game is played."

Right. When he thought about it, buying and selling entire companies wasn't so different from bartering at a local market. Know what the item is worth, then open the bidding at half the value. Just add about a half dozen more zeros behind the figure.

Tobin took a sip of the red wine Danny had ordered for them. It was delicious. Probably the best wine Tobin had ever had; not difficult when he never spent more than ten dollars on a bottle. The warmth of the wine coursed through him.

Being here with Danny, it was so easy to regress back to the little brother role he'd held for so many years. It didn't seem to matter that Tobin was proud of the adult he'd become. He was self-sufficient, successful in a job he enjoyed. Autonomous—for the most part—and he didn't have to answer to anyone other than himself.

Yet, Danny would always be older, more experienced, more worldly.

Maybe that was part of his appeal. Mysterious, slightly dangerous. The bad boy hidden beneath a veneer of polish. If anything, it made Danny even sexier than before, this backdrop of high-powered glitz and glamour.

Danny leaned forward, placing both elbows on the table

and tenting his hands. The look he sent Tobin was so intense Tobin stopped breathing.

"You know, I don't want things to be strained between us," Danny said. "Yes, we're both working with WesTec, and potentially at cross-purposes, but that doesn't make us enemies or competitors."

No, Tobin agreed. But what did it make them? Family friends? Childhood friends? Acquaintances? Former lovers? Maybe future lovers? Tobin pushed his plate away and took his time wiping his mouth with the cloth napkin. Danny's gaze followed his every movement, giving Tobin the courage to put himself out there.

He mimicked Danny's posture, leaning in to close the distance between them. "What does it make us, Danny?" he whispered.

Danny's Adam's apple bobbed, and Tobin's heart thudded with a lack of oxygen.

"Friends." Danny's voice cracked. He leaned back and cleared his throat. "It makes us friends."

Disappointing, to say the least. But if that was Danny's opening offer, then Tobin had a few ideas on how to counter.

"Just friends?"

Danny glanced across the restaurant as if there was anything more interesting than the conversation they were having. "Yes," he croaked.

He was bluffing, and Tobin saw right through it. Danny with his tough guy act, pretending he didn't feel the sexual tension in the air, the heat rippling in the space between them. It was a good act, Tobin could admit that much. It probably would have fooled anyone else. But Tobin wasn't anyone, and he planned on using that to his advantage.

He leaned back, again mimicking Danny's posture. "Okay, if you're sure."

Danny pinned him with a stare so potent, it was a wonder they didn't spontaneously erupt into flames. His jaw muscle contracted like he was trying to hold himself back.

Yeah. Tobin smiled.

Danny wasn't sure at all.

"Whatcha doing?" Monica plopped down on the couch with so much oomph Tobin almost flew off it. She snuggled in close, pressing thigh and shoulder to thigh and shoulder. She had never really understood the concept of personal space. That or she didn't care.

Probably the latter.

"Nothing." Would it be more or less suspicious if Tobin closed his laptop now?

"Liar." She leaned over him and peered at his computer screen. "You're doing something. I could see it on your face all the way from the kitchen."

So more suspicious. Tobin jostled her away and reached for the giant bowl of popcorn she'd brought with her. "If you're going to snoop, at least give me some of that."

"Who's that guy?" Monica wiggled her eyebrows at the picture of Danny with the twins.

"No one. Who? What?" He clicked away from the photo.

"Stop! Go back!"

Gah. He hadn't meant to stalk Danny on social media. No, wait. That was a lie. Constance, his sister-in-law, had posted a new picture of the twins and Tobin had a sneaking suspicion that clicking on it would lead to photos of Danny. He only ever showed up on social media in pictures with the kids. Tobin especially loved the one where Danny looked like the world's best uncle, holding one twin on each arm.

"Whaaat? It's no one. Leave me alone." He gave Monica another jostle.

"Shut up. Tell me who that is!" Monica poked him in the side. Bitch. She knew he was ticklish.

Tobin yelped and jumped at the same time, upending the bowl of popcorn.

"See what you've done?" Monica exclaimed.

"Me? You're the one who poked me."

"*You're* the one who won't tell me about the guy you're thirsting after." She started picking up crunchy bits of popcorn and tossing them on the coffee table.

"Okay, fine." He pulled up the picture again and crossed his arms. "It's Danny."

When he didn't elaborate, Monica pinned him with a look. "And?"

"And he's my brother's best friend."

"God, do I have to drag every word out of you? Don't make me poke you again."

Tobin wrapped his arms around the sensitive soft bits in his sides. He would never put it past Monica to tickle him where it hurt the most. "He's my brother's best friend and I had a childhood crush on him, okay? Happy?"

"Yes." She had the audacity to look smug. "So why are you stalking him now?"

"I'm not stalking him."

"Mmhmm, then why do you have a tab called 'Daniel Ip—Google Search'?"

Tobin slapped his palm over his screen. "No reason."

Monica stuck another piece of popcorn in her mouth and chewed loudly while staring at him wide-eyed.

"Yeah, okay, fine." He clicked over to the image search he ran earlier. There were plenty of pictures of Danny online. But they were all professional business headshots or photos from events where he was speaking onstage. Not that Tobin minded. The suave, put together, intense stare Danny had translated well into photos. But Tobin wanted more.

"Ooo, I like that photo." Monica pointed to one where Danny sat onstage, ankle on opposite knee.

Tobin rolled his eyes. "I need to find my own place," he mumbled, which only won him a hard slap on the shoulder.

"Shut up. You love me. I'm your best friend." Monica spoke to the screen as she scrolled through image after image. "Besides, you know you can't afford a place like this on your own."

She was right, as much as Tobin hated to admit it. They'd snagged a sprawling two-bedroom apartment in Metro Vancouver, close to public transit, a few months before rents really started skyrocketing in the city. Their place was now so below market neither of them had any hope of finding something comparable, even with full-time salaries.

"A guy can dream," Tobin shot back.

Monica looked from him to the photos of Danny and back. "Yeah, you can."

"Shut up." He gave her a shove and she toppled over giggling, popcorn everywhere.

Tobin sighed. He'd left Calgary feeling so confident and in control. Knowing Danny was still attracted to him had been a total power rush. But all that bravado hadn't quite made it across the Rocky Mountains with him. Maybe he'd dreamed up all that flirtation and innuendo. It could have been all in his mind.

Monica sighed, sobering. "You haven't answered my question."

Tobin grabbed the now empty bowl and set it on the coffee table. "What question?"

"Why you're stalking him *now*?"

There was only so much bush for him to beat around. Monica always got the story out of him anyway. "I ran into him when I was in Calgary last week. We had dinner."

She examined him a moment before speaking. "You really like him, don't you?"

"What?" Tobin closed the lid on his laptop. "No. I mean, yeah, he's hot. But it was a *childhood* crush. Hello, I'm not a child anymore."

Monica sat up, her face inches from his. A stray piece of popcorn crunched under her weight. "I don't believe you."

"What's there to believe?"

"You're hot for him, sure. But there's more, something you're not telling me."

"Since when did you become a mind reader?" Tobin tried to put some distance between them, as if that would make it harder for Monica to always know exactly what he was thinking.

"Oh, you know I'm the Tobin-whisperer."

God damn Monica always being so god damn right. "Maybe there is something else."

"Mmhmm." Her eyes sparkled with anticipation.

Tobin huffed and rushed the words out as fast as he could. "Before Calgary, the last time I saw him was at Wei's bachelor party seven years ago, and we had sex."

"What?"

He smacked a hand over the ear closest to Monica. "Ow!"

"I knew it! I knew it, I knew it, I knew it."

"You knew we slept together?"

"I suspected! You had it written all over your face." She shimmied her shoulders up and down in a little dance.

Tobin huffed. "Now you know."

"So, what's next?"

"What do you mean what's next?"

"Are you going to see him again?"

That *had* been the plan. But Tobin didn't know when or how or where. Going all the way back to Toronto for a booty call was too much, even for him.

"I don't know."

"But he's Wei's friend, right? You'll see him at some point."

"Maybe." Except Tobin had been really great at avoiding Danny for seven whole years. So not necessarily.

"Then what's the problem?"

"Who said there was a problem?"

She shot him an *oh please* look. He wasn't fooling her.

"Ugh." He buried his face into his hands. "It's not that simple. It's, like, complicated."

"Ooookay. Complicated, how?" Monica asked with genuine confusion.

"It just is, okay? Like, Calgary was a fluke. What are the chances we're going to be in the same city again? And…" Did he really want to go there? Put words to something he didn't even want to admit to himself?

"We grew up together and I was his best friend's kid brother. So, I don't know, I'm probably just some kid to him."

"Some kid he had sex with seven years ago? When you were what age?"

"Nineteen. I was legal."

"Yeah, barely."

Tobin pulled his knees up and wrapped his arms around them. "Okay, so what are you trying to say?"

"I'm saying…" Monica put a hand on his arm. "He probably doesn't think of you as a kid. If he was willing to bang when you were barely legal, he's most likely willing to bang now."

It was so irritating when Monica made so much sense. He knew her comment was supposed to be encouraging, but he'd worked himself up into such a frenzy, he couldn't accept the words for what they were. Tobin rolled his eyes. "Or maybe he's into pedophilia or incest or something." He regretted saying that even as the words were coming out of his mouth. Of course Danny wasn't like that; Tobin was being a brat.

"Um, ew." Monica's expression was disgusted and judgey

at the same time. "Maybe *don't* use those words when talking about queer people? You're lucky Ayán isn't here."

He was. Monica's girlfriend was the epitome of dyke and he'd probably get stuck washing her period underwear by hand as punishment.

"Sorry, sorry. I didn't mean that."

Monica sighed in solidarity. "Honestly, Tobi-wan Kenobi? You've got it bad."

He did. He really, really did. So much for growing out of a childhood crush. Now he was full-on adult obsessed. "So what do I do about it?"

"Scratch the itch?"

"But how?" he whined.

"Call him."

Did he hear that right? He looked over at Monica to make sure. She didn't look like she was joking.

"I'm serious. Pick up the phone and dial his number."

"And talk about what?" Tobin couldn't remember the last time he actually talked to someone on the phone—overbearing parents and brother notwithstanding.

"Anything!"

"That doesn't sound like scratching the itch. I mean, unless we have phone sex?" Which wasn't a bad idea. Danny had a deep radio voice that would sound so fucking hot over the phone.

"Not phone sex, silly!" She smacked him across the back of the head, but he was too preoccupied to feel it. "I mean, like, talk. About things. How's your day going? I was thinking of you. What are your hopes and dreams? You know, normal stuff."

She had to be joking. "Um, in case you haven't noticed, neither of us are lesbians. We don't scratch itches by talking."

"Fuck you." Monica jumped off the couch, popcorn crunching underfoot. That was going to be hell trying to clean up. "If you don't want to take my advice, fine. Don't come crying to me when you realize you're head over heels in love and you don't know what to do."

In love? That was kind of fast, wasn't it?

They'd just reconnected after years apart. Maybe Tobin had been in love with Danny before; after all, he'd known Danny better than he knew Wei. But that was so long ago and Tobin had been a kid. Whatever he felt now couldn't be love. It was lust and attraction, probably with a healthy dose of nostalgia thrown in to create that warm fuzzy feeling. Regardless, none of that mattered.

He could barely get Danny to admit he was attracted to Tobin. Love or anything remotely close to it was so far down the line, it might as well not exist.

Monica left him with the mess of popcorn and retreated to her bedroom. Sitting alone on the couch, Tobin opened his laptop again.

Danny with the twins. Danny with Wei and the twins. His whole family, with Danny standing off to the side. What would it look like if Tobin were in those pictures too? Maybe standing next to Danny, arm around his waist? Maybe each of them holding a twin?

God, Monica was right. He did have it bad. And not only physically.

He slammed his laptop closed and grabbed the abandoned popcorn bowl to start cleaning up. Seducing Danny for some fun between the sheets could be doable. But going out on a proper date? Being in an actual relationship? Out of the question. That would be some next-level imagination gone wild, science fiction fantasy, superheroes with magical powers type shit.

He'd settle for an *Up in the Air* type arrangement. Yeah, that he could do.

Tobin brought the bowl into the kitchen and dumped the popcorn into the garbage bin. Then he pulled out his phone, found Danny's number, and stared at it. His thumb hovered over the screen.

Do it. Just do it. His heart beat so loudly, he could hear the blood rushing past his ears.

Don't think about it. Touch the screen.

Tobin squeezed his eyes shut and twitched his thumb. When he dared peek at his phone, it was ringing.

Oh god, what did he do?

Chapter Four

Danny's phone buzzed and then stopped. A missed call popped up on the screen. From Tobin? Why was Tobin calling him? Was everything okay?

He hit the call back button before remembering his whole team was in his office. Shit. He went to the farthest corner, where a wall of bookshelves met the floor-to-ceiling windows of his corner office. Behind him, his team chattered away, but he couldn't care less about their discussion.

The phone rang, and Tobin picked up right away. "Uh, hi."

"Is everything okay?" Danny pressed the phone closer and plugged his other ear in an attempt to listen for background noise from Tobin's side. He couldn't hear anything suspicious.

"Oh, yeah, everything's fine."

He hadn't spoken to Tobin in seven years and now a call out of the blue? Right after Calgary? "Are you sure?"

"Yeah, yeah, of course. I, um, you know, butt dialed, that's all."

Butt dialed? Did that still happen with phones these days? "So there's nothing wrong?"

"No, nothing's wrong. I'm sorry. You must be so busy. I didn't mean to interrupt."

"No need to apologize." Danny meant it, especially now that his blood pressure was gradually returning to normal. "You can call me anytime."

"Really?"

He could imagine Tobin's mischievous smile. "Really."

"Okay. I um… I guess I wanted to say hi."

It was a simple greeting. One they'd technically already made. But it warmed Danny deep in that place that had felt so cold lately. He wished he could see Tobin's face. "Hi."

"Um, I'm really glad we ran into each other in Calgary."

"I am too." In fact, Danny hadn't stopped thinking about it since he got back. The way Tobin had leaned across the table and dropped his voice to a whisper. The not-so-subtle suggestion in his words. They were friends, but who was he kidding. Tobin was more than a friend; he was…special, beautiful, charming, smart, everything a guy could ask for wrapped up in a perfect package.

He was exactly Danny's type, if Danny was a relationship kind of guy, and if Tobin wasn't Wei's little brother. He propped his elbow on the ledge of a shelf to hold up his head. He was in dangerous territory, with all the alarm bells sounding. Everything felt dark and heavy, and right as he'd felt like chaos would consume him, Tobin appeared. A lighthouse shining through the storm.

Danny swam toward it. What choice did he have?

"So, I was thinking…" Tobin paused, and Danny let him gather his thoughts. "You said you're in Calgary pretty often, right?"

A spark of hope ignited in Danny and he felt like he could breathe for the first time in a long time. "Yes."

"Well, I'm going to be in Calgary, you know, on and off for the next few months. So, um, I was thinking, you know, maybe we could, I mean, if it works out and if you want to, maybe we could try to…meet up again?"

It was the best idea Danny had heard in ages. "Yes, let's do that."

"Really?"

"Really."

"Oh." Tobin actually sounded surprised. "Okay, well, um, when are you going to be there next?"

Danny tried to do a quick mental check of his schedule, then gave up. His schedule was so packed and convoluted, he was never actually free. He'd gotten used to working from wherever in the world he happened to be. "I can be there next week."

"Next week? Oh, um, that soon, eh? Uh…hold on a sec."

Danny held the phone an inch away from his ear as Tobin's mic picked up shuffling and tapping sounds.

"Sorry, I'm checking my calendar for next week. Next

week…is kind of booked up with some other projects I'm on." Tobin sighed. "I don't think I can do next week. Sorry."

"Don't apologize. How about the week after?"

"Week after?" More shuffling and tapping. "Yeah, I think I can do the week after. I'll have to move a couple things around. And I can probably dial into the meeting with Lonnie, she won't mind. Um, yeah, the week after should be doable."

Danny let out a breath he hadn't realized he was holding. "Excellent. I'll have my assistant send you the details."

"Your assistant, eh?" That flirty tone was back.

Danny let himself roll his eyes because no one was watching. "Yes, I have an assistant."

"Hm, maybe I can be your assistant. I'm good at assisting with things, you know."

Oh yeah, Danny's dick definitely knew. And his imagination didn't need any prompting to concoct all the ways Tobin and Danny could assist each other. "I might take you up on that."

"I hope you do."

Danny cleared his throat and adjusted himself.

"Anyway." Tobin's voice became bright and cheery. "You must be busy so I won't keep you. Talk soon!"

"Yes, yes, soon." It came out as a croak.

"Have a wonderful day."

"Yeah, you too."

Tobin hung up, leaving Danny with the worst case of blue balls he'd ever had.

He turned for his desk and came face to face with three pairs of eyes staring at him like he'd grown elephant ears.

Ah, shit.

He made a beeline for his desk. "Sorry. Personal emergency."

Miguel and Zahrah both looked away, but Ginika pursed her lips and cocked an eyebrow.

He hadn't fooled anyone.

"Where were we?" He put on his best big boss voice.

"We were going over this quarter's numbers." Ginika did not look impressed.

"Right. Yes. Continue."

"I was saying," Miguel jumped in. "That it's not all bad. Rio Dios met their KPIs this quarter."

"Barely," Ginika countered. "Only after they fired a third of their staff to cut costs."

"They needed to cut costs, anyway…"

Danny pinched the bridge of his nose, the warmth of his call with Tobin dissipating quickly. He felt like he was constantly having this conversation about quarterly performance numbers lately. They weren't quite where he needed them to be; they were tracking a little low. Basically, they sucked, and Danny had very little interest in doing anything about it.

"Listen." Ginika cut Miguel off with one raised finger. "Prosperity lost their largest client and missed the last three payments on their debt. Mekan-X can't maintain a steady supply of inventory from their China warehouses. They're blaming it on the Chinese, but I'm not buying it. Lux Brands had that epic public relations nightmare. They're being boycotted all over social media. It is an unmitigated disaster. Danny? Danny!"

"Yeah, yeah, I'm here." He got up from his desk and came around to the sitting area where the three of them were gathered. He perched on the back of an armchair opposite them.

Ginika and Miguel were his senior analysts and Zahrah a junior analyst who had joined them earlier that year. They were a good team. Smart, dedicated, skilled at their jobs. But even the best team faltered if they didn't have the right leadership, and Danny hadn't been a very good leader lately. Their abysmal numbers were proof.

"Zahrah, what do you think?"

"Oh, um…" She sent a panicked look in Ginika's direction.

Like a good mentor, Ginika nodded encouragingly, but didn't try to step in.

"Well," Zahrah ventured on, "I think the portfolio companies probably need more handholding."

When she didn't elaborate, Danny gave her a verbal nudge. "What kind of handholding?"

"That would depend on the company. Prosperity needs a dedicated business development team. Mekan-X needs someone who can speak Mandarin to handle their relationships with Chinese suppliers. Lux Brands should recruit a bunch of influencers to help clean up their public image." Zahrah stopped abruptly as if she'd caught herself rambling.

Danny waved her on. "Don't stop on my account. Those were good ideas." He knew he'd hired her for a reason. At least past Danny knew what he was doing.

"Basically, we need to revisit their business plans and recalibrate them individually. We should be doing more on-site visits to make sure they follow through," Zahrah concluded.

Which was what they were supposed to be doing all along. What Danny was supposed to be doing. Except, he…didn't care. No, that wasn't right. He wanted his team to be taken care of. He wanted to maintain his hard-earned reputation. But the work involved had lost all the excitement it once held.

"All right. Draw up detailed business plans for each portfolio company and get them back to me."

The three of them looked at each other, then back at him.

"What?"

"You already have them," Miguel said. "I put them on your desk two days ago and sent you an email to remind you."

Well, fuck. Danny ran a hand over his face. God, he was so tired. When the hell had he gotten so tired?

"Okay, sorry. I'll look at them tonight. Anything else?"

They muttered a chorus of *no*s, then filed out of his office. Danny stood and wandered over to the window overlooking Toronto's financial district. Thousands and thousands of people scurrying to and from buildings, banging out emails and taking phone calls. The economic engine churning away. Did any of them get tired? Or was Danny the only one?

A knock interrupted his dire thoughts. He turned to find Ginika closing the glass door behind her.

"I didn't want to say anything in front of them."

Danny crossed his arms to protect himself against whatever Ginika had to say. She didn't hold back—that's what he liked about her.

"Yes?"

"You've been distracted lately. I don't know by what, but it's dangerous. People have noticed."

"Who?" And why the hell were they entitled to an opinion?

Ginika glanced over her shoulder as if someone was eavesdropping. She continued with her voice lowered. "Everyone. It's filtering through the grapevine. 'Danny's lost his touch. He hasn't kept up with trends.' Shall I continue?"

"No. No need." He turned back to the window. So his fears weren't only in his head. Others were thinking exactly the same thing.

"What's wrong?" Ginika asked.

If only he knew. He closed his eyes and took a deep breath. He could do this. He could focus and get the fucking job done. It was what he did; it was who he was. Danny strode back to his desk with more determination than he felt. "Nothing. Don't worry about me. I'm fine."

Ginika was too smart to believe his bravado, but at least she didn't call him out on it. "If you say so." She turned on her heel and left.

The second the door closed behind her, Danny deflated into his chair. His desk was cluttered with piles of files and binders and paper. Somewhere in the midst of all that were business plans he needed to review. His phone buzzed with several new emails coming in.

It never stopped.

There was always more.

He should get back to it, keep chipping away at the

iceberg before it drowned him. But he couldn't find the strength to lift even one hand.

His phone buzzed again. But this time with a text message. From Tobin.

Danny picked it up to find a smiley face surrounded by hearts. Can't wait for Calgary.

He tapped out a quick response. Same here.

How did Tobin do it? Lift his mood with nothing more than a weird yellow face and four simple words? Whatever the key ingredient was, it worked.

Danny set the phone aside, took a deep breath with his eyes closed. When he opened them again, all the papers on his desk came into sharp focus. Ah, there were those business plans Miguel mentioned. He pulled out the first one, grabbed a pen to make comments, and began flying through the pages.

"Constance wants to set you up with someone." Wei spoke as if he was commenting on nothing more interesting than the weather.

"Oh?"

Wei shot him a curious glance over the patio set where they sat watching the twins—Peyton and Howie—run around the backyard. They were supposedly playing tag, but to Danny it looked more like a game of circling while screaming.

"Are you interested?"

"I didn't say that."

"But you didn't not say that."

Danny returned his look. "I don't know what you're talking about."

"Yes, you do. Don't play dumb."

"I'm not playing anything."

Wei gave him the middle finger and Danny didn't bother suppressing his smile. Constance was well-intentioned, but she was one of those people who thought all gay men liked each other. Definitely not the case with Danny. He'd been a good wingman when she and Wei had started going out, and reluctantly agreed to a couple blind dates when Wei begged him to. But nothing came of them. Nothing ever did.

"I'll tell her you're busy. I'm sure you've got a business trip coming up. Where are you off to next?"

"Calgary." Danny answered before he'd thought through the consequences.

"Oh yeah? You know Toby's going to Calgary a lot these days. You should call him up. See if you're ever in town at the same time."

"Yeah, that's a good idea." One he'd already done, joke's on Wei. But why he didn't come right out and admit it, Danny couldn't say. It wasn't like they were doing anything illegal or inappropriate. They were only meeting for dinner.

Wei yawned, checked his watch and drained the rest of his beer. "I should get those two in the bath."

Right on cue, Howie let out a wail. "Daddy!"

"Peyton, get off your brother!" Wei called out.

Peyton stood from where she had her brother pinned to the grass. "I was only playing," she complained.

"I don't wanna play anymore." Howie came running toward them.

Wei sighed and opened his arms to his sniffling son. "All right, time to go inside. Come on, both of you." He waved Peyton over.

"You go. I'll clean up here." Danny stood and stretched, feeling every one of his thirty-five years.

"Thanks, leave the leftovers on the counter for Constance when she gets home." Wei led the two munchkins inside and Danny watched as Wei lifted Howie over his head. The little boy let out a peal of giggles while Peyton jumped up and down for her turn.

Danny didn't envy Wei the amount of work that went into parenting twins. But seeing his best friend with his kids, Danny couldn't deny the pang of jealousy. Must be nice watching a little life grow and develop, to have a hand in shaping who they would become.

What was wrong with him? Danny shook his head as he gathered dirty plates and bowls covered in remnants of barbecue sauce. He was the last person in the world who should have kids. With the schedule he kept, constantly on the road, there was no way he'd actually be able to parent, and he wasn't about to shove that responsibility on a potential husband.

Husband? Danny almost laughed out loud. He couldn't keep a boyfriend happy, let alone a husband. It'd be a miracle if he ever found someone willing to marry him. Hell, he didn't even know if he wanted to get married.

He filled the dishwasher and set it to run a cycle, then headed upstairs.

Giggling and splashing erupted from the bathroom and Danny peeked around the corner to watch Wei wrestle two small people into some form of cleanliness. He looked like he was having fun. Peyton and Howie were lucky to have him as a dad.

Danny could never do what Wei did. He wasn't cut out to be a family guy. So why in the world did that make him so sad?

"Where's Uncle Danny?" Howie shrieked.

"That's a very good question." Wei turned his head toward the door and yelled, "Uncle Danny!"

"I'm here. I'm here." Danny stepped out from behind the doorframe.

The floor was practically a swimming pool. Wei's clothes were soaked. But the twins sported matching smiles, standing in puddles and wrapped in towels much too big for them.

"Can you take one?" Wei nudged Peyton toward him.

Danny knelt, ignoring the water seeping into his pant knees. "Come here, you." He wrapped Peyton in a big hug and rubbed her up and down while she wriggled underneath the towel. When he pulled it over her head to dry her hair, she giggled and ducked.

"I'm dry! I'm dry!" she cried.

"Dry enough for bed?"

"Yeah!"

"If you say so." He bundled her up and hoisted her into his arms, carrying her into the room the twins shared.

Together, he and Wei got the kids ready for bed. Danny had done it enough times to know how the ritual went.

Pajamas and stuffed animals, a story and then lights out. He retreated to the doorway while Peyton pondered which book she wanted Wei to read to them. With a child tucked into either side, Wei cracked open a picture book about cowboys and horses. Danny had picked it up in Calgary.

He turned away from the picture of domestic bliss and headed downstairs. He should tell Wei about meeting Tobin. There was no reason not to. What was so scandalous about a meal between old friends that he needed to keep it a secret?

He cracked open another beer while waiting for Wei. He was halfway through by the time Wei made it down.

Wei let out an exhausted sound as he collapsed on the couch, face down, one leg hanging off. "You're lucky you don't have kids."

Danny let out a laugh he didn't feel. "I was thinking that *you* were the lucky one."

"Oh yeah?" Wei propped himself up on his elbows. "I never knew you wanted kids."

"I don't."

"I don't know. I think you'd make a good dad."

Danny shot him a skeptical look even though the compliment hit something deep in his gut he didn't want to think too much about.

"I'm serious." Wei sat all the way up. "You would be. You're great with the twins. Honestly, why do you think I invite you over whenever Constance has a night shift?"

"Because I'm cheap labor."

"Yeah, you are. But good value cheap labor. Do you

think I'd let Toby watch them? Pssh, Toby practically needs a babysitter himself."

"That's not true." The need to defend Tobin was automatic. "Tobin's fully capable of taking care of himself and you know that."

Wei cocked an eyebrow. "Tobin, eh? Since when did you start calling him that?"

Ah, crap. "That's his name, isn't it?" Danny backpedaled.

"Yeah, but—"

"Anyway, I should go. I still have work waiting for me." He poured the rest of his beer down the sink, then pulled out his phone to call for a car.

Wei followed him to the front door and waited with him for the car to arrive. "Is everything okay?"

"Yeah, everything's fine." *Tell him about Calgary. Tell him about dinner with Tobin.* "I'm fine. Tell Constance I said hi."

He pulled Wei into a quick hug and then let himself out. Even as he made his way down the long driveway to the street, Danny kept telling himself to turn around and confess. It was not a big deal. Wei had suggested it himself. He would probably be thrilled Tobin and Danny were reconnecting.

But his car pulled up and Danny got in the backseat. As the driver pulled away from the curb, he waved back at Wei, who was still standing in the doorway.

Later. After. He would tell Wei once he got back from Calgary. There was nothing wrong with keeping some things to himself.

So why the hell did it feel like he was having a secret affair?

Chapter Five

The driver slowed to a stop in front of a house in the middle of a residential neighborhood and put the car in park. Were they there?

Danny had sent a message saying a car would pick him up in front of his hotel at seven o'clock to take him to dinner. The independent part of Tobin wanted to find his own way there, but the romantic side of him kind of liked the surprise. The only problem was, how did Danny expect him to pack when he didn't know what to wear?

The driver opened the back door before Tobin got to it.

"Oh, thanks." Tobin fumbled in his pocket. Was he supposed to tip the guy? Was that why the driver was smiling at him? "Here you go. Thanks."

A look of surprise passed over the driver's face, but he

still took the five-dollar bill Tobin handed him. "Thank you so much, sir. Have a wonderful evening."

Huh. Maybe he wasn't supposed to tip the guy? Oops. "Uh, thanks. You too."

It wasn't immediately apparent where Tobin was supposed to go now. He turned in a slow circle until a sign caught his eye. It was partially hidden by a bush with a weak spotlight illuminating the words *Chez Camille*. Was that the restaurant?

Tobin approached slowly, in case *Chez Camille* wasn't a restaurant but some other, perhaps more intimate establishment. But the brightly lit bay windows on the first floor revealed diners, fully dressed, with a single classic tapered candle between them. Tobin gave himself a mental slap. Of course it was only a restaurant. Where else would Danny take him?

He went inside before his imagination could start dreaming up answers.

A maître d' greeted him at the door. "Bienvenue à Chez Camille."

"Uh, hi…" He glanced past the maître d' hoping to spot Danny, but he was nowhere in sight.

"Are you looking for Monsieur Ip?" the maître d' asked with a heavy French accent.

"Ip. Yes, Danny Ip. Exactly. Yeah, thanks." Way to make a fool of himself. Ugh.

"Parfait. Follow me, s'il vous plaît."

They wound through tables set up for groups of two and four, each lit with a single tapered candle. Understated chandeliers hung from the ceiling and the walls were decorated with art—like, actual art someone had hand-painted and done up in gold wooden frames.

Tobin held his arms close to his sides and stepped carefully, the words *you break it, you buy it* ringing in his ears. He didn't think he could afford to replace anything in this place.

Near the back of the restaurant, in a secluded little corner, was Danny. He rose as Tobin approached, an easy smile on his lips and a look of wonder in his eyes. Tobin had a sudden flash of insight—was this what a bride feels like walking down the aisle to her groom? The maître d' gave them a mini-bow and melted into the background like he was giving Tobin away.

"Hi," Tobin whispered.

"Hi," Danny answered.

They stood there for a moment too long, soaking each other in. Whatever magnetism had drawn them together last time was no figment of Tobin's imagination. If anything, it was stronger today than it had been before. It would take one step for Tobin to close the distance between them, to feel Danny's body against him, the warmth of Danny's breath against his cheek. A cough in the background pulled Tobin from his reverie.

Danny held Tobin's chair for him and the small gesture was thrilling. Danny, the chivalrous gentleman; he almost giggled.

A candle flame danced between them, casting shadows on the table, against the wall, and across the planes of Danny's face. He was darkly tanned with laugh lines around his eyes and worry lines on his forehead. That closely cropped buzz cut kid Tobin loved petting. A little bit prickly and a little bit soft, it sent tingles up his arm whenever he brushed his palm against Danny's hair. Would it feel the same now?

"Did you have a good flight in?" Danny asked.

Casual, easy small talk. A gentle easing into whatever it was they were doing. Tobin's heart pattered away like he was on the edge of a cliff.

"Good. Uneventful. Yours?"

"Same."

Eyes locked. Breathing in unison.

"Thanks for coming."

Tobin nearly laughed out loud. "Of course. I pretty much invited you."

More silence held sacred between them.

"I ordered the tasting menu for us. I hope that's okay."

Tobin didn't even want to think about how much a tasting menu would cost in a place like this. "Perfect."

As if on cue, a waiter dressed in a crisp white shirt and matching white gloves appeared. He set plates in front of them. An oyster still in its mineral encrusted shell, sitting on a bed of lettuce with…was that beef tartare?

Another waiter came by and poured white wine into their glasses.

Tobin had always been an adventurous eater—honestly, most Asians were. Being intimidated by food was a new experience for him. He just hoped he didn't spill everything down the front of his newly dry-cleaned suit.

Danny didn't seem to have any such qualms. He picked up the oyster shell, held it to his lips, and tilted his head back. The collar of his shirt stretched against the thick column of his neck, sensual and strong all at once. Oysters were supposed to be aphrodisiacs, right? If the heat in Danny's eyes was anything to go by, they certainly were.

Tobin picked up his oyster shell and tipped the juicy meat into his mouth. Briny with a kick of sour and spice. It'd been a long time since he'd had a good oyster.

"Wow."

"Take a sip of the wine."

Tobin sipped and was assaulted by a sweetness that cut through the acidity of the oyster, leaving a pleasant reminder of something magical he couldn't quite put into words. "Damn. That's good."

Danny laughed. A low rumble starting in his chest and ending in the pit of Tobin's stomach. Danny never really laughed out loud. But somehow the sound always reverberated through Tobin at the exact frequency needed to melt his insides.

"I'm glad you enjoyed it," Danny said as he picked up his own glass for a sip.

His watch glinted in the candlelight. Silver with a bright royal blue face that couldn't help but attract attention.

"I usually eat whatever is cheapest," Tobin admitted. "It's a holdover from being a poor student."

Danny nodded, dropping his gaze to the table. "It's quite impressive, how you managed to support yourself."

Tobin's shoulder lifted and dropped in a self-conscious shrug. He knew it was impressive, but it was a rare treat to get that kind of compliment. "Thanks."

"I still can't quite believe that your parents let you get away with it."

Memories of their heated shouting matches over the phone came to mind. When Dad had accused him of being ungrateful for not taking their money. Mom exaggerating all the ways Tobin would starve and end up on the street.

"There were times I wanted to give in. Weeks of subsisting on nothing but the cheapest ramen can get to anyone. And, like—" he'd never admitted this to anyone, least of all his parents "—there were a few times I did use their money. But only because I had cash flow problems, and I paid them back as soon as I got my next paycheck."

Danny chuckled. "No one is going to begrudge you that."

"Maybe not. But still."

Danny clasped his hands in front of his mouth, his watch on full display. "You're not a poor student anymore."

"I'm not a lot of things anymore."

Danny's eyes darkened, and Tobin felt like he was getting physically pulled in. He leaned forward as far as the table between them would allow.

"No. You're all grown up now."

Tobin bit his lip. Fuck, how could those words be so god damn sexy? His dick stirred like it wanted to show Danny exactly how grown up it could be.

The waiter came by with the next course. A piece of foie gras sitting on a bed of toasted oats, with beets and figs, garnished with a creamy white yoghurt. Their wineglasses were switched out for something new. Tobin welcomed the interruption; it gave him a moment to get his dick under control.

Danny busied himself with the new wine, taking a sip that looked more like a gulp. "How's work going?"

He sounded so much like Wei in some ways Tobin had to laugh. "Good. It's going really well, actually. And I don't only mean WesTec," Tobin added quickly. "I'm lead on WesTec, but I'm supporting on like, three other projects."

"Sounds like a lot."

Tobin gave another self-conscious shrug. "It is. But nothing I can't handle. And Lonnie, my manager, she's really good about making sure I don't get overwhelmed."

"Having a good manager is important." Danny pushed a beet around his plate before stabbing it with a fork. Poor beet.

"Yeah, Lonnie's almost more like a mentor to me. I've been lucky. She's really believed in me, gave me opportunities to advance that would normally take years."

Tobin thought back to the video conference they'd had earlier that day. Lonnie had been a little skeptical about Tobin going back to Calgary so soon after his last visit with WesTec. He'd managed to come up with some random excuse he barely understood himself. He wasn't sure he had convinced her, though. He felt bad about it, but then, this was Danny.

"You're not lucky. You're smart. That's why you got the opportunities."

Tobin busied himself with slicing through the soft duck pâté. "Yeah, I know." It was weird saying stuff like that about himself. Until he went away for school, he hadn't had to work for pretty much anything in life. Everything he needed, and most things he wanted, were usually handed to him before he even knew to ask. Being born into those kinds of circumstances was luck, pure and simple.

"You like working for Paradigm," Danny stated.

"What, you looking to buy them up?" Tobin had meant it as a joke. But the way Danny's jaw stiffened, he didn't take it as a joke. "Sorry, not funny."

Danny breathed in and out, and the hardness softened. "That's okay."

"But yes, I like working for Paradigm. A lot."

"What do you like about it?"

Tobin thought for a second before answering. "It's what I had studied to do, and not a lot of people can say that. Accounting is like, the least cool major in school. But out there in the real world? People come to me like I've got the elixir for eternal youth. It's kind of nice."

"I'm sure it is," Danny said with amusement in his eyes.

"You must know how that feels, Mr. Hot-Shot-Private-Equity-Investor. I bet you've got people banging down your door vying for your attention."

Tobin couldn't quite read Danny's expression. It was a mix of wishful thinking and bashfulness. "What? Isn't it true?"

"Not quite banging down my door. But close enough." He reached for his wineglass and the candlelight caught on his watch again.

"That's nice."

Danny glanced at his wrist. His smile looked a little embarrassed. "Thanks." He adjusted the fit and tugged his sleeve over it.

"You were wearing a different one last time. With a gold

band, I think?" Tobin remembered how heavy it looked, like it could only be worn by someone strong enough to carry its weight.

"Perhaps, I don't remember." Danny folded his hands on the table with one of them covering the wrist where his watch sat.

"How many watches do you have?"

Danny squinted as he thought.

"Too many to count?" Tobin guessed.

"Something like that."

Tobin laughed. He shouldn't have been surprised. It fit Danny's shiny new image. Tobin held up his own wrist, pulling his sleeve down to reveal the scratched-up watch he wore. It wasn't even a real watch; more like an exercise bracelet that told the time. His parents had gotten it for him a couple Christmases ago—the only time he accepted expensive-ish gifts from them. "Maybe I need an upgrade."

Danny chuckled at the joke. Slowly, as if reluctantly, he pulled up his own sleeve and held out his hand. It looked dark and weathered against the bright colors of the watch. They shouldn't have matched, but somehow, they did—the rough Danny and the polished Danny, all in one.

Tobin reached for it, ostensibly to tilt the watch toward him for a better look. But his hand settled on top of Danny's and he left it there.

"I got my first watch with my first paycheck." Danny spoke with his gaze fixed on where they touched. "Then I started collecting them. Not on purpose. But before I knew it, I had maybe a dozen."

"All fancy ones like this?" Tobin ran the tip of his finger along the edge of the band where smooth metal met warm skin.

Danny's smile was a little smug, a little self-deprecating. "Fancier."

"Impressive."

"Not really." There was a touch of melancholy in Danny's admission. Something too tender and exposed, like Tobin had inadvertently peeled back the dressing on a not-quite-healed wound.

The waiter showed up again and they both drew their hands back into their laps. Plates appeared containing a bird of some kind with crispy brown skin, encircled by perfectly round balls of potato. "Quail," said the waiter as he bowed and backed away.

"Can I ask you a dumb question?"

To his credit, Danny only hesitated for a microsecond. "All right."

"When we were kids, you always stood up for me. Even against Wei. I mean, not that Wei was mean to me or anything. But you didn't treat me the way he and the other kids did. Why did you do that?"

Danny swallowed his bite of quail and wiped his mouth with a napkin before answering. "You were a good kid. I treated you like I would have treated anyone else."

That was probably accurate, but it didn't ring true to Tobin. Maybe it was his wishful thinking, but he could have sworn Danny had been kinder and more patient with him. He'd always given up his game console controller for Tobin. He'd stopped to help Tobin up when he fell. He'd even tried to teach Tobin how to skateboard a few times.

"Do you remember when you and Wei would come pick me up after school?"

Danny's laugh lines crinkled around his eyes. "Of course."

Wei was always trying to learn some trick on his skateboard while Danny stood facing the door, waiting for Tobin to come out. "You'd take me to the convenience store for candy and slushies."

Danny laughed, ducking his head like he couldn't believe he'd done that. "Wei would never let you get the giant gobstoppers. He thought you'd break a tooth and he'd get in trouble for it."

Tobin rolled his eyes. "But you'd get them and sneak one to me when Wei wasn't looking."

They laughed in unison. Getting a secret gobstopper from Danny had felt like winning the lottery back then. A precious gift only the two of them knew about.

"See? You were nice to me."

Danny tilted his head, lips curled in a nostalgic smile. "You were younger than the rest of us."

The warm fuzzy from their shared memory fizzled. Was that it? That he was the young one who needed special treatment? "I guess that makes sense. I should have thought of that." He stuck a piece of bird in his mouth and chewed.

"You always had such determination." Danny gazed off into the middle distance, as if retrieving snippets of memory from cold storage. "You had a late growth spurt, so you were a lot smaller than the rest of us for a long time."

"You used to give me piggybacks."

Danny laughed while shaking his head. "It was my way to weight-train."

Tobin rolled his eyes.

"But you never let that hold you back. You ran harder to keep up. Took risks you shouldn't have to prove you could. You wanted so badly to be one of us and you weren't going to take no for an answer."

Basically, Tobin had been a little shit. He knew that.

"Maybe that's why." When Danny looked at him, Tobin got the profound sense of being seen. Like Danny could sift through all his messiness and get to the core of who he was. No one else could do that. No one ever could.

Tobin broke eye contact first, blinking away the tears that prickled his eyes. Ah, crap. A little trip down memory lane and here he was tearing up. He wasn't usually so sentimental.

Danny reached across the table and, without thinking, Tobin slipped his hand into Danny's. Simple comfort offered and received. Leave it to Danny to know exactly what he needed.

"Well, whatever your reasons were. Thank you. I don't think I've ever told you that before."

Danny squeezed his hand. "You don't need to thank me."

"I know. But you deserve it." Tobin met Danny's gaze, and everything in the world faded away. The hum of diners in the restaurant, the clink of silverware against ceramic. Mouthwatering aromas drifting around them. The carefully designed lighting setting the mood. There was only the two of them, connected by their hands, but also by something more that dated back to those youthful, carefree days.

"Danny…" The words wouldn't come out. They were stuck in his throat and he couldn't breathe. Yet somehow it seemed Danny could read his mind and see how much Tobin appreciated him, admired him, adored him.

"I know," he whispered. "I know."

But that wasn't all, because the thought of leaving dinner and going back to their respective lives gripped Tobin with a panic he didn't fully understand. He squeezed Danny's hand, and Danny squeezed back.

Dinner wasn't enough. He wanted—no, he needed more. "Danny." His chest tightened. "I want...can we...?"

Danny didn't need Tobin to spell that out either. His eyes darkened, and his lips parted. Heat rose as if the candle between them was a raging fire. Time stood still as Tobin waited for a response. "Please..."

Danny shut his eyes; his fingers held Tobin's in a death grip. "I don't know."

"Yes, you do. I know you do."

Danny dropped his chin to his chest. "Wei—"

"Don't." Tobin cut him off. "Don't use him or my parents as an excuse. What do they have anything to do with us? I'm an adult. You're an adult. We're allowed to do whatever we want without their approval or even their knowledge."

Annoyance at his family getting in the way, once again, drove Tobin on. "I'm so sick and tired of them interfering with my life. Telling me what I can or can't do, like I don't know how to make my own decisions. Well, I've been living on my own for years now. And hey, I've got a job, and an apartment. I can take care of myself. I don't need them. And if they can't get that into their stubborn little heads, then that's their problem. Not mine."

He sucked in a breath and waited for the light-headed-ness to pass. When his lungs managed to resupply the dip in oxygen in his body, he looked up to find Danny watching him, a little taken aback.

"Sorry. I didn't mean to get carried away."

"Don't be sorry. You're right."

Tobin blinked, not sure he'd heard correctly. "What?"

"You're right. You're an adult and you can make your own choices." Danny said it so matter-of-factly that Tobin wasn't sure if that meant they *were* going to have sex or not. He liked the first option better.

"So then I choose you."

He waited again. Seconds ticked past. Their eyes locked in a silent battle between head and heart. Right when Tobin was sure Danny would say no, Danny gave him a small smile of surrender.

Tobin took Danny's hand and brought it to his lips for a simple kiss. A promise.

Chapter Six

The rest of dinner went by in a blur and suddenly they were in another town car, speeding away to…actually, Tobin hadn't asked where. They sat on opposite sides of the backseat, hands to themselves. Danny staring out the window with Tobin monitoring him out of the corner of his eye. He didn't dare speak. Nothing to interrupt the sacred silence that had settled between them.

What was Danny thinking? Was he having second thoughts? Maybe they were headed to Tobin's hotel where Danny would leave him standing alone on the sidewalk. Maybe he'd made a fool of himself at dinner and Danny was too much of a gentleman to reject him outright.

A hand closed over his own. "Whatever you're thinking right now. It's not true." Danny laced their fingers together and all the nervous energy and self-doubt seeped right out of Tobin. They stayed like that, hands linked, until the car pulled up outside Danny's hotel. The same one where they'd had dinner last time.

Valets rushed to open their doors. Tobin waited for Danny to come around the back of the car and as he strode past, he picked up Tobin's hand again like they'd practiced that move for years.

As they stepped inside the hotel, Tobin felt like a celebrity making his grand entrance on the arm of his leading man. Valets held the doors open for them, people in the lobby stepped aside to let them pass. He even caught the concierge tracking their progress across the room.

The elevator doors opened as if it'd been waiting for them to arrive. Neither of them spoke, but as they passed floor after floor, their grip became tighter and tighter until Tobin was convinced he'd have the shape of Danny's hand imprinted on his own for the rest of time.

Danny pulled a key card out from the inside pocket of his suit jacket. He swiped it against the card reader and pushed open the door all in one swift movement. He never broke his stride, never let go of Tobin's hand.

Danny's room was a suite. Mini-bar and living room. Heavy velvet drapes, dark leather couches, and a baby grand piano. A single solitary lamp lit the space with a warm yellow light.

That was the only glimpse Tobin got as they breezed through to the bedroom. Plush carpet, a padded headboard, and more heavy drapes. Rich, luxurious, opulent, and Tobin couldn't care less because Danny was looking at him like he was the most precious thing in the world.

Like he was the last morsel of food in front of a starving man. The last drop of water. The last gasp of air. Danny closed the distance between them and wrapped both hands around the back of Tobin's neck, bringing them even closer. With millimeters to spare, Danny paused. "You're sure?"

"One hundred percent."

Danny's kiss was all-consuming, rushing through him and tearing him apart until Tobin didn't exist anymore. There was only heat and sparks, want and need, the bitterness of their chocolate dessert and the sweet wine they'd washed it down with. Danny's kiss radiated from the tips of his hair down to the soles of his feet and back up again.

He whined when Danny broke the kiss. So Danny planted another quick one before setting to work.

Wordlessly, he stripped Tobin of his jacket, then his shirt. His shoes, his socks, and his pants went next until he wore nothing but emerald green briefs. Danny ran one finger down the length of Tobin's cock, already hard, and growled. Tobin's dick jumped in response and he bit his lip to keep from crying out.

"On the bed." The instruction was murmured in a soft voice, but Tobin felt the command in it all the same.

He moved quickly, scrambling onto the bed as Danny stalked toward him.

Standing at the foot, Danny began undressing. Slowly. Deliberately. Each article of clothing hitting the floor with a light thud that made Tobin's heart beat faster. By the time

Danny stepped out of his black boxer briefs, there was a sizable wet spot on the front of Tobin's.

"Don't move."

As if Tobin had anywhere else to be.

He watched Danny dig through a carry-on suitcase and pull out a strip of condoms and a bottle of lube. Somehow, Tobin was sure Danny didn't normally pack sex supplies for his business trips.

Danny tossed them onto the bed, then climbed on himself. He wrapped a hand around Tobin's ankle and yanked, sending Tobin sprawling backward onto the mattress. God. He loved getting manhandled. He loved that Danny was strong enough to manhandle him.

But Danny was more than only brute strength. He smoothed delicate touches over Tobin's feet, his calves, the backs of his knees, as if he wanted to learn the texture of every inch of Tobin's skin. And oh god, he loved that Danny was gentle enough to make every touch feel like heaven.

The air around them grew heavy and Tobin's head swam with desire. He ached for more of Danny. But he didn't reach for him, didn't rush him. He let Danny explore because it was delicious torture.

When Danny reached his sides, those sensitive, tender spots, Tobin couldn't help but squirm.

"Ticklish?"

Tobin bit his lip and shook his head.

Danny—the devil—ran his fingers up Tobin's sides again, lighter this time, and Tobin shrieked.

Out of an instinct for self-preservation, he scrambled to

the other side of the bed. "Okay, okay, I'm ticklish! Stop! Please! No!" He hugged his vulnerable sides, while Danny kneeled in the middle of the bed laughing.

"I'm not touching you anymore."

Tobin eyed him suspiciously and pouted. "Okay, but no tickling."

Danny held his hands up in surrender. "No tickling. I promise." He extended a hand in invitation, and after casting Danny one last disparaging look, Tobin went willingly.

"You don't have to run from me," Danny whispered as he drew Tobin near.

"I know."

Danny proved it with muscular arms wrapped with care around him, cradling him, as they kissed. Lips and tongue, drinking each other in and giving each other life.

Danny's cock pressed against Tobin's bulge, still trapped in his briefs. Hardness against hardness, but not nearly enough of it. He whined. The solution should be simple enough, but for the life of him, Tobin couldn't figure out how to get what he wanted.

Thank heavens Danny came to the rescue. He guided Tobin down until he lay on his back and helped him out of his briefs. When his legs were free of their restraints, Tobin spread them wide and welcomed Danny in.

Chest to chest. Thigh to thigh. Mouth to mouth and cock to cock. Danny used his weight to press Tobin into the mattress and he reveled in every pound. Tobin had dreamed of this for so long, but his memories paled in comparison to the real thing. The taste of Danny's skin on his tongue.

The dip of Danny's spine under his fingers. The smell of Danny's arousal in his nose. It was all utter perfection.

"Please, Danny."

"What do you want?" Danny asked between kisses down Tobin's neck. "Tell me what you want."

"I want… I want you to fuck me. Fuck me, Danny. Please."

"Yeah? How do you want me to fuck you? Hard? Slow? Tell me how."

How was it fair to ask him to decide? He wanted it all. Hard and slow and again and again.

"Come on, Tobin. Tell me how you want me to fuck you." Danny took one nipple between his teeth and nibbled, sending electric currents directly to Tobin's cock.

He dug his fingers into Danny's shoulders to keep himself from coming, releasing only when the waves of pleasure eased.

"Hard. Fast." Because he would never survive something soft and slow.

Danny reared up on his knees and reached for the condoms. He looked like a fucking god as he rolled it on. Broad shoulders, rounded biceps, a chest so defined it could have rivaled a marble statue. It should be illegal for someone to look so hot.

With a squirt of lube on his hand, Danny positioned himself between Tobin's thighs. The lubed hand went in search of Tobin's hole and the other directed Tobin's dick into Danny's mouth.

"Oh fuck." Tobin shut his eyes because the image of

Danny bent over his cock would have been enough for him to shoot his load.

He fisted the sheets beneath him as he suffered through wet, hot suction on his dick and thick probing fingers in his ass. One assault ricocheted off the other until Tobin was shaking with the need to come.

"God, Danny. Please. Fuck me, please."

"You want my dick?"

"Yes, please."

"You said hard, right?"

"Yes, hard, please."

Danny's cock was so much thicker than a few fingers could ever be. He pressed forward, inch by excruciating inch until the head popped inside. Still he pressed, not easing until he bottomed out.

Tobin sucked in shallow breaths. It was all he could manage with Danny's cock stretching him wide. So thick. So full. So perfect. He'd spent seven years trying to replicate this feeling, but no other cock and no dildo could even come close. Only Danny could fill up all the empty spaces in Tobin and make him complete.

He pulled Danny down for a kiss. Closed lipped, with noses smooshed together, Tobin poured all the emotions into it, happiness, joy, gratitude, and a whole bunch of others he didn't have the vocabulary for. He hoped Danny would understand.

Danny began to move. Slowly at first, despite Tobin's demand for hard and fast. Pleasure rippled through Tobin with every movement, washing over him until he couldn't breathe.

He rocked up to meet Danny, sending Danny's cock even deeper inside. He gasped, and Danny grunted, and they did it again. Picking up speed, they moved as one, furthering their connection with every thrust.

Danny's teeth sank into the meaty part of Tobin's shoulder. His nails scored paths down Danny's back. Their grunts and cries of pleasure filled the room, punctuated by the sound of skin slapping against skin.

It was hard. It was fast. But it was the most intimate lovemaking Tobin had ever experienced. Pleasure built inside him, straining against every muscle and every sinew, looking for a release valve. He didn't try to fight it, didn't try to hold back or drag it out. Instead, Tobin leaned into it, holding Danny closer as it burst from him and he came.

His body exploded into a million pieces. Stars danced in front of his eyes.

Above him, the sound of Danny's roar was muffled by the blood rushing through his ears.

Danny collapsed on top of him, hot heavy breaths against Tobin's neck.

Tobin ran his palm over the back of Danny's head, the prickly soft hairs tickling his skin. Danny practically purred at the caress. If the world ended now, Tobin wouldn't mind. He kissed Danny's temple and felt a kiss pressed into his collarbone.

"God, I've missed you." The words tumbled out before Tobin even knew what he was saying.

But it was too late. Danny heard, but did he understand? Did he know how much Tobin had pined for Danny when he'd gotten old enough to know what love and sex were? Did he know how freaked out Tobin had been the morning after, afraid Danny would awake furious at having been seduced? Did he know how much he still haunted Tobin's dreams in the years since, how hard and alone and empty it left Tobin?

Danny raised himself onto his elbows and slowly withdrew his softening cock from Tobin's body. He felt the loss immediately.

Danny climbed off the bed and dropped the condom into the wastebasket. He went out into the living room and turned off the light. When he came back, he had a damp towel and he silently, gently, wiped up the mess Tobin had made on his stomach.

If Danny had been anyone else, this would be when Tobin said thanks and left. He wasn't one to spend the night and he liked to sleep alone. At least, that's what he told himself.

With Danny, the thought of putting his clothes on and heading out made Tobin cringe. Still, he sat up and scooted toward the edge of the bed. Monica had said scratch the itch, and he'd scratched it. Now it was time to head back to reality.

Danny caught his hand. They sat facing away from each other, fingers intertwined behind their backs. "Don't go."

Danny's request was uttered so softly Tobin almost didn't hear him. He turned to make sure and what he saw cracked open something in his chest.

Danny's shoulders drooped, as if in defeat; head too heavy to be held up. But it was his expression that did it for Tobin. Sad and uncertain, a little fearful, like he wasn't sure he had the right to ask. This was childhood Danny in front of him, without the armor of expensive clothes and designer watches.

Tobin crawled back to him, coming up from behind to wrap his arms around Danny. He rested his chin on top of Danny's shoulder.

"I'll stay," he whispered and marveled as all the stiffness drained from Danny's body.

Chapter Seven

The bedside clock read four in the morning, but Danny was wide-awake. He hadn't slept for more than an hour combined the whole night. Tobin had no such problem, though. He'd been out like a light and had barely stirred since.

He should get up. Check his email and respond to messages that were undoubtedly waiting for him. But the bed was warm, the sheets were soft, and Tobin's gentle breathing was too enticing to leave behind.

Last night had been… Danny had spent all those waking hours trying to find the right words to describe it, but nothing could adequately capture everything he'd felt since the moment Tobin had walked into the restaurant. It'd been easy, fun, relaxed. The sex was hot—more than hot, mind-blowing. But all the vocabulary in the world paled to the actual experience of it.

Tobin was wonderful. He'd always been a cool kid and now he'd grown up into a man mature beyond his years. And not only mature, but smart, responsible, driven. In some ways, he reminded Danny of himself at that age, with the world at his feet and endless possibilities.

That felt like eons ago. What happened to that guy who thrived on hard work, always looking for the next challenge, eager to conquer every mountain before him? When had he faded into this shell of a man who wanted nothing more than to lie down and sleep?

Tobin was young. He still had so much to do and so much to experience. Danny wasn't old, he knew, but he sure as hell felt old. Jetting off somewhere at a moment's notice didn't sound like fun anymore. Staying up late to pull all-nighters in the office was a hard limit. Hell, he barely showed his face at Jade Harbour's Friday afternoon happy hours anymore. He'd rather go straight home.

Tobin would probably be better off with someone who had the energy to keep up. Someone who got as animated as he did when talking about his work, who was as keen and ambitious. Tobin would make a great half of a power couple.

Danny's battery no longer held a charge.

He ran a hand over his face before forcing himself out of bed and into the bathroom. Closing the door quietly behind him, he flipped on the light and winced as his eyes adjusted. God, he even looked tired. Like a dead man walking. A few years ago, he might have cared, might have tried to do something about it. Try to get more sleep, eat better, take vitamins and hire a personal trainer and all that.

Danny turned away from the mirror. Now? Eh, he couldn't be bothered.

He emptied his bladder, brushed his teeth, and splashed some water on his face. Flicking off the light before he opened the door, Danny leaned against the doorframe and watched the gentle rise and fall of Tobin's chest as he slept. Danny breathed with him, slowly in and slowly out, until all the thoughts swirling in his head settled.

There was no point in getting ahead of himself. For all he knew, Tobin was only looking for another one-night stand. The idea didn't sit right with Danny, rubbing him like sandpaper on the skin. But who was he to object? He wasn't boyfriend material, remember? He had a flailing career that needed saving and a team that depended on him to get the job done. He didn't have time for a relationship.

He grabbed his laptop and set up in the armchair by the window, Tobin still in his line of sight. Dozens and dozens of new emails were waiting in his inbox, the number of unread messages well into the thousands. He'd given up trying to clear them out ages ago. Danny worked, deleting emails where he could and ignoring others. The ones that needed a response from him got at most one sentence.

Quite a few of those emails were pitchbooks from companies who wanted Jade Harbour's money. But it wasn't that simple. They might be able to put together a glossy presentation, but that didn't mean those companies would be good investments. Buy low, sell high was the motto of the finance world. What novices didn't always understand was buying low was useless if you couldn't sell high.

Which was why WesTec was so pivotal even though

Cyrus West was an asshole. WesTec had the potential a lot of these other companies didn't have. Sure, there *might* be other good investments out there, but Danny had already spent months on WesTec and he couldn't afford to throw it all away for hypotheticals.

An email from Ginika popped up, the second draft of the business plans Danny had reviewed. He opened the attachments and scanned through each one, checking on the changes made and making more.

Behind him, the sky started to glow with the gradually rising sun. The morning rays lit up the Rocky Mountains, majestic as they towered above the earth. A wall of peaks topped with snow, silent and regal. They didn't care about EBITDAs and ROIs. They counted time by the centuries.

His inbox pinged with another incoming email. Joanna, asking for a WesTec update that didn't exist. Danny gazed out toward the mountains; he felt as old as they were.

On the bed, Tobin groaned and rolled over. The duvet slipped down to his hips, revealing his back, an expanse of soft skin over tight muscles.

"Working already?" Tobin's voice was groggy with sleep. Low and husky in that intimate way that only lovers heard.

"Always."

Tobin smiled, lazy and slow, and extended a hand in Danny's direction.

He shouldn't. The day had already begun and there was work to do. He'd already indulged last night and taking advantage in the morning was only pushing his luck.

Yet, Danny found himself setting his laptop aside and climbing back into bed.

"Mm, that's better."

As Tobin pulled him into a welcoming embrace, all thoughts of quarterly performance numbers, returns on invested capital, and cash burn rates fizzled away. None of that was important when he had Tobin underneath him, naked and hard, and so generous with his body. Danny drank him in.

He kissed his way down Tobin's neck, closed his lips around one pert nipple, then the other. Salt and musk and the smell of the sex they'd had the night before filled Danny's nose and made his head swim. Tobin moaned his encouragement.

Tobin's fingers were on his scalp, brushing through his short hair and firing nerve endings that sent Danny's eyes rolling into the back of his head. God, Tobin was so fucking intoxicating. He wanted more. He would never have enough.

Tobin's cock was hard and leaking pre-come onto his stomach. Danny swiped his tongue over the tip and a burst of flavor exploded in his mouth. Tobin moaned and lifted his hips for more. But Danny pushed him back down and nipped a little love bite on Tobin's hip. This was Danny's breakfast and he would take his sweet time enjoying the feast.

Tobin's balls were as hairless as the rest of him, two round orbs pulled up tight to his body. Danny took them in his mouth, alternating between sucking and lapping them with his tongue until Tobin writhed beneath him.

"Fuck." Tobin's eyes were squeezed shut, his head thrown back, mouth open. He was beautiful.

The thought hit Danny like an arrow through the heart. Tobin was so unbelievably gorgeous, and Danny was incredibly lucky to be in bed with him.

He pressed a kiss onto the inside of Tobin's thigh. Had anyone ever kissed him there before? Maybe Danny could claim that spot and leave a little piece of himself there. So when Tobin invited someone else into bed in the future, when that someone came across that spot, Danny would know he'd been there first.

"Danny?"

He lifted his gaze to meet Tobin's. Half-lidded and filled with the haze of desire, Tobin's eyes spoke volumes. Things that were too honest, too raw for Danny to listen to, not now when he so desperately needed to lose himself in Tobin.

Danny guided Tobin's cock into his mouth and closed his eyes to focus on making this the best blow job of Tobin's life. Tobin's dick was the perfect size and it tasted divine. He licked and sucked like his life depended on it, pulling out every trick he'd ever learned, and Tobin rewarded him with louder and louder cries.

"I'm coming. Oh god, I'm coming!" Tobin warned a split second before come flooded Danny's mouth.

He swallowed every drop.

Sitting back on his heels, he took in the sight of Tobin limp and covered with a sheen of sweat. Tobin wore a loopy smile and Danny returned it.

They should get up and shower. Life was waiting for them. Tobin had to get to WesTec and Danny had a slew of meetings lined up.

But when Tobin reached for Danny, he went willingly. He laid down and Tobin curled into him like two puzzle pieces fitting perfectly together.

Life could wait.

Danny had managed to avoid Joanna for nearly an entire week after returning from Calgary. But he could only put off the inevitable for so long. He hit the button to close the elevator doors, but they only got halfway before popping back open. In walked Joanna in a fitted pale blue dress, designer handbag on her arm.

"Joanna." Danny greeted her with a nod.

"Danny." She turned and stood next to him, both facing forward as the elevator shot up. "How was Calgary?"

Her way of saying, *what the fuck was going on with WesTec?* Danny had worked with her long enough to read between the lines.

"Fine. Great." He wasn't exactly lying. His meetings had gone well, and any time spent with Tobin was always amazing. But that hadn't really been her question.

She shot him a look, innocuous to anyone who didn't know her as well as Danny did.

He stood up straighter and adjusted his watch. "WesTec is coming along. We'll get there."

The line of Joanna's lips flattened a millimeter, but the doors opened before she could respond. She strode out first, her heels clicking on the tiled floor as an announcement of her arrival. Danny followed in her wake.

"What's the holdup?" she asked as she headed to her office.

Danny didn't need to be told to accompany her there.

"Cyrus West is reluctant to sell."

Joanna grabbed a bundle of mail and messages from her assistant as she walked past, no break in her stride. "Oh?" She breezed into her office, dropped her handbag on the couch, the mail on her desk, and drifted into her high-backed leather executive chair. With legs crossed and chin resting elegantly in one hand, she was power personified. No one messed with Joanna Chiang and got away with it.

Danny opted to stand behind the chairs in front of Joanna's desk. They were significantly lower than hers—probably by design. "I'll handle it."

She pinned him with a stare that was all the more unnerving because of her slight smile. Seconds ticked past and Danny resisted the urge to fill the silence. It must have been a full minute before Joanna spoke. "Brief Ray on WesTec. I want him to run point on opposition research."

Danny blinked at the verbal slap in the face. "I said I'll handle it."

"And I said, bring Ray in." Her smile was gone now.

Danny didn't have anything against Ray; as an operating partner, he was the best in the field. But Danny was the deal closer. He didn't care how good Ray was, he didn't need help doing his job. "Give me a little more time."

Joanna sighed and after a moment rose from her chair to come around the desk. "Danny," she said in a softer tone. "I've already given you months and quarters. I've defended you against our investors who want you out. This isn't about you anymore. *My* ass is on the line. So when I say I want Ray involved, that's not a request."

She took a moment to let that sink in before turning to her desk and pressing a button on the phone intercom. "Get Ray in here."

Danny couldn't see a way out of this. Joanna was right about his performance reflecting poorly not only on him, but on the firm as a whole. He'd been so distracted by his own pity party he hadn't realized what was so glaringly obvious. Still, it was a hit to his ego to have to rely on reinforcements and he couldn't help but bristle at having it forced upon him.

Joanna waved Ray in before he could knock on the glass door.

"You rang?" Ray sauntered in like he owned the place, exuding an air of confidence Danny had always envied. Ray came from generations of wealth and had never known a hard day in his life. The fact that he still worked for a paycheck was fodder for speculation and gossip in the industry.

"WesTec. What do you know about it?" Joanna fired off, retaking her seat behind her desk.

Ray let out a low whistle. "Cyrus West is a piece of work." He dropped onto the couch, spreading both arms across the back and resting his feet on the glass coffee table. "They call him the frat boy of Alberta's tech industry. Decently smart, entirely conceited. Wants to be the next Google, but word on the street is he doesn't have what it takes."

He looked at Danny. "You interested in WesTec?" At least he sounded impressed.

Danny crossed his arms. "It's got potential."

"I can ask around, if you'd like. See what I can dig up."

With his family's connections and his generally ruthless attitude, Ray had a reputation for digging up shit. As much
as he hated to admit it, getting Ray to do the dirty work
would make Danny's life a lot easier.

"Great." Joanna turned to her computer. Discussion over.
"Get leverage. Selling to us is in his best interest and if he
needs convincing, you know what to do."

Ray smiled like a cat about to shove an expensive bottle of champagne off the counter. There was nothing that
could stop him, and he knew it. Hell, he even rubbed his
hands together as he stood. "I'll get right on it."

Danny followed Ray out of Joanna's office. There was
no point in arguing. Sometimes they had to play dirty to
get the job done. If this was one of those times, then Ray
was the right guy to do it.

"Hey." Ray pulled Danny into a quiet corner. "No hard
feelings, yeah? You're Joanna's favorite and golden boy has
to keep his hands clean, if you know what I mean."

There was so much to object to that Danny didn't bother.

"I'll poke around and let you know what I find. Shouldn't
be too hard with Cyrus's reputation."

"Don't do anything without running it past me."

"Of course, man." Ray slapped him on the shoulder before heading off. "You're the boss."

If only.

Chapter Eight

"What's up with him?"

"Hm? Oh, he's probably looking at pictures of his new boyfriend."

"That explains the goofy grin."

"You'll never guess who it is!"

"I know him?"

"No, it's his brother's best friend!"

"Is that a good thing?"

Tobin looked up from his phone. "I'm right here, you know. I can hear you."

Monica and her girlfriend, Ayán, were sitting on the couch next to his armchair, Monica working on her latest cross-stitch and Ayán with a lap full of yarn. Ayán was here more often than she wasn't, and Tobin sometimes wondered why she didn't officially move in. He wouldn't mind; they had enough space, plus she was a wizard in the kitchen.

"Yeah, but you were preoccupied," Monica said, as if that was reason enough to talk about him like he wasn't in the room.

"That doesn't matter."

"You could have jumped in at any time."

Whatever. He went back to scrolling through Constance's social media, scouring it for pictures of Danny.

"You didn't answer my question about the brother's best friend thing," Ayán asked again.

"It's a little taboo," replied Monica.

"It's not taboo. It's not anything. And he's not my boyfriend." At least, Tobin didn't think he was? They hadn't talked about it before parting ways in Calgary last week, or during the few phone conversations they'd had since.

Oh, they'd talked about plenty of things. Like books they'd read—Danny was an audiobook fan, but honestly, listening didn't count as reading in Tobin's humble opinion. They'd talked about places they'd visited, like Tobin's last trip to Hong Kong to visit family, and Danny's Greek island hopping on a private yacht. According to Danny, that hadn't really been a vacation since a bunch of Jade Harbour investors had been aboard, but please: Greek. Island. Hopping. Private. Yacht. That sounded like a vacation to Tobin.

"If it's not anything, why are you so worked up about it?" Ayán and her damned logic.

"I'm not worked up about it!" Except both Monica and Ayán were staring at him like he was freaking out. "I'm not!"

"If you say so." Ayán went back to her knitting.

"You still haven't told us how Calgary went." Monica set her cross-stitch aside as if Tobin was going to tell her anything now.

"It was fine. I worked and then I went back to the hotel."

"To Danny?" Monica drew out his name like she was singing it.

An automatic denial was on the tip of his tongue, except Monica was right. "We had dinner," he admitted.

Now Ayán was putting her knitting aside.

"And?" Monica prompted.

"And I spent the night with him."

"See!" Monica gave Ayán a slap that was probably meant to be friendly but had Ayán wincing. Tobin knew how that felt—Monica and her over-excited slapping.

"Yeah, yeah, I believe you. Easy on the physical abuse." Ayán rubbed her arm.

But Monica was plowing full steam ahead. "And how was it?"

Amazing. Wonderful. Exquisite. "How was what?"

"Ugh, come on, Tobes. You know what I mean. Don't leave us hanging!"

Ayán jumped in quickly. "Leave *you* hanging, dear. I'm not a part of it."

"Yes, you are. Don't pretend you're not curious."

Ayán didn't look thrilled at the accusation, but she didn't refute it.

"To-kemon, spill!"

He wiggled deeper into the cushions of his chair as if they could hide him from Monica's questions. If it had been anyone else, Tobin would have already provided all the gory details; he and Monica were that type of best friends. But this was Danny and Tobin didn't feel like sharing him.

"Oh! He's blushing!" Monica was far too ecstatic about this whole thing.

Tobin buried his face into his hands.

"Damn. You're serious about this guy, aren't you?" said Ayán.

"Of course, he is!" Monica responded for him. "He's rich, you know. Like über-rich. He's like a corporate raider or something."

"He's not a corporate raider." Tobin jumped to Danny's defense, only to see a look of distaste flash across Ayán's face.

As a self-proclaimed feminist and all-around anti-mainstream anything, Ayán was highly critical of capitalism and the finance industry.

"He's not like that." Tobin doubled down.

"So, what does he do exactly?" Ayán asked.

It wasn't a trick question, but it *felt* like one. "He's a private equity investor."

"Which is a pretty way of saying corporate raider." She did not look impressed.

"That's how they ran into each other in Calgary," Monica chimed in again, bitch. "Danny's trying to buy Tobin's client."

When she put it that way, it sounded much worse than it really was. But Ayán didn't know that, and her eyebrows disappeared behind her bangs. "He's trying to buy what?"

"The company I'm consulting with. Not a person. That's

what private equity investors do. They buy companies, make them better, and then sell them again."

Ayán sent him a condescending look. "Yeah, I know what private equity firms do. They buy companies on the cheap with lots of credit, load them up with even more debt while firing everyone. Then they sell off bits and pieces of it to the highest bidder, rake in the cash, and leave everyone else devastated."

Okay, yeah, Tobin knew private equity firms had a bad rap with the bleeding-heart liberal crowd, but Danny didn't do any of that. Right?

"Listen, sorry to burst your bubble, Tobin." Ayán didn't sound the least bit apologetic. "Capitalism is an exploitative disease on society, rotting it from the inside out. If your boy is in on it, then he's rotten too."

"Fuck you." Tobin didn't care what Ayán thought about finance or private equity or Danny's participation in any of it. Danny was a good person. No one could convince him otherwise.

"Hey, don't shoot the messenger." Ayán picked up her knitting again. "One of these days, greed is going to kill us all."

Even Monica rolled her eyes. "No need for an existential crisis, babe."

"I'm just saying."

"Well, I'm sure Tobin's boyfriend isn't like that. Not all rich people are bad."

"Right. Like 'not all white people,' 'not all men.' Good people on both sides." When Ayán was on a roll, there really was no stopping her.

"Whatever." Tobin stood. "You don't know anything about Danny."

Monica mouthed a sorry to him as he headed toward his room. Except Ayán and her damn logic had planted a seed of doubt.

Finance was this huge industry, and yeah, some parts of it were pretty bad. But everyone had to make money somehow, right? Being exploitative and greedy wasn't the only way to work in finance—Danny must be one of the good guys. He had to be.

Except when Tobin plopped himself down on his bed, he wondered. He grabbed his laptop and pulled up a browser window. In the search bar he typed *Jade Harbour Capital*. After a moment's hesitation, he added *Daniel Ip*, and hit enter.

Jade Harbour's website was the first thing to pop up. A link to Danny's biography and head shot.

Then link after link of press releases and Bloomberg articles about Jade Harbour's business activities—how much money they'd raised from investors; the new companies they'd purchased and brought into the Jade Harbour family; portfolio company sales at huge multiples above the original purchase price. Interspersed were good public relation articles about the various charities they supported. Cancer research one year; a children's hospital the next. They even had an entire budget set aside for supporting women-owned small businesses.

See? They were doing good things. Nothing to worry about.

Yeah, yeah, don't believe everything written on the internet, Tobin knew as much. But after five pages of search results, not one even hinted at any remotely questionable behavior.

Tobin closed his computer. Ayán didn't know what she was talking about.

On his computer screen were WesTec's financial statements, budget to actuals for the past few years, and forecasting models for the next few years. Plus a few extra windows from other projects he was helping out with, for good measure. That way, if anyone walked past and glanced at his computer, he looked hard at work.

What they didn't see was Tobin's phone placed strategically in front of his keyboard and blocked from view by his body. He squinted at the screen and the maze of words he and Danny had built on the *Words with Friends* game board. Danny was kicking his butt with all his fancy advanced vocabulary. Tobin had gone into accounting for a reason, damn it.

He'd much rather they switch back to *Exploding Kittens*, but apparently all the screaming and laughing involved wasn't office appropriate enough for Danny. A strictly while-at-home game.

"Hey, Tobin."

He jumped, sending his phone tumbling to the floor.

"Sorry! I didn't mean to startle you. You okay?" Lonnie bent to pick up his phone for him—shit!

Tobin scrambled for it and managed to grab it before she could see what was on the screen. "Yeah, yeah, I'm fine. Sorry. A little lost in thought, that's all."

"No worries. Are you still good for our check-in?"

Check-in? Tobin glanced at the time. Ah, crap. He'd totally forgotten about his weekly check-in meeting with Lonnie. "Yes! Yes, definitely." He popped his laptop from its dock and stuffed his phone into his pocket. "Ready!" Though he was decidedly not ready.

She led the way to a small meeting room close by. "How's it going?" she asked as she sat.

"Good! Yeah, things are great!" Was he laying it on too thick? He coughed. "I'm good."

"Cool. The client's not giving you too much trouble, is he?"

Tobin had already told her about Cyrus West and his less than savory personality. She'd been careful to check in with him about it on the regular. "He's okay. You know, same old." In fact, Tobin hadn't spoken directly to Cyrus in a while. All his communication with WesTec had been filtered through the finance team, which he was more than happy about. The less interaction he had with Cyrus the better.

"Good, I'm glad to hear that. So, how about you walk me through what you've got so far?"

"Sure!" Tobin sorted through all the open windows trying to remember what they hell any of them were.

"Um, so, I've been going through their budget to get a sense of what their expenses are like. Most of it is fine. The more egregious expenses have to do with office perks, like daily hot breakfasts, weekly massages, stuff like that. But they're a start-up and I don't think they'll be willing to cut back on those."

Lonnie nodded, squinting at his screen. "Mmhmm, most don't. But if they want to grow past the start-up stage, they'll have to decide what's more important: profit or perks. What else have you got?"

"Um, well…" Tobin clicked away to another window, looking for something else he could talk about. "They've got a bunch of patents, but I haven't had a chance to go through them yet."

"Oh yeah? What kind of patents?"

"Well, some of them are promising." At least he hoped they were.

"Uh-huh."

"And obviously, they're using some of them. But again, I haven't had a chance to go through them yet."

"Okay, anything else?"

That wasn't enough? Tobin racked his brain. "Um… I heard they've got interest from an external investor."

That caught Lonnie's attention. Oops. She sat up a little straighter and looked directly at him. "Really? Do you know who?"

Shit. Shit, shit. As if Danny had telepathically eavesdropped on their conversation, Tobin's phone buzzed with a notification—most likely Danny completing his turn on *Words with Friends*. Yeah, Danny would not be okay with Tobin telling other people about Jade Harbour's plans. Private transactions like this were highly confidential until the official press release. And even then, details tended to be scant. "No, no, I don't know."

"Huh." Lonnie frowned. "Where did you hear this?"

Think. Think fast! "At WesTec." That much was true.

"Some people were whispering about it in the kitchen, but they didn't really know much."

Lonnie nodded. "Yeah, the regular staff probably don't know anything. They'd want to keep the information in a tight circle. Still, you've included that option in your analysis, right?"

"Yeah, of course, definitely. Although Cyrus didn't seem so keen on the idea." Shit. Why did he say that?

"You talked to him about it?" Lonnie looked a little confused.

Hell, Tobin was a little confused. "Not exactly. Just, you know, hypothetically." Tobin waved a hand around as if that was explanation enough.

"Right. Well, looks like you've got everything under control with WesTec."

Thank god.

Lonnie got up to leave but stopped with her hand on the doorknob. "Oh, I almost forgot," she said. "When are you going back to Toronto next?"

Tobin blinked. What did Toronto have to do with WesTec? Aside from Danny, that was. "Uh, I don't know. At least, I don't have any plans to take time off."

"It's not a big deal." She waved her hand to emphasize how not-important it was. "Let me know the next time you do. You should stop into Paradigm's Toronto office while you're there. Face time with the higher-ups and all that."

Ah, career progression. Trust Lonnie to be thinking big picture for him. "Got it. Will do."

"Perfect. Anything else you need from me? I'll be taking off early today."

"Nope! No, I'm all good. Thanks." Tobin closed his laptop and followed her out. She turned right to go back to her desk and Tobin turned left to go to his.

His phone buzzed in his pocket again. He pulled it out to find a notification from *Words with Friends* and a separate message from Danny. Your turn.

He slid his laptop back into its dock before sitting down to reply to Danny.

Yeah, yeah. *Some* people have to work for a living, you know.

He followed it up with a winking face with stuck-out tongue emoji.

Danny shot back quickly. *Some* people can work and play at the same time.

Ouch.

Three little dots blinked at the bottom of his screen before another message from Danny came through. About to head into a meeting. Will be incommunicado.

Good. That gave Tobin time to figure out his next move. And hopefully not lose quite so epically again. He navigated to the game app. Danny's last word was "acquisitions." Ugh. Of course Danny came up with a fancy-shmancy finance term. It was worth too many points for Tobin to even want to know.

Acquisitions. He paused.

He really hadn't meant to tell Lonnie about Jade Harbour's interest in WesTec. It was an honest-to-god slip of the tongue. But would Danny believe that if he ever found out how close Tobin had been to leaking news of his deal? Especially when Tobin never stopped going on and on about how adult and professional he was.

Yeah, loads adult, much professional.

Danny would probably be pissed, and he'd have every right to be. Tobin knew better. But it wasn't like Lonnie knew *who* was interested in buying WesTec; Tobin had at least managed that much. What were the chances Danny would find out, anyway? Unless Tobin told him, practically zilch. What Danny didn't know wouldn't hurt him, right?

Right.

Tobin went back to *Words with Friends*. He was sorely tempted to look up Merriam-Webster for word ideas. But that would be cheating, and Tobin wanted to beat Danny fair and square.

"Zex." That was a word, wasn't it? Maybe like "hex" but extra serious because it started with a "z"? Who knew. The game app accepted it, so Tobin would take it. Sweet.

He put his phone aside and turned to his computer again. Now, if only there was an app that could tell him how to fix WesTec.

Chapter Nine

Ray strode into Danny's office without knocking and dropped, uninvited, into one of the chairs opposite Danny's desk. "Got what you need." He waved a folder in the air.

Was it possible to feel dread and relief at the same time? He was getting nowhere with Cyrus West and with every day that passed, Joanna's approach felt like the only option.

Ray placed the folder in Danny's outstretched hand but didn't let go of it. "Fair warning, some of it is pretty nasty."

Danny expected nothing less. He took the folder and flipped it open. "What am I looking at?"

Ray slouched down in his seat, ankle balanced on opposite knee. "He's getting divorced and his wife is suing him for everything he's worth. She's going to win, if those photos are any indication."

The photos looked like they were taken with a pretty powerful zoom. They showed Cyrus getting handsy and intimate with young women—very young women.

"Is this what I think it is?" Danny held up one of them.

Ray cocked his head. "Could be. Or they could be very young-looking eighteen-year-olds."

"Where did the photos come from?"

"The wife hired a private investigator."

Danny shook his head. If he hadn't already been convinced Cyrus West was a piece of shit, this certainly confirmed it. "We need to send these to the police."

"It wouldn't solve our problem, though. All his assets are frozen because of the divorce."

The fact they were still worried about WesTec when Cyrus West was at best a sexual predator was disgusting. How had this become his life? He shuffled the photos to the bottom of the pile and picked up what looked like legal documents.

Ray continued, "Divorce proceedings spell it all out pretty clearly. She wants full custody of the kids, their big chalet up in Banff. Hell, she's even named which of their friends she's going to keep.

"As for WesTec, it's a part of his financial holdings, so she could get up to half the company by the time the divorce is finalized."

"Which is when?"

"Too far away to be any use to us."

Fuck. Danny ran a hand down his face. Cyrus couldn't sell the company even if he wanted to. "Unless we get his wife on board. Get her to agree to sell. With both of them signing off, the courts shouldn't have an issue with it."

"Yeeeep." Ray straightened in his chair and leaned forward, excitement in his eyes. "Anyway, the divorce and Cyrus West being the devil incarnate aside, there's something else."

"What?"

"There's a rumor going around that WesTec filed a patent a while back. No one really knows what it's for, but the word is it could change the industry. Here's the thing. Whatever it is they patented, they're not using it."

"Why not?"

"Cyrus and the project lead didn't get along. When they quit, everything they were working on got shelved. The rumor is he didn't like them because they were trans."

Danny dropped the folder onto his desk and pinched the bridge of his nose. Every time he thought Cyrus West couldn't get any worse, the asshole managed to prove him wrong. "Why am I not surprised?"

"I don't think anyone is."

Danny ran a mental scan of all the patents Miguel had dug up. "We've already gone through their patents, there wasn't anything revolutionary."

"Apparently it got filed under a different name. Whoever did the paperwork didn't want it traced so easily back to WesTec."

"Hm." The patent could be nothing. Or it could be everything. Danny didn't like the uncertainty.

"Can you find the person who worked on it?"

Ray shrugged. "I can ask around. The start-up scene in

Calgary isn't that big, I'm sure there's some way to track them down."

"Do it." Danny didn't like unknowns. If covering their bases meant having to delay their progress, it was worth it.

"And the wife?"

Leverage wasn't going to do any good if WesTec was locked up in divorce proceedings. But if the wife could be convinced to sell, a multi-pronged attack might do the trick. "Get in touch with her too."

"Consider it done." Ray stood and stretched. "So. When are you heading back to Calgary?"

Danny eyed him because Ray always had something up his sleeve. There wasn't a Calgary trip in his schedule, but he would be lying if he said he hadn't thought about it. Calgary meant more Tobin. "I've got New York and Montreal in the next couple weeks. Why?"

"Stampede is coming up soon. I can be your wingman." Ray pointed two finger guns at Danny as he backed toward the door.

"You mean you want to go fuck hot cowboys."

"You said it, not me."

No, Danny had no interest in fucking hot cowboys. Tobin dressed up as a cowboy, though? That was a different story. His imagination immediately supplied him with sample outfits and suddenly Ray's idea didn't seem so far-fetched.

Ray was already on the other side of the door, one arm extended to point at Danny. "Just say the word." And then he was gone.

Fucking Ray. How the hell was Danny supposed to work

now when all he could think about was Tobin in butt-less chaps and a red handkerchief tied around his neck. Tobin riding his cock. Danny riding his ass.

He reached down to adjust himself, thanking the heavens he was in the relative safety of his own office.

As if on cue, his phone pinged with a message. Morning babe. Followed by a selfie of Tobin still in bed, half asleep, shirtless. Tobin had taken to sending one of those every day and Danny couldn't deny he looked forward to them.

They were hot, sure, but they did more than give Danny an inconvenient chubby while at work. It was like the sun finally coming out after a winter in darkness. Tobin awake for the day meant Danny could breathe a little easier, could move around and work a little easier. Tobin was like a steroid, giving Danny the boost he needed to keep functioning.

Morning, he responded, resisting the urge to add an endearment at the end. This relationship—or whatever it was—had already gone much further than Danny had ever intended.

He walked over to the window. It was a rainy day in Toronto, the skies gray, umbrellas dotting the streets below. Who was he kidding? Danny hadn't thought through his intentions or their consequences when he'd agreed to take Tobin back to his hotel room.

He'd operated on instinct that night and had continued to do so ever since. With their nightly phone calls and silly games, this was way more than friends, more than a hookup. This was them getting attached to each other in a way that could only end in heartache and disaster.

He'd already lied to Wei about it more than once. Not

only that first time over barbeque, but also last week when Wei needed childcare backup and Danny had pleaded work so he could stay home to chat with Tobin. Wei was eventually going to find out. These things could never stay secret for long. And when he did? Pissed wouldn't even begin to describe it.

Danny could imagine it now. Wei's look of ultimate betrayal. Uncle Man's fury; Auntie Grace's sobs.

Don't take their generosity for granted, was what his mother had always said. *Don't take advantage, be respectful.*

Danny was doing the exact opposite. Not that this was the first time he'd disobeyed his mom's admonishments. She wouldn't have approved of all those under the table, "ah, it's nothing, take it, take it," gifts. It wouldn't have mattered that Danny had paid them back with interest since. She'd been a proud woman, and while Danny liked to think he was a lot like her, that was one area where he hadn't let pride stand in his way.

The Loks liked him well enough to adopt him as a charity case. But how would they feel when they found out the sponsor-child was fucking their little prince? Not ecstatic, would be Danny's guess. After all they had done for him, this was how he reciprocated their kindness?

No, he couldn't do that to them. He couldn't violate their trust. The honorable thing to do would be to end things with Tobin and then come clean, at least with Wei, if not Uncle Man and Auntie Grace. They might cut all ties with him—he wouldn't blame them if they did. The thought sent chills through Danny.

He'd gone through life as a loner, but the Loks had

been the one constant. They were his rock, his anchor. They provided a safety net when he hadn't even realized he needed one. Could he go on without them? Did he even know how?

He'd have to take the risk and figure it out. Danny went back to his desk and picked up his phone. He hit redial and Tobin picked it up on the second ring.

"Hey! What's up?"

The cheer in his voice made Danny smile. It chased away that icy chill and warmed him from the inside out. How could a simple greeting do that?

"Hello? Danny?"

"Hi, I'm here."

"Is everything okay?"

It was now that Tobin was on the phone. "Yes, everything's great." He could imagine Tobin's shy grin, the way he bit his bottom lip.

"Okay." From the background came the sound of shuffling, a door opening and closing, keys turning in the lock. "You want to keep me company on my way to work?"

"Sure." Danny would gladly keep Tobin company anywhere, anytime. Now, why had he called Tobin again? There was something he needed to talk about.

Ah, yes. "Have you ever been to the Calgary Stampede?"

"What? No! When is it?"

Guess Ray was good for more than only opposition research. "In a couple weeks. You want to go?"

"Do I want to go? Please, is that even a question? Of course I want to go. Oh, maybe I can schedule some meetings with WesTec and get Paradigm to pay for it."

Danny's cheery mood almost soured at the mention of WesTec, but he pushed it aside. "No need for that. It'll be my treat."

Tobin laughed out loud. "Thanks, that's very sweet of you. But I'm pretty sure I can pay my own way."

But hadn't he said he wanted to expense the trip to Paradigm? If it meant avoiding a meeting with Cyrus West, Danny would happily cover any costs.

"Seriously, Danny. Don't you dare try to pay for me."

Danny liked the idea of treating Tobin, but he wasn't going to force the issue if Tobin was going to be that adamant. "Okay, but don't book a hotel room. Stay with me."

Nothing but the sound of traffic from the other end. Had that been too much? It was only a hotel room that Danny would have to pay for anyway.

Tobin sighed audibly. "Fine. I'll let you pick up the hotel. And FYI, if you're staying in the same place as last time, that's not a room, that's a suite. Big difference."

Was it? Danny wasn't about to argue. "So you'll stay with me."

"Yeah, I will."

"Good." It felt like a victory, even if a small one. Danny would take every win he could get.

They chatted about anything and everything while Tobin made his way into the office. As they spoke, Danny turned his chair to face out the window. Gradually, sunlight broke through the heavy blanket of rain clouds, setting downtown Toronto all a-glisten.

They hung up when Tobin got to his desk, with the mutual promise of switching over to *Words with Friends*.

Tobin was getting better, but Danny still reveled in whooping his ass.

After making the first move, Danny set his phone down. The streets below were already drying. He was going to the Stampede with Tobin. A mix of anticipation and nervous excitement ran through him until he remembered the other reason he was going to Calgary. Right. He turned away from the window, the warm buzz giving way to dread. The folder sat on his desk, a glaring reminder that the trip wasn't going to be all fun and games.

"They don't want to talk," Ray said without looking up from his phone.

"Who?" Danny sat across from him, a low table between them.

A uniformed airport lounge staff member came by and collected their empty cups and plates. "Can I get you gentlemen anything else from the kitchen or the bar?"

"No, thank you." Danny responded for both of them since Ray was frowning intently at his phone, thumbs flying.

"The person who quit from WesTec."

"You found them?"

"Sort of." Ray sighed and put his phone down. "A contact of a contact found them. They sent word back they don't want to talk. Plus, they're not in Calgary anymore."

"Where are they? Why don't they want to talk?"

"Vancouver, apparently that's where they're from. They signed a non-disclosure agreement before leaving."

Unfortunate, but that didn't mean they were a dead end.

Plenty of people violated their non-disclosure agreements, they simply needed to be properly incentivized.

Ray was one step ahead of him. He held up his phone. "I've already asked if there's any way we can convince them. But we should look into other sources who might be able to get us the information."

Danny's mind immediately went to Tobin, but he ruled it out just as quickly. Tobin would have access to WesTec's intranet as part of his consultant role, but under absolutely no circumstances would he ask Tobin to be their inside source. Danny might be willing to play dirty, but even he had some lows he wouldn't stoop to. Dragging Tobin into this mess was one of them.

"What about the wife? Would she know?"

"Possibly. Not sure how involved she was with the day-to-day, though. Our meeting is set up for when we land."

"Good."

Ray had sent him more information on Marlena West. She looked like she could have been a regular on *The Real Housewives of Calgary*, complete with the big blond hair and slightly too puffy lips. But she was shrewd. Graduated top of her class and had an MBA from the University of Calgary. She came from a wealthy oil and gas family and had been the real source of financing behind Cyrus's business ventures. Looked like she'd gotten fed up with him after all these years.

If Danny had to choose a side, he was Team Marlena, hands down, no contest. It would make his life a whole lot easier if Marlena knew something about that patent.

"We should go," Ray announced, glancing at his watch. "They're boarding the plane now."

They made their way from the lounge to the gate and headed straight for the front of the line. Gate staff scanned their phones and minutes later they were settled into their business class seats.

"Mr. Ip, can I get you anything to drink while we wait for the rest of the passengers to board?" the flight attendant asked.

"Vodka tonic, please." So what if it was the middle of the day? Drinking rules didn't apply on airplanes.

Danny checked his phone for any emails that had come in during the walk down from the lounge and found a message from Tobin waiting for him.

Have a great flight! See you later tonight. :)

Danny smiled at the simple note and quickly tapped out a response.

Thank you. See you soon.

"Hot guy?" Ray was in the seat across the aisle from Danny.

"What?"

"I don't think I've ever seen you look like that before."

Danny tucked his phone away. "None of your business."

"Just saying." Ray smiled at the flight attendant who handed him his drink.

"And a vodka tonic for you, Mr. Ip."

Danny took the glass. "Thanks." This trip might turn out to be the best or worst of his life. He needed all the fortification he could get.

The door to the mansion opened as their car pulled into the driveway. Marlena West looked exactly as she did in her pictures.

"Gentlemen!" She waved to them from the porch. "Welcome!"

"Mrs. West." Ray led the way. "I'm Raymond Chao. We spoke on the phone. It's so lovely to meet you in person."

"Oh, please." She slapped Ray lightly on the arm. "It's my pleasure. And call me Marlena. We're not formal around here."

"This is Daniel Ip, my colleague I told you about."

Marlena held out her hand, palm down, as if Danny was supposed to kiss it. He took her hand, but pointedly did not kiss it.

"Very nice to meet you. Thank you for having us."

"Oh, look how sweet you two are. Come in! Come in! I've got some iced tea in the fridge. Or maybe you'd prefer something a little stronger?"

She ushered them into what Danny supposed was a sitting room. It was the perfect mix of modern and homey. Based solely on the mansion's exterior, he hadn't expected the inside to be so…normal.

"Iced tea will be fine," Danny answered.

"Wonderful! Make yourselves comfortable. I'll be back in a jiffy." She disappeared down a hallway.

"Nice," Ray commented as he went to peer out the windows. They looked out onto a backyard of endless green grass. "Big property. At least twenty million, I'd say."

Danny wasn't an expert on the Calgary real estate market, but that price sounded about right. Which put the rest of Cyrus West's assets into perspective.

Marlena came hustling back in carrying a tray laden with glasses and tea. "Come on over, boys. It's stifling hot outside. Here, I made the iced tea myself."

Danny and Ray settled into armchairs on one side of a coffee table while Marlena had the entire couch to herself. They accepted their glasses, had sips, and offered the obligatory compliments.

"Now, I know you didn't come all the way out here to taste my iced tea, as delicious as it is. What can I do for you?"

"We wanted to offer our condolences. We heard you're getting divorced." Ray got straight to the point.

Marlena patted her hair. "That's right. And no need for condolences. It's long overdue."

"We've been talking to Cyrus about a potential investment in WesTec. We think it's a very promising company, and Jade Harbour has the resources to make it a success." Ray took a breath before continuing. "But we understand WesTec could be part of the divorce settlement."

The housewife act evaporated. Marlena eyed them—oh, she understood what was going on, all right. "What kind of investment?"

"We're prepared to make a very generous offer," Ray said with a smile.

She responded with one of her own. "Cyrus, you know, he loves that company. Far more than he should."

"So you understand our predicament."

"I do."

Danny reached into his briefcase and pulled out the new term sheet his team had drawn up. It was a step above what he'd initially offered to Cyrus, but still left Jade Harbour with significant room for profit. "We were hoping you would be more levelheaded about it."

Marlena took the term sheet and flipped directly to the summary page. Her eyes flitted left and right as she read. Danny had no doubt she knew exactly what she was looking for. After a moment, she closed the booklet and set it on the coffee table.

"Oh, gentlemen, I'm only a simple housewife. I don't know much about these things. But it seems to me we might be able to find a mutually beneficial arrangement." She uncrossed and re-crossed her legs before taking a sip of her iced tea.

Ray glanced over at Danny, a satisfied look on his face. "We were hoping you'd say that."

"Mm, now. About those numbers…"

Chapter Ten

Tobin couldn't sit still, he was so beside himself. He couldn't remember feeling this excited since they'd gone on a family trip to Disney. Except he wasn't nine years old anymore and he needed to calm the heck down.

It was only the Calgary Stampede, after all. Only *The Greatest Outdoor Show in the World*. Plus with Danny, like a real couple going on a real mini-break. No big deal.

After the call with Danny, he'd debated whether he should tack on some work meetings with WesTec—not that he needed Paradigm to cover any of the costs, but he kind of felt bad taking vacation days in the middle of a project. But Lonnie hadn't blinked an eye and told him to have a good time. He hadn't even brought his work laptop with him!

Danny apparently wasn't so lucky. He'd been up and banging on his computer since before Tobin was awake. Impressive really, considering the late night they'd had after Tobin finally made it in from Vancouver. His bum was still a little sore from their enthusiastic reunion.

"Ready to go?" Tobin came up behind Danny and wrapped his arms around Danny's shoulders. He wanted to go to the hotel's annual pancake breakfast; he'd read that it was a Stampede tradition.

"Mm, give me a minute," Danny muttered, frowning at his screen.

"That's what you said ten minutes ago." He tried not to sound annoyed.

"Sorry, let me finish this one thing."

Tobin sighed and wandered over to the baby grand piano in the corner of their usual suite. Don't get upset, he told himself. Danny was always busy, always working. If he finished up whatever it was that needed his attention now, then they could have the day to themselves without interruption.

Tobin pressed a few keys on the piano. He'd taken lessons when he was younger, but he didn't remember much of anything. Except maybe "Chopsticks"? He tapped at the keys experimentally until he managed to piece together the melody.

Great. One distraction down. What time was it now?

Danny was still hunched over his computer.

Tobin pulled out his phone and scrolled through all his social media accounts, checking for notifications and spreading a few likes around. When he looked up again, another ten minutes had passed. He stared at the back of Danny's head. "Ready yet?" He held his breath.

"Yeah."

Really? He stood and walked up to Danny, who still hadn't budged. He didn't look ready. Forget this. "I can go by myself, if you're busy. Want me to bring something back for you?"

"What?" Danny looked surprised Tobin was standing above him. "Oh, no, that's okay. I'll come with you." He closed his laptop.

Finally.

Tobin stepped out of the door first and almost ran into another guest walking by.

"Oops, sorry," he apologized automatically.

"No worries. I'm Ray." The other man held out his hand and Tobin took it.

What a friendly guy. "I'm Tobin. And this is Danny."

"Ah, I know Danny."

Tobin turned to find Danny looking a tad sheepish.

"Ray's my colleague."

"Oh." Tobin's next question died on his tongue. Ray's expression said it all. "I didn't realize you were traveling with a colleague." Because this was supposed to be their mini-break, their little getaway, wasn't it?

"There's a few work things I need to take care of while I'm in town," Danny conceded.

"But don't worry." Ray jumped in as if he'd read Tobin's mind. "I have no intention of intruding. I've got my own agenda for the Stampede. Now, were you heading out?" He gestured toward the elevator.

They made small talk all the way down to the lobby. Had Tobin been to the Stampede before? *No, have you, Ray? No, it's my first time too.* Danny was silent for the most part, which annoyed Tobin even more.

First, he'd dragged his feet all morning, then Tobin finds out from Ray that he'd purposely planned work meetings on their mini-break. If Danny was going to be doing so much work, then Tobin might as well have brought some work to do too.

Ray left them in the lobby to search for pancake breakfasts on their own.

"Exactly how much work do you have to do while you're here?" Tobin asked as they walked to the hotel restaurant.

"Not much. Only a few things." Danny sounded a little too nonchalant about it.

A thought occurred to Tobin. "Is it WesTec work?" *Please say no, please say no.* After all, Danny had other portfolio companies in Calgary he could be meeting with.

Danny looked like he'd been caught robbing a bank.

"It is, isn't it?"

"Yes."

There's no reason why that should make things worse, but somehow it did. Here was Tobin trying to enjoy their time together away from all the stress and expectations of leading his first project. And there was Danny chipping away at his own agenda for WesTec.

It wasn't a competition; they'd both agreed. But in some ways, it kind of was, damn it. And Tobin felt like he'd been bumped off course so Danny could race ahead.

He mentally replayed all their conversations leading up

to the trip. Not once had Danny said Tobin shouldn't bring work; not once had he said he wouldn't bring work either. Had he read too much into Danny's invitation? Should he have treated this like any other work trip with a little fling tacked on rather than the other way around?

"Do you have anything else you need to do today? Do you want to stay here and work? I can go to the Stampede on my own."

Danny held Tobin's arms and turned him so they were facing each other. "No. No more work for now. I'm all yours."

The promise sounded nice, and Tobin wanted to believe, he really did. But he hadn't missed the "for now"—how long would now be?

"I'm sorry," Danny continued. "I didn't mean for work to distract me. Let's get pancakes and head down to the fairgrounds, okay? We're here to have fun."

Despite the warning bells chiming in Tobin's head, he didn't bother arguing. He did want pancakes and he did want to wander the fairgrounds with Danny. And if this was all he could get for today, he'd take it.

Tobin gasped and squeezed Danny's hand.

"What? What's wrong?"

"Mini donuts!" He dragged Danny toward the food stand, dodging other Stampeders along the way. "This place is supposed to be a local favorite."

"It is?" Danny peered at the bright red and yellow sign with unbridled skepticism.

"It is." Tobin had done his research. Mini donuts were a

must-try, as was one of those giant cups of root beer. And the barbecue, of course. They had to save room for ribs.

Tobin reached for his wallet, but with how tight his jeans were, it took longer than normal to get it out. Danny beat him to it. "Hey, I've got this." He pushed Danny's wallet away.

For a moment, Danny looked like he was going to object, but then he relented and put his wallet back. "You know it's okay to let others treat you every once in a while." He actually sounded a little grumpy.

Tobin's eyebrows shot up. Was he serious? "I know. I let others treat me. But there's a difference between being treated and mooching off others. I've got a full-time job with a decent salary. I can buy my own donuts."

"Of course you can. But sometimes it's not about whether you can afford it. It's about why the other person wants to treat." Danny stood with hands in his pockets, gaze fixed on the ground like he was moving past grumpy and onto upset.

How had Tobin become the bad guy for wanting to pay his own way? "So...why do you want to treat?"

Danny stared at him like the answer was the most obvious thing in the world. "To be nice."

To be nice. Okay. Nice was holding the door open for the person coming through after you. Or flagging someone down when they hadn't realized they'd dropped something. Danny wasn't always paying for stuff and buying expensive gifts just to be nice. But the cashier for the mini-donuts interrupted them before Tobin could counter.

It didn't take long to get a paper bag full of piping hot

golden donuts coated in some mysterious seasoning, and by then, Tobin had more important things to worry about than arguing with Danny. He popped a donut into his mouth and groaned. "Ohmygod, it's so good." He held the bag out to Danny, who picked up a donut with much less enthusiasm.

Danny took a small bite and made an "mm" sound that was somewhere between *wow, that's gross* and *I'm going to hurl.*

"You don't like it?" Tobin couldn't believe what he was seeing. What kind of taste buds did Danny have?

"It's edible."

"Fine. I'll keep the rest for myself."

Danny didn't put up a fight.

They wandered past a food stand selling some sort of corn dog wrapped inside bacon wrapped inside a pickle, and another selling more traditional pizzas. On the other side of the Midway were the classic game stalls like ring toss and darts.

"Let's check out the games." Tobin led the way and they watched as a row of kids aimed water guns at a target in an attempt to get their ship across the finish line first.

"Do you want to play?" Danny asked.

"Of course, I want to play. What kind of question is that? You can't come to a place like this and not play games."

From the look on Danny's face, that must be exactly what he did.

"Come on, we're both playing." He pushed Danny into one seat, then took the next one over.

The teenager running the game explained how to use the

water guns and then they were off. A hidden sound system played a ringing bell, while brightly colored wooden ships wiggled their way across the booth. On the other side of Danny, a kid screamed at the top of his lungs. Ten seconds later, it was all over.

"And the winner is this gentleman here." The teenager gestured to Danny, who stared back at him like he was speaking an alien language. "You can have your pick of these prizes."

Danny's eyes widened at the row of small stuffed animals, like they were going to jump down and eat him alive. Tobin resisted the urge to pull out his phone and snap a picture. Instead, he took pity on him. "He'll take the unicorn."

The teenager grabbed the white unicorn with a rainbow spike coming out of its forehead and handed it down. Danny muttered a thanks as he took it and turned to Tobin. "Here, you can have it."

Tobin put a hand to his chest. "Who, me? But you won it fair and square."

Danny frowned. "What am I going to do with this?"

"What am *I* going to do with it?" Tobin shot back. He might secretly like unicorns, because hey, what kind of gay didn't? But that didn't mean he wanted a plushie of one. He was an adult, excuse him.

Danny dropped his outstretched hand. "Oh, sorry, I didn't mean to imply—I shouldn't have assumed—"

Tobin stopped him, taking the plushie and tucking it under his chin. "I'm kidding. I'd love it. Thank you." He leaned in and gave Danny a quick peck on the lips. "See? I can accept gifts once in a while."

If Danny was the type to roll his eyes, he probably would have rolled them so hard.

But Tobin spun away before Danny could respond.

"How are you with rides?" Tobin asked, eyeing something called The Tornado.

Danny followed his gaze. "No, absolutely not." The terror stamped on his face vetoed any thought of rides.

"Okay! No rides, then. At least, not scary ones. Maybe something a little tamer?"

"I'm starting to think coming here was a bad idea."

"Hm, yeah, you're not much fun."

It took Danny several seconds too long to figure out Tobin was joking.

"I'm teasing you!" But only sort of. They'd both been on edge all day, throwing barbs at each other that didn't necessarily hurt, but were certainly uncomfortable. Tobin knew he was being a brat, but then so was Danny. What had happened to the easy-going flow they'd always had? Was it Danny? Was it him? Both of them? Maybe they simply didn't get along as well as they used to.

No, Tobin refused to believe that. They were having an off day, that's all. Everyone had off days. They'd get through it and everything would be fine. "Let's go in there." Tobin pointed to a building on their right. "I think it's like a petting zoo."

Calling it a petting zoo was like calling Disney World a playground. As they entered, Tobin was hit by the earthy musk of farm animals and the woodsy fresh scent of saw dust. The enormous exhibition hall was divided into sections by animal type—lambs, pigs, cows, horses in stalls erected specifically for the event, and even alpacas.

"Look! Alpacas!" Tobin marched over to the gentle, fluffy creatures with long necks and curly tufts over their eyes. A baby sat near the fence and Tobin bent down to pet it. It turned to Tobin, gave his hand a sniff and a lick, then ignored him. "He's so soft!"

Danny stood behind him, gazing down at the cute little animal with absolute indifference. "How do you know it's a he?"

Tobin huffed. "I don't know. Could be a she." He stood. "It's still soft. You should pet it."

"I'm okay." Danny checked his watch.

It was the third time he'd checked it in the past thirty minutes. Tobin had been fighting the urge to ask Danny about it, but this time, he lost.

"Do you have somewhere to be?" He couldn't keep the annoyance out of his voice.

"No." Danny genuinely looked confused.

"You keep looking at your watch."

Danny's hand flew to his wrist like he might have forgotten to put his watch on that morning. But it was there, all right, Tobin had no doubt. "Oh, um…"

Whatever. If Danny was distracted by work things, fine. Work was always at the top of Danny's mind; that wasn't news to Tobin. But that didn't mean Tobin couldn't enjoy himself. "Never mind. I want to see the pigs."

Most of the pigs were kept behind glass with heat lamps

to warm them. The mamas were huge, lying on their sides while all their piglets clambered over each other for a teat.

"Look at those little tails! So curly!" Tobin said more to himself than anyone else.

"I know, right?" A little girl next to him chimed in. She had her face pressed right up against the glass, which probably wasn't the most hygienic, but hey, he wasn't her mom. "This one is so much smaller than the rest."

"The smallest one is called the runt," Tobin explained. "Sometimes they need extra care from the farmers because they're so tiny."

"Oh, but it's the cutest."

"I think so too."

The little girl smiled up at him and then ran off to find her parents.

"You're good with kids."

Tobin hadn't realized Danny was watching the exchange. He shrugged. "They're just miniature humans."

"You'd be surprised at the number of people who don't know how to speak to kids."

"You speak to them like you would adults. Just use shorter words." Tobin cocked his head as a thought occurred to him. "Do you want kids?"

That question clearly caught Danny off guard. He blinked like he couldn't quite connect the dots. "Kids aren't in the books for me."

"Why not?" Now that he thought about it, Danny would make a great father. Look at how he'd treated Tobin when they were younger. Plus he was great with Peyton and Howie. He could see it already, Danny helping Peyton learn how to ride a bike. Danny teaching Howie how to hold a pencil.

God, when was the last time he'd seen the twins in person? It felt like ages. They'd already grown so much since then, if their photos were any indication. Wei let them video chat with Tobin every once in a while, but it wasn't really enough given how quickly kids changed at that age. Danny for sure knew them better than Tobin did. Not that Tobin begrudged him for it, but he did miss the little monsters now and then. Not getting to see them more often was probably the only drawback of living in Vancouver.

"I'm too busy." Danny answered his question. "My job is too demanding." He sounded dismissive. Like he was trying to convince himself rather than Tobin.

"You could always get a less demanding job," Tobin suggested as they wandered toward the horses.

"A different job?"

Obviously, Danny had never considered that. He frowned like Tobin wanted him to settle on Mars.

"Yeah, a different job. Maybe one where you don't travel so much?" It seemed like a no brainer to Tobin. Danny had the expertise and experience to go anywhere and do whatever he wanted. Hell, he could probably retire early if he made anywhere near the amount of money Tobin suspected he did. Why stay at a job that took over his entire life?

"I like my job." Danny couldn't have said that with any less conviction.

He must have liked his job at some point, maybe even loved it. But from their conversations recently, that love had faded to practically nothing. Danny always sounded so exhausted whenever he talked about work, and yet, he never seemed willing to stop. Tobin had his own opinions about that, but who was he to voice them?

Tobin had never given kids much thought either, to be fair. He assumed he'd have kids one day. Wasn't that what people did? Got married and had kids? It wasn't like being gay was an issue anymore. Plenty of gay couples adopted or used surrogates.

What if he and Danny had kids together? What a wild idea. Suddenly, Tobin's imagination replaced Peyton with a different little girl and Howie with a different little boy. Danny could teach their daughter how to ride a bike, while Tobin watched through the window. Danny could help their son with writing, while Tobin made dinner for the family.

Yeah, right. In his literal dreams.

The wide open space of the exhibition hall gave way to long corridors of stalls. Horses big and small poked their heads through the gates, nibbling on treats from their admirers.

Tobin stopped in front of one gate and peered inside. A giant black horse with a long beautiful mane came up to him.

"Hi," he whispered. "You're gorgeous." Slowly, he reached out his hand and placed it gently on the horse's nose, giving him a few soft strokes.

He would love to bring his kids here someday. To the Stampede or some other fairgrounds with horses. He would pick them up, so they could pet the horse and feel how velvety its nose was. He would buy treats for them to feed the horse and giggle at the tickle of lips on their palms. Tobin sighed, and the horse did too.

"He likes you."

Tobin glanced back at Danny. "How do you know it's a he?"

Danny pointed to a sign on the stall. "Stallion."

"Show off."

The horse took a step sideways and extended its neck far enough to give Danny a headbutt, as if demanding pets.

"The stallion knows what he wants," Tobin said.

Danny obliged, giving the majestic animal a few strokes between its eyes. Danny's expression softened, and his lips curled into a small smile. The horse blinked slowly, once, twice, as if soothed to sleep by the attention.

Danny would be there too, in Tobin's fantasy visit to the fair. He could hoist up the kids, one at a time, so they could sit on his shoulders above the crowd. He would win them little stuffed unicorns and frown disapprovingly when they insisted on getting mini donuts.

Okay, enough already, overactive imagination. Tobin stored the image deep inside his heart where he kept his most precious longings, and then escorted his imagination out of his brain.

Chapter Eleven

The crowd roared as the gate popped open and a cowboy riding an angry bull burst into the arena. A plume of sawdust followed the pair around as they twirled in circles until the bull finally won and the cowboy was flung from his back.

Tobin hid behind Danny's arm, clutching his bicep while peeking out to watch the action. "Jesus fucking Christ! That's terrifying."

Having Tobin use his arm like a pillow during a scary move thrilled Danny more than was logical. "They've got a mechanical bull around here somewhere."

"Oh yeah?" Tobin's eyes lit up. "We should do it!"

"You can do it. I'm too old for that." The thought of climbing on a machine designed to toss him in the air held absolutely zero appeal for Danny.

They turned back to the arena, where the next bull rider was getting ready. Tobin squealed as the gate flung open and man and animal leaped out. "He looks like he's going to break in two!" He turned his face into Danny's arm for a split second and then peeked out again.

Danny smiled and patted Tobin's hand. "There, there."

"Shut up."

"They're professionals. They'll be fine."

"It's still scary!"

Ray popped out of nowhere before Danny could respond. "Howdy, folks!"

"Uh, hi?" Tobin greeted him.

"Now don't you look at me like that," Ray said with a horribly fake Western accent. "I'm getting into character is all."

"That's...great." Tobin was nice enough to humor Ray.

Danny, not so much. "Do you have anything?"

Ray dropped the act. "I do." His head tilt was subtle.

He turned to Tobin. "Will you give us a minute? It's a work thing. I won't be long."

Tobin frowned, and a pang of guilt shot through Danny at leaving him alone. All day, Tobin had alternated between annoyed and upset. Who could blame him? Danny had tried to push Cyrus West out of his mind and let Ray handle things, but it was more easily said than done. Twenty plus years in the work force was difficult to shut off.

He gave Tobin's hand a squeeze before heading off to find a secluded spot with Ray.

They had been pretty certain Cyrus West would be at the Stampede. Nearly all of Calgary was here, but the business elite were known to host their own exclusive parties. Ray had been working his contacts to find out when Cyrus was holding his.

"It's tonight." Ray got right to the point. "Not on the fairgrounds. At a hotel nearby. Apparently, they've booked the Bacon Brothers as the musical act."

Danny didn't care who they'd booked as long as Cyrus West was there.

"You got us on the list?"

Ray eyed him for a second before speaking. "I didn't know if you wanted to bring Tobin."

Danny wasn't sure either. They had planned on cornering Cyrus at the party, which wasn't something Danny wanted Tobin to witness. But leaving him alone in the hotel wasn't an option either. There was no way Tobin would agree to that. "Yeah, I'll bring him."

"Okay, just double checking." Ray shot him a look that had *this is a bad idea* written all over it. "Well, you go back to your beau. I've got my own boy toy to entertain." He turned and sauntered off.

Danny made his way back to Tobin, but he'd lost the thrill of watching the rodeo somewhere back where he'd convened with Ray.

"Everything okay?"

He tried to play it cool. "Yeah, everything's fine. A minor scheduling issue."

Tobin's expression was suspicious, and he had every right to be. What was that saying about using lies to cover up lies and before long nothing was real anymore? Yeah, Danny was experiencing that first hand. "How about we go to a party tonight?"

Tobin blinked at the sudden change of topic. "A party?"

"Ray got us invited to some exclusive event nearby." He should admit it was a WesTec party, hosted by Cyrus. After all, Tobin already knew he was here on WesTec business, why not come clean? But Tobin looked like he was on the verge of walking out on him and Danny lost his nerve.

It took a moment, but Tobin broke out in a grin. "Okay, sure. Party means dancing, right? I'll get to see your moves."

Not at this party. "I don't know about that."

"Just you wait. I'll get you going." Tobin spoke with so much confidence that Danny felt even more like shit.

He had to tell Tobin the truth. He would find out eventually. It's not like Danny could blindfold him at the party, and waiting until they got there would be so much worse than hashing things out now.

But then Tobin planted a quick kiss on his cheek and turned back to the show. The moment slipped away, and Danny didn't know how to get it back. Shit. He was in so much trouble.

Danny looked up as Tobin emerged from the bedroom and did a double take.

He was clad head to toe in leather. Bright yellow leather. Tight pants stretched across his crotch, highlighted by a giant belt buckle sparkling with rhinestones. Fringe flowed down either side of his legs and yellow snakeskin boots peeked out under the hem. On top, Tobin wore a matching cowboy vest with fringe across the chest, a black handkerchief around his neck...and nothing else. His stomach, chest, and arms glistened as if he'd applied some kind of sparkling lotion. He'd lined his eyes heavily in makeup and completed the outfit with a black cowboy hat.

Standing in the middle of the living room, Tobin did a slow spin. "What do you think?" He hooked his thumbs into the belt loops, bringing the waist of his pants dangerously low.

What did Danny think? Danny's brain wasn't capable of thinking, but his dick was whole-heartedly on board. Where the hell had Tobin come up with that outfit? Fuck it. Danny didn't care. The more important question was how quickly he could get his cock into Tobin's ass.

Tobin strode over to where Danny sat on the couch and bent to bring their faces level. With one finger, he gently nudged Danny's chin. "You're gaping, babe."

No shit. What else was Danny supposed to do? He cleared his throat and shut his laptop. He'd been in the middle of composing an email, but whatever it was for, it wasn't important now.

"Hm, I like the rugged cowboy look you've got going too."

Danny glanced down to remind himself what he was wearing. Black jeans and cowboy boots. A black Western style shirt with pearl buttons down the front and white piping detail. He didn't look too shabby, he supposed. He stood to his full height and grabbed the white cowboy hat sitting on the coffee table. He stuck it on his head and Tobin straightened it for him.

Danny brushed his hand across Tobin's cheek, gazed into

his eyes and leaned in for a kiss. A simple one with heat sizzling underneath. Danny's gut tightened with need. Fuck the party. Fuck Cyrus West and WesTec. Here in his arms was a man sexy beyond Danny's wildest imagination—why should he share him with the rest of the world?

A knock on the door disabused Danny of any ideas of playing hooky. He was technically on the clock and work called, no matter how delicious Tobin looked.

"Ready to go?" Danny asked.

"Mm, if we have to."

"Unfortunately."

Tobin let out a dramatic sigh. "Okay, fine."

Ray stood in the hallway waiting for them. He let out a low whistle when they emerged. "Look at you two. Power couple."

Danny felt simultaneously proud and embarrassed. Of course he was delighted to be seen on Tobin's arm. But Ray's comment reminded him that Tobin wasn't his to show off.

That convenient lie of omission from that afternoon? Yeah, Danny hadn't worked up the courage to tell Tobin the truth yet. At this rate, he'd be lucky if Tobin was still speaking to him in a few hours.

"Why, thank you, sir." Tobin tipped his hat at Ray, who laughed and led the way to the elevator.

The ride to the party was hell and Danny debated the whole way whether he could justify turning the car around. The other two didn't seem to pick up on Danny's unease, chatting animatedly with each other. But Danny couldn't even follow the conversation.

The leather of Tobin's outfit was soft and buttery, carefully molded to his body like a second layer of skin. Danny couldn't keep his hands to himself. Then he pictured Tobin's expression when he spotted the WesTec logo at the party and connected the dots. All that smooth leather slipped right out of Danny's hands.

The car pulled up to the hotel and valets rushed to open the doors. Tobin moved to get out, but Danny grabbed his hand and held him in place.

"What's wrong?"

Say it. Say it, damn it. "I…"

"Danny?"

Ray was already at the hotel entrance, looking back at the car with curiosity. The driver and the valets were doing their best to pretend nothing weird was going on.

"What is it?" Tobin's expression was quickly morphing into worry.

Danny ran a hand over his face. God, why was this so hard? He'd done plenty of hard things in the past but coming clean with Tobin felt impossible.

"Hey, hey." Tobin pulled Danny's hand away from his face. "Did something happen? What's going on?"

"I'm sorry. I'm so sorry."

"About what? Danny, you're freaking me out."

He couldn't say it. He didn't have the words or the guts to do it. Instead, Danny tugged on Tobin's hand and they exited the car together.

"Danny!"

As they strode past Ray, Tobin shot him a bewildered look, but Ray only shrugged and followed them inside.

Danny didn't have to go far. Right inside the entrance there was a table set up to register guests as they arrived. A giant sign with the WesTec logo hung in front of the table.

Tobin gaped at it. "Is this what we're here for?"

"Yes."

"And you're freaking out because you conveniently forgot to mention the party is hosted by WesTec?"

"Yes." God, he really was the scum of the earth.

Tobin let out a single chuckle, covered his mouth and stepped away from Danny like he wanted nothing to do with him.

Danny didn't blame him. Hell, he'd probably be doing the same thing. Yet, seeing Tobin look at him like he was a stranger cut Danny to the core. "I can explain."

Tobin let out another chuckle. "Oh, *now* you can explain. Not this afternoon, not when I got dressed up in this ridiculous outfit, not back there in the car. No, you have to explain *now*. Yeah, I don't think so." He pivoted on his heel and stalked back toward the doors.

"Wait, Tobin, wait." Danny caught up with him outside and managed to slow him down before Tobin climbed into a taxi and out of his life. "Listen, I'm sorry. I really, really am. I should have told you it was a WesTec party. I don't know why I couldn't."

"Couldn't? Or didn't want to." Tobin crossed his arms.

Hell if Danny knew. The words literally would not come out of his mouth. But how did that make any sense? If he really wanted to, wouldn't he have found a way? "I don't know."

Tobin squeezed his eyes shut and scrunched up his face

like he could wish himself away from all of this, from Danny.

"Please." He took Tobin by the arms. "You have to believe me. I never wanted to lie to you."

"But you did," Tobin said in a small voice. "You lied to me. The least you could do is tell me why."

The full answer was too long to give in the middle of the parking lot, with hotel guests streaming past, people eyeing them, trying to figure out what the lovers' spat was about. "Cyrus won't grant us a meeting. We need to talk to him." That was the best Danny could come up with.

"That's it?" Tobin shook his head in disbelief. "You needed to talk to Cyrus so you decided to lie to me?"

"No, I mean, I understand that's what it looks like. But it's more complicated than that—"

"So uncomplicate it for me."

Danny went to pinch the bridge of his nose and his hand hit the brim of his hat. He tore it off his head. "Yes, I can do that. I *want* to. Just, not here."

Tobin glanced around as if only then realizing where they were. His shoulders sagged. "Why did you even invite me here? Like, if you needed to be in Calgary for work, then come for work. Why ask me to take vacation days and pretend this is some sort of getaway for the two of us? Why go to all this trouble?"

Finally, the words came on their own. "Because I wanted to see you." It was the most honest thing Danny had said all day.

His phone buzzed in his pocket, loud enough that Tobin heard it too. Fuck. It was probably Ray, wondering where the hell he was. Danny froze. If he reached for his phone, he was sure that would be the end of it for him and Tobin.

An icy chill settled in the space between them before Tobin spoke. "Go ahead. Answer it."

Danny hesitated. It felt like a test—one he was bound to fail. The phone buzzed again.

Tobin rolled his eyes. "Just check it."

"Don't leave."

"What?"

"Please, don't leave. Wait for me. I only need a few minutes with Cyrus and then we can go, and I'll explain everything."

Tobin stared at him like he'd grown antlers. "You are unbelievable. You're kidding, right? Why in the world would I wait for you to go do whatever the hell you're planning to do?"

It was a long shot, Danny knew that, but he didn't know what else to do. He'd get down on his knees if he had to. His phone buzzed again.

"Jesus Christ," Tobin muttered. He slipped past Danny and strode back toward the hotel entrance. "Pick up the damn phone before Ray loses his shit."

Danny pulled out his phone and hit ignore before stuffing it back into his pocket. "Where are you going?"

"Oh, wouldn't you like to know?" Tobin pushed open the door but didn't bother holding it for Danny.

He deserved that.

He followed Tobin across the hotel lobby to the lounge at the back of the building. Tobin made a beeline for the bar.

"Go do whatever the fuck it is you and Ray need to do.

I'm going to stay here, get drunk, and maybe find a hot guy to flirt with. I did not get all dressed up only to turn around and go back to the hotel."

"What?" Danny's hackles rose.

"Oh, like you have any right to be upset." Tobin stepped up to the bar and leaned over it to give the bartender his order. "Sex on the Beach, babe. Keep the change." He handed over a twenty. The bartender gave him a once-over and smiled like he was going to put some extra sex into Tobin's drink.

"Tobin." Danny tried to turn him around only to have his hand shrugged off.

Tobin waved a finger in Danny's face in warning. "Uh-uh, no marking your territory. I am not yours tonight." He looked Danny up and down, expression bordering on disgust. "What are you still doing here? Don't you have some ass kissing to do upstairs?"

Not quite ass kissing. But either way, he didn't want to leave Tobin like this. "Don't leave without me, okay?"

"You are in no position to make any requests, mister."

"I know. I'm sorry. But please. I won't be long."

The bartender came back, and Tobin took a slow sip of his drink before answering. "No promises." He stared resolutely over Danny's shoulder.

That was about as good as he could hope for. Leaving Tobin alone in a hotel bar was one of the most difficult things Danny had done in a long time. But he had no one to blame except himself. His own foolishness and coward-ice had brought him here. How he was going to dig himself out, he had no idea.

But first. Ray and Cyrus and WesTec. All waiting for him upstairs. He'd deal with that then come back and figure out how to fix things with Tobin.

"I'm sorry," he tried one more time, but Tobin was already walking away.

To his credit, Ray didn't say a word when Danny arrived at the party alone. He simply nodded toward a group gathered on the opposite side of the room and led the way.

Danny tried to get his mind in the game. Confront Cyrus West, let him know they'll do whatever it takes to convince him to sell, then leave. Simple. Easy.

Except Danny couldn't care less whether Cyrus sold, whether WesTec rose to the top of its sector or crashed and burned. At that moment, he didn't even care what Joanna would do if his career careened off course. Tobin was downstairs, pissed at him, hurt because of him.

He walked straight into Ray, who had stopped up ahead.

"Hey." Ray put a hand on his shoulder. "You okay?"

No, he wasn't fucking okay. "Let's get this over with."

"Do you want me to take the lead?"

It was probably the smarter option, given Danny's mood. But he needed to take his frustration out on something and Cyrus would do just fine. "I've got this."

He marched toward the circle of people surrounding Cyrus, moving with such intensity the crowd parted naturally for him.

"Cyrus."

To say Cyrus was shocked was an understatement, but he recovered quickly.

"Danny-boy," he said with a sneer. "I didn't realize you were on the invite list."

"You've got to pay more attention, Cyrus." Danny clapped a hand on his shoulder and clamped down as hard as he could. "The world's moving fast these days, you never know what might be headed your way."

Cyrus gave him a cold stare and Danny sent a colder one back. He wasn't here to play nice and he didn't care about saving Cyrus's face. "How about we take a stroll?" It wasn't an invitation.

They locked eyes in a staring contest Danny had no intention of losing. It wasn't difficult. Cyrus caved barely a second in. He let out a nervous laugh and turned to the group around them. "Gentlemen, if you'll excuse us a moment. Please, help yourself to the food and drinks. The line dancing should start soon!"

Danny guided Cyrus away to a quiet corner, his hand never letting up on its grip of Cyrus's shoulder. The second they were clear of the crowd, Cyrus shrugged him off and spun to confront him. "What the hell do you think you're doing here?" he hissed.

"Cyrus West, meet my colleague Raymond Chao. Ray, this is Cyrus, CEO of WesTec."

Ray tipped his hat. "Nice to meet you. Great party you've got here."

Cyrus didn't return the greeting. "I said, what the fuck do you want?"

"A meeting, that's all. It seems like we've been playing a bit of telephone tag." Danny widened his stance and crossed his arms. The brim of his hat left his eyes in shadow and suddenly he understood the appeal of Stetsons.

"We don't need a meeting. There's nothing to talk about."

"I beg to differ. We have plenty to discuss. You never got back to me about WesTec." Danny put a hand to his chest. "That hurt, Cyrus. That really hurt."

"I told you, you asshole. I'm not selling my company."

Danny threw up his hands. "Ah well, that's too bad. It really is. You know, the funniest thing happened yesterday. We ran into your wife—or I should say your soon-to-be ex-wife. She's quite the woman."

Cyrus's already furious eyes darkened even more. A vein running across his forehead bulged dangerously.

"She was telling us about your chalet up in Banff. Personally, I've been thinking of buying some property there. Apparently your place is going up for sale soon. Oh, and your horses too; your wife showed us pictures. I think they'd be perfect for my niece and nephew. Marlena said she'd be willing to sell them to me at a steep discount. Isn't that nice of her?" Danny gave Ray a light pat on the back. "She took a shining to you too, didn't she, Ray? Now, you see, Ray loves golf, and we were hoping to catch a game before we head home. Marlena recommended your club, the Rolling Hills Country Club. We had a lovely chat with the club manager about you."

Cyrus looked from Danny to Ray and back. "Are you threatening me?"

Danny didn't pretend to look shocked. "Threatening? Ray, did you hear that? Would I ever threaten anyone?

Don't you know I always get what I want?" He paused for effect. "Let's just say you have something I want, Cyrus. You could cooperate, we'll put in a good word for you around town, and we'd all be better off. Or...we'll find some other way to get what we want."

"Fuck you."

"Sorry, job's taken."

Cyrus drained the last of the beer he'd been holding and slammed the glass down on a nearby table. "You're not going to get away with this." He started to walk away, only to have Ray catch him by the elbow.

"About that golf game. We have an early morning tee time reserved under your name. I understand Rolling Hills has a very strict no-show policy." Ray sounded like he was having the time of his life.

Cyrus blanched and wrested his arm away. "Fuck you. Fuck both of you."

Danny and Ray watched Cyrus stomp off into the crowd.

"Think he'll show up tomorrow?" Ray asked.

Danny almost hoped he wouldn't.

Chapter Twelve

Tobin was on his third SOTB and Danny still wasn't back yet. Angry didn't even begin to describe how he felt. Betrayed wasn't quite right either. He felt like a kid again, going along his merry way, thinking everything was fine. And then, boom, the big kids say he can't come with them to the park or something.

God, he was such a fool. Getting all dressed up for a night out on the town. All the while Danny had been scheming behind his back.

It was partially his own fault. He'd seen the signs, heard the alarm bells sounding, but he'd ignored them. Because Danny was supposed to be better than that. The problem was, if Tobin had been wrong about this one thing, what else could he be wrong about?

Ayán's criticisms came back to haunt him. What if Danny really was one of the bad guys? Could Tobin live with that? Wait, why was he even considering it?

"Still not back, eh?" The bartender had been checking in on him between taking orders from other customers.

"Nope."

"Rough."

"Yeah."

The bartender leaned toward Tobin from his side of the bar. "Want to talk about it? I hear bartenders are great listeners."

Tobin appreciated the attempt at levity, but he was beyond saving. The bartender was cute, though, kind of like a snuggly teddy bear type with rosy rounded cheeks. His name tag said Devon.

"Thanks, Devon." Tobin sighed. "But I don't even know where to begin."

"The beginning usually works."

Which beginning? When Danny had invited him to the Stampede? Or when they'd fucked seven years ago? Or even further back to Tobin's childhood crush? What was the point, even? It was clear he didn't mean anything to Danny. Only a piece of ass to tap when Danny felt horny.

"Does it have anything to do with the guy who left you here?"

Apparently, their little disagreement hadn't been as discreet as Tobin had hoped. "Yeah, that guy. He's a private equity investor and wants to buy up this company. But I was hired by the company to figure out how to save the business without selling it…"

Devon's eyes glazed over. He had no idea what Tobin was talking about.

"Never mind. Basically, he invited me to this fancy party upstairs. Turns out it wasn't only to have a good time. He's here for business and he didn't tell me."

Devon nodded sympathetically. "So he lied to you."

"Yup."

"That's not cool."

"Nope."

"Why did he lie?"

An excellent question Tobin didn't have the answer to. Would it matter, even if he did? A lie was a lie, and Danny wasn't the man he thought he knew. "I don't know."

"Hey." Devon reached across the bar and clasped Tobin's hand lightly. "You'll figure it out. And if not, dump his ass because you deserve better."

Not that Devon knew him from Adam, but the affirmation felt nice. "Thanks."

Devon's gaze shot past Tobin's shoulder and his eyes widened. "Let me know if I can get anything else for you."

The buzzy effects of the SOTBs dissipated at Danny's return.

"Making friends?" Danny's voice was stony.

"Shut up. You don't get to tell me who to talk to."

Danny let out a heavy sigh. "You're right. I'm sorry." After a beat, he continued. "Can we talk?"

No, go fuck yourself, was what Tobin wanted to say. But had he really waited around all this time only to blow Danny off? He could have done that without embarrassing himself in front of the bartender. "Fine. Talk."

Danny surveyed the increasingly crowded bar. "Can we go somewhere quieter? There are some empty seats by the window."

"Ugh." The last thing he wanted to do was to make things easier for Danny, but he didn't really want to have this conversation where anyone could walk up and over-hear either. "Fine." He dragged himself to his feet and followed Danny across the room to a grouping of armchairs and love seats around a low table.

He sat down on one side of the love seat, scooting as far to the edge as he could. Thank the heavens Danny didn't try to crowd him. He was not in the mood for Danny's touch.

"I'm sorry I didn't tell you about the party."

Tobin waited for him to continue. One sorry wasn't going to cut it.

"I didn't because…god, I don't even know why. I wanted to, I really did, but I…" Danny braced his elbows on his knees and buried his face in his hands.

Tobin was supposed to be angry and he was. But seeing Danny so torn hit him in that soft spot he'd always have for Danny. As much as he didn't want to feel it, sympathy started mellowing his anger.

Danny sat up straight and stared out the window toward the fairgrounds sprawled before them. "I really need Cyrus to sell WesTec to us. My—I haven't been doing very well at work for several quarters now. My portfolio is falling apart, and Jade Harbour might lose some of our financial backers because of it. If I don't pull off a win with WesTec, I might be done."

"Done, like fired?" That seemed harsh. But then, maybe that was the push Danny needed to start taking care of himself a little more.

"Not in such crude terms, but essentially."

That didn't answer Tobin's question, though. "So why lie about it? Why didn't you tell me?"

Danny dropped his gaze to his hands, studying as he rubbed them against each other. "You were so upset with me already. I didn't want to make things worse."

Tobin's eyebrows shot up. That was the weakest excuse Tobin had ever heard in his life. "Yeah, I was upset with you. Because you didn't tell me shit that you should have told me. Why would you think keeping more stuff from me would make me feel better?"

Danny didn't look up. "I didn't tell you the other stuff because it's pretty ugly."

"What do you mean by that?"

Danny sighed, and his jaw clenched. "We have information we're leveraging to force Cyrus to sell."

Warning bells again. "Information?"

"I can show you, if you want." He looked so serious, like he was talking about nuclear launch codes rather than a midsized start-up company in Calgary. "It's back at the hotel."

Did Tobin want to see? Hell yeah, he did. Who wouldn't want to see information so sensational Danny thought Tobin needed protection from it? He popped up from the couch. "Fine, let's go."

"Now?" The look of surprise on Danny's face would

have been laughable if there was anything funny about the situation. What else did they have to wait for?

"Yeah, now. Unless there's something else you'd like to confess."

"No, nothing."

The denial came a little too easily and a little too fast. Tobin didn't know why he thought so, but something about Danny's eagerness didn't sit quite right with him.

In the sky above the fairgrounds, fireworks exploded in bright reds, greens, blues, and whites. The sound of them reverberated through the entire building. Normally, Tobin loved fireworks. All that power constrained to form shapes and patterns, filling the great big sky above him. This display was impressive, but it only made Tobin more bitter.

This trip was supposed to be fun, romantic even. How had it ended up like this?

Tobin flipped through page after page in the file Danny had given him. Court documents, bank account statements, property deeds, pictures. It looked like a private investigator had gone through Cyrus West's whole life.

"I don't understand."

"His wife is filing for divorce."

That must be the court document. "So?"

"All of Cyrus's assets, including WesTec, are frozen until the divorce is finalized."

"Which might take a while?"

"Exactly."

There was so much more going on with WesTec than Tobin had realized. His own project with the company felt irrelevant in comparison. How was he supposed to advise WesTec properly when he didn't know all this stuff was happening around it? Hell, was there even a point in trying to save the company when there were so many people fighting to get their hands on it?

"What are these?" The photos showed Cyrus embracing a number of women who looked too young to be a Mrs. West.

"He's been sleeping around."

"They look a little young."

"They might be. Or they could be young-looking eighteen- and nineteen-year-olds."

"Are they trafficked?"

"Could be. We don't know for sure."

Tobin dropped the pictures as if he would be implicated simply by holding them. He closed the file and pushed the whole thing to the side. The farther away he got from it, the better.

"God, he's a pervert." He leaned back and wrapped his arms around his middle. "Have you reported him?"

At least Danny had the decency to look ashamed. "Not yet."

"Why not? Those pimps move the girls around all the time. If the police don't get on it right away, they could be gone already." Hell, Tobin would take the pictures directly to the police station now if he needed to.

Danny shook his head. "These photos are from months ago. We only got them last week. Besides..."

"Besides what?" What other consideration could there possibly be?

"Marlena wants to settle the divorce first."

"Who the hell is Marlena?"

"His wife. She's the one who hired the private investigator. She's trying to squeeze every last penny out of him, and then she's going to the authorities."

Tobin shot up from his chair and stuck his fingers through his hair as he paced around in a circle. What kind of fucked-up black market underground bizarro world had he found himself in? WesTec was supposed to be a simple first project for him to lead. This week was supposed to be a fun getaway with his hot lover. And now suddenly, there's a greedy ex-wife and possibly trafficked sex workers, and everyone seemed to be okay with it, except him.

"Ray and I paid her a visit before you got here."

"Oh, great, there's more."

Danny looked at him, face carefully blank as if any small misstep could ignite Tobin's anger again. Well, he was right to be careful. Tobin felt strung out like a tightwire about to snap. "Go on."

"Since WesTec is frozen with the rest of Cyrus's assets, we couldn't buy it off him even if he was willing to sell. We'd need Marlena's sign-off on it too."

"Hence your visit."

"Yes."

"Did she agree?"

"She's willing to discuss it."

God, Tobin could use another drink. All the buzz from those Sex on the Beaches had long worn off. He stalked over to the mini-bar and grabbed the first hobbit-sized bottle of alcohol he could get his hands on and downed it like a shot.

Danny frowned at him, but fuck Danny. He didn't get to tell Tobin when or how to drink. Not after all the shit he'd been pulling.

"So what does all this—" he waved his hand in the direction of the folder "—have to do with the party tonight?"

"Like, I said, Cyrus wouldn't grant us a meeting. We had to go to him and make sure he knows what we know."

"Blackmail." Maybe there were more tasteful words for it, but that's what Danny was doing, essentially. He was blackmailing Cyrus to get to WesTec.

Tobin sighed. "I'm tired." He rubbed his eyes, and his fingers came away black with smudged makeup. He didn't even care. "I'm going to bed."

"You haven't had dinner."

Tobin headed toward the bedroom. "I'm not hungry."

"Wait."

What now? He stopped in the doorway to the bedroom, back to Danny, waiting for whatever bomb Danny wanted to drop now.

"Tomorrow morning. I, uh, have a meeting."

What else was new.

"It's with Cyrus."

Of course it was.

"I'll be gone pretty early."

Tobin waited one second and then another. When Danny didn't have anything else to add, he slipped into the bedroom and shut the door behind him. He shouldn't be upset Danny had an early morning meeting with Cyrus. That had been his reason for coming to Calgary in the first place, hadn't it? Tobin was only the convenient entertainment in between his work obligations.

He went through his bedtime routine in a daze, mind blank from being overloaded with information. Danny and Ray and Cyrus and WesTec. Marlena, an ugly divorce, and human trafficking. Where the hell did Tobin fit into all of it? He didn't—wasn't that always the problem? He never really fit in with the big boys.

Sleep came quickly. At some point, Tobin didn't know when, the bed behind him dipped and warm arms pulled him close. He turned into them, clinging to a dream that was less and less possible with each passing day.

Chapter Thirteen

Danny had never been a fan of golf. Too much walking around and talking. If he wanted to play a sport, he preferred the full heart-racing, brow-sweating experience. But knowing how to swing a golf club half-decently was a necessary skill in finance, so he'd forced himself to learn years ago.

He wasn't a fan of country clubs either. They were all the same, no matter which club it was or what city it was in. The staff were always dressed in white and a little too polite. The guests seemed to revel in the attention they received. Danny reached for his watch and adjusted its fit on his wrist.

He was never really in the mood for golf. Today? He definitely wasn't in the mood.

Tobin had pretended to be asleep when Danny left in

the morning. The stilted breathing, the slightly stiff limbs. Danny hadn't bothered to call Tobin on it; he'd deserved it after the debacle around the WesTec party.

He'd sent a good morning text message to Tobin. No response yet. Checking his phone constantly wasn't making Tobin respond any faster.

Ray was leaning against the reception counter, one foot crossed over the other, arms folded casually across his chest. The young woman on the other side of the counter looked flustered at Ray's flirting, which Danny supposed was what Ray was going for.

They were waiting for the Wests—both of them.

What a fucking mess he'd made of things. He wouldn't blame Tobin if he didn't want to see him again. He never should have started down this path. He'd known it would end in disaster, and sure enough, here they were. Yet, Danny couldn't muster up regret for what little time they'd had together. There were moments, entire evenings and nights, when Danny had felt happier than he'd been in a long time. Holding Tobin in his arms, kissing him—Danny couldn't regret knowing what that felt like. He'd treasure those precious memories forever.

Cyrus came striding in, scowl on his face. Marlena wasn't with him, but that wasn't surprising. They'd heard Cyrus had moved out of the big house and was living in a condo downtown.

"Cyrus! So glad you could join us!" Ray's voice boomed across the lobby and Cyrus cringed in response. "Hey now, you're not hungover, are you?"

His eyes were bloodshot, and his skin looked a little ashen. "Fuck you."

"Oh, come on. How is that a way to greet your business partner?" Ray's smile never budged, and Danny had to admire him for it.

"We're not business partners."

"Eh, I would beg to differ." Ray glanced past Cyrus's shoulder to where Marlena was headed toward them.

Cyrus followed his gaze only to spin back to Ray. "What the fuck is she doing here?"

"We need a fourth person for the game," Ray said, unfazed.

If smoke could actually come out of someone's ears, it would be gushing out of Cyrus's.

"Marlena, good morning. So glad you could make it." Danny greeted Marlena with a quick cheek-to-cheek kiss.

"Nonsense, it's my absolute pleasure to be here, Daniel. Who in their right mind would turn down a lovely game of golf with you handsome gentlemen?" She turned to her husband, her pleasant façade dropping away. "Cyrus."

"Marlena."

Ray clapped his hands together and rubbed them back and forth. "Now that we're all here, I believe this nice young woman has been holding our tee time for us." He led the way down the hall, Cyrus and Marlena behind him, Danny bringing up the rear.

Their caddies were already waiting for them. Normally, Danny didn't like using caddies. He could carry his own damn golf clubs. But the young man who approached him had such a huge smile on his face, Danny didn't have the heart to dismiss him. He recognized the hustle, the scrappiness and determination in the young man's eyes. He remembered what it was like.

"I am Arif." The caddy spoke with a slight accent. "I can help with anything. Just tell me."

"Thank you, Arif. How much do you know about golf?"

Arif brightened at the question. "I read a lot on the internet. And I learn a lot from the club. You can ask me anything."

"Great." Danny followed the rest of their party out to the greens where two golf carts sat waiting for them. "I hate golf. You can help me play."

"Sir, why do you play if you don't like golf?"

Danny had to smile at Arif's confusion. He nodded toward the others. "Business."

That was all it took for understanding to dawn in Arif's eyes. Smart kid. No doubt he was filing it away for future use.

Danny slid into the passenger side seat while Ray and Marlena chatted away in the back. Cyrus drove them out to the first hole in silence and Danny didn't try to break it. They had all day.

Cyrus lasted until the third hole before he caved. "I know what you're trying to do," he said as they stood back and watched Ray adjust Marlena's swing.

Danny didn't take the bait.

"It's not going to work." Though Cyrus didn't sound quite so confident. "Even if I wanted to sell, which I don't, the lawyers would never agree to it."

"The lawyers work for you. They'll do what you tell them to."

That seemed to stump Cyrus, who stalked away.

A few holes later, he came back. "You know, I asked around about you."

Danny used to be pretty confident in what people were saying about him, but with his recent dip in performance, he wasn't so sure anymore. "Oh?"

Cyrus looked annoyed. "Jade Harbour's got a good rep." As if he'd been hoping they didn't.

Danny quietly let out the breath he was holding. "We do."

"But you can't come storming into my office and demand to buy my company out from under my feet."

Hardly. But Cyrus sounded like he was about to dig himself into a hole and Danny had no intention of stopping him.

"I can't bend over backward and let you fuck me up the ass."

Danny's eyebrows shot up. Interesting choice of words.

To Cyrus's credit, it only took him a split second to realize what he'd said and who he'd said it to. "Uh, I mean… I didn't mean…you know what I mean."

Cyrus's already pale complexion paled even more in the face of Danny's stony silence. He laughed nervously. "Hey, buddy, I don't like, hate gays, or anything. My cousin's gay. He's a great guy!" He cleared his throat.

Danny decided to let it slide. He could deal with Cyrus's micro-aggressions after he'd secured WesTec.

"We're proposing a win-win situation here," Danny said.

"Right now, you have a bunch of WesTec shares locked up in your divorce proceedings. You have no idea what those shares are worth and how that might affect the way your other assets are split with your wife. If you sell to us, we'll give you a good deal. You get a lump sum of cash and then you and Marlena can sic your lawyers on each other for all we care." Danny pinned Cyrus with a look. "By the way, Marlena's already on board."

Cyrus looked over to his wife, who was giggling at something Ray had said. She noticed his attention and wiggled her fingers at him. "Figures she'd sell out."

"Your wife is a smart woman, Cyrus." Danny clapped a hand on Cyrus's shoulder and squeezed. He was beginning to like that power move. "You'd do well to learn a thing or two from her."

Danny could almost hear Cyrus sending him a mental *fuck you* as he walked away.

The club's general manager was waiting for them when they got back to the clubhouse.

"Oh, hi, Gerald. Thank you so much for meeting with us." Marlena went up and greeted the older man.

Cyrus shot a look at Ray and Danny. They stared right back at him. Maybe Ray knew what Marlena was up to, but Danny had no clue.

"Of course, Mrs. West. It's my pleasure. How was your game this morning?" Gerald spoke with a delightful English accent.

"Wonderful! Wasn't it wonderful, darling?" Marlena

took Cyrus's arm, though the endearment she used didn't sound at all endearing.

"Yeah, wonderful."

Marlena barreled full speed ahead. "Gerald, I don't want to waste any more of your precious time, but I'm afraid we need your assistance with our membership."

"Oh?" The change in Gerald's expression was subtle, but enough that Danny had to feel bad for the guy. Changes to membership usually meant cancellations. "Why don't we speak in my office?"

"That's a lovely idea." Marlena followed Gerald and Cyrus had no choice but to tag along.

"What is that all about?" Danny asked.

"Your guess is as good as mine. She said she had everything under control. Maybe this has something to do with it."

"Hm." Danny was more than happy to leave it in her capable hands. He turned on his heel and went in search of Arif.

When he said he'd done a lot of reading on golf, Arif hadn't been exaggerating. He knew what he was talking about, knew how to talk to people, how to strike that precarious balance between friendliness and professionalism that some would never master. Danny wouldn't be surprised if Arif was a guest at the country club one day.

He found Arif wiping down the equipment by himself.

"Mr. Ip, sir!"

Danny reached for his wallet. "Arif, thank you for your hard work today." With a practiced motion, he folded a few bills into his palm and held out his hand for a shake.

Arif's eyes bugged out of his head. He must have seen what Danny pulled out of his wallet. "Oh, Mr. Ip. Thank you so much."

"It's nothing." It was less than what he could drop on a weeknight dinner at one of Toronto's more exclusive restaurants. Danny pulled out a business card before putting his wallet away. "Take this too. If you ever need anything. Anything. Give me a call. That has my direct line."

Arif took the business card with more reverence than he'd taken the tip. He stared at it as if committing every detail to memory. "Yes, sir. Thank you, sir."

"You're welcome, Arif. You did good today."

They shook hands again, a nice solid hold, direct eye contact between two people who knew what it was like to fight their way to the top. Who had the conviction to do what it took to get there and stay there. At least, Danny used to.

He rejoined Ray as Marlena and Cyrus were emerging from Gerald's office. Marlena looked like a cat who ate the canary. Cyrus looked like he needed to lie down.

"Is everything okay?" Ray asked. The question was directed to Marlena even though Ray eyed Cyrus with concern.

"Oh, he'll be fine." Marlena waved a dismissive hand. "We were working out the details of separating our couple's membership. The club has a few options and I wanted Cyrus to know which one I preferred."

From Cyrus's expression, it sounded like a euphemism for something much less pleasant, but if it meant Danny could get his hands on WesTec, he wasn't about to ask too many questions.

Cyrus glanced from his wife to Ray and finally to Danny. Without a word, he spun on his heel and slunk away. The three of them stood and watched until he was out of sight.

"Are you sure he's okay?" Ray asked again.

Marlena cast him an *oh please* look. "You're sweet, dear, but he'll survive. He's got too much cockroach in him to succumb so easily."

Danny was no fan of Cyrus, but even he felt bad for the guy. Getting Marlena onside was one of the more brilliant ideas he'd had in a long time. Why do the dirty work himself when there was an ex-wife who was ready and willing?

"Give him time." Marlena brushed some invisible dust off her shoulder. "He'll come begging."

Danny had no doubt.

By the time Danny got back to the hotel, Tobin was gone. He'd expected as much. A part of him was even glad. Things had been so tense between them the past couple days—all Danny's fault, he knew—but he didn't like arguing with Tobin. What with all the maneuvering around WesTec, Danny really didn't want to come back to more fighting.

He needed to pack up his shit and get to the airport for his flight. Instead, he stood at the foot of the bed with the covers twisted in a pile, remembering Tobin lying there. If he closed his eyes and tilted his head just so, he could still smell the scent of Tobin's deodorant in the air.

He'd really fucked things up, hadn't he? It couldn't have been worse if he'd tried. Perhaps the only silver lining to the whole situation was Wei didn't know about it; at least, not yet. He could still find out and Danny wasn't looking forward to that possibility, but he'd deal with it when the time came.

Danny grabbed his suitcase and started throwing things inside. He needed to get out of the suite where every corner reminded him of Tobin. Tobin's smile and his laugh. Tobin's scowl when he was pissed—was it pathetic Danny missed even that?

Maybe the fiasco with Tobin was a blessing in disguise. The WesTec deal was finally gaining momentum and he needed every ounce of energy to focus on it. He couldn't afford distractions.

He pinched the bridge of his nose. He used to love this. The anticipation of closing a deal, the thrill of negotiating, the excitement when all the papers were finally signed. This time, he felt like he was stuck in a pit of quicksand; the harder he tried to climb free, the deeper he sank.

He zipped up his suitcase and dragged it out of the room. No more Calgary. No more Tobin. He needed to get his head in the game and get the job done. It used to be more than enough, and it would have to be this time too.

Because Danny didn't have anything else.

Chapter Fourteen

Tobin turned the corner on his way back from lunch and stopped short. There was a huge bouquet of red roses sitting on his desk and it could have only come from one person.

His heart thumped wildly. His coworkers were watching him with amused expressions, no doubt waiting for him to react. It was a big fucking romantic gesture that under normal circumstances would have Tobin swooning. But after last week, he had no interest in being charmed.

He steeled himself and marched up to his desk. A small card sat in the midst of the red blooms. *I'm sorry.*

Tobin tossed the card on the desk. He was sorry? That was it? An entire week of lies and deception and the best he could come up with was he was fucking sorry?

Tobin should take the flowers and toss them out. Just

on principle. That's how Tobin felt about Danny's pathetic apology. But that wasn't fair to the roses. And it'd raise more questions than he was ready to answer.

"Wow, these are beautiful!"

Tobin pasted a smile on his face and turned to greet Lonnie. "Thank you."

"Who are they from?" she asked, leaning in to take a sniff.

What did you call a childhood friend you'd been fucking, but who'd then turned around and stabbed you in the back? "Oh, um, some guy."

Lonnie wiggled her eyebrows at him. "Some guy? Must be pretty special."

He was. Emphasis on *was*.

Lonnie took one last sniff of the apology roses and sighed. "Anyway, you ready for our check-in?"

"Sure." As if Tobin had any other choice. He used to enjoy these little one-on-ones with Lonnie. He'd always been able to ask her anything and she always gave him great advice. Everything from how to think through a complex project and how to talk to clients, all the way to which managers he should suck up to for better visibility in the company. But Danny'd had to go ruin that too.

Now, every time the name WesTec came up, even in casual conversation, Tobin wanted to physically run away. How was he supposed to lead a project when he wanted nothing to do with the client?

"How's WesTec doing?" Lonnie asked as Tobin closed the meeting room door behind him.

He cringed. "It's fine," he responded. In reality, who the hell knew? Certainly not Tobin. Apparently, there was very little going on at the company he was actually privy to. "I've started reviewing their patents." In fact, he'd spent the morning giving himself a crash course on intellectual property law and how to read patent filings. He knew way more than he needed to—but hey, procrasti-work for the win.

"That's great! Anything interesting?"

Not unless Lonnie was curious about the nuances of patent versus trademark law. "I've just started, so not yet."

"Sounds good. And what about that external investor you mentioned last time? Any news?"

Ha. Too much news and not enough, all at the same time. But did he dare tell Lonnie? She'd want to know where he got his information from, and how would Tobin explain it? *Oh, you know, I've been fucking around with my brother's best friend, who I thought was a decent guy. But turns out he's pretty adept at blackmail and he has his sights set on WesTec. So yeah, he's got all this dirt on Cyrus West and I should hate him because apparently, he's totally not the man I thought he was. Then he sent that giant bouquet of roses and as much as I want to hate him, I'm really only seriously annoyed, so I'll probably forgive him eventually. And what the fuck does that say about who I am, hm?*

Yeah. As much as Lonnie was a good mentor and friend, Tobin didn't think that kind of outburst would go over well.

"External investor. Yes. It's Jade Harbour."

Lonnie sat back in her chair as she processed the new information. "Jade Harbour. Wow. They're a big deal."

"So I hear."

"And the client still doesn't want to sell?" She sounded surprised.

"As far as I know. But I haven't spoken to him lately."
No, he'd been actively avoiding Cyrus, hiding in a hotel
bar while dressed as a sexy cowboy.

"I wonder what the issue is. Most start-ups would kill
to get a backer like Jade Harbour." Lonnie frowned as if
trying to puzzle it out.

"From what I can gather, pride probably has something
to do with it."

"Pride?"

Tobin thought back to the power struggle he'd witnessed
in the meeting room that morning. When he'd been so
impressed and enamored by Danny's display of authority.
How long ago had that been? It felt like years and eons
had passed since. Like Tobin had shed his naïve rose-tinted
glasses to finally see the world and Danny for what and
who they were.

"I don't think Cyrus wants to admit he needs external
financing to keep the company afloat."

Lonnie cocked her head and Tobin could see the wheels
turning. "Every company needs external financing at some
point. Even if it's from the founder's personal assets. If that's
where WesTec is, then Cyrus is only shooting himself in
the foot by rejecting an investment offer, especially if it's
Jade Harbour knocking at his door. What we need to figure
out is whether WesTec needs an external infusion of cash,
and if so, whether Jade Harbour is a good option for them."

Put that way, the informational debris Tobin had been
wading through for days suddenly reorganized itself into
neat rows. How did Lonnie do that every single time?

"That...that makes a lot of sense. Thanks."

Lonnie waved it away. "You would've gotten there eventually."

"Still. Thank you."

"No problem." Lonnie stood. "Who knew this WesTec project would get so exciting, eh? Let me know if there's anything else you want to chat about." She let herself out of the meeting room and Tobin took his time following.

Exciting was one way to put it. Stressful and exhausting were good descriptors too. Was this the norm for every one of Danny's deals? If there was so much cloak and dagger all the time, no wonder Danny looked like he was barely holding himself together.

Back at his desk, Tobin stuck his nose into one of the rose blossoms and breathed in deep. Maybe he'd been too harsh on Danny. Hell, if Tobin was under that amount of stress day in and day out, who knew what kind of shit he would resort to.

Danny had said he'd been trying to keep Tobin away from the ugliness. It hadn't worked, but maybe Tobin should be grateful he tried?

So Danny wasn't exactly the heroic, could-do-no-wrong teenager Tobin had looked up to and loved. So what? Tobin wasn't the same person he'd been back then either. People grew up and life demanded things that yeah, maybe they weren't proud of, but were necessary if they wanted to survive.

Danny was nothing if not a survivor. Wasn't that also something Tobin had admired?

He traced a finger along a rose petal and picked up the card again. Danny had said he was sorry. He'd sent flowers to apologize. Tobin had never gotten flowers at work before. He snuck a few glances around at his colleagues.

Danny wasn't perfect. Neither was he. No one was. If Danny could admit he'd made a mistake, then Tobin could take him at face value and forgive him.

Tobin stretched and glanced at the time. The roses sat in a vase next to his computer screen. They had all bloomed, perfuming the air with their naturally sweet scent. He'd spent all day scouring WesTec's patents; some interesting stuff, but nothing too surprising. He wanted to go home and veg out.

But there were still a few hours left in the workday and all around him, people were hunched diligently over their desks. Couldn't hurt to get through the last one, he supposed. Tobin sighed and opened up the next patent folder.

At first, it looked like all the others. Diagrams and descriptions that almost read like a different language. But the longer Tobin stared at it, the more confused he got. He read through every document in the file, then read through it all again. It didn't make sense—the algorithm covered in the patent sounded like it could spin gold out of straw, but as far as he could tell, WesTec wasn't using it.

He pulled up file after file, checking and cross-checking until he was sure. Then he picked up the phone and called Lonnie. "Do you have a minute? I think I have something here."

She showed up at his desk before he could hang up the phone. "What's up?"

"Not sure. Might be nothing." He pointed to some code

on his computer screen. "This is the program WesTec uses to process all the data they collect. Then their analysts interpret the data and make recommendations to their clients on how to invest in the stock market."

Lonnie nodded. "Okay, I'm with you."

"Now this..." He clicked over to the patent. "Is another piece of code that kind of does the same thing, but on a bigger scale."

"Okay..." She didn't look like she was with him anymore.

"It's like this." Tobin started talking with his hands. "Normally, alternative data pulls a bunch of information together and makes inferences about how any particular stock on the market will move."

"Right."

"Now think of this patent as alternative data plus. It takes all those inferences and pieces them together to form an even bigger picture. Like, consumer spending, real estate trends, road traffic patterns—basically anything you can think of—and churns out a macro-level analysis of where the economy is going." Tobin's hands really started flying. "The alternative data industry to date has only been able to give us vague predictions, there's still such a high degree of uncertainty in the analysis it produces. But this? This brings together multiple data points, all reinforcing each other, so what it spits out is pretty much guaranteed."

"Okay." Lonnie still looked confused. "If this is such a game changer, why is WesTec struggling so much?"

"That's the thing!" Tobin dropped his voice into an excited hush. "WesTec isn't using this technology."

"What? Why not?"

Tobin shrugged. He hadn't figured out that part yet. "I don't know. But they're not. I've double- and triple-checked it."

Lonnie cocked her head. "Do you think Jade Harbour knows about this?"

The question was like a bucket of cold water tossed in Tobin's face. He'd been so excited about his find he hadn't even thought about Danny. Danny and Jade Harbour definitely had their own sources of information—no one could be where they were in finance without an established network. But unless their sources had access to WesTec's networks, would they know about this patent? It'd been buried so deep Tobin would never have come across it if he hadn't been going through WesTec's server with a fine-toothed comb.

"It could be why they're going after WesTec even though it's such a hard sell," Lonnie mused.

It made sense. It could explain a lot of things. "Could be."

"Hm." She nodded. "Good find. Really, Tobin, this is great. Keep at it. I think you're on to something here."

The compliment did little to lift Tobin's spirits. If pressed, he would guess Cyrus didn't know about the patent. It sounded implausible, but if he did know about it, why would he let it sit there gathering dust?

Then there was Danny and Jade Harbour. Tobin would bet money Danny knew about the patent. He was too good at his job not to. Everything started falling into place. Danny had been cagey because he couldn't risk Tobin finding out about the patent. Sure, that irked Tobin a bit, but he could understand.

He was obligated to include the implications of the patent into his analysis of WesTec. It wouldn't have mattered how he'd found out about it. If Danny had leaked it to him, then he'd have had to report it to WesTec, which could have derailed Danny's entire deal.

Tobin studied the roses on his desk. Danny had been pretty torn up the night of the WesTec party. He'd gone to the trouble of sending the massive bouquet of flowers. He'd texted a few times too, which Tobin had ignored.

But now he felt bad. If it had all been because of this patent, then could he really blame Danny at all? Hell, maybe he should be thanking Danny—no, that was a little too far. But it could very well be that Danny was looking out for Tobin's best interests, not wanting to put him in a conflicted situation where he had to choose between Danny and his professional integrity. That sounded a lot more like the Danny he knew.

Yes, that had to be it. Tobin picked up his phone to respond to Danny, only to have it start buzzing in his hand.

Wei. Shit. He'd messaged a while ago, but Tobin was so focused on work he'd forgotten to reply.

He tapped the accept button. "Hi."

"Hey, how's it going? Just checking in. You know, make sure everything's okay." Wei sounded like he was driving. Tobin could hear the twins trying to sing along to some song in the background. "Kids, say hi to Uncle Toby!"

"Hi, Uncle Toby!" they both yelled in unison.

"Hi!" he whisper-yelled into the phone while hightailing it to the closest empty meeting room.

"So what's going on? Haven't heard from you in forever."

"It's hasn't been forever. You only messaged me a couple hours ago! I happen to have something to do called work."

"Yeah, smart aleck, I know. I also have something called work. And I still manage to respond to family members when they text."

"Doesn't count when you work from home." Tobin crossed his arms, leaned against the wall and stared out the window at his coworkers wrapping up for the evening.

"Excuse me, you entitled little—you know what. Working from home is still working. I've got clients all around the world and I'm on call 24/7. When I'm not telling clients to turn their machines off and on again, I've got two toddlers to run after, who are arguably more work than my actual work. So don't give me any of that Gen Z—poop."

"Uncle Toby did a poop?"

"Did Uncle Toby use a potty?"

Tobin cringed. This was really not the conversation he wanted to be having.

"Great. See what you did?" Wei muttered. "No, Uncle Toby did not poop. And yes, if Uncle Toby needs to poop, he will use the potty."

"Are you driving? You shouldn't be on the phone while you're driving. I should let you go." Any excuse he could find to hang up.

"I'm going to Mom and Dad's." The sound of the car's turn signal clicked in the background. "Constance has her monthly girls' night out and Danny's been too absurdly busy at work to come help me with the twins."

"Yeah, I know," Tobin replied before realizing the implications of what he'd said.

"You do?" The engine fell silent on the other end. "No, wait! Don't climb out by yourself. I'm coming!"

Saved by the twins?

"Okay, I've got to go. Talk soon."

"Bye!" But Wei had already hung up.

Disaster narrowly avoided. Tobin dropped his head forward only to snap it back up when someone knocked on the door. It was Lonnie.

"Oh, sorry, Lonnie. Did you need the room? I'm done in here."

"Nope. A few of us are going to grab drinks. I wanted to see if you'd like to come."

He did. It'd been a while since he'd been out to drinks with his coworkers. One of the senior managers usually picked up the tab for everyone, which was especially nice. But he wanted to call Danny, tell him everything was forgiven and water under the bridge.

Lonnie was looking at him, waiting for a response.

"Yeah, sure. Let me grab my stuff."

He'd call Danny later; he could suffer a little longer.

Tobin snort-laughed at something Lonnie said and then started coughing as he got beer up his nose. He doubled over, and the rest of the group erupted in another round of laughter.

"You okay, Tobin?" Lonnie leaned in to be heard over the noise of the bar.

"Yeah, yeah, I'm good. Thanks."

She laughed and turned to speak with someone else.

God, he'd missed this. He'd been so caught up in work

and Danny and WesTec he hadn't been out to one of these happy hours in ages. It was seriously good for the soul to hang out, have fun, and not have to worry about a single thing other than when the next round was being poured.

In his pocket, his phone buzzed, then buzzed again. Shit—he knew who it was, and he had no desire to answer the call. How the hell did they do this every single time?

He let the call go to voicemail only to have his phone notify him of a new voicemail waiting. Then his phone buzzed again. Seriously?

Tobin dug it out of his pocket and smashed his finger against the accept key. "Hello?" he shouted into the mic.

"Toby? Toby! Are you there? Toby!"

Tobin didn't bother smothering his groan. It's not like his mother would hear it. "Yes, I'm here!" He made his way toward the front of the bar, draining the last of his beer as he went. He stepped out into the cool summer evening. "Yeah, what do you want?"

"Ah, Toby. Where are you? So loud!"

"I'm out, Mom."

"Out? It's so late! Have you had dinner yet?"

"It's not late, Mom. It's only six o'clock here. Did Wei tell you to call?" It would be so quintessentially Wei to get her worked up about nothing.

She conveniently ignored his question. "You have to eat, okay? And rest. Prepare for tomorrow."

"Tomorrow is Saturday." But she didn't hear him.

"I have this new eye mask made with carbon. It's good for dark circles. I've been wearing it to sleep for a week now and my eyes look so much younger. You want I send one to you? Oh, and some for Monica and her girlfriend too. What's her name?"

"Her name's Ayán. But they don't want eye masks. I don't want eye masks. Please don't send eye masks." Why did he even bother? Chances were they were in the mail already.

"Here. Talk to your daddy."

Tobin sucked in a deep breath and reined in his temper. They meant well. They missed him. This was how they showed him they loved him. Repeating it to himself helped...a little.

"Wai? Toby?"

"Hi, Dad."

"You okay?"

"Yes, Dad."

"Need food? Money?"

"No, Dad."

"Your boss happy with you?"

Tobin cringed. "Do you mean how's work going? It's going fine, thanks for asking."

"Your English okay? Not too hard?"

Tobin slapped himself on the forehead. Hard. "Yes, Dad. My English is fine. They're not sending me to ESL classes during lunch."

"Okay!" He didn't even bother saying goodbye before handing the phone back.

"Wai? Everything okay?" his mom asked again.

Hadn't he answered that a million times already? "Yes, Mom. Everything is okay. I have food and money. I'm eating, and I will get some rest. Tell Dad not to worry whether my English is good enough to keep up with the white folks. And *please* don't send the eye masks."

"Aiya, Toby, I went to postal office already! If you don't want, then give to your friends. It's good eye mask!"

"Yeah, okay. I will. Thank you."

"Okay, bye-bye!" And the line went dead.

Tobin stuffed the phone into his pocket. So much for happy hour. Now he was so wound up he wouldn't be much fun.

He should just go home. He turned to head back inside only to be met with Lonnie and the others heading out.

"Oh! There you are!" Lonnie said. "We weren't sure where you disappeared off to."

"Yeah, sorry. My parents called."

She gave him a sympathetic smile. "They're doing well?"

"Yes, they're great. Thank you for asking."

"I'm glad to hear that. Anyway, we're all heading home. Don't worry about the bill. I got it." She gave him a quick pat on the arm. "Have a great weekend! See you next week!"

"Thanks! You too!" he called after her as everyone filed down the street. Guess that was it for the evening. Tobin sighed. Time to eat and rest and prepare for tomorrow. Too bad the eye mask was still in the mail.

Chapter Fifteen

"You talk to Toby lately?"

Danny choked on the beer he was drinking.

"Whoa, easy there." Wei pounded him on the back, which only made Danny cough more.

Danny shrugged him off.

"You all right?" Wei laughed.

"Yeah, fine." He cleared his throat.

In the yard, Peyton and Howie let out coordinated shrieks of joy. "Be careful!" Wei shouted without even sparing them a look.

"Why do you ask?"

"What? Oh, Toby?" Wei opened the barbecue to check on the meat. "I don't know. Just wondering."

Had Tobin said something to Wei? It seemed unlikely

given how Tobin felt about his family interfering with his life. But who knew? Maybe Tobin was pissed at him enough to go venting to Wei.

Either way, Danny should have come clean a long time ago. "Actually—"

Wei's head snapped up and he narrowed his eyes at Danny.

Shit. Maybe he shouldn't have said anything. But it was too late to back out now. "I saw him in Calgary."

"I knew it!" Wei waved the barbecue tongs in his face.

"Whoa. Easy with those." Danny took a step back. "You knew what?"

"I mentioned to him you've been busy lately and he said, 'I know.'" Wei looked triumphant, like he'd solved a tricky crossword puzzle or something.

"Okay, so?"

"So, I knew you two had been in contact! Why didn't you tell me?"

Because the type of contact they'd been in involved no clothing and bodily penetration. "I don't know. It didn't seem like a big deal." Liar, liar, pants on fire.

Thank god Wei seemed to take it in stride. "Yeah, but still. Let a guy in on the secret, why don't you."

Danny rubbed the back of his neck and took another sip of his beer. "Yeah, sorry. It slipped my mind. You know, with work."

Except he hadn't been too busy to send the most expensive bouquet of flowers he could find. It was one of those Valentine's Day arrangements that was somehow still on sale in the middle of summer. He hadn't heard from Tobin since.

Which was fine, he kept telling himself. Tobin didn't owe him anything, certainly not forgiveness. Yet every time his phone buzzed, he found himself hoping it was Tobin.

"So what did you do in Calgary?" Wei asked.

"What?"

It was a harmless question. Wei was only curious. Like a "how was your vacation?" type of question.

"Didn't you go during the Stampede thing?"

For someone who always looked a little frazzled running after his kids, Wei managed to remember a lot of details.

"Oh, uh, yeah. You know, rodeo and that type of stuff."

"Cool. Can you grab the twins for me?" Wei started pulling food off the grill and piling it onto plates.

Danny breathed a sigh of relief. Corralling the twins was much preferable to answering Wei's questions. It wasn't even difficult. The second Danny stepped off the patio and onto the grass, Peyton and Howie came rushing over to him, nearly knocking him to the ground.

"Uncle Danny!" With a toddler latched onto each leg, Danny made a loop around the yard while making loud growling sounds. They giggled and screeched, a soothing balm to his constant fatigue. He crouched down, pulling them both into a tight embrace. Two pairs of tiny arms wrapped around his neck, soft hair brushed against his cheeks.

"Love you, Uncle Danny!"

"Love you, Uncle Danny!"

His throat tightened. "Love you both too." He planted a kiss on the top of each innocent head.

"Food's ready!" Wei called out and the twins scampered off to their dad.

Danny took a moment on the grass. He really did love those two terrors. He hadn't realized quite how much until things with Tobin had imploded. Every time he thought of how badly he'd botched it all, his first instinct was to call Tobin for a little pity party and some consoling. But that wasn't about to happen when Tobin was the one he'd pissed off. The next best option—and only by a hair—had been the twins. They were so carefree and joyful. Danny envied the simplicity of their lives. It wouldn't always be that way, but Danny would do everything in his power to protect them for as long as he could.

He joined Wei and the kids at the patio table. There was one chair empty, one that usually belonged to Constance. But in Danny's mind, it was Tobin's.

It would be nice to share easy evenings like this with Tobin. Comfortable and relaxing, with nowhere to be and nothing to prove. Danny could imagine Tobin running around the backyard with the twins, hoisting them up to the sink to wash their hands, cuddling with them while reading a bedtime story. He'd be the uncle they'd go to for dating advice and fashion advice. He'd be their confidant when their parents were being overbearing.

Did Tobin know how much of their lives he was missing out on? Was that something he thought about? If it were Danny, the toughest of Stampede bulls wouldn't be able to pull him away from this, not if he had a choice.

His phone rang with an incoming call. Tobin's face popped up on the screen. Danny grabbed it off the table as fast as he could, but it was too late.

Howie saw it. "It's Uncle Toby!" he announced.

"Uncle Toby!" Peyton echoed. Neither of the twins noticed the frown on their dad's face, but it wasn't lost on Danny.

He couldn't very well excuse himself from the table to answer it now. Ah, crap.

He answered it and immediately put it on speaker. "Hey, I'm at Wei's. The twins want to say hi."

"Hiiiiii!"

"Hi hi hi hi hi!"

"Oh, hello!" Thank god Tobin was quick on his feet. "Are you keeping Uncle Danny busy?"

"We're having dinner with Daddy and Uncle Danny," Howie explained.

"We're having barbecue," Peyton clarified.

"That sounds delicious! I wish I could have some too!"

"We'll bring you some!" Peyton turned to her dad. "Can we? Please please please?"

Wei and Danny exchanged a look before Wei patted his daughter on her head. "Uncle Toby lives a little too far for us to drive, sweetie."

She looked positively crestfallen.

"That's okay, Peyton! I'll get some barbecue on my own and I'll think of both you and Howie while I'm eating it."

"Yay!" Howie held two sauce-covered fists in the air.

"Is everything okay?" Wei asked, staring at Danny's phone. It wasn't a video call, but Danny could have sworn he could hear Tobin roll his eyes. "Yes, everything's fine. Don't worry about me."

Tobin didn't know about Danny's earlier conversation. "I was telling Wei we met up at the Stampede."

Silence from the other end before Tobin recovered. "Yeah, we did. That's actually why I'm calling...actually. I wanted to thank you for the, uh...donuts you bought. They're really, um, delicious, and I really appreciate it."

Danny could feel Wei staring at the top of his head, but he couldn't bring himself to make eye contact. He wasn't the blushing type, but under the right circumstances...

"Yes, you're very welcome." Danny racked his brain. Donuts must mean the flowers because Tobin had very distinctly rebuffed his attempts to purchase donuts at the Stampede. Donuts were made with flour, which sounded like flower, right? "I'm glad you enjoyed them."

"Yeah, you know, I was, um, skeptical at first. But uh, I have to say, you've won me over."

Did "won me over" mean Danny was forgiven? Did the flowers work?

"Daddy, I want donuts," Howie whined.

God, why were they having this very poorly coded conversation in front of everyone?

"Not now, buddy."

Danny risked a quick glance in Wei's direction and immediately regretted it. The twins might have been fooled, but Wei certainly wasn't. "That's great to hear. I'm really happy that worked out."

"Yeah. Okay, I'll talk to you later then."

"Yes, yes, later. We can talk later."

"Okay. Bye."

"Bye." Danny tucked his phone away where observant little kids wouldn't be able to completely blow his cover.

"I want donuts too." Now Peyton.

"Maybe Uncle Danny can get you donuts. Seems like he knows a good place."

Danny kept his gaze lowered strictly to the level of small children. "Yeah, sure. I can get you as many donuts as you'd like. Whatever flavor you want."

That did the trick. They started spouting off increasingly inventive flavors, filling the very awkward silence between the adults. Danny chanced one more look in Wei's direction. Fuck, he was so screwed.

They managed to get through dinner and washing up and putting the kids to bed, with Danny promising donut flavors he was pretty sure didn't exist. Wei normally would have come to his rescue with some explanation for why Uncle Danny couldn't pull donuts out of thin air, but Danny had no such luck this time.

Wei waited until the twins were tucked in before bringing it up. "What the hell's going on?" he asked the second they made it back downstairs.

There was no point in lying about it now. Where had all his lying gotten him recently? Nowhere he wanted to be. "I ran into Tobin in Calgary, but it was before the Stampede. We've seen each other a few times since."

Wei pulled the garbage bin out from under the kitchen sink and tied the liner shut. "I figured as much. But what's with the donuts? And don't tell me it was donuts, I'm a little more perceptive than a couple toddlers."

Danny's palms grew clammy and his stomach fluttered with butterflies. God, what was wrong with him? He felt like he was going to his first job interview straight out of undergrad—but worse. Because if he fucked up the interview, there'd always be another one. If he fucked things up with Wei, there was only one Wei.

"I'm waiting." Wei had perfected that annoyed parent tone.

Danny swallowed, but his throat was dry. "They're uh… flowers." He stuck his hands in his pockets to keep them from shaking.

Wei dropped the bag of garbage on the kitchen floor. "Flowers."

"Yeah."

"Why the hell are you giving Toby flowers?"

Danny glanced over to make sure he'd heard correctly. Why else would he be giving Tobin flowers? "We're, um, sort of, seeing each other?"

Wei's mouth gaped, and his brows scrunched together so hard the two sides were almost touching. "You're what?"

"We're seeing each other." Danny hoped that was explanation enough, because if he needed to go into more detail about what "seeing each other" entailed, then he was out of there.

"Like, not as friends?" Wei had his eyes squeezed shut now and Danny couldn't tell if he was trying to imagine what that looked like or trying *not* to imagine it.

But his question stopped Danny short. He and Tobin had never discussed what exactly they were. "Definitely more than friends." But how much more? Danny realized he had no clue where Tobin stood.

Wei snapped his mouth shut, then opened it again before covering his face with both hands like his brain was melting inside his head. "You know Toby's always had a crush on you, right?"

Now it was Danny's turn to frown. What did that have to do with anything? "Yes."

"And now you're—" He waved his hand around, but Danny got the message.

"Y-yes."

Wei shook his head as if he'd smelled something rancid and was trying to get the scent out of his nose. "I don't—I can't—what the fuck do you think you're doing?"

Wei didn't really swear anymore, what with having two small children around. That combined with the way he shouted had Danny taking a step back. Wei didn't wait for a response.

"You have got to be kidding me. This isn't happening. You *know* Toby's always had a thing for you. Yeah, at first it was cute. You know, it was a little kid crush and we all thought he'd grow out of it. But no, he didn't. And now you're—I don't know what, playing along? Is that what this is? How could you—when you know—I can't believe you're taking advantage of him like this!"

Danny staggered backward until he bumped into the kitchen counter. Every single word was a knife in his gut until Danny felt like his insides were spilling out onto the floor. He'd known this would happen. Wei would flip out, accuse him of all the things he'd been beating himself up about.

"Daddy?" Peyton's quiet, uncertain voice sliced through the tension in the room.

Wei immediately turned to his daughter, all evidence of anger, disappointment, and disbelief vanishing, and he scooped her up in his arms. "Hey baby girl, what are you doing down here?"

"I heard shouting. Are you okay?"

He kissed the top of her head and started back up the stairs. "Yeah, yeah, I'm fine. Uncle Danny and I were talking about a few things."

Danny didn't hear the rest of it. He was already halfway out the front door, feeling like he'd left huge chunks of himself inside. He'd known this was coming. He had no one else to blame but himself.

He climbed into his car, started the engine and stomped on the gas. He made it around the corner before slamming on the brakes. He was shaking so hard he could barely keep the steering wheel straight.

Fuck. Fuck fuck fuck.

Twenty-two. Twenty-four. Twenty-six Maple. There it was. Danny pulled his rental car over and put it in park. The neighborhood looked like every other Vancouver suburb Danny had driven through, and this house looked like every other house on the street. But according to the address Marlena had given them, this was the right place.

It turned out Marlena had no knowledge of any patent, but she knew the person who'd been working on it. Apparently, Cyrus wasn't shy about broadcasting his opinions about trans people.

Ray had offered to come along, since they'd been working the deal together for a while now. But Danny declined. There were other things he needed to do in Vancouver and he didn't want Ray getting in the way.

Things like sitting down with Tobin and having an honest heart-to-heart. Something that was long overdue. Tobin would hate it, but the whole "taking advantage" thing was real, and having Wei scream it in his face made Danny realize he couldn't ignore it anymore.

They'd had a good time. It'd been fun. But it was time for them to confront the facts. Their little affair involved way more people than simply the two of them. Their actions and decisions affected Wei and Uncle Man and Auntie Grace. To deny that was the epitome of selfishness.

Danny wasn't looking forward to that conversation. But first—River Teegee.

He got out and strode up the driveway. A car was parked there; good since he was showing up unannounced. Ray had tried reaching out to River repeatedly with emails and phone calls, but hadn't gotten a response. So their last-ditch attempt was Danny coming in person to plead their case. He rang the doorbell and a muted ring sounded inside. Floorboards creaked under footsteps before the door opened only a crack. Barely enough to reveal a face framed with long black hair and big gold-rimmed glasses. They eyed Danny up and down. "Can I help you?"

"My name is Daniel Ip, from Jade Harbour Capital. I'm looking for River Teegee."

They narrowed their eyes. "I don't have anything to say to you," they said and then shut the door in his face.

Danny had expected as much. He knocked on the door and rang the bell again. "Please, I could really use your help. It'll only take a moment."

No response. He knocked again. "Any information you can give me will be kept strictly confidential. No one will know we spoke."

Nothing. He knocked on more time. "At least listen to what my questions are."

Next door, a screen door creaked open and an old woman with white hair stepped out. She glared at Danny. "What's all this racket? Do I need to call the police?"

Shit. The last thing Danny needed was getting the police involved. "Sorry, ma'am. Everything's fine. Sorry to disturb you." He took a few steps backward, only to have River's door open again.

They peered out at the older woman. "Mind your own business, Karen." Then to Danny. "Get in here before the cops start showing up."

Thank heavens for Karen.

Danny followed River to a tiny office at the back of the house. Metal shelves lined the walls and the floor was covered in cardboard boxes. Electronic odds and ends filled the space.

River cleared some debris off a chair and gestured Danny into it.

They sat in an office chair that had seen better days. "You can talk, but no guarantee I'm going to answer any questions."

Fair enough. "I wanted to ask you about WesTec."

They shook their head. "I'm not supposed to talk about that."

"I know." Danny relaxed into the metal folding chair as much as was physically possible. "And I promise you word will not get out that we've spoken. I will be discreet."

They seemed to consider for a moment before crossing their arms. "What do you want to know?"

"You were working on a project while at WesTec. A patent was filed for it, but not under the WesTec name. I was hoping you could tell me about it."

River's gaze was like lasers burning holes into Danny's face. This was it. He was going to get kicked out with nothing to show for it.

River sighed, muttered something that sounded like a curse, and started talking.

Danny stepped out into the sunshine thrumming with energy. If what River had told him was true… Fuck. He hoped to god it was true.

They had a bona fide unicorn on their hands. True untapped potential that was sure to net them billions and launch Danny and Jade Harbour into the next level of the private equity world. Forget Canada—they'd be competing with the global heavy hitters.

He climbed into his rental car and pulled out his phone to call Joanna. She needed to know about this right away.

But then he noticed the time. Shit. He was late to meet Tobin. He tossed his phone into the passenger seat and started the car. He could drive and talk at the same time.

Joanna's assistant patched him through. "Yes?"

"Joanna, it's Danny. I've got great news." He slowed to a stop at a traffic light. "I spoke with River Teegee, the former WesTec employee Ray dug up."

The light turned green and he stepped on the gas. "The patent is better than we thought it was going to be. Cyrus West is a fucking piece of shit."

"We knew that already."

"Yeah, well, he's an even bigger piece of shit because of this. He shelved the project because he and River butted heads. When River finally quit, Cyrus refused to let anyone else pick it up. So it's been sitting there collecting dust while WesTec bleeds money." Danny slowed, checked for oncoming traffic and then turned right.

He heard the sound before he felt the impact, before he even saw anything fly past the front of the car. The scrape of metal against metal that never meant anything good. He threw the car into park and scrambled out. On the ground, in front of his bumper, was a cyclist on his back, holding his shin. The bicycle was twisted up beyond repair.

"Jesus fucking Christ." He rushed over to the cyclist. There was blood everywhere and the guy was sitting on the ground holding his shin. A crowd of spectators gathered. "Someone call 911!"

Danny pulled off his sport jacket and pressed it against the cyclist's shin, which he assumed was the source of all the blood. "I'm so sorry, man. I'm so sorry."

"Fuck you!"

"I know, I know. I'm so sorry. I fucked up." In the distance came the wail of sirens. "The ambulance is on its way. Hold on. Everything's going to be okay."

"Fuck you, you fucking asshole driver. Not fucking watching where you're going."

"I am an asshole. I'm so sorry. Hold on. Paramedics are almost here."

The cyclist started shaking. Tears trailed down his face, mixing with the blood and dirt on his skin.

Fuck. Fuck. Fuck. What had he done? He was in so much fucking shit.

"Paramedics. Move out of the way." Someone pushed him to the side and Danny tumbled to the ground.

Sitting in the middle of glass and metal shards, Danny held his head in his hands. The sound of the bicycle crumpling under the car. The reverberation of the impact ringing in his bones. The smell of blood and burned rubber.

One of the paramedics came over and crouched down in front of him. "Sir, are you okay? Are you hurt anywhere?"

Danny shook his head. He was fine. But the guy... "Is he...will he be okay?"

"We're taking him to the hospital." The paramedic looked into Danny's eyes. "Do you want to go too? Just to be safe?"

"I'm going to need to take his statement." The voice came from above Danny's head. A police officer Danny hadn't even known was there.

The paramedic scowled at the officer. "You can take it at the hospital. He's in shock. We shouldn't leave him unattended."

The officer shrugged. "Fine, whatever. I'll need his name before you take him."

"D–D–Daniel. Ip," he managed. His tongue was numb, and his teeth were chattering.

"How do you spell the last name?"

The paramedic rolled her eyes.

"I. P."

"All right. Come on. Let's get you in the ambulance." The paramedic steadied him as Danny rose to his feet.

He felt like he was floating, like his limbs weren't under his control anymore.

The paramedic led him to the back of the ambulance where the cyclist had already been loaded in. He climbed up and wrapped his arms around himself.

"Wait!" He raised his hand to keep the paramedic from shutting the door. "My phone. It's in the car."

She glanced back at the car, engine still running, driver's side door hanging open.

"It's on the passenger seat. I need it." He needed to call Tobin, Joanna, the rental car company, his insurance company. His mind snapped into sharp focus and he moved to jump down from the ambulance.

"Whoa, whoa. You sit tight." The paramedic pushed him back into his seat. "I'll get it for you. Just the phone? Anything else?"

Danny thought hard. "And…and my bag. It's also on the passenger seat." All his other stuff was at the hotel—at least he was pretty sure it was.

The cyclist groaned, and Danny turned to find his face all scrunched up. His leg looked mangled. The other paramedic noticed Danny's attention.

"Don't worry. I've got him hopped up on morphine. He shouldn't be feeling anything in a moment."

"Here." His bag and phone were dumped into his lap and the door of the ambulance shut before he could check everything was there. He clutched his phone to his chest; it still buzzed every few minutes. But he couldn't bring himself to look at it. All he could do was stare at the poor cyclist's leg, bandages now covering the wound.

The bone must be broken. It would take months for it to heal, and then many more months for rehab. Would the guy be able to walk normally again? To cycle again? Had Danny ruined his life? Fuck. Fuck. Fuck.

Chapter Sixteen

His phone rang, and Danny's name popped up on the screen. Tobin was so tempted to let it go to voicemail. It was what he deserved for not showing up when he was supposed to and not picking up his own damn phone when Tobin called.

Ugh. He couldn't *not* answer. "Hello?" He put every ounce of his annoyance into the one word.

"Hi." Danny's voice was small, shaky, more of a squeak than anything else.

Tobin had never heard him sound like that before. All his annoyance evaporated. "Are you okay? What happened?"

Danny's breathing came across loudly, as if he was blowing directly into the phone. "I'm fine."

"Bullshit. You're not fine. What happened?"

"I, uh…there was an accident."

"An accident?" Tobin jumped to his feet and searched his room for his wallet. "What kind of accident? Where are you?"

"I'm at the hotel. And I'm fine. I, uh…" Danny took an audible breath. "I hit a cyclist."

"Shit. Are they okay? Which hotel?" Tobin grabbed his keys from the top of his dresser.

"He's… I…"

He stuck his feet into shoes and ran out the door. "Which hotel!"

"You don't have to come over."

"Like hell I don't. Save us both some time and tell me." He jabbed the elevator button.

Danny let out a sigh like he was letting go of everything inside him. "The Oceanic Hotel."

"Oceanic. Got it. Don't go anywhere. I'm on my way."

"Danny?" Tobin rapped his knuckles loudly on the door. "Danny! It's me. Open up."

It took a moment, but then the dead bolt slid open and the doorknob turned. Tobin didn't wait for Danny; he pushed it open himself.

"Danny?" He sucked in a breath, his heart twisting in his chest.

He didn't look nearly as bad as Tobin's wild imagination had suggested. But he didn't look good either. He had smudges of dirt and blood on his face. His shirt looked like he'd been rolling on the ground. There was a rip across one knee of his pants.

"Jesus." Tobin took him by the arm and led him back

inside. The door swung shut behind them with a thud. "What the fuck happened? No—don't answer that. You need to take a shower first."

Danny held a glass in his hand, still half full of what was probably whiskey.

"Give me that." Tobin took it and Danny surrendered without a fight. "Bathroom, bathroom. Through here?" He led them toward a set of French doors he guessed was the bedroom.

In the bathroom, he propped Danny up against the counter. He looked like shit. Like a zombie. His eyes were vacant, and his arms swung heavily by his sides.

Tobin's heart ached at the sight of Danny so broken. He ran his hands over Danny's head, his face, looking for cuts and bruises, any sign of damage, but he didn't find anything. "Let's get you out of these clothes, okay?"

He didn't respond, but he didn't stop Tobin either. Carefully, with fingers that trembled, Tobin undid the buttons of his shirt and peeled the fabric off him. Then came Danny's belt and pants, socks and underwear.

The last to go was Danny's wristwatch. A worn leather band and a crack across the glass face. The time was still set to the Toronto time zone, but the second hand had stopped ticking. Tobin laid it on the bathroom counter then turned to help him into the shower.

Danny shivered as he stepped onto the cold tile.

"Yeah, it's cold, isn't it?" Tobin reached in and turned the water as hot as it would go. "Give it a minute."

Danny's head was lowered, like it was too heavy for his neck to hold up.

"Do you want me to help you?" Tobin reached for the hem of his shirt without waiting for a response.

"No. I'll manage." Danny didn't lift his head, but the emotion wafting off him hit Tobin like a tidal wave. "Thank you."

Tobin took a step back as Danny closed the glass shower door and stepped under the spray. Danny would be okay, he had to be. There was barely a scratch on him. And emotionally, well, that was only shock. Nothing a good night's rest wouldn't cure.

Tobin gathered Danny's soiled clothes and dumped them into the laundry bag he found in the hotel closet. He doubted Danny would want to keep any of them.

Then he went back to the living room. The bottle of whiskey sat on the coffee table next to the glass Tobin had set there. Had Danny eaten anything? Tobin searched for the room service menu and called down an order.

What else? What did Danny need? What could Tobin do to keep his hands busy and his mind occupied?

The shower was still running.

Should he call Wei and tell him what happened? But Tobin didn't even know what happened. And what could Wei do all the way from Toronto anyway? No, Tobin would handle this on his own.

He went to check on Danny. The bathroom was filled with steam, so much so it was a little hard to breathe.

"Danny? You still in there?" Tobin tried to wave the steam out of his face. "You okay?"

Danny stood under the water, head tilted back to catch

the full force of the spray. Had he been standing like that the whole time?

Fuck it.

Tobin stripped as fast as he could and pulled the shower door open. Danny's hands were by his sides, fingers curled into fists. Tobin ran his hands down Danny's arms and wrapped his fingers over Danny's. Slowly, ever so slowly, he relaxed enough for Tobin to intertwine their fingers.

He pressed his chest against Danny's back, his cheek against Danny's shoulders. After a moment, the tension in Danny eased and he leaned back into Tobin. They stood there as the water fell over them, washing everything away.

They technically hadn't spoken since that weird phone call about donuts. Tobin had hoped Danny would call back, so they could have a proper conversation without the twins and Wei listening in. But instead, he'd texted, saying he was going to be in Vancouver for work and would Tobin be willing to meet up.

Tobin had been tempted to ask what kind of work he was in town for but had decided against it. Sometimes the less he knew the better. Besides, WesTec didn't have a presence in Vancouver as far as Tobin knew.

Tobin had planned on giving Danny a hard time, just because. But in reality, Tobin had already forgiven him. Patent and apology flowers aside, Tobin didn't think he could ever stay angry at Danny for long.

He reached for the soap and gently ran it over Danny's body. He was careful to cover every inch, careful to keep his touch light. After he finished with the back, he turned Danny around.

Danny's gaze followed him as he moved. Shoulders to chest to stomach. Tobin kneeled on the tiled floor to wash Danny's legs. First the left, then the right. He returned to Danny's groin, running a soapy hand over Danny's dick and balls. Nothing sexual. Nothing meant to arouse.

He made Danny turn around in the water so every last sud was rinsed off.

"Ready to get out?" Tobin asked.

He nodded.

Tobin helped him towel off and wrapped him in the bathrobe provided by the hotel. "Come on. Let's get you into bed."

Danny didn't resist, climbing under the covers and letting Tobin tuck him in.

A knock sounded at the door and Danny frowned.

"Room service," Tobin explained. "Give me a second." He shut the bedroom door on his way out, pausing a second to catch his breath. God, it was so hard to see Danny like this. But he could do it, he would be strong, so Danny could be weak. Except, as he cinched his own bathrobe a little tighter, tears stung his eyes.

No crying, god damn it. Tobin swiped angrily at his cheeks and yanked the suite door open. The hotel staff outside looked up in surprise.

"Oh, hi. I've got room service here." He lifted a tray from his cart and took a step forward.

"Actually, I'll take it." Tobin took the tray from him. "Do I need to sign anything?"

"No, you're good, sir."

"Thanks." Tobin stepped back and let the door swing

shut. Oh wait, should he have given the guy a tip? Ah well, too late now. He took the tray into the bedroom where Danny was in the exact same position Tobin had left him in. Flat on his back, staring at the ceiling.

"Want some food?"

"Not really."

"Tough, you should eat something anyway." Tobin helped Danny sit up in bed, stuffing pillows behind his back, and then handed him a bowl of soup. Tobin had wanted chicken noodle, but the kitchen didn't have any, so he'd settled for minestrone. From where he sat on the other side of the bed, it smelled good. He hoped it tasted good too. "Want to tell me what happened?"

Danny rested the bowl in his lap. "I was on my way to your place, making a right. I didn't look before turning. I was watching for oncoming traffic." He stopped, took another sip of soup, and put the bowl down again.

"I hit the front wheel of his bicycle. It was completely mangled."

"Shit," Tobin muttered. "And the cyclist?"

"Fractured his leg, but I don't know how badly. The doctors wouldn't tell me anything." Danny paused before continuing. "I was on the phone with Joanna when it happened."

Tobin frowned. "Joanna?"

"My boss."

Ah. Work. As always. Tobin should have guessed. But it wasn't only work this time, was it? It'd also been him. The missed call and follow-up text asking where the hell Danny was, which must have made Danny rush over. If he'd been taking his time, he might not have hit the cy-clist. Tobin ran a hand over his face. What a mess.

"The police came to the hospital to question me," Danny continued while stirring his spoon through the soup. He didn't seem interested in eating it.

"You were at the hospital? What did they say?" Could Danny get arrested? Would he go to jail?

"Doctors checked me over. I'm fine. In shock, but they said to sleep it off. Police asked what happened and gave me a ticket."

"That's it? That doesn't sound too bad."

Danny lifted defeated eyes to him.

Oops. "I mean…it could have been worse, right?"

"Yeah, it could have been worse." Danny put the half-eaten bowl of soup on the nightstand. "I'm kind of tired," he said, as if surprised by his fatigue.

"You should definitely sleep. Doctor's orders, right?" Tobin helped Danny get settled in, duvet tucked tightly around him.

Danny's eyes drifted shut almost immediately, but his brow was still furrowed, like demons haunted his dreams. Tobin ran the pad of his thumb over Danny's forehead in an attempt at soothing out the creases. Danny's breathing slowed at Tobin's touch and he seemed to sink deeper into the mattress.

Tobin turned off the bedside lamp and tiptoed toward the door.

"Don't leave?" The request came quietly, hesitantly, like Danny wasn't sure he was allowed to ask.

But it wasn't even a question for Tobin. Of course he would stay.

Tobin rounded the other side of the bed and slipped under the duvet. With their roles reversed, Tobin as the big spoon and Danny as the small, Danny finally succumbed to sleep.

He ran a hand over Danny's hair, the bristles soft against his palm. Danny let out a delicate meow so unlike his public persona that Tobin had to smile. His big tough lion was nothing more than a kitty cat on the inside.

They really had made a mess of things, hadn't they? What was that saying about work and play not mixing? But WesTec was only a blip on their timeline. They'd known each other long before WesTec came into their lives, and they would know each other long after. Why should they let this one company stand between them and what they wanted? It wouldn't—not if Tobin had anything to do about it.

He pressed a kiss onto Danny's temple. "It'll be okay," he whispered. "I promise. Everything will be okay."

Chapter Seventeen

Danny woke with a start at the sound of crunching metal. His heart raced, and his lungs sucked in air like he was in a vacuum. It took a full second for him to realize he was in bed and another second to remember it wasn't his bed at home.

Then it all came back to him. He rubbed his eyes. He needed a shave. He felt like he'd been hit by a truck. Damn it. Bad analogy, brain. He'd been the one doing the hitting. Fuck.

Danny sat up before he noticed Tobin still in bed with him. Fast asleep with one arm thrown above his head. He looked peaceful. Danny hoped his dreams were too.

It was nice of him to come over at a moment's notice. Sweet. Thoughtful. A Lok through and through.

Danny leaned forward, massaging his temples. A light throbbing pulsed through his head. He wanted to sleep for another few weeks. Hell, a few months sounded good at this point. Maybe when he woke up, the whole WesTec debacle would be a thing of the past and Wei would have forgotten how Danny had betrayed his trust. If only he was that lucky.

God, what time was it? His hand went to his wrist, but he wasn't wearing his watch. He reached for his phone on the nightstand, but it wasn't there either. He didn't want to get out of the warm, comfortable bed, especially not when Tobin was lying there next to him.

But Joanna must be eager for an update. His team was probably freaking out that he'd fallen off the face of the earth. And he should check if his insurance company had gotten back to him. Danny took a breath. He could do this. Get the fuck out of bed, go find his phone, and come right back. Three minutes. Five minutes, tops. No big deal.

Quietly he lifted the covers enough to swing his legs out, careful not to jostle Tobin awake. The living room was cold and dark. A tray of uneaten food sat on the table alongside a half-empty bottle of whiskey.

Phone. Where the hell had he left his phone? He'd called Tobin from the couch. It took a few minutes of sticking his hand between cushions before he found it. He tapped the screen, but the battery was dead. Great.

Charger. Where was his charger?

He padded back to the bedroom and rummaged through his suitcase as silently as he could. Without the lights on, he resorted to feeling around with his hand until it closed around the charger. Finally.

With phone in one hand and charger in the other, Danny turned to find Tobin awake and watching him. "Hi."

"Hi." Tobin's voice was groggy with sleep. "Work?"

How could such an innocent innocuous syllable sound like an insult? Yes, work. It was what he knew. And until recently, it was the one thing he was good at, the one thing that was predictable.

Tobin held out a hand, an invitation Danny understood without a single word. Put down the phone. Come back to bed. Work can wait.

Could it? The tug-of-war between his heart and his head pulled Danny so taut he couldn't physically move.

What was a few more hours without checking his inbox? Dozens, if not hundreds of emails, that's what. Most of those wouldn't even be directed to him—he'd end up deleting them anyway. But there would be plenty that required his attention. His team needed him to be present, to lead; getting distracted was what had gotten him into this fiasco in the first place.

Danny put the phone on the nightstand but didn't plug it in to charge. He sat on the edge of the bed and Tobin came over to hug him from behind. He was warm and solid, and Danny leaned back and closed his eyes. Maybe a little longer. He'd relax a few more minutes before getting back to it. He did feel like shit, after all.

He didn't protest when Tobin guided him down onto the bed. He didn't even open his eyes when Tobin tucked himself under Danny's arm and swung a leg over Danny's thighs. They were made to fit like this, so yes, work could wait.

★ ★ ★

The next time Danny opened his eyes, Tobin was sitting in bed next to him with a laptop open, typing away. The curtains were drawn over the windows and the lamp on Tobin's side of the bed was on.

How long had he slept? It felt like days. His limbs were heavy with slumber, his mind slowly crawling back into consciousness.

"Morning, sleepyhead." Tobin leaned over and planted a quick kiss on his forehead.

"Is it morning?"

Tobin checked the time on his computer. "Not anymore."

Danny sat up and groaned. He really needed to pee. Standing in front of the toilet, his bladder aching with relief, a sense of deep-seated dread settled over Danny.

A terrible thing had happened. He'd managed to hide from it for a while. But now it was time to go back into the real world and face up to it. The office must be impatient to hear from him. They needed to know what to do about WesTec. He hadn't even told them about his meeting with River Teegee yet.

His insurance company should have gotten back to him by now with next steps. Would he have to coordinate with the rental car company? Should he check in on the poor guy in the hospital? He was probably going to get sued. Hell, even if he didn't, he'd insist on paying. Medical expenses, lost wages, emotional and psychological harm—he owed the guy *at least* that much.

Danny washed his hands and looked at himself in the

mirror. He'd always had dark shadows under his eyes, but now he looked like he'd been punched in the face. He hadn't shaved in a few days and a patchy goatee was forming on his chin. He tried straightening his posture, shoulders back and chest forward, but after a second, he collapsed back into the slouch. It was more comfortable that way.

"You hungry?" Tobin asked from the door. How much had he seen? Oh, who cared? What did Danny have to hide anymore, anyway?

He didn't feel hungry, but his stomach growled in disagreement. "Maybe something small."

"I'll grab the room service menu."

While Tobin did that, Danny put some clothes on and pulled back the curtains. The window revealed a stunning view of the water, shimmering blue green. The sky was painted with wispy white clouds and the sun shone brightly like it had not a care in the world.

"Here." Tobin came back and held up a leather-bound binder with the menu inside. "Let me know what you want. I can call down."

Danny didn't take the binder. He knew what he wanted. "Grilled cheese sandwich. And chips."

"Huh." Tobin flipped through the menu. "I don't think they have that…"

"It's okay. Tell them what room we're in and have them ask the kitchen to make it."

Tobin's eyebrows shot up. "And they'll make it for you? Even when it's not on the menu?"

"What do you think I pay the premium room rates for?"

Tobin gave him a single nod. "Right. Got it. Grilled cheese sandwich and chips. Anything else?"

"A Coke."

"Coke. Check." He paused. "I thought you'd order something fancy like a filet mignon or something."

He usually did. But he had a craving for something simpler, something that grounded him and reminded him of life before everything got so complicated. "My mom used to make me grilled cheese sandwiches and chips. It was her go-to dish because anything else took too long."

Tobin put one hand gently on his arm and leaned in for a quick kiss. "Grilled cheese it is."

The coffee table was littered with the remains of their lunch. Plates with crumbs, empty chip bags, a row of soft drink cans. They'd sat side by side all afternoon, each with a computer on their lap, typing away. Sometimes Danny got up to make a phone call. Sometimes Tobin put in headphones to sign into a video conference.

They didn't speak to each other much—there was no need. They worked, and in between work, they touched, kissed, hugged, held hands. It was so comfortable Danny couldn't quite believe it. He hadn't been so productive in ages.

His phone buzzed with a text message from Ray. Made contact with the hospital. Dude fractured both bones in his shin, but the breaks look clean, so they slapped a cast on him and sent him home.

Danny hadn't told Ray what happened. It must have been Joanna who'd looped him in. Wonderful. The last thing Danny needed was news about the accident filtering through the office grapevine. Still, though, he appreciated Ray's initiative; he didn't want to know how Ray found that information. The cyclist's injury could have been so much worse. Danny could have killed him.

"You have much more to do?"

"What?"

Tobin had shut his computer and set it aside. "It's five o'clock. Time to stop working."

If it was five in Vancouver, then it was eight in Toronto. Danny was still getting emails from the office.

Tobin took one look at his face. "What's wrong?"

Danny held up his phone. "Message from Ray."

Tobin sobered. "WesTec?"

"No. The cyclist. His leg is broken, but they've already sent him home."

"Oh." Tobin's shoulders dropped. "That's good, right? He didn't need surgery or anything?"

"I guess not." Small comfort. But even clean breaks could have complications down the road. Clean breaks didn't dissolve him of responsibility.

"Hey." Tobin took Danny's face in his hands. "There's nothing you can do about it now, right?"

He didn't want to admit it, but Tobin was right. He nodded.

"And you'll have to eat dinner at some point, right?"

He had zero appetite, but Danny guessed he should eat something. He nodded again.

"Awesome. So let's go get dinner."

Go get dinner? As in leave the suite? Could he be trusted to set foot outside that door?

"Go where?"

Tobin took Danny's laptop and stashed it with his own. "Don't worry. I've got it covered." He dragged Danny toward the bedroom. "You're always planning big fancy dates, but now it's my turn. You're in my city, so I'm in charge."

Tobin had an outfit laid out for him on the bed already. Jeans and a T-shirt with a light sweater. No one had ever done that for him before, not even his mom. It didn't feel weird, though. It felt nice, not having to make decisions for once, not having to be in control.

Danny changed while Tobin…did whatever he was doing out in the living room. When Danny emerged, Tobin had his shoes on and was waiting by the door. "By the way," Danny asked as he followed Tobin out. "How did you get your laptop?"

"Oh, Monica and Ayán brought my stuff over."

"Who?"

Tobin cast him a confused look. "Monica, my roommate? Ayán, her girlfriend?"

"You've never talked about them before." At least Danny didn't remember Tobin mentioning them.

"Oh." Tobin cocked his head. "Well, they were pretty impressed with this place. Penthouse suite at a fancy downtown hotel and all that."

There was something in Tobin's voice, perhaps a touch of mockery or sarcasm. But Tobin continued before Danny could put a name to it.

"Anyway, you were asleep, so I didn't let them come in and make a fuss."

"I'd like to meet them. To say thank you, at least."

"Thank you for what?"

"For bringing your stuff."

Tobin waved him off. "It's fine. It's only Monica and Ayán."

"Even so. Should we invite them to dinner?" They'd made it to the lobby and Tobin stopped him with a hand to the arm.

"You want to invite Monica and Ayán to dinner?" he asked, as if Danny had suggested they sail around the world.

"Yes, is that not appropriate?" The thought of meeting Tobin's friends left a funny feeling inside, almost like getting a chance to flip through photos of Tobin when he was a kid, if Danny didn't already know what those looked like.

"No, it's fine. It's just, maybe not today?" Tobin cast a pair of doe eyes at him.

"Sure, whatever you'd like." Danny reached for Tobin's hand as they stepped out onto the sidewalk. A car pulled up in front of them.

"I called the limo company you use," Tobin explained as he opened the door for Danny. "I hope that's okay."

"Of course."

They climbed in and Tobin leaned forward to speak with the driver. "You have the address, right?"

"Yes, sir," the driver responded as he pulled away from the curb.

"Where are we going?" Danny asked.

Tobin smiled mischievously. "You'll see."

Chapter Eighteen

"Right here! You can stop right here. Perfect. Thanks!"
Tobin scrambled out of the car and turned to take Danny's
hand as he emerged.

"Where is this?" Danny looked around as if boogeymen
were going to jump out at him.

"Japanese hot dogs!" He pointed to the sign above the
storefront. It was one of Tobin's favorite places to eat in Vancouver. Who didn't like a good old hot dog? Then pile on
a whole bunch of Asian toppings to kick things up a notch.

"What's a Japanese hot dog?" Danny scanned the interior like he was looking for exits.

"You'll see!" Tobin deposited him at a table by the window and went to order.

It felt nice to show Danny something new, to be able to

take care of him and treat him, rather than the other way around. Danny was always so put together, so *I'll handle things*, but he was only human like the rest of them, wasn't he? He couldn't handle everything all the time. He needed to have things taken care of for him sometimes too.

Tobin brought back two hot dogs and an order of fries.

Danny stared at the tray of food with a touch of fear. "What is this again?"

Tobin rolled his eyes. Danny was such a food snob. He pointed to one hot dog. "This is a pork hot dog with Teriyaki sauce, mayo, and seaweed. This other one is a hot dog with rice and barbecue beef on top. And these fries have been flavored with butter and soy sauce."

Danny looked at him like he was speaking a foreign language. "How do we eat it?"

"Put it in your mouth and chew, silly."

"I don't think that will fit in my mouth."

Tobin held up a couple of forks. "That's what these are for." He handed one to Danny and dug in.

The smoky earthy flavor of umami hit Tobin's tongue, mixing with the juiciness of the hot dog underneath. Like an orgasm in his taste buds. "This was my go-to spot after exams every year. Go on, give it a try." Tobin felt like he was trying to get a toddler to eat something new.

With the fork, Danny carefully loaded up a perfect morsel and took a bite.

Tobin watched his expression change from skeptical to impressed. "See? It's good, right?"

"It's not bad."

"Not bad? Not bad!" Tobin threw up his hands. "You're impossible."

A grin tugged at the corner of Danny's lip, making all this worthwhile. He tried a fry and the hint of a grin blossomed into the full thing. "That's quite good."

"Told you."

Their eyes locked for a few moments before Danny dropped his gaze. He reached for another fry and his watch caught Tobin's attention.

Tobin pointed to it. "I think your watch is broken."

Danny tapped on it as if that would fix anything. "Hm, I hadn't noticed." He stared at it for several more seconds before pulling it off with a tug on the strap. He placed it face up on the table between them. "I don't know why I put it on."

"Out of habit." Tobin took the watch, the leather and metal still warm from Danny's skin. "It's nice. Maybe you can get it fixed."

"Perhaps."

Something about Danny's tone suggested he wouldn't bother. Considering how many watches Danny said he had, Tobin shouldn't have been surprised. Besides, it probably reminded Danny too much of the accident. A physical representation—frozen in time, forever marking the moment of the disaster. Tobin wouldn't want to keep it either. He placed it back on the table.

Suddenly the hot dogs and fries didn't taste quite so delicious.

"I'm sorry."

Danny cocked his head. "For what?"

Hell if Tobin knew. "For everything. For being angry you

were running late that day. That you have to go through all this."

"Don't be sorry. None of it was your fault. I should have been more careful, paid more attention." Danny pinched the bridge of his nose.

"Still." Tobin pulled Danny's hand away from his face and intertwined their fingers.

A beat passed before Danny spoke. "Thank you." He squeezed Tobin's hand like he had something else to add.

Tobin waited in silence, giving him all the time in the world to pull his thoughts together. After such a rough few days, who knew how far they'd been scattered.

"I'm sorry too."

Tobin's heart skipped a beat. Oh yeah. The whole reason why he and Danny were supposed to meet up. "I know."

"No, I mean it. I'm sorry. What I did in Calgary was completely unacceptable."

Tobin squeezed Danny's hand back. "It's okay. I understand."

Danny studied him like he couldn't believe what Tobin was saying.

"I'm serious, Danny. It's fine. You were in an impossible situation. I probably would have done the same thing if I were you."

"Really?" Danny frowned.

Tobin shrugged. They would never know for sure, but Tobin liked to think he could be equally as protective as Danny. The past few days were a case in point. Tobin wasn't always the one who needed taking care of, he could be the caretaker too.

"You know what? Let's not ever talk about WesTec again,

okay? That company and Cyrus—they're not worth it." Tobin rushed on when it looked like Danny was going to protest. "I mean, I know we both still have to do our jobs, but we don't need to let that get in our way. It's not like WesTec is going to be in our lives forever. Once it's done and over with, we can go back to normal. In the meantime, I'll do my thing and you do yours and we'll agree not to talk about it."

Danny didn't look at all confident in Tobin's suggestion. But it made complete sense to Tobin. He only had at most a month or two of work left on WesTec, by which point, they should know whether Cyrus was going to sell to Jade Harbour or not. "Why ruin what we have for something so…temporary and…inconsequential, in the grand scheme of things?"

Danny gazed down at their half-eaten meal. "What do we have?"

What did they what? "I don't understand."

"What do we have?" Danny repeated. "You said we shouldn't let WesTec ruin things for us and I agree. But what is it we don't want them to ruin?"

Tobin blinked. "Um…"

Danny pulled his hand away to sit back in his chair and Tobin immediately felt the loss. "Wei knows about us. After your call that day, I told him."

Tobin cocked his head, trying to keep up with Danny as he jumped from one topic to another. "Okay."

"He was not happy."

Tobin had expected as much. "That would explain why he hasn't texted me in a while."

Danny crossed his arms over his chest, gaze still fixed on the table. "He accused me of taking advantage of you."

"What?" Tobin's volume was a little too high and the people at the next table turned to cast curious glances in their direction. He leaned forward and lowered his voice. "He said what? Who the hell does he think he is to say something like that?"

"He's your older brother."

"And I'm not a freaking child anymore, in case you haven't noticed."

Danny finally looked up and pinned him with an expression filled with pain and confusion and want. "I know."

Some of the anger drained out of Tobin. "I know *you* know. I wish Wei knew." Tobin slapped a hand over his face and breathed through the urge to go strangle his brother.

"Am I taking advantage of you?" Danny asked in a voice so soft, it sliced through Tobin like a razor's edge.

He dropped his hand to find a tortured Danny. "No. Absolutely not. Why would you think that?"

"Come on, Tobin. You know why."

Always the same old arguments coming back to haunt him. "I thought we'd moved past this."

"Have we?"

Hadn't they? But then, they'd never really talked about it.

Danny took a deep breath and let it out slowly. "You're important to me. And so are Wei and your parents. I can't afford to lose—" Danny stopped short and cleared his throat. When he continued, he spoke with a clenched jaw. "Wei was furious. I've never seen him that angry before. I thought he was going to hit me." He ran a hand over his face. "God, I wish he had, it would've hurt less."

Tobin's throat closed at the thought of Danny and Wei fighting over him. He'd never expected that to happen.

They were best friends, closer than even Tobin was to Wei. In hindsight, he should have known better. Wei with his overblown sense of responsibility, as if he had to personally oversee each and every little thing in Tobin's life. If Wei thought Danny was taking advantage of him, then yeah, he could see Wei absolutely losing his shit.

If he came between them, if their friendship ended because of him, even for as ridiculous a reason as Wei's misplaced guilt, Tobin wasn't sure he could live that down.

"You're not taking advantage of me," Tobin said in a small voice. Hell, if anything, he was taking advantage of Danny. He'd known all along how uncomfortable Danny was with lying to Wei, and yet, he'd insisted everything would be fine.

Well, they weren't fine anymore. So what the hell were they going to do about it?

Tobin planted his elbows on the table and propped his head in his hands. The walls felt like they were closing in on him, the air felt too thin. He needed to get out, he needed to move, he needed to scream.

Tobin sat straight up and nodded at the food still left on their table. "Are you going to finish that?"

Danny glared at the pieces of hot dog and fries. "No."

"Good." He gathered up the leftovers and marched them over to the garbage bin, feeling only mildly guilty for wasting perfectly good food. He didn't wait for Danny to follow him out of the restaurant.

They fell into step, walking down the sidewalk, hands to themselves. Tobin didn't have any particular destination in mind, but the fresh air helped clear the jumble of thoughts wrestling in his head.

Danny didn't speak; he didn't either. What else was there to say? If they wanted to save Danny's friendship with Wei, the only realistic option was to end things. Neither of them had put it in such concrete terms, but Tobin knew. And he knew that Danny knew.

They walked for about twenty minutes before Tobin saw a sign for a bike rental place. They were close to Stanley Park now. He stopped. He'd always wanted to take one of those romantic bike rides through the park with a guy. Some part of him had hoped it would be with Danny. Maybe this was his chance. If not now, then never.

Danny followed his gaze and seemed to understand without Tobin needing to ask. He blanched. "I don't know about bikes right now."

"Please?" Tobin put every ounce of pleading he could muster into it. "Think of it as facing your fears?"

For a second, Tobin didn't think Danny was going to go for it. But then he sighed.

"Okay, fine."

Danny on a bike was one of the more amusing things Tobin had seen in a long time. With his bulk balanced on a mostly two-dimensional vehicle, he looked way too top-heavy. It shouldn't have worked—but he managed to pull it off. Better than Tobin did, anyway.

That saying about never forgetting how to ride a bike? One hundred percent a lie. Tobin had forgotten.

"You all right back there?" Danny had stopped ahead of him and was watching Tobin struggle up an incline.

He couldn't even call it a hill. If he'd been walking, he

probably wouldn't have noticed the slope. Who'd come up with this humiliating idea for a ride through Stanley Park, anyway? So much for their one last romantic jaunt.

"Yes," Tobin managed to mutter, and he pumped his legs. Why in god's name was this so hard? Everyone else kept zooming past him.

"Keep your head up. Don't look at your feet. Focus on where you want to go."

"I'm trying!"

Danny looked like he was working really hard to suppress a laugh. At least one of them was having a good time. Jerk.

His foot caught on the pedal and the bike veered off to the right. Tobin caught himself before flopping onto the pavement, but Danny still rushed over, eyes a little frantic.

"Are you okay?" He ran his hands all over Tobin, checking for injuries.

"I'm fine." Tobin pushed Danny's hands away and picked the bike up. "Not even a scratch." He walked the bike the rest of the way up the incline, Danny by his side still checking for signs of distress.

"Seriously. I'm okay."

"Maybe this wasn't a good idea."

Never mind Tobin had been thinking the same thing. He glared at the bike as if it were purposefully trying to sabotage their remaining time together. "We are riding around this damned park if it takes me all freaking night."

"I can hold the back of your seat for you."

Tobin whipped his head around and pinned Danny with a stare. He had a blank expression on his face, but Tobin knew what to look for. "Was that a joke?"

A twitch of Danny's lips gave him away.

"Ha. Ha. Very funny."

Danny's smile was more of a smirk and it was all Tobin could do to keep up his pretense of annoyed frustration.

"Sure. Laugh away." Tobin swung one leg over the seat and braced a foot against the pedal. "It's your fault anyway. You should have done a better job teaching me when we were kids."

"I did a fantastic job teaching you." Danny returned to his own bike. "It's not my fault you didn't practice."

He took off and this time Tobin managed to keep up. They rode along in silence, Tobin focusing on not falling on his face. Other cyclists passed them, sometimes a little too close for Tobin's comfort. Seagulls chirped overhead, and water lapped gently against the stone seawall.

The more he focused on his surroundings, the more his muscles relaxed, and the easier riding became. He even managed to look up every few seconds to enjoy the view. He took a deep breath, forced his shoulders away from his ears, and released the death grip he had on the bike handles.

This wasn't so bad after all. And just like that, a reminder of why they were there hit Tobin like a spear through the heart. Riding alongside Danny, joking with Danny—it was all so easy and carefree. Like it had been when they were kids.

But they weren't kids anymore, and being an adult wasn't easy or carefree. He'd created a life for himself in Vancouver and Danny had his own back in Toronto. Even without the complication of Wei and his parents, what had Tobin expected? He wasn't about to give up his freedom and he couldn't ask Danny to walk away from everything he'd built.

At the far side of the park, Danny slowed to a stop. Tobin braked a little too fast and almost went flying. Instead, he knocked the wind out of himself, but at least he was in one piece.

He glanced at Danny, who was wincing. "I'm fine." He disentangled himself from the bike and they walked over to a bench overlooking the Pacific.

Danny sat down, elbows braced on knees, and gazed out onto the water. Tobin sat next to him, close but not touching.

"You okay?" Tobin asked.

Danny nodded.

The sun was low in the sky, casting pinks and purples across the landscape. The light breeze off the ocean washed them with the briny scent of salt water. It was pretty perfect. If only they could freeze time.

They sat there for who knows how long. The sun dipped even lower, the pinks and purples morphed into oranges and reds. Tobin shivered as the chill tickled his bones. He stuck his hands into his armpits and bounced his knees. He didn't want to leave yet.

He didn't want to leave ever.

The sun was a mere sliver in the horizon, casting the last of its rays as it gave way to night. Danny stood. Tobin followed suit.

Without a word, they headed out of the park.

Chapter Nineteen

Tobin was in the bathroom filling the giant Jacuzzi while Danny checked his inbox. There were a ton of messages, but thankfully only a few required his immediate attention. He tapped out quick responses then slipped his phone into his briefcase and did the same with his laptop. The world could wait for one more night.

The water stopped running in the bathroom. "Danny!"

"Coming!"

They hadn't said a word to each other since leaving the park. There hadn't been any need. They both knew what had to be done. Why make their last evening together more difficult by talking about it?

Tobin was already in the tub when he got there, nothing more than a head and feet sticking out of a mountain of bubbles. The air smelled like roses. Candles flickered everywhere. Danny stood by the door to admire it all. Might as well pull out all the stops if this was going to be their last chance.

Danny grabbed the hem of his shirt and pulled it over his head in one swift motion. He was rewarded with a sharp inhale from Tobin's direction. His belt came undone with a practiced tug, and he pushed his jeans and briefs down all at once. He stepped out of them and strolled over to Tobin, who watched him with lust-filled eyes and a parted mouth.

He really was gorgeous, with cheeks red from the heat of the water, beads of sweat forming on his temples. Tobin lifted one hand and Danny took it as he stepped in. Bubbles and water gushed over the sides of the tub as Danny sank down next to him. Slick skin, slippery limbs. They slid together like the smoothest of silk. Their lips found each other, and Danny poured all he was into it.

All his regret and remorse, his gratitude and his appreciation. A part of him wanted to say fuck it, throw caution to the wind and steal Tobin away to some far-off location where no one could find them. They could have bubble baths every night. Danny could teach Tobin how to ride a bike again.

Running away sounded nice, but that wasn't reality. No one could run from the world forever, life always caught up. Besides, he couldn't take Tobin away from everything he loved—his job, his friends, his independence, his freedom. It wasn't fair.

And Danny was deluding himself if he thought he could walk away from his work that easily. He'd spent years on it and sacrificed so much; work had made him what he was today. He wouldn't be the same person without it.

If they had one night, then Danny would commit every second of it to memory.

He pulled Tobin to him, back to chest, tucked in between his legs. He let his hands roam—shoulders, stomach, hips. Tobin's head dropped back to lean on his shoulder and Danny planted kisses along Tobin's jaw, nips on his ear.

His dick was caught against the small of Tobin's back, providing just enough friction in the water to tease. Tobin reached up and grabbed the back of his head. The brush of his palm against Danny's hair sent tickles across his scalp, down his spine, and straight to his dick. It jumped, and Danny's hips bucked as a sharp spike of desire ran through him.

"Danny."

He understood the urgency in Tobin's voice. The desperation. He felt it himself.

"Fuck. Danny."

He'd closed his hand around Tobin's dick. He couldn't see it under all the bubbles, but that only made it hotter somehow. A slick, hard rod in his hand. Tobin responding to every tug, every squeeze. Tobin's fingers returning the favor across the back of his head.

Fuck was right. Danny had never needed to fuck someone so badly in his life.

Danny nudged Tobin to stand and followed him up. More water went sloshing over the side of the tub. He stepped out carefully and held Tobin's hand to steady him.

Fluffy towels hung within arm's reach and Danny

grabbed one to wrap around Tobin. He dried him off, being sure to cover every inch, inspecting his work with his lips until he was on his knees in front of Tobin. Tobin's dick stood up proud and Danny took it into his mouth.

"Oh fuck." Tobin's fingers dug into his shoulder.

He worshiped Tobin's cock, lavishing it with all the tender loving care it deserved. Plenty of tongue, plenty of suction until Tobin was pulling away from him. "I'm going to come if you keep it up."

Danny liked the sound of that. The taste of Tobin's come on his tongue. The way Tobin tensed when he orgasmed. The sound he made.

"Nuh-uh." Tobin pulled him off his knees. "I want to come with your cock in my ass."

Danny liked the sound of that too.

Tobin marched him back into the bedroom. He was still damp from their bath, but things were getting so heated, it hardly mattered. Tobin pushed him down onto the bed and motioned him to spread out. Then Tobin proceeded to torture him—a toe to head bathing with mouth and tongue, leaving not one inch of skin untouched.

Need burned in Danny's gut, stoked by a gentle and steady stream of Tobin's ministrations. Every hair follicle stood on end as goose bumps broke out over his skin. His dick was so hard it hurt.

But Tobin ignored it, scampering off the bed to grab the necessary supplies. It felt like eternity as Danny lay spread eagle on the bed. He sighed with relief when Tobin returned, the dip in the mattress a comforting reminder he wasn't alone.

Tobin squirted a generous helping of lube onto his hand and smeared it all over Danny's cock. He stroked it, squeezing and tugging as if he was trying to milk it. Pre-come gathered at Danny's slit. His hips lifted off the bed as he shut his eyes and tried desperately not to come. Tobin's other hand cupped his balls, alternating between a gentle massage and sharp tugs. The pleasure-pain combination fucked with Danny's head as much as his body. He couldn't tell what he wanted more, what he needed more.

"Fuuuck." He was going to come. It was building deep in his gut and it promised to be explosive. He shook as Tobin drove him ever closer to the edge.

And then it stopped.

Danny blinked, balanced precariously on the precipice of an orgasm. Straddling his thighs, Tobin wore a look of profound satisfaction as Danny groaned his frustration.

In a deft move that spoke of practice, Tobin ripped open a condom packet with hands still slick with lube. He rolled the condom onto Danny so quickly it was also clinical. But he didn't mind. The faster they got the logistics over with, the faster he could get inside Tobin's ass.

Then, with yet more lube, Tobin took his own dick in hand and stroked it. He angled it down and used his thumb to massage the tip until pre-come oozed from it. Tobin's eyes were dilated, his lips parted; he looked like he was halfway to nirvana. Danny couldn't decide what was sexier—Tobin's expression of utter pleasure or his cock growing with every stroke of his own hand.

Tobin reached behind himself.

Oh fuck.

They locked eyes.

Tobin dropped his jaw, but no sound came out. His chest rose and fell rapidly as he shuttered. A fine sheen of sweat developed on his skin.

God, what Danny would give to see Tobin's fingers at work back there. How many fingers was he using? How deep did they go? Was he twisting them? Scissoring them? Tobin let out a whimpering sound and squeezed his eyes shut. He sucked in a deep breath and let it out in shudders.

Danny dug his fingers into Tobin's thighs. His skin was hot to the touch, burning like a coal heated in fire. If that's what his skin felt like, Danny could only image how hot his ass would be.

Tobin placed one hand over Danny's and nodded.

It was time.

Tobin shuffled forward until he was aligned ass to dick. With one hand braced against Danny's chest and the other guiding Danny's cock, he slowly lowered himself.

It was like slipping his dick inside a tiny furnace. Whatever prep Tobin had given himself wasn't nearly enough for Danny's girth. It was so tight, Danny wasn't sure he'd make it all the way in.

Tobin's expression was some hybrid of absolute torture and absolute bliss. His eyes were shut tight, brows furrowed, mouth agape. His chest rose and fell in slow steady breaths.

Danny ran his hands up and down Tobin's thighs, his sides, his arms, soothing him until he adjusted.

It didn't take long.

When Tobin started moving, pleasure rocketed through Danny like he'd never experienced before. He clenched his jaw, fisted the sheets, ran basketball statistics—anything to keep from exploding right then and there. Tobin was hot, tight, magnificent. Nothing before and nothing after would ever compare.

Tobin danced above him, undulating with a grace Danny could never hope to achieve. He drove them to the brink and pulled them back, over and over until Danny lost count of how many times he'd almost come. This wasn't merely edging. This was practically inhumane.

"Tobin. Please, Tobin." He wasn't normally one to beg. He was always in full control. Except tonight was anything but normal.

With their hands clasped, Tobin drove them onward, fucking himself with remarkable speed and accuracy. They filled the room with the sound and the smell of sex, with their cries of passion, with the desires of their hearts.

When Danny came, it wasn't only physical. It was every cell in his body bursting, releasing atoms and molecules until he dissipated into thin air. He was no more, and all that remained was an emotion too honest and too raw for Danny to put a name to.

"Shh."

Fingers brushed across his face and his temples. Lips pressed against his, then drifted to his nose, his eyelids.

"It's okay, baby. It's okay. Let it all out."

There was movement around him and then covers being draped over his body. Comforting arms drew him close and he curled into their familiarity.

"I'm right here. I've got you."

More kisses. Soothing touches. Slowly, the sobs eased,

and he settled into a semi-conscious rest. Danny clung tightly to Tobin; he would hold on for as long as he could.

He drifted in and out of a fitful sleep. Whenever his brain surfaced enough for thoughts to form, panic sent him in search of Tobin. Tobin was always right there, within arm's reach, touching him. And every time, Tobin would whisper hushed words of reassurance until he slipped into darkness again.

When finally Danny drifted toward wakefulness for the last time, he didn't want to open his eyes. The bed was still warm. The room still seemed dark behind his eyelids. But he knew.

He stayed still, willing himself to sleep again. Maybe, if he slept and woke up again, everything would be different. To no avail. He shifted one arm, and then a leg. There was no responding movement in the space next to him. Reluctantly, he opened his eyes to confirm what he already knew in his heart. The bed was empty. Tobin was gone.

Chapter Twenty

Yeah, okay, it'd been the cowardly thing to do, but if Tobin had waited until Danny woke up, he'd never have had the strength to leave. He'd have ended up making a scene and then Danny would have had to put him in his place, and no one wanted that kind of awkward goodbye. It was much better this way—a quiet slip out the door and they could each go on their merry way.

At least, that's what Tobin told himself. It didn't necessarily make him feel like less of a piece of shit. He pushed open the door to his apartment and dragged his suitcase in behind him.

Ayán's face popped out from the kitchen. "You're back. I didn't realize you were coming back so soon."

"I wasn't." Tobin kept his head down and made a beeline for his room. He had absolutely zero desire to talk to either of them.

"Monica! Tobes is back!" Ayán announced.

"He is? How come? Did he forget something?"

Tobin closed the door to his room, stripped off all his clothes, and climbed into bed. He was exhausted. Not only physically from barely sleeping the night before. But also emotionally from…the past several months. He pulled the pillow over his head so he wouldn't have to hear Monica and Ayán muse over why he'd come home so early.

His eyes were sore with fatigue; his joints ached with it too. The bed was a comfortable relief, but as much as he wanted it, sleep wouldn't come. His brain flitted from one thought to another, never lingering long enough for any to form into something coherent.

A soft knock sounded at his door. Maybe if he ignored it, Monica would go away. Yeah, right. She knocked again and when Tobin didn't respond, she cracked the door open anyway. "Hey."

"Go away."

"I thought you would say that."

Tobin grabbed one of his many spare pillows and tossed it in the direction of the door.

"You missed."

"Fuck you."

Monica chuckled quietly, which was not the effect Tobin was going for. "Anyway, Ayán and I are heading out. There's some stuff to make a breakfast burrito in the kitchen if you're hungry. And leftover takeout in the fridge too."

"Thank you."

There was a moment's silence but no sound of his door closing.

"You'll be okay?" Monica asked.

Would he? Eventually, sure, but Tobin wasn't so certain about the twenty-four-hour forecast. "Yeah."

"Okay. I'll see you tonight?"

"I don't have anywhere else to be."

"Okay. See you later."

The door closed softly. Tobin held his breath as he listened for sounds of Monica and Ayán leaving. Feet shuffling and keys jingling and finally—finally—the front door closing behind them.

Tobin pulled the pillow off his face and slammed it down on the mattress. He wasn't going to be able to sleep. He rubbed his eyes with the heels of his hands. God, he wished he could, so badly. Anything to not have to deal with the last few days.

He sat up. There was no point in lying there with so much running through his head. Besides, he still had to email Lonnie and let her know he was working from home. There was no way in hell he was dragging his ass into the office. With limbs that felt much heavier than they were, Tobin dragged himself out of bed, sent a quick note to Lonnie, and headed to the bathroom.

The hot water was as cleansing as it was scalding. Tobin welcomed the burn. It hurt less than the emptiness in his chest. He stood there until the bathroom filled up with so much steam it was difficult to breathe. With his head spinning from lack of oxygen, Tobin leaned against the cool tile wall and slid down to the floor. He pulled his legs up and wrapped his arms around them, forehead on knees.

The air was cooler down here, the spray a little less forceful. It was easier to breathe, but also easier to think. With his eyes squeezed tightly shut, tears mixed with water and both were washed down the drain.

Other than the first *hey* and *how's it going* when Tobin got into Wei's car, they hadn't said a word to each other. Tobin told himself he didn't mind; hadn't he always wanted Wei to leave him alone? But after weeks of no messages, it'd started to get to be a little much, even for Tobin. He actually had to call Wei and ask for a ride from the airport, since Wei hadn't automatically offered one himself.

Maybe he shouldn't have come back to Toronto for Thanksgiving. He and Monica usually threw Friends-giving parties at their place. But this year she and Ayán had flown down to Mexico City, and all his other friends had miraculously disappeared to their respective families. Which left Tobin alone and for once in his life, that hadn't sounded appealing.

He rolled the passenger window down even though it was freezing outside. But the interior of the car was suffocating, and Tobin wanted to feel the biting wind on his face.

"What are you doing?"

"What does it look like I'm doing?"

Wei rolled his eyes, shook his head, and shut his mouth. That seemed to be the response Tobin got from everyone these days. Even Ayán hadn't bothered trying to poke him in her lesbian feminist way.

But he'd heard her and Monica whispering behind his back. When was he going to snap out of it? Did they need to stage an intervention? He'd gotten so fed up one day he marched into the kitchen and stated they should definitely not stage an intervention because he was going to snap out of it when he damn well felt like it. Thank you very much.

That had silenced the whisperings for about a day. But then it got worse—everyone left town, left him. He'd almost been relieved when his mom had called and asked if he was coming home this year. He hadn't even tried to put up a fight.

But now, sitting in the car with Wei, Tobin felt like running away again. This wasn't the warm, fuzzy, homecoming he'd been hoping for.

Wei cranked up the heater. Tobin rolled the window down lower.

More silence before Wei finally spoke up. "Don't know if Mom told you, but we're all going out for dinner tonight."

"No." She never told him anything. "Who's we?"

"Us. Constance and the twins. Danny."

Tobin's heart skipped a beat at the mention of Danny's name, and a mix of elation and dread flooded his system. Of course he knew he'd see Danny this week. It would have been impossible to avoid him. But today? Right after he landed? Ugh. If it'd only been the big Thanksgiving dinner his parents planned every year, then Tobin would at least have had a slim chance.

Still, there was a part of him that wanted to see Danny.

Was he as miserable as Tobin was? Or had he moved on with his life? Maybe if Tobin saw Danny happy, then he could finally get over this weird funk he'd been stuck in.

"You going to be okay?" Wei asked, the question taking Tobin aback.

"What do you mean?" What did Wei know about how "okay" Tobin was doing?

"You know, with you and Danny."

"I could ask you the same thing," Tobin shot back, feeling the need to poke and draw blood.

Wei, to his credit, looked guilty. "We haven't really spoken."

A weird sense of gratification rose up in him at the knowledge that he wasn't the only one hurting in all this, but then what the hell had he put himself through if Danny and Wei weren't going to make up?

"So why is he coming tonight?" Tobin crossed his arms, knowing full well he looked like a petulant child.

Wei snuck a glance in his direction, as if the question was absurd. "He's family."

That was a good answer. Not even Tobin could find fault with it.

Wei slowed the car as they approached the turnoff for their parents' house. He pulled out a remote control, pressed the button, and the double gates slowly swung open.

This was the house Tobin had grown up in. He knew it like the back of his hand. But after being away for a while, the size and scale of it always slapped him in the face. God, it was so monstrous. Too big for a family of four. Way too big for his parents now that it was an empty nest.

The three-door garage stood off to the side, a path connecting it to the main house. But Wei parked right at the front door and turned the engine off. Neither of them spoke. Neither of them moved.

"I don't like the idea of...you know," Wei spoke softly.

Guess they were doing this now. Better than inside with mom and dad getting in the way.

"Why not?" The question had been nagging Tobin for ages. "And why is it any of your business?"

"Of course it's my business. You're my brother."

"That's not a reason. Being my brother doesn't give you the right to anything."

Wei physically shifted away from Tobin as if he'd actually struck him. He looked confused. Genuinely puzzled at Tobin's statement.

"What's so hard to understand about that?" Tobin threw his hands up and let them fall heavily on his thighs. The movement let out a tangible release in energy, and everything that he'd bundled up inside him came spilling out. "You have always been like this, no matter how many times I've tried to explain. I get I'm younger than you. And I get your big brother routine. But I'm an adult. I can make my own decisions and if they're the wrong ones, I can handle the consequences. You can't keep treating me like a kid forever."

Wei looked like he was about to launch into a counter-argument, but then he snapped his mouth shut and turned to stare out the window. "So what are you saying? This crush you've always had on Danny, is it the real thing? Do you love him? Are you going to rearrange your life so you can build one together with him?"

Now it was Tobin's turn to gape. The real thing? Building a life together? Love? Who knew? It might have been, but he and Danny never got the chance to get that far.

Wei interpreted Tobin's silence. "Yeah, that's what I thought." He opened his door and climbed out of the car before Tobin figured out what he was talking about. He slammed the door shut so hard Tobin flinched.

What the hell was that? He scrambled out after Wei, but Wei already had his suitcase in hand and was walking it up the stairs to the front porch.

The front door flew open before either of them reached it.

"Toby!" Their dad stepped out of the house and came to pat Tobin on the back.

"Hi, Dad."

"So glad you're back from Vancouver. Please thank your boss for giving you time off." His dad ushered him inside like he was some sort of guest of honor.

"Actually, I still have to work this week." Tobin had made the mistake of telling Lonnie he would be in town and she had conveniently notified Paradigm's Toronto office.

"Toby!" His mom came shuffling from the kitchen. "Ah, you are home! How was your flight? No delay? Did you eat? You want food? There's leftover fried rice in the fridge from yesterday. I can heat up in microwave for you."

"Mom, aren't we going to dinner, like, now?" Wei had followed them inside and closed the door.

"But maybe Toby's hungry now. He can eat more at dinner later."

"It's okay, Mom. I'm not hungry." He straightened from taking off his shoes and realized his dad had disappeared up the stairs. "Dad, I can carry the suitcase." Not like it was going to make a difference. He was already halfway to the second floor.

Tobin followed his dad to his childhood bedroom, mostly stripped of his youthful fingerprint. A stack of plastic tubs in the corner held all the things he hadn't brought with him to Vancouver but couldn't bear to throw out. The wall above the bed held a single remaining poster of Zayn Malik.

His dad patted him on the back a few more times. "You rest, okay? We go to Congee King later for dinner, okay? Okay! Bye!" He shut the door behind him.

Right. Tobin flopped down on the bed. A couple glow-in-the-dark stars still clung to the ceiling. He felt like he was in the twilight zone, all right.

What had Wei meant back in the car? That's what he thought? What did he think? How was Tobin suddenly the bad guy in the whole scenario?

The stairs creaked under the weight of footsteps. If Tobin had to guess, he'd say it was Wei. He held his breath. *Don't come in. Don't come in. Please, at least knock.*

No such luck. His door squeaked as it opened and in popped Wei's head. "Hey kid—"

Tobin groaned at the annoying nickname.

"Listen, I'm sorry, okay? I don't want to make this week any more onerous than it's already going to be. Let's forget it, okay?" He sighed.

"Yeah. Fine." Not that it solved anything. But Tobin wasn't in the mood for more heavy discussions.

"We're cool?"

"We're cool."

"Good. Because everyone's here and we're heading out."

Tobin groaned. Didn't he just lie down? He wasn't ready for this. "Okay, let me use the bathroom first."

"Yeah, take your time. But don't take too long or Mom's going to come looking for you."

Tobin went to relieve his bladder in the bathroom that connected his and Wei's old bedrooms. As he washed his hands, he caught a glimpse of himself in the mirror. Ouch. He looked a little too far beyond disheveled. He shouldn't care, it was only family. Only family and Danny.

Screw it. He grabbed his toiletry bag from his suitcase. He splashed some water on his face, then fixed his hair and reapplied a bit of makeup. A little concealer for his dark bags and the red splotches around his nose. Eyeliner to make his eyes pop and a smidge of tinted lip balm.

He stepped back and tilted his head. He should change too.

Dressed in a fresh pair of jeans and a flannel button-down decorated with fish, Tobin headed downstairs with an air of confidence he didn't feel. Before he even made it to the last step, he was greeted by a harmony of squeals and the pattering of tiny feet.

"Uncle Toby!"

"Peyton! Howie! No running!"

Too late. Two hurtling balls of energy glommed on to his legs and Tobin didn't think he was getting them back.

"Hey!" He gazed down at two sets of wide innocent eyes and four cherub-shaped cheeks. "What are these two things stuck to me? Are they octopuses?"

"No!" Peyton looked up at him with more exasperation than a toddler should have. "We're not octapusases. I'm Peyton. He's Howie."

"Oh! I get it!" Tobin pointed to Howie. "He's Peyton. You're Howie."

"No!" Peyton grabbed Tobin's finger and pointed it at herself. "*I'm* Peyton." Then pointed his finger at her brother. "*He's* Howie."

Tobin shook his head and threw his hands up in defeat. "This is too confusing. I give up."

"All right, now. Enough torturing Uncle Toby." Constance came up to rescue him. "Hey, Tobes." She gave him a quick hug before corralling her kids out the door.

His mom followed close behind, going on about something to do with jackets and the wind. His dad and Wei were next, debating something about sports ball. Which left Tobin standing in the front foyer...with Danny.

"Hey."

"Hi. I trust you had a good flight?"

"Yeah, it was fine."

"Good. I'm glad."

Was this what they'd been reduced to? Small talk and pleasantries? Sadness and rage bubbled under the surface, begging to be let out, but Tobin tamped it down. They didn't have time for this. He wasn't even sure if there was any point.

"Hey, come on, slows pokes!" Tobin's dad called to them from the porch, where he was waiting to lock the door.

Danny gestured for Tobin to go first. In the driveway, there was a heated debate about which vehicles to take and who would sit where. Constance was already strapping the twins into car seats in the back of a giant SUV. Tobin's dad went automatically to his own decades-old BMW and no one stopped him—he was the worst backseat driver in the world.

"Okay!" Wei shouted over the mêlée. "Everyone take their own car. That way everyone's comfortable and we can all head off to wherever after dinner. Jesus."

Except Tobin didn't have a car.

"You can come with me, if you'd like," Danny offered at a volume only Tobin could hear.

Yes! Every cell in Tobin's body screamed. God, he was such a sucker for punishment. He met Danny's gaze and saw the exact same bittersweet tension in his eyes. It was going to hurt to be in such close proximity to Danny, but he couldn't for the life of him say no.

He nodded and was rewarded by a small smile from Danny.

Tobin followed Danny to his car and noticed Wei tracking their progress across the driveway. He ignored it. Wei could think whatever the fuck he wanted.

Chapter Twenty-One

"Nice car," Tobin said, sass in his voice and a smirk on his lips.

If Danny had long hair, he probably would have flipped it. "Thank you." He hit the ignition button and the engine purred to life like a giant cat.

Out of the corner of his eye, Danny could see Tobin watching his every move. Putting the car into drive, gunning it around the roundabout and down the driveway, Danny felt like a peacock, his feathers on full display.

It didn't take long for the air in the small enclosed space to get warm. It was like Tobin was setting him on fire with his eyes. Dampness collected around the back of his neck. Heat pooled low in his groin. Danny gripped the wheel and forced himself to ease off the gas. The last thing he needed was another accident.

"You look good," Tobin said, and Danny laughed in response.

Good was generous. Danny looked like shit and he knew it. Tobin, though, looked fucking amazing. Gorgeous. Delicious. Danny was sorely tempted to have Tobin for dinner instead. "You do too."

Tobin's smile was so smug, Danny wanted to kiss it off his face.

God, what was he doing? They'd ended things back in Vancouver. They were finished. He had no right flirting with Tobin like this.

Tobin started it.

Danny shut down his inner hormonal teenager. Not helpful.

"Wei said you two haven't been talking," Tobin said, effectively dousing Danny's libido.

"No, we haven't."

"Why not?"

He sucked in a breath and let it out. Why not, indeed. "I'm not sure." He'd tried to broach the topic with Wei a couple times, but Wei kept finding ways to excuse himself. There was no fighting, no arguments; Wei was generally civil to him. But they hadn't said more than a few words to each other in passing for more than a month already.

"I'm sorry."

"Don't be. It's not your fault he won't talk about it."

Tobin's hand closed over his own and Danny clung to it like a lifeline.

"Fucking Wei," Tobin continued. "Why did we go through all this if he's going to be an asshole about it?"

"He's still processing. Give him time." Danny had no idea why he was defending Wei. Why *had* he and Tobin broken up if Wei was never going to forgive them?

"Still."

Yeah. He might not say it out loud, but he felt exactly the same way.

They held hands the rest of the way to the restaurant. It didn't take them long. In fact, Danny would have preferred another couple of circles around the block. He pulled into an empty spot, turned the engine off, but didn't get out.

Danny glanced over at Tobin and found him looking back. Danny's mind swirled with one "what if" after another. If they didn't have Wei in between them; if Danny's job wasn't so all-consuming. But what did any of it matter? They couldn't change what was.

"We should go."

Tobin nodded quietly, and they headed inside.

They took the last two empty chairs at the table, Auntie Grace to one side of Tobin, Uncle Man on Danny's other side. Under the table, obscured by the tablecloth, Tobin's leg brushed against Danny's. He didn't pull it back, so Danny hooked Tobin's ankle with his own.

Around them, the Loks were busy shouting at one another over the din of the busy restaurant. Wei poured tea for everyone while throwing glares in their direction. Constance and Auntie Grace were busy keeping the twins occupied and Uncle Man squinted at the specials menu.

It was like a choreographed dance they performed with a chaotic ease that Danny admired. Things were always one second away from an argument, and every argument was one "aiya" away from being water under the bridge. Danny had witnessed it many times with his own eyes and still, he marveled. There was an unspoken understanding that family fought and forgave, that conflict was inevitable but could never sever the bonds connecting them.

He was lucky the Loks invited him to dinners like this. They'd made him feel like an honorary member of the family—but honorary wasn't the same as the real thing, was it?

Tobin joined in on the ruckus like he'd never left, giving as good as he got. He might love complaining about his family, but he looked like he was enjoying himself. That's what Danny wanted, to know he was a part of the unit, that no matter what happened, they would always be there. Short of that, he would content himself with whatever the Loks had to spare.

Dinner was delicious. Peking duck made three ways, sweet and sour pork for the kids—though Tobin helped himself to plenty too. Snow pea sprouts lightly sautéed in garlic, a whole steamed fish. Peyton and Howie got to eat the eyeballs to help them maintain healthy eyesight.

About halfway through, Danny excused himself to go to the bathroom. He took the long way there, detouring to the front counter with his wallet. When he got back to his seat, Auntie Grace descended on him with scolds.

"Aiya, Danny! Not again! I told you not to pay for us!"

Uncle Man shook his head and piled more and more food onto Danny's plate as if to compensate Danny with food he'd paid for. "Aiya, here, eat, eat. It's too much, Danny. It's too much."

It was the least he could do.

★ ★ ★

Everyone was standing in the parking lot for the after-dinner ritual of saying goodbye but not going anywhere. Uncle Man and Wei were studying his sports car as if they hadn't seen it at least a dozen times before. But Danny obliged their questions and pointed out features he knew he'd already shown them.

"Okay, okay." Auntie Grace came over to physically drag her husband away from the car. "Time to go home now! Come, come, come!"

"Okay, okay!" Uncle Man shooed her away. "I'm coming. I'm coming." He waved to Danny and slapped Wei on the back. "Toby, come on."

"Actually." Tobin took a step backward. "I'm going to go with Danny."

What?

"What?" Auntie Grace frowned at him in confusion. "With Danny?"

"Yeah, don't worry. I'll see you later." Tobin walked around to the passenger side of his car and gave Danny a pointed look.

He cleared his throat. "I'll, uh, get him home soon."

For a second Auntie Grace looked like she was going to argue, but then she shook her head. "Okay, okay, don't be too late, okay?" Then scurried after her husband.

Wei glared at Tobin, then Danny, then Tobin again.

"What?" Tobin shot at his brother so forcefully even Danny flinched.

"Oh, come on, hun. Leave them alone." Constance had

a twin in each hand and did not look like she was prepared to have her husband get in an argument in the parking lot.

Wei didn't bother saying good night, simply spun on his heel and marched after his family. Danny let go of the breath he'd been holding. Thank god for Constance.

"Come on, what are you waiting for?" Tobin sounded more tired than annoyed.

Danny unlocked the door and they both climbed in.

"Can we go to your place?"

Did he hear that right? His place? As in, not Tobin's parents' house? "Sure."

Tobin slouched down in the seat, chin tucked into his chest. He leaned his head back and stared out the window as Danny started the engine and put the car in reverse.

It was a fairly long drive from the suburbs to Danny's condo downtown and they made most of it in silence. He switched the sound system to some random playlist he had saved on his phone but turned it down low. Light from passing street lamps flashed over them at regular intervals, giving Danny snapshots of Tobin's profile out of the corner of his eye. He looked more than tired now, more than fatigued. He looked almost defeated.

Danny wanted nothing more than to pull Tobin into his arms and chase away whatever was bothering him. To wrest the bully's name from Tobin so he could go beat up anyone who'd dared hurt him.

But he didn't have the right to comfort Tobin or to defend him—at least not in that way. And besides, Tobin didn't need him to. If the past several months had taught Danny anything, it was that Tobin could defend himself.

As they got farther downtown, Tobin seemed to come a little more alive, tilting his head to gaze up at the skyscrapers lining the streets. He even looked a tad impressed when Danny turned onto the ramp leading down to his building's underground parking garage.

Danny's spot was near the elevator and once inside, he pushed the button for his floor.

"Penthouse, eh? Figures." The flirt was back.

"Of course. Why would you assume otherwise?"

Tobin rolled his eyes and shook his head, but his smile grew a little more.

The ride to the top didn't take very long and the doors opened onto Danny's personal landing. The building's management company kept an arrangement of fresh flowers on the side table, leaving a hint of floral perfume in the air.

"Fancy." Tobin eyed the flowers as Danny unlocked the front door.

It was. And not something Danny had asked for. But it was included in his astronomically expensive building management fee, so why not take advantage?

Tobin's eyes grew wide as they entered, and Danny tried to see his apartment from Tobin's perspective.

Dark hardwood floors extended throughout the open-concept space. A large fireplace dominated the far wall, rising up the full two-story height of the room. Floor-to-ceiling windows offered a bird's-eye view of the city, with the waves of Lake Ontario in the background and the pointy tip of the CN Tower off to the side.

His couches were leather, worn and distressed, with blankets thrown over the backs. The coffee table was made from a massive slice of a tree trunk, its distinctive rings on full display.

Most of this had been the doings of the celebrity interior designer he'd hired. She was worth every penny Danny had spent, had captured his taste with only the minimum amount of direction from him.

"Damn." Tobin toed off his shoes and wandered into the living room with a look of awe, as if he was entering a cathedral. He caressed the back of a couch. "Nice."

Tobin turned to his left where the living room morphed into the connecting kitchen. This was one of the few places Danny had given his designer very specific instructions. Sure, he technically needed a kitchen, but he didn't need it to look like a kitchen. The only thing that gave it away was the copper spout of the sink's faucet, curving up and over the middle of the kitchen island. Otherwise, sleek paneling hid the fridge, the dishwasher, and the oven. Even the range was little more than four discreet gas burners barely protruding from the polished countertop.

Tobin ran his hand along the paneling, opening every cabinet until he found the fridge. "Takeout boxes and condiments. Why am I not surprised?"

"I'm too busy to cook."

"Sure." Tobin raised one eyebrow and gave Danny a pointed look as he shut the fridge.

Around the corner was a dark, narrow hallway leading to Danny's office, the guest bedrooms, and the master suite. Tobin threw a sly look over his shoulder before continuing. Warm lighting slowly brightened the hallway as they moved down it. "Motion sensors?"

"Energy-efficient."

"Right. Like your hydro bills are your biggest concern." The hint of laughter in Tobin's voice made Danny smile.

He didn't bother telling Tobin that the costs of the lights themselves far outweighed any savings on his electricity bill.

Tobin poked his head into the first door they passed: Danny's office. "Whoa."

His interior designer had done a good job filling the floor-to-ceiling bookshelves with interesting titles. Reading all of them was on Danny's bucket list—one day, perhaps. His desk was a little embarrassing, though. The mahogany monster sat impressively in the middle of the room, but equally impressive were the stacks of folders and papers covering its surface. Maybe he should figure out a better filing system than piling things up until they toppled over.

The guest bedrooms weren't much to gawk at. Danny never had guests. He barely remembered what they looked like himself. But he was quite proud of his own bedroom. He'd actually found the time to go shopping for it and had personally picked out the four-poster bed and the plush area rug underfoot. Both appealed to him on a tactile level he hadn't fully understood. Sometimes, when he closed his eyes, he could imagine the softness of the carpet under his bare feet, the warmth of the wood under his hand.

Seeing it now, Danny's toes curled at the image of bending Tobin over the mattress, his fingers tingled at the thought of using those sturdy posts for leverage. Despite all his wild fantasies about Tobin, he'd never once allowed himself to dream of him in his bedroom, of all the things he'd love to do to Tobin here. Tobin's cries of pleasure fill-ing the air; the scent of Tobin's arousal marking his sheets. Even the thought of it now was making Danny hard.

Why had Tobin wanted to come here? What good did it do them to spend time around each other? It only made things more difficult, testing their self-control.

"Danny." Tobin's voice was husky.

He closed his eyes and clenched his jaw.

"Danny?" Tobin was closer now, close enough Danny could hear the sound of his breathing.

No, they shouldn't. They couldn't. But he was only a man, damn it. A man who was desperate for Tobin.

"Danny," Tobin whispered against his lips. Fingers trailed lightly down his chest, their final destination obvious.

Danny caught them before Tobin could reach his hard-ening cock. "Tobin," he said, putting as much warning into his voice as possible.

"I know," Tobin responded. "I know. But… I've missed you so much."

Danny had missed him too. More than he could accu-rately describe. More than he wanted to admit to himself.

On the outside, he looked like he was pulling himself together. Things were slowly getting back on track with work; his team was working with Ray to draft the latest proposal to take to WesTec, and Marlena had assured them she and Cyrus would take any offer they made seriously. Joanna had finally gotten off his back.

But inside, Danny had never felt so empty and devoid of life. He'd spent every waking moment thinking about Tobin, and every sleeping minute dreaming about him.

Knowing Tobin reciprocated those thoughts was like having a sledgehammer smash through the buttresses keeping Danny upright.

He tried to resist. He really fucking tried. But there was only so much he could take. Danny met Tobin's gaze and gave him one last out. "Are you sure?"

And like he'd done all those months ago, Tobin replied, "One hundred percent."

Chapter Twenty-Two

They shouldn't be doing this. This was a very bad, no-good, terrible idea.

But god, the strength of Danny's arms around him, the force of the kiss, the way Danny bent him backward like he was as malleable as putty. Tobin's erection was raging, and he was too fucking selfish to stop now.

He wasn't even sure how they'd ended up here. Why had he asked to ride in Danny's car? Or to come see Danny's place? Who the hell knew?

No, that was a lie. It was because of Wei and the dark cloud that had been hanging over him all through dinner. Tobin had tried to ignore it, tried to focus on the unusual pleasure of having his whole family around the same table. They were obnoxious, sure, but they were his brand of obnoxious. Trading barbs with them was like slipping on an old abandoned sweater to find it still fit perfectly.

But even then, Wei's perma-scowl had worked its way under Tobin's skin. If he was going to be so uptight about it all, then Tobin might as well indulge himself while he was here.

Danny spun him around and pushed him up against the bed post. Fuuuck. Tobin clung to it as Danny yanked down his pants and briefs in one swift motion.

Smack. Tobin flinched more at the sound of palm meeting flesh than at the actual sting. *Smack.* His other ass cheek smarted at the same treatment. Then Danny's large hands covered the heated globes of his ass and pulled them apart.

Oh fuck. Oh fuck. Oh fuck.

It was an attack, an onslaught. Danny's tongue versus his hole, and Danny was winning. Wet and forceful, there was no denying Danny entrance to his body and Tobin had absolutely no desire to do so. He dropped his head forward as Danny expertly reduced him to a shuddering mass of need.

Danny dragged his chin across Tobin's hole. He'd kept the stubbly goatee he'd developed in Vancouver and the bristles on Tobin's sensitive skin sent fire shooting up his spine and down his legs. Thank the heavens for the post, or else he'd have collapsed by now.

Something thicker, more insistent wiggled its way into Tobin. As wet and loose as he was, Danny's finger had no trouble slipping in. First one, then two. Danny finger fucked him until Tobin was practically horizontal, his grip on the post slipping as he stuck his ass out. Then Danny hit his prostate and Tobin nearly came.

"Fuck!" His whole body convulsed with the almost-orgasm.

"Fuck," Danny echoed and emphasized his point with teeth into the meaty part of Tobin's ass.

He couldn't take much more of this. His legs were noodles. His hands were so slick with sweat holding the post was impossible. He needed to come so bad his stomach was practically cramping.

He whined. What else could he do?

Danny slowly extracted his fingers and helped Tobin stand up straight again. "I've got you," he whispered into Tobin's ear. Danny pressed himself against Tobin, full body contact with Tobin caught between a post and a wall of muscle. He wasn't going anywhere; there was nowhere else he wanted to be.

At some point Danny had pulled his dick out of his pants; it fit perfectly between Tobin's ass cheeks. Smooth as silk. Hard as steel. Danny rubbed it up and down, back and forth, and it was driving Tobin fucking out of his mind. *God, stick it in already.*

Tobin reached up and grabbed Danny by the back of the neck. "Fuck me," he demanded between clenched teeth.

Danny had the audacity to laugh. Asshole. Tobin tightened his grip on the back of Danny's neck, letting his nails sink in.

Danny tried to pry Tobin's hand away. "Got to get a condom, babe."

Fuck condoms. They didn't need them. He needed to get railed now.

"Babe." The gentle admonishment in Danny's voice

made Tobin growl with frustration. "I'll only take a second. Promise."

Screw Danny and his being all responsible. "Fine. Hurry."

The comforting weight of Danny on his back disappeared, leaving Tobin feeling adrift. But true to his word, he was only gone a moment. Tobin reached for him. He needed him. Needed the connection. Needed to be joined together.

Danny chuckled before sinking his teeth into Tobin's earlobe. "Hold on a minute."

Foil crinkled. A lid popped. Squirt and cool wetness between his ass cheeks. Tobin leaned into it.

"Enough already." Tobin fumbled for Danny's dick and aimed it at his hole.

Danny pushed his hand away. "Okay, okay. So impatient."

Tobin sighed with relief as Danny entered him. The press and stretch and fullness were everything he loved and dreamed of and hoped for. God, he'd missed this so fucking much.

Danny clamped one hand onto Tobin's hip, wrapping his other arm over the top of Tobin's shoulder and around his chest. Tobin was caught, and he wouldn't have had it any other way. Slowly, Danny pulled his dick out until only the head was still inside. Tobin waited for it. Knew it would be good. The anticipation was killing him.

Danny snapped his hips forward, slamming Tobin into the bedpost with a loud smack.

It was better than good. It was absolute bliss.

Again and again Danny thrust into him. Hard and vicious. Unrelenting and possessive. Tobin cried out, incoherent sounds forced out of him with every surge of Danny's cock. It was all he could do to hang on and stay conscious.

Danny shifted behind him, the change in angle bringing his cock directly in line with Tobin's prostate. Every single muscle in his body contracted at the contact and lights exploded in his eyes. His head spun, and his lungs couldn't suck in oxygen fast enough. Over and over Danny hammered his prostate until Tobin was nothing more than skin and flesh and bones held together by the sheer strength of Danny's arms.

Tobin's orgasm started in his mind. A blinding flash of pleasure short-circuiting every neuron in his brain. It rippled down his body, zapping every nerve ending from the tips of his hair to his baby toe. And only then did his cock erupt in streams of come, as if every cell in him was being forced out the tip of his dick.

A roar sounded, and Tobin was slammed into the bedpost one last time. The last jab of Danny's cock on his prostate hit Tobin straight in the heart. But he had nothing else to give. Danny had taken it all.

Tobin was limp as Danny moved him onto the bed. His pants were stuck around his ankles and he'd sweated through the shirt he was still wearing. Danny didn't look like he'd undressed at all. They lay in each other's arms, dosed with the smell of their joining.

It was probably the hottest sex they'd ever had. It was definitely the worst idea Tobin had had in a long time.

All they'd done was hit pause on life for long enough to come. But life was waiting impatiently on the other side of Danny's door. Hell, they were lucky Wei hadn't shown up, all decked out in his knight in shining armor costume.

Slowly, his brain recovered enough oxygen to function again, but Tobin only snuggled in closer. "I should go."

Danny tightened his hold. "I know."

"I don't want to go."

"I don't want you to either."

They breathed together, in and out, in and out, a few times before Tobin mustered up the strength to pull away from Danny. He eased himself off the bed as Danny rolled onto his back.

"We need to fix things with Wei," Tobin said as he put himself back together.

Danny's eyes were still hazy with lingering passion. "We do."

"I don't know how."

"We'll figure it out."

Tobin pushed back the hair that had fallen into his eyes.

Danny stood and tucked himself back into his pants. "I'll drive you back."

Tobin put a hand on Danny's chest. Broad, muscles, solid and sturdy. "I can grab a cab."

Danny took his hand. "Let me call you a car."

They locked eyes, but there was no struggle in them. Simply an easy meeting halfway that felt natural and normal. Tobin nodded. "Okay."

It was always weird visiting the Toronto office, kind of like stepping into a parallel universe. The decor was similar, the logo on the wall was the same, everyone used the company jargon, but it all felt a little off. Tobin sat at one of the empty desks, doing more daydreaming than work.

The office wasn't far from Danny's place. It'd be easy to walk to and from work every day. There was a massive food court in the underground maze connecting most of downtown. He wouldn't even have to go outside in the winter for lunch. The people were nice—a bit more type A than Tobin was used to, but it wasn't anything he couldn't handle.

Wait. What was he doing? He wasn't moving back to Toronto. He wasn't moving in with Danny. Tobin dropped his face into his hand. It was too early to be awake. Which genius had come up with time zones, anyway?

It didn't help that he'd stayed up all night replaying the sex he'd had with Danny. It had been hard and fast, and a necessary relief from the tension that had been building all day. But in hindsight, it only made things worse. Look at what it'd done to Tobin, making him dream about an imaginary life in Toronto that would never materialize.

Damn Danny and his magic penis. He should have stayed in Vancouver.

Tobin shook his head and forced himself to look—really look—at the presentation he was working on. The one he was due to present to WesTec in just over a week. All the hard work was done, picking through document after document, crunching the numbers, and running one financial model after another. Lonnie had already reviewed it and given it a thumbs-up, so now all he had to do was throw it into a presentation deck and make it look pretty.

It shouldn't have been this hard!

Tobin planted his wrists on the desk and forced himself to type.

Recommendation number one: exploit the patent. Financing options: bank loan, private loan, private equity.

Like Jade Harbour.

Hm... Danny. That bed sure was something. If Tobin ever had the room for it—and the budget—he was definitely getting himself one of those.

Stop! Focus!

Patent. Right. Tobin's calculations had assumed Jade Harbour knew about the patent—he had no reason to believe they didn't. If they ended up offering what he thought they should offer, it might actually be the best option for WesTec. But no one would know for sure until Jade Harbour's final proposal came through.

Someone tapped him on the shoulder and Tobin practically jumped out of his seat.

"I'm so sorry! Are you okay?" Aisha was one of the few Toronto-based colleagues Tobin had met before. She was basically Lonnie's counterpart in Toronto and had come out to Vancouver several times.

"Yeah, sorry. I was distracted."

"I'm sorry to interrupt. A few of us are going to grab lunch at the food court downstairs. Did you want to join us?"

Any excuse to stop working on the damn presentation. "Sure!" Tobin followed her out to the office lobby.

She was tall and slim, and her hijabs always matched her outfit. Today, it was a cheetah print scarf over a super sleek black turtleneck and black wide-legged trousers, cinched at the waist with a thin gold belt. Damn girl, she made Tobin feel frumpy in his hastily thrown together going-to-be-late pants and a button-down. If he was going to work in Toronto, he'd have to up his fashion game.

Except he *wasn't* going to work in Toronto; he mentally slapped himself.

Waiting for them by the front door were two colleagues Tobin recognized but had never met before. Aisha introduced them as Kenya and Barry. Kenya was a Black woman who wore her hair in thick spiraling twists. Barry was a petite white guy with shocking orange-red hair made all the more shocking by his pale complexion.

They led the way and Tobin trailed behind with Aisha. The food court was really more of a mall, with dozens of stalls lining the two sides of a giant space running the length of the building. On offer was cuisine from every corner of the world and every counter had a line of people, ten to twenty deep. Walking through the throng was like trying to play dodgeball with human bodies.

"Is it always this busy?" Tobin shouted above conversations held in French, Spanish, Korean, Arabic, Chinese, and a few he couldn't place.

"Yes," Aisha shouted back.

Somehow, they found a table with four empty seats, tucked away in a quiet corner.

"It's probably just as busy in Vancouver, eh?" Aisha asked as they snagged the table.

Tobin surveyed the circus around them. "Maybe it is in the business district, but our office is a little more out of the way. We're in an artsy neighborhood."

"Ugh, I'd love to be anywhere but in this part of Toronto. I hate downtown." Barry ran a hand through his bright orange-red hair, making it stand up on end.

"At least it's close to the train station," Kenya piped in. "Imagine having to take the subway after sitting on the GO Train for an hour?"

"Yeah, at least there's that," Barry agreed.

"Why don't you two go get food?" Aisha motioned to Kenya and Barry. "We'll hold down the fort." Once they left, Aisha continued. "So, Tobin, how long are you in town for?"

"Until the weekend. I'm back for Thanksgiving with the family."

"Right. Your family is here, I remember now."

Had Tobin ever told her that? He wasn't sure he had, but then again…

"Have you ever considered moving back to Toronto? You could transfer to our office." Aisha had a glint in her eye, like she knew something Tobin didn't and was having a hard time keeping it to herself.

Had he ever considered? What had he been doing all freaking morning? But when confronted with the question point blank, Tobin hesitated. "Oh… I don't know."

"We have an opening." Was she offering it to him?

"Really?"

Aisha nodded. "I've been approved to hire a junior analyst, but what I really need is someone who can take projects and run with them. We're so swamped with work, I don't have time to train someone new."

"Yeah, that makes sense."

"Lonnie's been saying great things about you."

Lonnie had been talking about him? Was this why she'd made him spend the whole week here? "Huh, I didn't know that."

"If it's something you'd be interested in exploring, I can go back to the management committee to revisit the budget. Make sure it's something worth your while."

"Wow." Tobin didn't know what else to say. Daydreaming aside, a transfer like this could be a pretty big deal. Would it be considered a lateral move? Or a step up? Paradigm's Toronto office was about three times bigger than Vancouver's and a lot more high-profile. This could give Tobin more room for growth and a clearer trajectory to a promotion.

But then, he'd have to move back to Toronto. He'd have to leave behind his friends and the life he'd built in Vancouver. He'd be coming back to his family and Wei, ugh. But also Danny...

Kenya and Barry returned before Tobin could voice any of his questions. So instead, he wandered into the fray, trying to imagine—for real this time—this as his everyday life.

His parents would definitely be thrilled with the idea. They'd most likely want him to live at home. Wei would probably rope him into babysitting for the twins. Though, Tobin honestly didn't think he'd mind. They were growing up so fast and there was something sad about missing out.

What would Danny think? Tobin sighed. Would it make things easier or weirder?

After lunch, as they headed back up to the office, Aisha

leaned in and whispered, "I was serious about earlier. Let me know if you're interested and we can talk more."

Tobin smiled his appreciation. Was he interested? If only it were so simple as yes or no.

Chapter Twenty-Three

Thanksgiving at the Lok house was a big deal. They filled the bona fide mansion with extended family, friends, co-workers, classmates, and basically anyone they could convince to show up. There were always at least two giant-ass turkeys, plus a honeyed ham, and all the traditional sides and dressings. On top of that came the Chinese food, enough for a wedding banquet.

Danny hadn't missed a year since he could remember. It was one of the only times when his mom booked a holiday from the nursing home so she could go too. He remembered standing in the corner of the kitchen, marveling at her socializing with all the other aunties, chatting, laughing, cooking a huge meal.

Watching the aunties now, Danny could almost imagine

his mom among them, fussing over the right way to mash potatoes. He could hear her laugh, loud and boisterous, ringing above all the other voices in the room.

Happy Thanksgiving, Mom. However the afterlife worked, Danny hoped she was someplace comfortable, pain-free, and joyful. He hoped she could see this gathering of friends and family and smile.

"Danny, look at you, such a good young man." Auntie Grace patted him on the cheek. "Your mommy would be so proud of you."

He hoped so. Though, what exactly he'd done to earn Auntie Grace's praise today, he had no idea.

"Remember, don't work too hard, okay? Any boyfriend yet?"

Danny choked on his own saliva. "No, no boyfriend." At least, if he didn't count her youngest son, whom he'd fucked and then sent packing the other night.

Tobin was in the backyard with Wei and some of their cousins. They were throwing around a football, but Tobin was curled up on a lawn chair, wearing two coats and three scarves.

"Aiya, you see? You are working too hard!" Auntie Grace slapped him on the shoulder.

"That's what Mom did."

She cast him a disapproving look over the rim of her glasses. "Yes, so you don't have to. Now go!" She made a shooing motion with her hand. "Go outside with the boys. You are in the way."

As if on cue, the twins came bounding into the kitchen toward him.

"Uncle Danny! Uncle Danny!"

He bent down in time to catch them in his arms. "I'm here. I'm here."

They both tried climbing on top of him at the same time. Except they'd grown past the size where he could comfortably carry both of them and they all ended up in a pile on the floor.

"Aiya, not in the kitchen! Go outside. Outside!" One of the aunties—Danny couldn't tell which—shouted at them.

"All right, you two. Let's get out of their way."

He let the kids lead him down to the basement, the designated under-eighteen zone. Older kids were playing video games in the home theatre or pool on the billiards table. The youngest kids were corralled around a few couches where their adult supervisors were chatting. The in-between kids were wreaking havoc everywhere else, bouncing off the walls like the air had been laced with sugar. When Danny made an appearance, at least half a dozen came toward him like heat-seeking missiles. Apparently, it was time for a wrestling match: Danny against anyone between one and three feet in height.

He roared as he picked up one child after the next, hoisting them above his head like he was a gorilla, then setting them down with a tickle. There was a lot of squealing, often in his ear. He got elbows in his side, heels against his shin. One kid tried to bite his arm. By the end, Danny ended up on his back, flat on the floor, while the little monsters tugged on limbs and tried to use his stomach like a trampoline.

"Uh, are you okay?"

Danny turned toward the question, barely audible above the din. Tobin was standing next to him, staring down with a mix of concern and amusement.

"Yeah. Ow." Danny winced as one kid's skull connected with his.

"Okay, I think that's enough beating up Uncle Danny." Tobin started pulling them off and distracting them with other toys until Danny managed to sit up.

He was going to be covered in bruises tomorrow.

Tobin squatted down to brush invisible dust off Danny's shoulders and back, and ran his palm quickly over Danny's head. "No permanent damage?"

Danny chuckled. "No. Nothing permanent." He hoisted himself up to standing, his not-that-young-anymore muscles immediately groaning in protest. "I thought you were outside."

Tobin rolled his eyes. "It's cold outside. And it's not like I was going to play."

Danny remembered. Tobin had never been a fan of catch, especially not when he always ended up as the monkey in the middle.

His hair was a little messy today, probably on purpose. He had eyeliner on too, a little heavier than usual, and something on his lips glinted if he stood in the light at the right angle.

Danny shouldn't have noticed, but he couldn't help it. Especially not after their little quickie at his place the other night. In fact, Danny kept reliving it every time he'd stepped into his own bedroom. Hell, he kept reliving it every time his mind drifted to Tobin, which was often. Danny cleared his throat and turned away.

"Want to get out of here?"

Danny snapped his head back. The soft look in his eyes and his slightly pursed lips told Danny exactly what Tobin meant by his question. Danny answered it with a smile of his own.

They were halfway up the basement stairs when they ran into Wei.

"Hey." Wei glanced back and forth between them. "What's going on?"

"Nothing." Tobin immediately adopted a tone of utmost annoyance. "Why do you think something's going on?"

Wei's suspicious look hardened.

"Are you going to let us through?" Tobin asked, taking a step up and physically trying to move his brother to the side.

Wei relented, but not before throwing the stinkiest of stink-eyes at Danny as he too squeezed by.

"Don't go disappearing," Wei called up to them. "Food's ready. Everyone's gathering."

So much for getting out of there. Danny followed Tobin into the big dining area off of the kitchen where a buffet spread was laid out. They took up position along a wall, shoulders pressed together.

Auntie Grace clapped loudly for everyone's attention. "Okay, okay!" Everyone quieted, even the kids who had come clambering up the stairs.

"Today is Thanksgiving, which is the day we say thank you to our family, to our friends. Thank you to mommies and daddies for their hard work. Thank you for food, for house, for jobs. So thank you for everyone coming today to celebrate with everyone." Auntie Grace clapped once. "Okay! Eat!"

Chaos erupted as people lined up for plates and cutlery, reaching across the big dining room table for the dishes they wanted. Constance and a couple other moms were helping the older kids fill plates while Wei and the dads brought the younger kids back to the basement.

Danny and Tobin hung back. As a middle-of-the-road generation, they had last priority. The crowd eventually cleared as everyone took their food elsewhere to sit and eat. Danny stepped forward and handed a plate to Tobin. In silence, they moved around the table, serving themselves stuffing and fried rice, green beans and Chinese broccoli, slices of dry turkey and juicy barbecue pork. By the time they were done, every other room on the first floor was full.

"Come on." Tobin led the way through the house and up the stairs. Below them, aunties, uncles, cousins, and kids laughed and argued with each other. But upstairs in Tobin's room, with the door closed, it was actually quiet.

There was nowhere to sit except the bed, but the single mattress was too small to fit both of them. Danny folded his battered body down onto the floor and sat against the wall. Tobin slid down next to him. Together they ate.

After a moment, Tobin reached over and skewered a piece of barbecue pork off Danny's plate and popped it into his mouth. He smirked as he chewed, and Danny narrowed his eyes. It was going to be like that, huh?

Danny surveyed Tobin's plate and stole a dumpling. To-bin's eyebrows shot up with indignant rage, but Danny chewed away happily. Pork, shrimp, and chives. His favorite.

Tobin stuck his fork into the mound of candied yams on Danny's plate. Jumping into defense mode, Danny tried to stop him, but he still managed to get half a forkful.

He went after Tobin's mac n' cheese next, but his fork got caught on a roasted potato and when Tobin tried to counterattack, the plastic broke, leaving him holding only the handle. He held it up. "Now look what you've done."

Tobin blinked big doe eyes at him before serving up a nibble of mac n' cheese with his still-intact utensil. "Peace offering?"

Danny let Tobin feed it to him, wrapping his lips around the fork as if it was some other delicious appendage. "You're going to have to do better than that."

Tobin bit his bottom lip and skewered a brussels sprout. He held it up with a questioning look, but Danny shook his head. Tobin pointed to a piece of sweet and sour pork, but Danny shook his head again.

"So what do you want?"

Danny's gaze dropped to Tobin's lips, rosy red from where he'd worried it. He couldn't have what he wanted, shouldn't even be thinking about it. But Tobin was sitting so close to him, thighs touching, shoulders touching. It would be so easy to lean over and take.

Danny squeezed his eyes shut and swallowed the lump in his throat. Being up here, alone with Tobin, was danger-ous territory. They were tempting fate by even contemplating it. Tobin dropped his head onto Danny's shoulder, and Danny tilted his head over to touch. They really couldn't be trusted to keep their hands off each other. If only they didn't have to.

The image of a ragey Wei circled with images of Tobin's seductive eyes. Maybe if they could convince Wei to stop being mad at them. Maybe if Danny stopped caring what Wei thought. Would that be enough?

Perhaps to ease Danny's guilty conscience. But to what end? So they could keep hooking up in random hotel rooms around the country? Tobin deserved more than that, except Danny wasn't sure he could give more.

Tobin reached out and took Danny's hand, intertwining their fingers. They sat for long moments, the silence punctuated by the second hand of the wall clock and the occasional burst of laughter from downstairs. Neither did anything to provoke it, nothing to stoke desire or want. But simply being in the same room, touching, was enough.

Danny's dick perked up at the scent of Tobin. His gut clenched with need. He wanted Tobin in his arms, under him, gasping, pleading. He gripped Tobin's hand tightly and Tobin squeezed back just as hard.

With his free hand, Tobin took Danny's plate and set it on the floor, out of the way. Then he rose up onto his knees and straddled Danny's thighs.

"Tobin." He tried to put as much warning into his voice as possible, but it still sounded much too husky for the right effect.

"Shh." Tobin put a finger over his lips. "I know."

They gazed at each other, mere centimeters apart. It

wasn't fair. God damn it, it wasn't fair. Why did Tobin have to be Wei's kid brother? Why did Danny have to love him so damn much? Fuck.

The realization snapped into place, crystal clear and undeniable. He loved Tobin; he always had. Sure, at first it was platonic and friendly, even brotherly. But he'd been drawn to Tobin from the first, and it had only intensified over the years. It explained so much. Why Danny couldn't keep his hands off Tobin; why Tobin haunted him day and night. Why Danny so often made a fool of himself to keep Tobin from finding out how little he measured up.

Danny pulled Tobin's fingers off his lips to say something. Anything. But nothing came out, except the name Danny held so close to his heart. "Tobin."

That was all Tobin needed to close the distance between them. When their lips met, whatever brain cells Danny had left popped, leaving him acting on instinct, drive, passion.

He wrapped his arms around Tobin's waist. So slim and lithe, corded muscles running up his back and down his thighs.

Tobin dragged his hands across Danny's neck and over his scalp, igniting all those sensitive nerves. Tobin's tongue teased his lips until Danny let him in. He could still taste the sweetness of the candied yams. Marshmallows and caramel, a sugar high Danny never wanted to come down from.

He pulled their bodies closer. Danny's head tilted all the way back while Tobin bent over him. A protruding bulge rubbed against Danny's stomach. Tobin was hard for him and Danny's dick filled in response.

He would never be able to get enough of Tobin. Not

physically; not emotionally. Not when his whole world had flipped upside down with the revelation of his love for Tobin. It didn't even matter if Tobin didn't feel the same way. Danny would never hold it against him. It would be enough to call Tobin a friend, to have him in Danny's life in whatever way he could get him.

He squeezed Tobin tight and flipped them over so Tobin was on his back and Danny on top of him. Their arms wrapped like tentacles around each other, legs entangled.

Danny took over the kiss, deepening it as the sounds of the party below melted away. He shifted to insert a knee between Tobin's thighs. Tobin gasped in response, arching up for their erections to meet. Danny met him halfway and pressed him back down.

Tobin whimpered and squirmed like the greedy little thing he was, and Danny couldn't keep their cocks lined up. So he grabbed both of Tobin's wrists and brought them overhead, pinning them to the floor with one hand. Tobin settled, relaxing as Danny let him take his entire weight. Chest to chest, groin to groin, lips locked in a kiss so all-consuming neither needed air.

Danny rocked against Tobin, their dicks iron rods trapped under clothes. Tobin rocked back, matching Danny in an easy rhythm that quickly grew urgent. All the blood in his body flowed to his cock until his head spun and his limbs were numb. He rested his forehead against Tobin's as they each breathed heavily against each other.

"I'm going to come," Tobin warned in a whisper.

"I am too."

"Fuck."

Danny smashed his mouth against Tobin's, pouring out every ounce of love he'd ever had for Tobin. Years and decades, all their stolen moments and secret touches. Care and gratitude, admiration and appreciation. Tobin made Danny whole in a way no one else could.

He was there. He was almost there. Just a little more.

"What the *fuck*?"

Chapter Twenty-Four

One minute Tobin was on the verge of another amazing Danny-induced orgasm, the next minute Danny was gone and the empty space chilled Tobin to the bone.

A door slammed, and the same question came again in a whispered shout. "What the fuck are you doing?"

It took a moment for the haze of pleasure to clear from Tobin's mind and for Wei's voice to register. He stood back against the door as if keeping a mob out, more furious than Tobin had ever seen him before. Danny had scrambled clear across the room, a look of horror branded on his face.

"There's a house full of people downstairs and you two are up here…" He waved his hand toward the floor.

"I can explain." Danny climbed to his feet, both hands raised as if to ward off a physical attack.

Wei pointed a finger in his face. "You said it was over!"

"I did. It is."

Danny's words were true, but that didn't soften the impact when they slapped Tobin across the face. Whatever lingering sex-haze he had was definitely cleared out now. He jumped up, hands balled into fists by his sides, not knowing who he wanted to argue with more—Wei or Danny.

"Then why did I find you two humping on the floor?" Wei's volume increased.

Danny winced, but Tobin stepped into his brother's face and matched it. "Why did you come barging in here in the first place?"

"Because I couldn't find you downstairs!"

"Why do you need to know where we are? Why can't you mind your own business?"

They were full-on shouting now, no attempt to keep the argument under wraps.

Danny stepped between them, a hand on each of their shoulders. "Calm down. Please."

Both Tobin and Wei shrugged him off with identical shoulder movements. Danny meant well, Tobin knew that, but this was between him and Wei. He'd put up with Wei trying to boss him around for too long and they were going to settle it once and for all.

He poked Wei in the chest. "You need to back off. Don't you have your own shit to take care of?"

Wei smacked his hand away. "I wouldn't have to take care of your shit if you grew up and acted like the adult you keep claiming to be."

"Guys, please," Danny tried again.

"Shut up—"

"Stay out of this—"

The door cracked open again. "What is going on here?" Mom stage-whispered as she slipped inside. "Everyone can hear you!"

"Why don't you ask them?" Wei gestured to Danny and Tobin before turning away and running a hand through his hair.

Oh, great. Mom.

"Toby? Danny?" She looked genuinely concerned. "What's wrong?"

"Nothing's wrong, Mom! Wei needs to stay out of my life!"

"Toby!" Mom gasped at his outburst.

He wanted to say that she did too, but he knew a hard limit when he saw one.

Wei let out a humorless chuckle as if to say Mom was on his side. The problem was, he was probably right.

"Danny." She went over to Danny, who was sitting on the edge of the bed, head in his hands. "What happened? What's wrong?"

Danny dropped his hands and glanced quickly up at Mom before lowering his head again. Tobin's heart caught in his throat at the look of pain and defeat in Danny's eyes, all tinged with a palpable fear. He wanted to go to him, to hold him and tell him everything would be okay. Instead, Tobin turned to Wei. "This is your fault. You did this to him."

"Me? What did I do? I don't have anything to do with this!"

"You have everything to do with it! You and your delicate sensibilities. And you're telling *me* to grow up?"

"Stop, stop." Mom came in between them. "Why are you yelling? It's Thanksgiving. You have to be thankful."

"Yeah, like I have anything here to be thankful for." He didn't really mean it. It'd just sounded like a good jab in his head. Well, it did the trick. Mom's jaw dropped, her posture stiffened, and her eyes focused into two lasers. He'd stepped over the hard limit.

The door opened yet again, and Tobin had never been so happy to be interrupted.

"Mommy, why is everyone shouting?" Dad didn't bother closing the door behind him. "People are asking if we want them to go."

Mom stared at Tobin, eyes unblinking, instilling the fear of an Asian mom in him before finally relenting.

"Daddy, you talk to them." She waved one dismissive hand before marching out of the room and down the stairs, grumbling something about wishing she'd never had children.

Dad looked from Tobin to Wei to Danny and back. Scowl fixed in place for no other reason than because Mom was upset. No one dared speak. Hell, they barely breathed.

He raised a hand and Wei and Tobin instinctively inched backward. Tobin wouldn't put it past Dad to try to spank them.

"I don't know what happened here. Don't make me find out. Okay?"

"Yes, sir," all three of them muttered, eyes lowered obediently to the ground.

Dad stood up tall, barely reaching Tobin's shoulder. He pointed out the door. "Downstairs. Now."

"But—" Wei cut himself off when Dad pinned him with a glare that would make any grown man wither. Wei inched past him and then practically stomped his way down the stairs.

Dad turned to follow Wei, shouting over his shoulder, "You two. Same thing. Come on."

Tobin drew in a breath and exhaled all the tension in his body. The spike and crash of adrenaline made him a little light-headed.

Danny stood from the bed, looking ashen.

"Hey." Tobin went to him, holding Danny's face between his hands. "It's okay. Everything's going to be fine."

Danny met his gaze and immediately Tobin knew everything was not going to be fine. "Danny." Panic sent his adrenaline spiking again.

Danny closed his strong fingers around Tobin's wrists and gently drew them down. He dropped Tobin's hands and stepped back. It was a simple movement, but it felt like Tobin was being let out to sea without a safety line.

"Danny. No, whatever it is you're thinking. No."

Danny shook his head. "I can't do this."

"You can. *We* can. We'll figure it out. We'll deal with Wei. This is fixable."

Danny kept shaking his head. "Didn't you see what happened? I've never seen you and Wei fight like that. I can't be the cause of it." Danny stepped back again, and Tobin wanted to follow him, but his feet were glued to the floor.

"I know we ended things so Wei and I could repair our

friendship. But I'd gotten it all wrong. We need to end things so you and Wei don't damage your relationship. Family is too important, Tobin. We can't risk that. *I* can't risk that."

Danny ran a hand down his face. It was a mannerism Tobin was used to. Except this time there was a finality to it that Tobin had never seen before. He wanted to protest; he wanted to scream *NO!* But all he could do was stand there.

"I'm sorry. I should never have let things get this far. If I'd had more self-restraint, been more responsible, none of this would've happened. I'm sorry." Danny spun around and nearly ran down the stairs, like he couldn't get away from Tobin fast enough.

Tobin stared at the empty doorway, waiting for Danny to come back with some sort of April Fool's joke even though it was the middle of October. He waited and waited, but Danny didn't reappear.

Tobin crumpled to the floor. His face was wet. He felt nauseous. What was going on?

Danny's words made no sense. None of what happened had anything to do with Danny's sense of responsibility or his self-restraint. If anything, Danny was *too* responsible. If he hadn't cared so god damn much about Wei's feelings, they could have carried on without it all blowing up in Tobin's face.

And why the hell were Wei's feelings so fucking precious? What about Tobin's feelings? What about what Tobin wanted? It was always Wei getting worried or upset. It was Wei's protective streak they needed to coddle. Well, fuck that. Tobin was done caring about Wei. And if no one else was going to care about him, then they could all go fuck themselves too.

The little simmer of anger urged Tobin to his knees and he crawled across the floor to his suitcase and started throwing things in. He didn't care whether clothes were folded, or how things fit. As long as he could zip the damn thing shut, that'd be good enough. He climbed to his feet and stumbled into the bathroom for his toiletries.

Coming to Toronto had been a mistake. He should have known better—nothing good ever came out of being in Toronto. Staying in Vancouver might have meant doing Thanksgiving alone, but it would've been better than this fucking disaster. God, he must have been high or something to think he'd have a good time spending the holidays with his family. He'd left for a reason; he needed to remember that.

Tobin had to sit on the suitcase to get it closed, but it worked. Everything else he stuffed into his laptop bag. It might be impossible to change his flight over Thanksgiving weekend, but he'd spend the night in the airport if he had to. He needed to get out of there, stat.

"Shh!" Tobin stumbled into the apartment with some random guy's hand down his pants.

What was his name? Conner? Corey? Whatever. It didn't matter. What mattered was the big bulge he sported underneath his spandex tight jeans.

C-Dude landed a hard smack on Tobin's ass, making him yelp and crash into the coffee table. Tobin's shin collided with the edge and when he toppled over, his hip caught on the corner.

"Ow!" He sucked in a breath, though the pain was thankfully dulled by the copious amounts of alcohol he'd managed to funnel into his system. Sweet.

"Tobes?" Monica's door opened, and light spilled into the living room. "Oh, hi."

"Hey, what's up." At least C-Dude had manners.

"Tobes, are you okay?" Monica asked.

"I'm fine!" Though he was still on the floor, sprawled out now because getting to his feet was simply too much work.

"Are you sure?" Monica came over and stood above him. She looked at C-Dude. "How much has he had to drink?"

C-Dude shrugged. "He was pretty wasted when I met him."

"I'm fine!" Tobin tried to swat Monica's ankles, but she sidestepped him with an agility he hadn't known she had. "Help me up." He stuck his hand up into the air.

C-Dude grabbed it and with a simple tug, Tobin came flying off the floor.

"Whee! See?" He giggled. "That's why I picked you." He let the momentum of the tug drive him into C-Dude's arms. The guy had a broad chest and thick biceps. He made for a decent cushion, but not great. The bumps and dips didn't fit with Tobin's in the right way. It was like wearing someone else's shoes.

"I don't think this is a good idea." Monica crossed her arms as she slipped into protective best friend mode.

He groaned. Not another one. There were way too many over-protective people in his life already.

"It's a *great* idea. It's the best idea in the whole wide world. Because you see…" Tobin looked at C-Dude and wracked his brain for the poor guy's name. Nothing. "You see, my friend here—" he patted the solid chest under his hand "—is a very nice guy with a very big dick and he's going to stick it in my ass and we're going to have a great time. It's called a hookup."

He reached out to give Monica a placating pat, but his arm must have shortened since the last time he'd used it. Weird. It fell limply by his side. "It's okay, Monica. I know you don't know about hookups. You're a lesbian."

"What the hell is that supposed to mean?"

Oopsie. He'd made her mad.

"Uh…actually." C-Dude tried to interject, but honestly, he needed to stay in his lane.

"Shh." Tobin put one finger over his lips. "No talkie. Just fuckie." He turned toward his room and took one step before stopping. The floor shifted under his feet. His stomach felt like it was going to come out of his mouth.

"Whoa." C-Dude steadied him. "You're right. I don't think this is a good idea."

"I said, shh!" Tobin pushed C-Dude away. What the hell? He didn't need his nameless, faceless hookups to have consciences and talk.

"Yeah, I'm out of here." C-Dude backed away as if Tobin was going to jump him. In his dreams. Tobin didn't want some good guy tapping his ass. He'd had enough of good guys.

He let out a frustrated growl. If he couldn't get some real live dick, at least he had some dildos.

"Tobin." Monica's tone was less offended and a little more resigned. "You're just going to ignore me?"

"Is it working?"

She sighed. "Are you going to puke? Do you need me to check on you to make sure you don't choke on your own vomit?"

Tobin shut the door in her face. What did she care what happened to him? What did anyone care? He was little baby Toby who didn't know any better, didn't know what he wanted, who needed the grown-ups to dictate his life. Little baby Toby who could be dismissed with a wave of a hand when he got too inconvenient. Fuck all of them.

He'd show them. He could be happy. He didn't need them. He could do what he wanted and be the king of the world!

He lifted his arms as if he were on the bow of the Titanic and then flopped backward onto the bed. He stank of the club. His hair was greasy. Who knew what kind of germs were on him. So what?

When he'd disappeared after Thanksgiving, his phone kept blowing up with messages. He'd blocked everyone's phone numbers, including Monica's and Ayán's. He couldn't avoid the lezzies at home, but it was time he started looking for his own place anyway.

His chest hurt. His stomach hurt. Something was gnawing away at his insides. His limbs were heavy, almost too much for him to move. He felt like he was dying. It sucked.

Tobin flipped over and buried his face into his pillow.

Don't cry. Don't cry. Don't cry. He didn't even know what the fuck he was crying about. Life was better this way, wasn't it?

When would it fucking stop?

He punched his mattress over and over again until he didn't have the strength to lift his fist.

Not fucking soon enough.

Chapter Twenty-Five

Danny sucked in a breath and proceeded to cough all the oxygen back out. Everyone around the conference table stopped and stared at him.

"Shit, Danny. That doesn't sound good," said Ray from right across the table.

Danny popped a throat lozenge. "I'm fine. Keep going."

Miguel glanced at Ginika, who nodded for him to continue. "So, given what we know about their patent, I think it's fair to increase our offer price to at least ten times EBITDA."

"I disagree." Ginika swiveled in her chair. "We should play dumb and keep the offer price low. WesTec hasn't been exploiting the patent, so why should we pay for it?"

"You have a point," Ray chimed in. "I'd be inclined to

keep the price low too. As it is, it's going to cost a fortune to build out the infrastructure needed to utilize the patent."

All eyes turned to Danny. He was the investment lead on the deal. He needed to have an opinion. Except he couldn't remember what the hell WesTec's earnings were and, maybe for the first time in his life, he didn't care.

"Are you sure you're okay?" Ray asked again.

Danny opened his mouth to answer and ended up bent over with his elbow covering his face as his lungs tried to escape his body. After the fit eased and his head stopped spinning from lack of air, he tried to speak, only to trigger another coughing fit. When he finally looked up, everyone had backed several feet away from him. He waved in Miguel's direction.

"Me?" Miguel pointed to himself. "My idea? Increase purchase price?"

Danny nodded.

The team launched into another debate about whether it was a good idea and if they *had* to increase their offer, how much they should increase it by.

Danny tuned it out. He was shivering. It was freezing in there. Hadn't the building turned the heat on yet?

The room fell silent. Everyone was staring at him. Had he missed something?

Ray cleared his throat. "We need an executive decision. Investment committee meeting is tomorrow."

Danny fucking well knew when the investment committee meeting was. Danny pointed at Miguel. "You said ten times EBITDA."

Miguel nodded.

"And what do you say?" he asked Ginika.

"No more than six point nine."

"Split the difference." Danny shut his laptop and stood. He'd made it to the door before the room exploded in questions.

"What does he mean, 'split the difference'?"

"Can he do that?"

"He's the boss. He can do whatever he wants."

"Danny!"

He slowed his trek toward his office but didn't stop. Ray fell into step next to him.

"Jesus, that's bold, even for me." Ray sounded impressed. "Take the high, take the low, split the difference and offer the midpoint. I guess that's one way to do it."

Danny fought back another coughing fit. "Marlena?" he croaked.

Ray frowned at him and inched away. "I think she'll be happy with that. It's a decent jump from the offer we showed her."

Danny nodded as they reached his office. As long as they had Marlena, it shouldn't be too difficult to make sure Cyrus fell in line too. He set his laptop down on his desk and collapsed into his chair.

"You know, you should get that checked out."

Danny glared at Ray. It would be the smart thing to do, but who the hell had time to go see a doctor?

"I'm serious. You should probably go home too. Whatever it is you've got, it sounds contagious and I sure as hell don't want to get it."

"Then you should stay the hell away."

Ray spun on his heel. "Already on it!"

Danny doubled over with another coughing fit as Ray left. This time gooey, slimy phlegm escaped his lungs. He spat it out onto a tissue. It was a disgusting green-yellow. Fuck.

Danny popped a couple of prescription antibiotics and chased them with a throat lozenge. Then he climbed into bed and shivered against the cool sheets.

His head weighed a million pounds, his joints ached, and his lungs had gone on strike. Was pneumonia supposed to feel this bad? Apparently yes, according to the real-life doctor and the random internet searches Danny had done after getting home.

He sipped on his mug of hot water with lemon and honey. At least he'd figured out where the kettle was and how to use the damn thing. When he didn't feel like an iceberg had taken up residence inside his body, he set the mug aside and grabbed his laptop.

He might have been banned from the office, but he could still work.

He opened his inbox and scanned through the bolded subject lines. Ignore, ignore, ignore. Wait. This one was from his lawyer, the one he'd retained after the car accident because he knew this was coming.

Danny was getting sued by the cyclist he'd hit. His lawyer had attached the claim, but he didn't need to read it. Whatever the cyclist wanted, he told the lawyer to agree. If insurance couldn't or wouldn't cover the whole amount, then Danny would make up the difference himself.

The screen blurred as his eyes grew heavy. How was it even possible to be this tired and still alive? Danny rubbed his eyes, trying to get them to focus, but it only made things worse. Fuck it. He was done. He set his laptop aside and was unconscious by the time his head hit the pillow.

It was the banging that woke Danny. Loud, yet muffled, like his ears were stuffed with cotton. As his brain slowly clawed its way back to the world of the living, he realized where the banging was coming from.

His front door.

"Fuck," he muttered.

No one ever came to his place. Why the hell did they have to come now?

Very carefully, he sat up. Bad idea. Very bad idea.

All the muscles in his chest and abdomen seized, trying to cough out whatever was in his lungs, but he couldn't suck in enough air to cough, so he ended up gagging. By the time it stopped, Danny was so light-headed he almost flopped back down onto the bed.

After a moment, he tried again. The air was so cold it had penetrated his bones and he was being frozen from the inside out. Yet, his skin was tacky with a layer of sweat.

More banging.

"I'm coming. Jesus."

His bathrobe was at the foot of the bed and he wrapped it around himself, little good it did. He shuffled out of his bedroom, wincing when his bare feet hit the cold hard-wood floor, then shuffled some more until he made it to the door.

He flipped the dead bolt and but didn't bother opening the door. Whoever was on the other side got the idea and opened it for him. Danny was already halfway down the hall back to his warm, soft bed.

"Jesus, what happened to you?" Wei. Fuck.

"He's got pneumonia." Ray. Double fuck.

"It's a furnace in here. What temperature did you set it at?" Was Wei asking him? Because he didn't remember setting the temperature to anything.

Footsteps followed him down the hall and into his bedroom.

"Shit. It's a mess in here."

Danny would have told Ray to fuck off, but his lungs picked that moment to do their happy dance. He braced himself on a bedpost, wincing as his organs tried to detach themselves from each other.

"Danny?" Wei touched him gently on his shoulder. "Are you okay?"

"Does he look okay to you?"

A pause, then, "Who are you again?"

"I'm Ray. Coworker. Boss sent me over to check on him because he went MIA."

"Well, he's got a fever." Wei pressed the back of his hand on Danny's forehead. "He's not doing any work today. Probably not for the rest of the week either."

"Hm. Joanna won't be happy about that."

Wei guided him toward the bed and Danny was too exhausted to resist him.

"I'm okay." It sounded like he had a frog in his throat.

"I don't think so." Wei nudged him onto the mattress

and Danny lay where he landed. "Come on, buddy, help me out here. You're heavier than a pickup truck." Wei hoisted Danny's left leg then his right one onto the bed.

"You're not much help, you know."

"Hey, I was sent to make sure he was still alive. I'm no nurse."

"Well, neither am I." Wei tugged at the duvet Danny was lying on top of. "Jesus, how does Constance do this?"

Danny summoned all his strength and rolled away so Wei could get the duvet unstuck. "She's a better person than you," he mumbled.

"You got that right." Wei tucked him in like he was one of the twins. "I'm sending her over next time." He turned to Ray. "You should call Joanna or whoever your boss is and tell them Danny's out of commission."

"No." He shot straight up in bed, only to have Wei push him back down. "I can do it."

"What? What can you do?" Wei was in full dad mode now.

Danny groaned. Something to do with a deal or something. "WesTec." That's it.

"What's that?"

Ray jumped in. "A deal we're working. We're supposed to be in Calgary next week."

"Calgary?" Wei looked back at Danny. "You're not going to Calgary next week."

Not if Danny had anything to say about it. "I'm coming."

"No, he's not."

No wonder Tobin thought Wei was bossy. He was.

"Yeah, you two can figure that out among yourselves. I'm going to call Joanna."

"Wait! Ray!" Danny tried to shout, but it ended up as more of a croak.

"Save it," Wei said.

"Fuck you."

"Yeah, I've been hearing that a lot lately." Wei disappeared into the bathroom and reemerged with a glass of water he set on the nightstand. He picked up the bottle of prescription antibiotics and gave it a shake. "You saw a doctor already?"

Danny moaned something along the lines of an agreement.

Wei took his phone out and snapped a picture of the bottle. "Go to sleep. I'll send this to Constance and see if she thinks you need to go to the hospital."

"No hospital." The last thing Danny needed was to be admitted for some minor case of pneumonia.

"We'll see about that."

Wei slipped out of the room before Danny could stop him to argue. Damn it. He should get up before those two assholes took over his life. He should try to get in some work. But instead, his eyes drifted shut and his brain switched off.

The next time Danny opened his eyes, he felt like he'd been run over by a train, but at least he wasn't freezing, and he could see straight. The sheets were damp and so were his clothes. His muscles ached like he'd run a marathon the day before. He sat up slowly, thanking the heavens when the room didn't spin.

Oh so carefully, he made his way to the bathroom, emptied his bladder, and took a shower. Feeling semi-human again, he risked a check-in with the mirror. He might have felt better, but he still looked like death. Whatever.

He was starving but also positive there was no food in the fridge. He made his way to the kitchen only to stop short when he got there.

"What are you doing here?"

Wei spared him a brief glance before turning back to the stove. "Oh good, you're alive."

Danny surveyed his kitchen. Cutting board and chef's knife, remnants of food packaging. Wei was stirring something in a giant pot. This was the most use the kitchen had been put to since...forever.

"How long have you been here?" Danny asked. He had some vague memory of people arguing in his bedroom, but had chalked it up to hallucinatory dreams.

"I stayed the night." Wei started chopping green onions. "I called Constance and she said it'd be best if I stuck around to monitor you. Mom went over to help with the twins."

Danny dropped onto a stool on the other side of the island, dumbfounded at how quickly they'd mobilized around him. All for a little pneumonia. "You didn't have to do all that."

Wei shot him an incredulous look. "What are you talking about? Do you know how close you were to going to the hospital? Frankly, I wanted to bring you in, but Constance convinced me to wait until this morning to see if your fever broke. Dude, pneumonia is no joke."

Had he really been in such poor shape? Maybe that's why he felt worse than shit on the bottom of someone's shoe. "You could have called an ambulance to take me."

Wei set the knife down hard enough that the metal rang against the hard surface of the countertop. "You've got to be fucking kidding me. I'm not sticking you in an ambulance to pass you off to hospital staff. Do you think I'd do that to Constance? The twins? My parents? Even fucking Toby when he's being a little shit? What makes you think I'd do that to you?"

The answer seemed obvious to Danny, but his sense of self-preservation prevented him from voicing it out loud.

"Yeah, I know what you're thinking." Wei waved the pointy end of the knife in his direction. "And you need to wipe the thought from your mind. You're family. This is what family does."

Everything inside Danny wanted to protest. So much so his brain sputtered and stalled trying to form arguments from thin air.

"Save it." Wei used the knife like an extension of his hand, waving it to dismiss Danny before he spoke. "You think I don't know what you think? Please. How long have we known each other? I should be insulted, really. Stick you in an ambulance. Please."

He set down the knife—gently this time, much to Danny's relief—and switched it for a ladle. Then he grabbed a bowl and filled it up with aromatic congee from the pot. A sprinkle of green onions on top and Wei set the bowl down in front of him. So that's what that mouth-watering scent was.

"Eat."

Danny didn't dare disobey.

Wei made up a smaller bowl for himself and ate it while leaning against the counter. When he finished, Wei set his bowl aside and watched Danny as if making sure he ate every last drop.

"Look. I'm sorry about how I reacted with the whole you and Toby thing. I'm not sure what got into me."

Danny folded his arms on the counter and waited. He would have held his breath if his lung capacity was anywhere near normal.

"Toby's my brother and you're pretty much my brother, so the thought of you two together was…hard to get my mind around. Not in any weird incest kind of way or anything. But, like, you have this place in my life—" Wei gestured with his right hand "—and he has this place in my life—" he gestured with his left. "But bringing them together—" he interlaced his fingers "—didn't make sense. I think that's why I freaked out."

Danny could understand that, to an extent. The dynamics between them were shifting and it could be difficult adjusting to changes in relationships.

"Anyway." Wei dropped his hands. "I'm sorry."

Danny was about to say thanks when Wei continued.

"At the same time, it was a pretty shitty thing you guys did, running around behind my back. I don't care what your excuses were or how you justified it to yourselves, but it wasn't very nice." Wei crossed his arms. "I would have appreciated a heads-up."

Danny refrained from pointing out how poorly Wei had reacted. But maybe it wouldn't have been so bad if they'd been up front with him right from the beginning. "Speaking of which...shit." Danny cleared his throat and ran a hand down his face. "Um, about that. We, um..."

"Oh my god, what is it now?"

"Remember your bachelor party?"

Wei put the heels of his hands to his eyes. "Yes?"

"That was the, um, first time, um, we..."

Wei got the idea. "You've been sleeping together for seven years?"

"No. No. We haven't." Danny sat up straighter. "The bachelor party was only one time. We've barely seen each other since then, you know, until earlier this year."

"Oh my god." Wei braced both hands on the edge of the counter and bent at the waist. "Oh my god, how old was Toby back then?"

"He was nineteen! He was definitely nineteen! And it was completely consensual. You can ask him. Please, ask him." Oh fuck. Danny covered his face with a hand. He sounded no better than Cyrus fucking West.

"No shit, Sherlock, I know it was consensual. As if you could ever live with yourself if it wasn't." Wei shook his head. "He was probably the one who initiated, wasn't he? God, that boy never knows when he's going too far."

They fell silent. Wei had apologized. Danny had apologized. So what did they do now? Carry on as if nothing had happened?

"I don't want either of you to get hurt," Wei whispered.

"We ended things. For real this time." Danny's chest tightened at the words, but he wrote it off to the pneumonia.

"But that's it, isn't it?" Wei cast a penetrating look at Danny, one so much like Tobin's. "You're hurting now because you ended things."

His chest tightened even more, and Danny forced himself to take long, slow breaths in and long, slow breaths out. This definitely wasn't the pneumonia. Pneumonia had never been this soul-damagingly painful.

"I know you guys broke up because of me. Or at least, partially because of me." Wei let out a heavy sigh and started cleaning up the kitchen, tossing utensils into the dishwasher. "But I don't want to be responsible for your misery. I've got two kids; I'm already going to be responsible for their therapy bills when they get older. I don't need you and Toby on my conscience too."

Danny swallowed around the lump in his throat. "What are you saying?"

"What I'm saying is none of us know whether you and Toby can actually make this thing work. Honestly, I have my doubts—Toby's still got some growing up to do and you're married to your job. But if you're not going to work out, it's not going to be because of me."

"Tobin's plenty grown up. He's a lot more mature than you give him credit for."

Wei sighed. "Maybe. But my point still stands."

What point was that? Danny watched as Wei finished clearing up the kitchen. If they weren't going to work out, it wasn't going to be because of him. So Wei wanted them to get back together? To give it a try?

Wei finished putting everything away, ran the dishwasher, and then came around the island to sit next to Danny. "So yeah, not that you need it or anything. But if you wanted my blessing or whatever, you have it." He didn't sound all that enthusiastic, but Danny figured he could only ask for so much. "And in case you were wondering, don't worry about Mom and Dad. Dad's oblivious to stuff like this and Mom will probably start planning your wedding."

A wedding. The unusual sensation of hope filled Danny's heart at that word. He'd never considered it for himself before, but he kind of liked the sound of it now. If only Tobin would take him back after the way Danny had left him last time.

But there was something else Wei had said that bugged him. "What do you mean I'm married to my job?"

Wei burst out laughing.

"What's so funny?"

"Oh god." Wei dropped his head back like he was pleading with some higher power. "You—" Wei poked him in the arm "—have always been so hung up on all the money shit."

Danny sat up straighter at the accusation. He wasn't hung up. Money wasn't something to be flippant about. But before Danny could object, Wei kept talking.

"Hear me out." Wei held up one hand to keep Danny from interjecting. "Everyone knows Auntie Helen was a single mom. Everyone knows why you spent so much time at our house. But so what? We're all friends—no, we're more than friends. We're family. And families share what they have with one another. Dad got rich on some weird marketing scheme that to this day I couldn't explain to you if I tried. Does that make him or any of us better than you or your mom? No! Of course not! But you're the only one who seems to care about it so damn much."

Danny tried to go in for a rebuttal, but his lungs chose that moment to remind him they were still unhappy. Wei waited until his coughing fit stopped and kept going.

"Case in point. Remember when we were in under-grad? It was so obvious your scholarships weren't covering everything, but could we just dole out a bit of cash to help you out? Nope. Mom had to go all covert and invent ways to 'accidentally' give you money. She even made me swear it to secrecy in case your ego got bruised." Wei shook his head. "There's no shame in accepting help, you know."

Danny got up from his seat to pace around. He'd always assumed Wei knew about the mysterious gifts that ended up among his things, but it didn't sit right to talk about it out loud. Oh god, Wei was right—even now his ego bris-tled at the mention of needing help.

"I've tried to repay them," Danny said, more to ease his own discomfort than anything else.

"See? This is my point. You don't need to repay them! You don't owe them anything. They're happy you're suc-cessful. We all are. You don't need to keep killing yourself at work to prove it was all worth it." He gestured to Danny as another coughing fit took over.

This one didn't let up.

"Okay, that's enough for now. Let's get you back to bed." Wei took him by the arm and led him toward the bedroom.

Danny had more questions, but whatever energy he'd gotten from the congee was starting to wane. He let Wei usher him back into bed, took a couple antibiotics, and pulled the duvet up to his chin.

With Danny all tucked in, Wei stood next to the bed. "You love him, don't you?" he asked with a satisfied grin. "I can tell from the look on your face."

Danny met his gaze and nodded. "I do."

Wei patted his shoulder. "Welcome to the club."

Well, he'd made it to Calgary. Against Wei's vehement objections, but Danny had taken enough of Wei's advice lately.

Ray kept casting him suspicious sidelong glances the entire way there. As if Danny would keel over at the slightest gust of wind. He was still coughing, but it wasn't nearly as bad as it had been the week before. No more of that whole-body-turning-inside-out stuff, so he'd cleared himself for work travel.

"Give me a signal or something if you need me to take over," Ray said in the elevator as they rode up to Wes-Tec's office.

"I'm fine."

"I'm just saying. If you need me, I can jump right in."

"I won't." Danny dug a lozenge out of his briefcase to prove how fine he was.

The elevator doors opened, and they stepped out to find Tobin in the lobby. Danny was so dumbstruck the elevator door almost closed on him. Wei had said he was going to reach out to Tobin and patch things up. Danny had been waiting for the go-ahead from Wei before doing his own reaching out. He hadn't heard from Wei yet.

"Oh hey! Tobin, right?" Ray greeted Tobin with a handshake. "Great to see you again. You here for WesTec too?"

"Yeah." Tobin shook his hand much less enthusiastically. "Good to see you again." He didn't even deign to look at Danny.

"Okay," Ray muttered beneath his breath.

"Hi, folks. Welcome to WesTec. I can take you into the meeting room now." A young woman with a friendly smile addressed them.

Tobin led the way and Danny gestured for Ray to go ahead of him. He wasn't surprised when they were all ushered into the same meeting room. Of course Cyrus would try to pit them against each other.

Or maybe it'd been Marlena's doing. She was certainly shrewd enough. Her name hadn't been included in the official meeting invite, but Ray had confirmed she'd make herself available.

Tobin continued to ignore them after they were left alone, eyes downcast and focused on getting himself set up.

"What am I missing here?" Ray asked.

Tobin sat down, back ramrod straight, lips in a thin line. His hands were clutched tightly together, and Danny had to stop himself from marching over and pulling Tobin into a comforting hug.

Ray glanced back and forth between them before thankfully dropping it. "Never mind."

Marlena came bustling in with a whiff of perfume strong

enough to set off Danny's coughing. "Oh my, darling. Are you okay?" She came over and pounded on Danny's back. It didn't help.

Ray came to the rescue. "Marlena! It's so wonderful you could make it today." He escorted her to the other side of the conference table and pulled out a chair for her.

"Likewise!" She patted Ray on the cheek and took the seat he offered. "You know, I figured, if I'm going to own half the company anyway, I might as well see what you folks are willing to pay for it. Oh, and I can't wait to see my precious Cyrus's face." She lowered her voice. "I didn't tell him I was coming today."

Danny resisted the urge to pinch the bridge of his nose. This was going to be one hell of a meeting.

"Mrs. West?" Tobin circled around to where she sat.

Marlena gave him a quick once-over. "For now. But please, call me Marlena."

"Hi. I'm Tobin Lok from Paradigm Consulting."

"Oh yes, I know about you. Thank you so much for all the work you've done for us. I'm sure it was no easy task."

Tobin smiled and stood a little taller. "It's entirely my pleasure."

"How darling." Marlena smiled at him before surveying the rest of the room. "Isn't it wonderful we're all here. Now if only my husband would show up when he's supposed to."

"Marlena?"

"Speak of the devil."

"What are you doing here?"

"Why, Cyrus, what a silly question! I wouldn't miss this

meeting for the whole wide world!" She shot him a look that said *shut up and sit down*.

Cyrus complied.

Danny stifled a cough.

"Well, now that everyone is present, why don't we get started?" Marlena took charge of the meeting to absolutely no one's surprise. "Tobin, dear. Won't you be a darling and go first?"

Tobin looked from Marlena to Cyrus to Danny and back. "Sure." He cleared his throat and handed out a presentation deck. When he got to Danny and Ray, he only had one left for them to share. "Sorry, I didn't realize I needed extra copies."

Ray flashed him a smile. "No worries."

Tobin settled back into his seat before starting. "If you'd like to flip to page three…"

Danny tried to pay attention to Tobin's presentation. He really did. But the sound of Tobin's voice, the way he conducted himself and held the attention of the room, that was so much more interesting than expenses and budgets. He was self-assured and confident in the quality of his own work. He knew what he was talking about, there was no doubt about that.

Danny's mind drifted back to his conversation with Wei. Maybe Tobin still had things to learn about being an adult, but didn't they all?

Tobin had moved away from home at the tender age of seventeen, cut all financial ties with his family, and figured out how to support himself, all while attending classes full-time. He would have needed serious grown-up skills to do all that without a support system. Danny certainly hadn't been able to manage it entirely on his own.

But Wei had mentioned something about Tobin always trying to play catch-up when he'd already caught up. Danny had never interpreted Tobin's independent, chip-on-the-shoulder streak in quite that way, but he could understand it. Maybe all Tobin needed was a little affirmation he'd become one of the big boys he'd been so desperate to impress.

"Any questions?" Tobin asked, drawing Danny back from his ruminations.

"Yes, I have one." Marlena took off her bedazzled reading glasses.

She seemed much more on the ball than Cyrus was. He was still frowning at the presentation deck like he couldn't figure out what it said.

Marlena looked Tobin straight in the eye. "Tell me more about this patent."

Oh, shit.

Chapter Twenty-Six

Tobin took a deep breath and willed himself to stop shaking. He knew his shit. Marlena looked impressed. So why was his adrenaline still running so fucking high?

"Of course." Tobin had read that patent backward and forward and could probably recite it out loud if she wanted him to. "It's the next level of alternative data, like a 2.0. You'd be taking the results from the first round of analysis and feeding them through the algorithm to gain even more insight into market movements. The inputs are still the same, but you're essentially squeezing more profit out of them."

Marlena looked like she'd discovered a giant chunk of diamond buried in her backyard. "No one else in the world is doing this?"

"No, ma'am." Tobin paused, resisting the urge to glance in Danny's direction. "At least not yet."

"Hm." She tapped a perfectly manicured nail against her chin. "That sure is something."

Something that could potentially make Jade Harbour's offer look like peanuts, if Tobin had done his job correctly. "Like I said, it'll require a significant amount of investment before WesTec can take full advantage of the patent. But once you're up and running, the upside is substantial."

"So you recommend we pursue this in-house?" Marlena asked.

Tobin didn't hesitate, not even for a second. "Absolutely."

Her smile was so smug that it helped ease some of Tobin's pent-up nervous energy.

"Well." She patted her blond curls. "Aren't I glad I showed up to this meeting?"

Tobin was glad she'd shown up too. He felt like he'd found an ally. Cyrus was slouching in his seat, glowering at her. He hadn't said a word since they'd gotten started.

"Ray, Danny, what do you have for me?"

Cyrus huffed. Ray chuckled out loud. None of them missed Marlena's specific choice of words.

"I think you'll be very pleased with what we have." Ray made the rounds and handed out their deck.

Tobin flashed a tight smile when Ray handed him one too.

Danny cleared his throat and popped something in his mouth. When he started speaking, he sounded like his vocal cords had been shredded. What the hell had happened to him?

"Jade Harbour has a reputation for helping struggling companies reach their full potential. Which is why we're here. We believe WesTec can do much more, and we want to partner with you in creating that success story."

A polished pitch if Tobin had ever heard one. But Marlena only seemed to be half listening to him. She nodded along, flipping through the presentation and scanning each page like she was a speed-reader.

"Where's the patent mentioned in here?" she interjected before Danny could continue.

Ray jumped in. "I believe it's on page sixteen."

Aha, so Jade Harbour *did* know about the patent.

Marlena found the page, read it, then flipped back to the offer summary. "Have you incorporated the value of the patent in your offer price?" she asked with a frown.

Tobin caught the look Danny exchanged with Ray. Oh, some shit was going down and strangely enough, it put Tobin more at ease. If Jade Harbour was in trouble, it'd make him look less disheveled.

Sure, on the surface, Tobin had managed to pull his life back into some semblance of normalcy. He showed up for work and got the job done. At home, Monica and Ayán had finally stopped hovering around him like he was about to do something inadvisable.

But he still hadn't unblocked his parents and Wei's phone numbers—he couldn't bring himself to talk to them. And he always felt like he was one misspoken word away from crumbling. Sometimes he woke up shaking with an anger that dissolved into tears.

"We have," Danny said, which garnered him a very

pointed look from Marlena, made all the more brutal with her reading glasses perched on the end of her nose. Tobin never thought he'd see the day when Danny squirmed. Served him right.

"Are you sure?"

The room fell into deadly silence. Marlena locked eyes with Danny and perhaps for the first time in Danny's life, he flinched.

Danny cleared his throat. "Keep in mind this offer isn't final. We want to find a solution that is mutually beneficial."

Marlena stared at him for a moment longer before taking off her glasses and flipping the Jade Harbour presentation shut. "Thank you for that, dear. It's always nice to know we've got friends we can count on." She checked her watch with a deliberate motion and Tobin could have sworn the look of surprise on her face was practiced.

"I am so very sorry," she said, "I just remembered I have an appointment to get to. This esthetician is always booked out months in advance and I can't afford to lose my spot in her schedule."

That was it? She wasn't going to hear Danny out? It was no skin off Tobin's back, but it hardly seemed like a fair fight. She'd given Tobin at least thirty minutes to plead his case. Damn. If Marlena had been running the show instead of Cyrus all these years, there's no way WesTec would have ended up where it was.

She stood, and everyone stood with her, even Cyrus, who didn't bother saying goodbye and stalked out the door.

"So lovely to meet you, dear." Marlena offered her hand to Tobin.

He took it. Fuck, he almost kissed it. "The pleasure is all mine."

"Well, gentlemen, I'm sure Cyrus will be in touch with you soon. He's so busy these days, sometimes it takes a little time for him to go through things, you know. But don't you worry. I'll make sure you get your answers before too long." She tucked the presentations into her bag, wiggled her fingers at them, and left as abruptly as she'd shown up.

"That went...well." Ray had a grim look on his face as he tucked his hands into his pockets.

Danny glared at him.

Tobin didn't know about Jade Harbour, but it'd gone better than well for him.

When Danny had stepped off the elevator earlier, it'd thrown Tobin for a loop. He'd been working so hard at putting Danny out of his mind and focusing on the presentation, only to have Danny stroll back in at the least opportune moment. Not that Tobin had been *nervous*, necessarily. But he certainly hadn't needed Danny breathing down his neck and judging his every word.

"Tobin, you have plans for dinner tonight?" Ray asked as they filed out of the meeting room.

He didn't. But neither did he want to spend a second longer than necessary in Danny's presence. Danny had made his opinions very clear on Thanksgiving and Tobin had no intention of wasting his time on people who didn't think he was worth their effort.

"I have some work I should catch up on." Including some TV-binging in the hotel bed.

"You should join us," Danny said in that half-croak of a voice. He must have noticed the question on Tobin's face. "I had pneumonia."

"What?" Tobin scanned him like he could find evidence of the illness on Danny's immaculately tailored suit.

"He did. You should have seen him last week. He looked like the walking dead. We had to send him home so he wouldn't infect the entire office." Ray punched the elevator button.

"I'm fine now."

The elevator arrived, and they piled in. Under the startling white lights shining overhead, Danny did look a little gaunt, like he'd lost weight in the couple weeks since Tobin last saw him.

"Barely." Ray chuckled as he spoke.

Danny leaned against the wall as if he needed the support. In fact, the farther away the elevator took them from WesTec, the more exhausted Danny looked.

"Maybe you should rest." Tobin could stop by to help him order room service. Make sure Danny stayed hydrated. He could even draw a bath. Should pneumonia patients take baths?

What the hell was he doing? The last thing he needed was to play nursemaid to Danny and then get tossed out on his ass again.

"I'm fine," Danny croaked again as the elevator arrived on the ground floor.

"Either way, you should have dinner with me." Ray

flashed Tobin a smile that suggested he had more than dinner in mind.

Danny scowled like he wanted to rip Ray in two. "He's not having dinner with you."

Tobin blinked. No, Danny did not just try to tell him what he could or could not do. Fuck that.

"You know what, Ray? I would *love* to have dinner with you."

It didn't take long for the news to come in. Thanks, but no thanks, Jade Harbour, they were going to give it a go on their own.

Tobin had been lying spread eagle on his hotel bed staring up at the ceiling, mind blank. Nervous energy still skittered across his skin and it was all he could do to breathe in for three and out for three. Rinse and repeat.

He'd been contemplating whether he should cancel on dinner with Ray when his inbox had chimed with the incoming message.

Suddenly that shaky restlessness solidified into genuine excitement. "Ahh!" He let out a squeal even though there was no one there to hear him.

It was from Marlena, with a WesTec email address. She'd taken over the company in the time it took for Tobin to get back to his hotel room and zone out for a bit. The incriminating evidence of Cyrus sleeping with trafficked girls had been submitted to the police, and Marlena had cancelled the divorce to retain control of their assets while he rotted in jail. She'd even managed to convince her dad to bankroll the implementation of the patent. Best of all?

She wanted Tobin on a long-term contract to guide them through the project. Him!

He'd never had a client ask for him by name before! Would he get a raise from Paradigm? Maybe a promotion? At the very least, he should get a decent bonus at the end of the year. Tobin spun around in a circle a few times before collapsing back onto the bed.

He'd done it. He'd really done it.

Little baby Toby had taken on a project all on his own, did all the hard work, and the client wanted him back for more. External validation had never felt so good.

Tobin had his phone clutched to his chest and it buzzed with an incoming call. No Caller ID. Maybe it was WesTec?

"Hello?"

"Hey, kid."

Fuck. How did Wei get through? How did he crush all of Tobin's happy vibes with two simple words?

"What do you want?" Tobin pressed a thumb and forefinger into his eyes. This had to be Danny's doing. It was too much of a coincidence that Wei would find a way around his blocked number on the same day Tobin saw Danny again.

"To apologize."

Tobin frowned. Wei's words said one thing, but his tone said another. "For what?"

Wei sighed heavily, like the phone call was asking too much of him.

"Dude, you called me. If you don't want to talk, we don't have to talk." Tobin seriously considered hanging up on him.

"Sorry! Sorry, I want to talk." Wei's tone changed. "Listen, I was wrong about you and Danny. I reacted badly. I made assumptions I shouldn't have. And you're right. I do see you as the baby of the family, and yeah, I am overprotective."

This was the strangest apology Tobin had ever heard. "Okay."

"You remember how I said before that I didn't think you were ready for a relationship with Danny?"

He remembered something vaguely along those lines. "Mmhmm."

"Well, I still believe that. But—and it's a very valid *but*—I also think you've got the guts to give it a try...and succeed."

Tobin started shaking again. He thought he knew what Wei was saying, but he didn't want to go there on the off chance he was interpreting Wei wrong.

"So, I'm sorry for underestimating you. For not trusting you to make good decisions." Wei swallowed audibly. "I spent my whole life trying to make sure you didn't get hurt. But I think what I should have done was let you get hurt and then make sure I was there after to help you get better. So yeah, I'm sorry."

Tobin rolled over and buried his face into a pillow. Fuck Wei and his fucking sincere apology. Tobin held his breath until his lungs burned because if he breathed now, he'd be letting the flood gates open too.

"Hello? You still there?"

Tobin screamed into the pillow.

"Uh... I'll take that as a yes?"

Tobin dropped the phone on the mattress and ran into the bathroom for tissues. How many years had he been waiting to hear those words from Wei? Why had it taken so god damn much to get him to finally say them? Tobin sat on the floor, ugly crying until there were no more tears to shed and his nose was red and raw.

On unsteady legs, he made his way back to the bed. The call was still connected.

"Hello?" he whispered into it.

Wei answered immediately. "Hey, you okay?"

Tobin sniffled. "Yeah."

Wei sighed, sounding relieved. "Okay, good. I figured you were, you know."

"Yeah, I was."

"Right."

After a moment of silence, Tobin whispered, "Thank you."

Wei chuckled. "God, don't thank me. I'm the older one, you'd think I'd be the smarter one."

"I'm definitely the smarter one. And the better looking one."

"Yeah, yeah," Wei joked. "You won the genetic lottery."

They fell silent again.

"There's one more thing," Wei continued after a second. "I know why you did it and I'm not angry or upset or anything. It's just… I would've thought you and Danny could've come to me right from the start. Like, yeah, I get I reacted badly and all that. Gah, what I'm trying to say is don't feel like you need to hide stuff from me, okay? I'm going to try to not be an asshole."

Tobin wasn't sure Wei would want to hear all the things all the time, but he could appreciate what Wei was saying. "Yeah, okay. I'll try."

In the background, a door opened, followed by two screaming young voices.

Tobin couldn't help but laugh. "I guess that's our cue."

"Yeah, no shit. Sorry."

"No, no, it's fine. Go deal with the twins. Thank you for calling."

"Thanks. Talk soon, okay?"

"Yeah, talk soon."

Tobin hung up feeling like he needed to crawl under the covers and sleep for a month. He'd had enough ups and downs for at least that long.

His phone buzzed. Oh god, now what?

He grabbed it to find a text message from a number he didn't have saved in his phone. Hey Tobin, it's Ray. Confirming dinner at six. I'll meet you in your lobby.

Fuck. Dinner with Ray. He'd totally forgotten. Could he beg off?

Tobin checked the time. It was only twenty minutes to six. Probably too late now. Fuuuuck. He dragged himself into the bathroom. *Fuck*. He'd just spent the past thirty minutes ugly crying on the bathroom floor. His whole face looked like an allergic reaction. His eyes were puffy, and his lips were swollen. He couldn't go out in public like this!

Tobin switched into overdrive, splashing cold water on his face and pulling out all his makeup tricks. He changed in record time, and with minutes to spare he stood in front of the mirror. He didn't look fabulous, but at least he was presentable. It'd have to be good enough.

Ray was already in the lobby when he got downstairs, flirting shamelessly with one of the valets. When he saw Tobin approach, Ray slipped something to the poor guy and leaned in close to whisper in his ear.

Tobin scanned the lobby. "No Danny?"

Ray chuckled. "And here I thought you were having dinner with me."

"I am! I mean, sorry. Of course I'm having dinner with you." He was genuinely surprised. He would have bet money Danny was behind the call from Wei, which would make more sense if Danny had planned on being at dinner.

Ray shook his head as he turned for the entrance. "You two need to get over yourselves."

"What does that mean?"

"It means…" Ray held the door open for him. "That it's obvious to everyone you're both head over heels in love with each other."

In love? What the hell did Ray know about him and Danny?

Ray led the way to a black car parked a few spots down the driveway and opened the backseat door for Tobin. He slipped in, only to find Danny waiting for him.

Chapter Twenty-Seven

"Hello." Danny's heart thudded in his chest at the sight of Tobin. He was gorgeous, as always, perhaps even more so tonight given everything that had happened.

"Hi." Tobin eyed him suspiciously. That was okay; he had good reason.

"Congratulations." Danny meant it wholeheartedly. When he'd found out WesTec had rejected their deal, once and for all, a huge weight had miraculously disintegrated from Danny's shoulders. He hadn't realized how heavy it'd been until it was gone.

"Thank you."

The driver pulled the car away from the curb, but Ray was still standing out there. "Isn't...?" Tobin craned his head around as they left Ray behind.

"No." Danny smiled sheepishly. "He made other plans." It was a bit underhanded, but he had very little confidence Tobin would voluntarily see him again.

Tobin let out one chuckle and shook his head. "Guess I was played."

"Sorry." He had a lot of apologizing to do tonight. Might as well start early.

Tobin cast Danny a glare out of the side of his eye and huffed a sigh. "It's fine." He sounded resigned. Danny would take that over furious.

"How are you feeling?"

Danny shifted the throat lozenge around with his tongue. "Mornings are the worst. The coughing dies down half-way through the day."

"I don't think I've ever seen you get sick before."

"I don't get sick." He cleared his throat. "Until now."

"Everything finally catching up with you," Tobin said. A statement. Not a question.

"Something like that."

Maybe it was his ready admission or something in his voice, but Tobin eyed him for a second before turning in his seat to study Danny. He could almost feel Tobin's gaze as it scanned every inch of exposed skin, like he was testing to make sure Danny was still Danny. He was. And he wasn't.

"What... You look..." Tobin scowled like he'd been presented with low grade fake merchandise.

Danny chuckled softly. "Yeah, I know." His hand went automatically to his wrist that was now bare.

"You're not wearing a watch."

Caught in the act, Danny clasped his hands together. "I thought I'd try going without for a night."

Tobin's eyebrows shot straight up. "You're telling me you purposely didn't put a watch on when you left your suite."

"Is that so hard to believe?"

"Yes."

Danny laughed out loud. It felt like giant bubbles releasing from somewhere deep inside him. "That's fair."

"Who are you and what have you done to my Danny?" Tobin wore a semi-horrified look on his face.

He'd said, *"my Danny."* Was Danny his?

God, he hoped so. "I'm right here."

Tobin shook his head like he didn't believe. Danny could barely believe it himself.

In the couple of hours between leaving WesTec's offices and when Marlena had emailed, Danny had had a very honest conversation with Joanna. Regardless of how the WesTec deal panned out, he needed a break. At least six months, ideally a year. He wouldn't take a paycheck either, if that was an issue. He'd barely taken any vacation since joining Jade Harbour, and now he was calling it all in.

Joanna hadn't sounded very surprised, almost as if she'd been expecting it for a while. Sure, she pressed him, trying to negotiate reduced workloads, but Danny knew he'd never adhere to those limitations. If he was in work mode, he'd be on at one hundred percent.

Wei was right—he was married to his job. It was all he'd known for so long and he'd poured so much of himself into it. And for what? Prestige and recognition, money and status; all those things were fine, but they weren't making him happy. When Danny thought about happiness, the first thing that came to mind was Tobin.

Tobin had never been attracted to his money or his status. He couldn't win Tobin over by showering him with gifts. Danny still couldn't say for certain what it was Tobin saw in him, why in the world Tobin would want him over anyone else. But if there was even the slightest chance Tobin still had feelings for him, then Danny had to take it. And if that meant quitting his job so he could devote himself to meeting Tobin where he was, then Danny had to do it.

Danny dropped his gaze to where Tobin's hand rested on the seat between them. When he looked up again, Tobin's bristly armor had softened. Did he understand? Could they try again?

Without a word, Tobin flipped his hand over, palm up, and Danny took it. Their fingers slid together like they were designed to dock with one another.

It was physiologically impossible, but Danny thought he could feel Tobin's heart beat through their touching palms. They breathed together, in and out, and slowly their hearts synced up too.

A smile tugged at Tobin's lips and Danny returned it. This could work. They could get this to work. They had to.

The car turned off onto a gravel road and Tobin looked out the window at the old-growth forest around them.

"Where are we?"

Danny had to hand it to him for not asking until now. Danny's first instinct was to give some vague answer so he wouldn't ruin the surprise. But Tobin glanced at him with

an expectant look. Right. That was old Danny. He needed
to be new Danny.

"Kananaskis, west of Calgary. There's a nice restaurant
out here."

Tobin cocked one eyebrow. "Nice?"

"Very nice," Danny conceded.

They pulled up to a giant log cabin with a wide wrap-
around porch lined with Adirondack chairs. As Danny
emerged from the car, nature assaulted his senses. Pine and
dirt and a touch of winter in the air.

He waited for Tobin to come around the car and offered
an outstretched hand. To his absolute delight, Tobin slipped
his hand in without a second of hesitation.

Inside, they were greeted by a host who brought them
all the way to the back of the building. It extended out
over a lake, the pristine blue waters reflecting the peaks
of the Rocky Mountains back at them. The dining room
was small, almost family-sized rather than restaurant-sized.
But the ceiling soared above them with exposed wooden
beams and chandeliers made from antlers. They were led
to a table by a roaring stone fireplace, the heat chasing
away even the slightest suggestion of cold. Opposite them
were wide windows offering uninterrupted views of the
outdoors. The place was the epitome of rustic charm, with
staff wearing red and black checkered lumberjack shirts.

Danny had made sure they were the only ones there.

Once they were settled with menus and glasses of water,
Danny took a deep breath. It was now or never. "Tobin."

He paused in his perusal of the menu and peeked up

through mascara lined lashes. "Yes?" Oh, Tobin knew something was up. There was no point in trying to hide it.

"Wei called you."

Tobin closed the menu and set it aside. He cocked his head. "I was wondering when you'd get to that."

Danny nodded, though the blame wasn't entirely on him. "He was supposed to have called you earlier."

All humor drained from Tobin's face. "You two are co-ordinating your phone calls to me?"

Shit. "No. Well, in this case, yes. But—"

Tobin sat back in his chair and crossed his arms. Unimpressed didn't even begin to describe him.

Danny sighed and ran a hand over his face. When he looked up again, Tobin's expression had softened, but only a smidge. "Maybe I should start at the beginning."

"Maybe."

"Right. After Thanksgiving—"

"After you walked out on me."

Danny cleared his throat. So it was going to be one of those kinds of conversations. Okay, he could work with that. "After I walked out on you, I got pneumonia." He gestured to his chest, in case there was any doubt about where his pneumonia was. "And Wei came over to check on me." He paused, but Tobin didn't seem to ascribe significance to that development.

"When he was over, we had a talk. Wei apologized for being a dick. I apologized for being a dick—"

"You made up."

Short and to the point. "Yes, we made up. I also told him about our hookup at his bachelor party."

Tobin covered his face with one hand and groaned. "Sorry."

Tobin shook his head but didn't drop his hand. "Keep going."

"He accused me of being married to my job."

That caught Tobin's attention. His head shot up and he stared intently at Danny. "And? What did you say?"

Danny didn't think what he said at the time mattered as much as what he eventually decided to do. He hummed and hawed a bit. "I...came around to the idea."

"What does that mean?"

Danny heaved a sigh. Here it was. "I'm taking a sabbatical from work. Six months to start, with the option to extend to one year."

Tobin blinked, then his jaw dropped like it'd taken him a moment to process the information. "Seriously? You're taking time off work? Like for real?"

Danny laughed. "Yes, for real."

Tobin uncrossed his arms and leaned forward again. "Wow, that's...that's amazing. It's fantastic. Congrats."

Danny wasn't sure taking unpaid leave was worthy of congratulations, but he wasn't about to correct Tobin. "Thanks."

"Did they...put up a fuss?" Tobin propped his chin in his hand, elbow on the table.

Danny leaned forward to meet him. "A little. But I can be persuasive."

"Sure, right. Of course you can." Tobin rolled his eyes before narrowing them again. "What else did you and Wei talk about?"

Danny braced himself. "You."

Tobin didn't appear the least bit surprised. "Uh-huh. What about me?"

"How you're all grown up."

Tobin cocked one eyebrow.

"How we sometimes treat you like you aren't."

Tobin pursed his lips.

"And how we need to do better." Danny lowered his voice and put everything he was into his next words. "How *I* need to do better."

Tobin blinked once, twice. Then looked everywhere else but at him.

"Tobin." Danny reached across the table and grasped Tobin's hand. Thank god he didn't pull it away. "I was a complete asshole to you these past several months. I lied to you, went behind your back. I put my own needs above yours."

"Fuck," Tobin muttered as he tightened his grip on Danny. With his free hand, Tobin grabbed the napkin off the table and dabbed at his eyes. "I put on all this makeup too."

Should he stop? The last thing Danny wanted was to make Tobin cry.

When he didn't continue, Tobin glared at him. "Keep going. I didn't tell you to stop."

Danny swallowed the laugh that wanted to bubble up at the command. "I, um…" What the hell had he been saying? Oh yeah. "I told myself I had to do all those things because otherwise I'd lose my job. And I thought my job was the most important thing in the world. But I was wrong. You're the most important thing in the world."

Tobin sniffled loudly and pulled his hand away to blow his nose into the napkin. When he reached a hand out to Danny again, it was a little damp, but Danny took it anyway.

Danny took another steadying breath before continuing. "I know you've liked me for a long time. To be honest, I still don't entirely understand why."

Tobin pinned him with an *are you kidding* look. But Danny held him off with a wave of his hand. He needed to get the rest of this out. "At first, I thought, maybe it was the bad boy thing. Then I thought maybe it was because I was successful."

"It's not any of those things," Tobin interjected with a voice full of emotion.

"I know. But a part of me thought I could make myself more deserving if I was successful. But in order to be successful, I wouldn't have time for anything else. So, yeah…"

Tobin blew his nose again and Danny handed over his own napkin just in case.

"What about all the Wei bullshit?"

"The Wei bullshit." Danny nodded. "I mean, Wei was legitimately upset when he found out about us."

Tobin rolled his eyes.

"But…" And here was the truth Danny had spent the last couple days drawing out from the deepest depths of himself. "It was easier to use Wei as an excuse than to own up to how inadequate I felt."

His throat closed, and his eyes prickled. Tobin reached out and they held their grimy hands together in the middle of the table.

"Tobin, you're the most important person in the world to me. More important than Wei, than your parents. More important than my job. I was scared if I let myself want you too much, and then I lost you, I wouldn't survive. So I thought, I have Wei and your parents and my job. These are all things I'm lucky to have. Why try to push my luck?"

Tears started filling Danny's eyes, not enough to spill over but enough to make his vision blurry. "But that's not fair to you, is it? You deserve more than me settling for what's safe. You're worth the risk of trying, even if things don't work out. Tobin—" Danny blinked, and the tears fell. "I love you."

Chapter Twenty-Eight

Tobin dropped his head forward. He'd known this was coming. From the second he'd gotten in that god damn car, he'd known. Only a fool wouldn't have, and despite all the foolish things he'd done and believed in the past several months, he wasn't a fool.

Why else would Danny and Ray go to all that trouble to trick him into getting in the car? Why else would Wei have called exactly when he did?

The chip on his shoulder bristled at the thought of three older men coordinating behind his back to get him where they wanted him. They could have come directly to him, treated him like an equal. But then, if Tobin was honest with himself—and wasn't that what they were all doing today?—he probably wouldn't have listened to them. The chip needed to calm the fuck down. Sometimes people co-ordinating around him wasn't such a bad thing; sometimes it meant they cared.

"Tobin? I love you," Danny repeated himself.

"Yeah, I heard you." Tobin pulled his hands away from the messy pile of palms and fingers they'd made, leaned over and grabbed a clean napkin from the table next to them. His makeup was shot, but that was the least of his worries now.

He tried to clean himself up the best he could, then took a breath and stood up. He laughed at the look of alarm on Danny's face. "Relax, big boy. Come on. Follow me."

Tobin grabbed his coat from where it hung on a hook near their table and tried one of the doors leading out to the patio overlooking the water. The sun had dipped be-hind the mountains, casting long shadows everywhere. The wind was picking up and the trees rustled around them. Tobin pulled his coat tightly around him, raised his face, and took a deep breath of the cold, crisp air.

He felt a little hollow, like his gas tank was empty and he'd been running on fumes for a while. WesTec and Danny and Wei, the half-truths and the lies—it was all so exhausting. Tobin would never admit it to anyone, but there were times he wished he was a kid again; no respon-sibilities except to play and try not to get grounded. Adult-ing was hard and sometimes he wanted a break.

Danny's admission felt like that break, like a rest stop along the side of the highway where Tobin could pull over and refuel. Was that what being an adult was really about? Working together, depending on each other, mu-tually supporting? All it needed was the acknowledgment that, hey, Tobin couldn't do it alone. And of all the people in the world, he'd rather head back onto the road with Danny at his side.

It couldn't be that simple, could it? The answer had been sitting right in front of him this whole time. His childhood infatuation with Danny that only grew stronger the older he got. It had been love all along, except he'd been too stubborn to admit it. Maybe he'd been too scared too.

Danny came to stand beside him, and Tobin let him stew. Tobin had stewed for weeks while Danny figured his shit out, Tobin deserved a few more minutes. To his credit, Danny didn't rush him. It was only when the chill started penetrating Tobin's wool coat that he turned to lean one hip on the railing, facing Danny.

He knew it was true; it'd been true for as long as he could remember. The excitement at the mention of Danny's name. The pure joy that filled Tobin to overflowing when he was in Danny's arms. The satisfying comfort that came with being in the same room as Danny. It might have been the truth, but it was still terrifying to say out loud.

Tobin's gut twisted, and he could've sworn his heart stopped beating for a second. He forced his tongue to move. "I love you too, you fucking asshole."

What he wouldn't have given to capture the expression on Danny's face. It went from cautious to elated to confused with a touch of offended. Tobin laughed out loud, overcome with a lightness that moments before he would have said was impossible.

"Yeah, you heard me right. You're a fucking asshole and I love you." Now that it was out in the open, it was easier to say. Hell, he wanted to say it again and again, to scream it to the mountains.

Instead, Tobin took a step closer so they brushed against each other. He rested his hands on Danny's chest, rising and falling. Tobin matched his breathing to Danny's. "I always have. I didn't know what it was called as a kid, but I knew the feeling. It's the same feeling I have now."

Tobin tilted his head. "You're not the only one to blame for the fiasco we've made of things." Because adults owned up to their mistakes.

When Danny opened his mouth to object, Tobin put a finger on it to stop him. "You've had your turn, now it's mine." Danny pressed his lips together and nodded for Tobin to continue.

He was shaking again, like he'd been in the morning at WesTec. Danny took his hands, wrapping them in strong steady fingers, and slowly the shaking eased.

"I was scared too. I've spent my whole life trying to be one of the big boys, but what if I never measured up? What if I'd always be little baby Toby?"

Danny worked his jaw, like he had something to say and was trying really hard not to say it. Tobin smiled and kept going.

"Everything I've done as an adult is to prove to everyone that I'm an adult. But what if the only one who needed the proof was me?" Tobin took another step closer. "Adults admit when they're wrong, they admit when they need help. Adults work together and live in community and support one another. Or, at least healthy adults do."

Subdued laughter burst from Danny and Tobin returned it.

"I think I've been doing a pretty decent impersonation of being an adult. But I also think it's time I actually grew up."

Danny flashed a smile. "You're probably not the only one."

"I guess that means we should both try to be healthy adults?"

Danny nodded. "Yeah, we should."

"I love you, you fucking asshole."

"I love you too, little baby Toby."

"Fucker."

"You love me."

"Yeah, I do." Tobin closed the remaining space between them and pressed a snotty wet kiss to Danny's lips. It was the best kiss of Tobin's life. Warm and intimate, it sent a soul-deep satisfaction spiraling through him until he felt like he was floating on thin air.

When they finally came up for oxygen, the smile on Danny's face lit up the darkening sky. Who needed the sun when he had Danny?

"So," Tobin asked. "What are you going to do with all your free time now?"

Danny pretended to consider it. "I might travel. Take up yoga. Go vegan. I heard there are some places out west that are good for that kind of lifestyle."

"Oh yeah?"

"Yeah." Danny led them back inside. "You know of any?"

"Hm." Tobin relinquished his coat to Danny, who rehung it on the wall. "I don't know. I'll have to give it some thought."

They took their seats again. Their place settings were immaculate with fresh napkins and topped up water glasses.

"I'll probably need a roommate. You know, now that I'm unemployed."

"Oh sure, I can ask around for you. See if anyone has a spare room for rent."

"Make sure it's big, though. I'll be bringing my four-poster bed."

Tobin smirked. "I'm sure that can be arranged."

"Shh." Danny whispered against his mouth, but how the hell was he expected to stay silent when Danny was on top of him, fucking him into the mattress?

Danny thrusted and his thick cock grazed Tobin's prostate at exactly the right angle. He let out a whimper that was probably too loud. He was trying, he really was.

"Monica and Ayán are going to hear us again."

That's it. Tobin pushed Danny away so Danny was propped up on his hands. His cock was still buried in Tobin's ass, but it wasn't going to be for long if Danny kept this up.

"Enough about them. I don't need to hear their names when I'm getting railed by my boyfriend."

Danny glanced at the wall in the direction of Monica's room. "But they're going to hear us."

"Who cares? Do you know how many times I've heard them having sex?"

Danny winced, and Tobin's erection waned at the memory. Danny's did too, and he slipped out of Tobin's body.

"Sorry." Danny moved off Tobin, flopping onto his back.

So much for their daily sex-cap. They'd been horny as fuck the first week after Danny had moved out to Vancouver. Morning quickies before Tobin headed off to work. Discreet car sex when Danny picked him up from the office. Full-on, marathon-level lovemaking almost every night.

But then the realities of living with another couple had started sinking in, and the once spacious two-bedroom apartment was now much too cramped for four fully grown adults.

"We need to get our own place," Tobin said. It'd been their intention all along. After all, Danny had brought his four-poster bed—or rather, he'd ordered a replica of it— but it was too big for Tobin's bedroom.

If it'd been up to Danny, they'd probably already have a gorgeous penthouse condo set up and be moved in by now. But no, Tobin wanted to be involved in the whole process, wanted to make sure he could pay his fair share.

Danny had been good about it, going through the steps at Tobin's pace, even though Tobin could tell he itched to take the whole situation and handle it. Even now, he didn't say anything though Tobin could practically hear him think.

Maybe he needed to get over himself. Let Danny find them some extravagant condo. Because this current situation was driving everyone up the wall. "Sorry," he muttered.

Danny turned to look at him. "For what?"

Tobin smiled. That was sweet. "You know what."

"No, I don't. You'll have to tell me." Danny sat up and plucked his boxer briefs off the floor. "Be right back." Danny let himself quietly out of the room.

God, he must have done something right in a past life to end up here with Danny. When Danny had first brought up moving to Vancouver for Tobin, he'd been skeptical. Danny was used to a life lived at one hundred and fifty percent. What was he going to do with himself as an unemployed millionaire in sleepy Vancouver?

Apparently, Danny had that problem handled too. He'd had teaching gigs lined up at UBC, volunteer hours scheduled with local youth organizations, and was working with some big names in the Vancouver business community to establish a mentorship program for young entrepreneurs. He'd even taken up yoga. Danny's version of relaxing didn't sound all that relaxing to Tobin. But hey, who was he to judge?

WesTec had signed a new contract with Paradigm, and Tobin's travel schedule had him flying out to Calgary every other week. Danny had met him there a couple times before he'd relocated to Vancouver. They'd replayed some of their greatest hits.

Hm, Tobin's dick stirred at the memory. What was taking Danny so long? Tobin could give it another go.

"Ahh!"

"Ahh!"

Tobin jumped out of bed and rushed to the door. Wait, he was naked. Underwear. Where was his underwear? Ah, fuck it. He grabbed the duvet off the bed and wrapped it around himself.

"Jesus fucking Christ." Ayán was braced against the wall, hand covering her eyes.

"I'm sorry. I'm so sorry." Danny, dressed in nothing but boxer briefs, looked like he was trying to make himself as small as possible.

"What happened?" Tobin asked as Monica poked her head out of her bedroom door.

Danny looked sheepish. "I didn't turn the light on in the bathroom—"

"Or close the door! How was I supposed to know someone was in there if the door is wide open and the lights are off! How do you even pee like that! Gross!" Ayán still had her hand over her eyes like she literally could not stand the sight of Danny.

"Sorry." He genuinely looked remorseful.

"Okay." Tobin found the opening in his makeshift duvet toga and dragged Danny back to his room. "Sorry about that! Won't happen again!"

"Wait! You have to clean up the toilet! I still need to pee!" Ayán yelled after them.

Danny pulled away from Tobin and grabbed more clothes. "She's right. I can't leave it like that."

"Like what? What did you do?"

The embarrassment on Danny's face said it all.

"Never mind. Cleaning supplies are under the sink."

"When was the last time I cleaned a toilet?" Danny muttered as he left again, fully clothed this time.

Tobin shook his head. His hang-ups be damned. They were going to find their own place tomorrow.

Epilogue

Danny had never been so nervous in his entire life. Not when he first went to university with all the fancy rich kids. Not when he was interviewing for jobs. Not when he went into his first meeting as Joanna's shadow.

"Dude, relax." Wei clapped both hands on Danny's shoulders and gave him an impromptu and very ineffective massage.

He couldn't. Not when Tobin's flight had landed moments ago. Danny mentally calculated the time it would take for Tobin to get off the plane, make it through the airport corridors, collect his luggage, and meet Uncle Man, who was picking him up. Then it would take about twenty-five minutes for them to drive back to the Lok house—that is, if they didn't run into too much traffic.

"It's not like he's going to say no," Wei reminded him.

"You guys are already living together. And you're moving back here next month."

The rational part of his brain agreed. But the old Danny, the one who still couldn't quite believe how this was all turning out, wouldn't shut up and leave him alone.

He would have been more than happy to stay in Vancouver and play house boyfriend while Tobin won their bread for them. The students and youths he was working with were a good bunch and it was gratifying to be able to bring up the next generation of business leaders—and hopefully, help them avoid his own pitfalls along the way.

But then Tobin had sat him down one day with an idea. Paradigm had offered him a transfer to Toronto. He could continue his work with WesTec easily from there. The twins were growing up fast and he'd missed out on a lot already. And he was feeling like he'd outgrown Vancouver somehow.

Danny had recognized that ambitious itch for something more. And if that meant moving back to Toronto after a year out west, Danny couldn't say he minded. Toronto was still home, after all.

"Danny! Come here. Take this," Auntie Grace called to him from the foyer. She shoved a wrapped package into his hands before taking off her winter coat.

"What is it?"

"Open it!" she demanded, shuffling him into the living room where everyone was gathered.

The package was rectangular, with raised edges and a glass front. He turned it over and carefully peeled off the tape holding the brown paper together.

"Aiya, so slow." Auntie Grace took the picture frame from him the second the last of the paper fell away. "Look! Look!"

She held it up against her chest and Danny's breath caught in his throat.

He didn't remember the photo. It was old, the colors muted and the image a tad grainy. Danny's mom had a big smile on her face, and her arms were wrapped around a very young Danny standing in front of her. He'd still had his baby fat then; his cheeks were pudgy as he smiled.

His mom's hair must have been freshly permed, curling into a halo around her head. She wore the same oversized glasses Danny remembered from when he was a kid.

"Where—?" He searched the photo for clues of when it had been taken but came up empty.

"I found it in the basement," Auntie Grace proclaimed in triumph. "You don't remember?"

"No. Where was it taken?"

"Aiya, in Algonquin Park! Your mommy almost didn't make it. She got a call from work that morning, but she said she was busy."

Danny's mom never did that. She picked up every extra shift she could get her hands on. He took the photo from Auntie Grace, careful not to drop it or get finger smudges on the glass.

He had a vague recollection of that trip. They'd rented canoes—he and Wei paddling with Tobin sitting in the middle in a life jacket several sizes too big. He didn't re-member her being there, though. He felt the loss so viscerally, like someone had physically siphoned the memory from his brain.

"She is with you, eh, Danny?" Auntie Grace said in a lowered voice. "She always has been and always will be. She loved you so much."

Danny nodded. He knew she did. He only wished they'd had more time together.

Auntie Grace pulled him into a hug and it was almost like she was channeling his mom. "She was so proud of you, you know? You did so good in school and you got a good job. She's proud of you now too." Auntie Grace pulled away to pat Danny on the cheek. "We're all proud of you, okay? You were always my third son. And today you become legally my son!"

Well, it didn't quite work that way, but Danny wasn't about to correct her.

"Okay, come." She took the frame from him again and marched over to the family piano, an old upright Wei and Tobin had been forced to play as kids. "We put mommy here, okay? That way she can see everything."

She placed the photo in an empty spot on the already crowded piano top, almost as if the spot had been waiting for a photo of Danny's mom. It was surrounded by pictures of the entire Lok clan, including grandparents who were no longer with them and distant aunties and uncles.

Now Danny and his mom were part of the family too.

Danny glanced down the length of the piano at all the other photos. He'd seen them before; they'd been there for as long as he could remember. But this time, as his gaze wandered from one frame to the next, he realized he was in more than half of the pictures.

He was wrong. He'd always been a part of the family. The proof had been sitting right in front of him the whole time and he hadn't recognized it. God, what a fool he was.

But no. He pushed the thought away. That was the past and he was focused on the future. His hand drifted to the small box in his pocket, making sure it was where he had left it.

"They're getting close!" Wei announced.

Someone let out a little shriek and everyone shuffled into their places. Auntie Grace directed him to his spot closest to the front door. She stood right next to him, and on his other side was Wei, who gave him one last encouraging slap on the shoulder.

Constance and the twins were there, the kids leaning over the back of the couch to peek out the window. Monica and Ayán rounded out the group. After the bathroom incident, Danny had slowly but surely won Ayán over, and they'd jumped at the offer of a free trip to Toronto.

Danny took the box out of his pocket and popped it open to make sure the ring was still inside. A burst of doubt flashed through him. Was he ready? Was Tobin ready? Maybe he was rushing this, and he should wait until they'd settled back in town.

But damn it, they'd already waited most of their lives. What else was there to wait for?

"You got this," Wei whispered behind him.

Danny nodded. He was shaking. This was the single scariest thing he had ever attempted in his life. Everyone fell silent. The wall clock ticked away the seconds as Danny held his breath.

Finally, a car pulled into the driveway and the engine cut out. Doors opened and slammed, accompanied by muffled voices.

"Jesus, it's cold!"

A chorus of snickers echoed at Tobin's loud complaint, only to be silenced by Auntie Grace's "shh."

"Why the hell did I agree to move to this arctic tundra?"

Danny's head spun, his heart raced. He forced himself to take in a lungful of air.

Then the door opened. The room erupted. Tobin shrieked at the top of his lungs.

"Ahh!" He flung his arms in front of him in self-defense, and the suitcase he was dragging crashed to the floor with a bang. "What the fuck!"

"Toby! Language!" Auntie Grace rushed forward and grabbed Tobin's arms to lower them.

"What is going on? Mom?"

"Aiya, go inside. I can't close the door with your suitcase blocking it." Uncle Man pushed him forward, muttering something about the heating bill.

Auntie Grace dragged Tobin further into the house while waving Danny over. "Danny has something to say."

"Danny?" Tobin looked like he was about to smack him. "Oh my god, what is everyone doing here?"

So much for the romantic proposal Danny had envisioned. But somehow, this was better. It was now or never.

"Tobin." It came out as a croak. Danny held out a hand.

Tobin reached for it the way opposite sides of a magnet reached for each other.

Danny cleared his throat and tried again. "Tobin." He could do this. He *had* to do this. "I've known you since the day you were born, and I've had the honor of watching you grow up from the annoying little kid brother into the amazing man you are today."

Tobin's eyes grew wide and he took a step backward. "What?"

Danny took advantage of the extra space and got down on one knee.

"Oh my god. Ohmygod, ohmygod, ohmygod." Tobin leaned away from Danny but kept his grip on Danny's hand as tight as ever.

Behind him, their family and friends provided a soundtrack of whispers, giggles, and sniffles. Better than any love song Danny could think of.

"Danny?" Tobin's voice was small, no more than a squeak, and he started blinking rapidly, the way he did when trying not to cry.

"Growing up, I thought I didn't have a family because I didn't have a big house filled with parents, siblings, and a ton of relatives. Instead, I tagged along with your family, waiting for the day you would realize I was an interloper and kick me out. But you never did. You invited me deeper into the fold even when I resisted, even when I didn't believe I deserved it."

Tears trickled down Tobin's cheeks and Danny reached up to wipe them away with his thumb.

"You recognized something in me I didn't know existed.

Your bravery forced me to face my own insecurities. Your love gave me the courage to go after my heart's desire."

Fuck, now he was crying too. Danny sniffled. "Tobin—"

"Oh god." Tobin covered his mouth with his free hand.

Danny's voice shook. Hell, his whole body was shaking. "Tobin Lok, I love you."

A sound halfway between a sob and hiccup escaped from Tobin.

"You are the best thing that has ever happened to me."

Tobin squeezed his eyes shut and sniffled loudly.

"You taught me what family is, and I wouldn't have one if not for you."

Tobin gave Danny's hand a hard shake. He got the message—*hurry the fuck up.* Danny wrested his hand from Tobin's grip of steel and opened the box.

On the white satin-covered padding sat a thin black band with black diamonds set at regular intervals all around.

Tobin gasped loud enough to silence the entire room. His eyes looked like they were going to pop out of his head.

"Tobin, will you be my family? Will you marry me?"

Tobin nodded, looking from the ring to Danny and back again, like he wasn't sure if he wanted to kiss Danny or kiss the ring.

Thank god Danny won out.

Tobin threw himself into Danny's arms, pressing a messy, snotty, teary kiss onto his mouth. Danny pressed an equally messy, snotty, teary kiss back. He hugged Tobin like he never wanted to let go—he didn't, and he wouldn't. He'd spend every second of the rest of his life making sure Tobin was happy. Because Tobin made him happier than he ever thought possible.

When they finally broke the kiss for some air, someone asked, "Is that a yes?"

"It's a fuck yes! About time!" Tobin shouted.

"Aiya, Toby. Watch your language. I should have taught you better."

Tobin ignored Auntie Grace and pressed his forehead to Danny's. "Yes, yes, always, forever." He gave Danny another quick kiss before letting out a squeal. "Let me see that ring! Oh my god, you didn't!"

Danny took the ring from the box and slid it onto Tobin's finger. A perfect fit. Like the two of them.

"I love you." Danny kissed Tobin's hand where the ring met skin.

Tobin took Danny's hand and kissed where a matching ring would eventually sit. "I love you too."

★ ★ ★ ★ ★

Dear Reader,

Hard Sell was inspired by my years working in the finance industry, rubbing elbows with the rich and über-rich. I never made it anywhere near Danny's level of success, but I experienced that initial fascination and wonder of taking off to a different city every week, staying at hotels way out of my personal price range, and tossing down credit cards like the plastic grew on trees.

Eventually, like Danny, all that glitz and glamour wore off. I've spent entire days in an airport waiting for a delayed flight; scrambled for a last-minute hotel room when I got stuck in a foreign city; and woken up having no clue where in the world I was. Border agents would ask me where I was headed and I'd draw a blank; "I don't know, wherever the plane spits me out." No amount of platinum credit cards could make up for the grind.

Do you know what that's like? If you can sympathize, I'd love to commiserate with you. You can find me on Twitter, Instagram and Facebook at @HudsonLinWrites or through my website at www.hudsonlin.com.

If you'd like more of the Jade Harbour world, Ray's story is coming up next in *Going Public*.

Happy reading!
Lin

Acknowledgments

This book wouldn't exist if it weren't for Stephanie Doig, reaching out to me while I was in the dredges of the day job, desperately looking for a way out. She offered me an opportunity to pitch for Carina Adores and I decided to funnel my day job frustrations into a romance novel. If I couldn't have a work-related HEA, at least my characters could. Thank you for holding my hand throughout and putting up with my author drama.

Thank you to Tanya, Allison, Jenn, Roberta, Mel, Sadie, Nazri, and Sam for listening to me gripe and validating all my woes. Thank you to Margrit, Jane, Shirley, and Jess for encouraging words and cheering me on all the way to the end.

Oscar is a grouch. Jack is an ass. Together, they're a bickering, combative mess…until a one-night stand that might just lead to more feelings than either of them are ready for.

Keep reading for an excerpt from
The Hate Project *by Kris Ripper.*

Once upon a time there was a grumpy old thirty-something called Jack and a tragically misunderstood (but younger) hermit called Oscar and they bickered so much that their friends told them to get a room, so on a particularly bad night they did. Stay tuned next week to see what happens to our hero (Oscar) and The Broker Who Pitied Him (Jack).

Not that I'd ever go on a show about relationships and neither would Jack. It's one of the few things we have in common. And before you say no one would do that in real life, one of my closest friends found the *cough, gag* love of his life on a YouTube advice show. He actually fell for the advice-giver, which should be against the rules, but apparently isn't.

Anyway, this thing with me and Jack started out as a one-off after yet another cutesy gathering hosted by Dec and

Sidney, my "YouTube brought us together *aww*" friends. For two people who didn't technically cohabitate they co-hosted a lot of crap, and this particular event was in my honor.

Or rather, in honor of me being laid off and falling into a pit of despair. I know pits of despair are about as clichéd as bell jars, but if the metaphor works, why screw around?

First I should say this: I hated my job. Hated-hated it. Hated it so much that there were days when I seriously considered driving into the cement barriers on the side of the freeway because the thought of literally dying sounded better than going to work for another nine hours of sitting in a cubicle taking customer service calls. And I'm not saying that like it's a joke to me; I've had intense anxiety all my life and thinking, *Death would be better than this excruciating (mundane) situation I must now force myself to endure* isn't actually all that rare.

I try not to let it get to the point where I'm fantasizing about the impact of my vehicle hitting a solid object, but I had nightmares about my job. Nightmares during which customers yelled at me for sending them a pillow in the wrong shade of periwinkle blue, or tried to return things because this blanket didn't feel soft as a baby's bottom (was that a common blanket-softness standard? and if it was: *creepy*), or that picture frame was *white* not *white-washed* like the description on the website.

Those are actual situations that happened, which became nightmares later. Or does that make them flashbacks? Whatever they were, I'd wake up sweating and nauseous like the customer was still on the phone demanding I go back in time and psychically intuit that when they clicked "twin size" on the Thomas Kincaid knockoff duvet cover they were ordering, they really meant "king size." *Shudder.*

I was sitting at my desk in my cubicle ("my" in a loose sense—we were not permitted to "personalize" our "work-spaces" in any way) on a Friday afternoon when an email popped up from my direct supervisor, Brad. He'd been my supervisor for about three weeks and he was *such* a Brad. He had that non-threatening straight guy thing going for him that seemed statistically likely to mean he was a serial killer.

Or, okay, not really, but serial killers were statistically likely to seem non-threatening, right? And Brads are, by their nature, a non-threatening branch of the human tree. He was the everydude.

Brad, being a supervisor, had a very small office. More of an upright coffin for a very large person. The chair he invited me to sit in had to be moved to the side in order to close the door and then, uncomfortably, it blocked the door when moved back into position.

"This seems like a fire hazard," I said as I sat down.

"A...what?"

"A fire hazard. As in, if there was a fire it would be hard for us to get out of this room."

"Why would there be a fire?" he asked. As if *I* was the idiot.

"I think most fires in office buildings are unplanned." I thought I'd mostly managed to keep the *you idiot* addendum from my tone, but maybe I hadn't.

"I don't think we have to worry about a fire right now, Oscar."

I shrugged. "I'm sure that's what nearly anyone would say right before burning to a crisp in a fire, but okay. We won't worry about it." Obviously I'd already mentally re-hearsed how I'd stand, turn, push the chair aside, swing the door open, and bolt for the stairs, but since everyone else would also be bolting for the stairs *and* they'd have the advantage of not having to escape from an upright coffin, I doubted my chances.

It should probably be noted that I was never A) athletic or B) of a particularly spry build, but even if I was both of those things, I'd still be seriously screwed by the misfor-tune of being wedged in Brad's office.

At which point I realized he was looking at me a bit too intently. "Did you hear what I said? About the papers?"

"Uhh. Papers? No, sorry." *Too busy thinking about where they'd find my remains, but I'm pretty sure they'd find yours right here in your office.*

"I know this is a difficult time—wait, I think I said that already—"

A difficult time? I should have been paying closer at-tention. "Can you start over?" I asked as he ran one fin-ger with stumpy, straight-guy nails down an actual script.

This did not bode well. There couldn't be too many dif-ficult times your supervisor needed a script for.

"We're in a very challenging position right now," he said earnestly. "The economy being what it is, and consumers not buying as many home goods, you understand our po-sition in the market has been challenging."

It was like a slow-motion train derailment; I knew what was coming, but I couldn't help hoping that at the last mo-ment something would change and the train would stay on the tracks.

"Which is why I need to tell you that—" quick check of the script "—your time here has come to an end."

I stared at him for a long moment. "I think I would have preferred the fire."

I drove home in a daze, trying to figure out what this meant. It was a terrible job, a job I wasn't suited for, that had given me panic attacks on a near-daily basis for the first three months I'd worked there. Which would have probably sent me looking for another job if it wasn't for two things: my loathing for and increased anxiety about job hunting, and the lack of assurance I had that the next place wouldn't be equally bad.

There are people who have a lot of anxiety and can also go to work like normals. (And yes, blah internalized blah blah, but I don't mean "normal" like it's better than being an anxiety-ridden wreck. I *like* being an anxiety-ridden wreck. Wouldn't have myself any other way.) My friend Dec has a certain type of anxiety and you wouldn't know it to look at him. But me?

Let's just say if you saw a round, soft, eye-contact-avoiding guy walking down the street, hands in his pockets, head down, skirting to the edge of the sidewalk to not get too close to people, you might think to yourself, *Hey, that guy looks anxious.* And if that guy was me, you'd be right. Or you'd think, *Hey, that guy might be a serial killer,* in which case you'd be wrong because they usually look normal, like Brad.

You see what I mean about not wanting to be one of the normals?

All that to say this: I hated my job. If ever there was a

job that a regular person would *want* to be laid off from, it was this job. Which I hated. And yet all I could think about as I was driving home was how terrible it would be to look for a new job—I'd have to go to interviews, shake hands with people I didn't know and then sit there trying not to be distracted by the fact that I'd just touched some random and their skin flora was now co-mingling with my skin flora like an invasive species of plant, out of my control and changing things that didn't need to be changed.

Shaking hands is one of the worst forms of "politeness" ever invented. What is the point, other than the gratuitous touching of strangers? Saying "Hi, good to meet you" isn't enough, you gotta add some unnecessary physical interaction in there? You realize that even if the person you're shaking hands with washed after taking a shit, the other eight hundred people who also touched that bathroom door today didn't 100% comply with the signs, and even if most of them *did*, there are actual procedures to that sort of thing, soap coverage and friction and duration and…

Why is shaking hands even a thing? I don't want to touch your hands. No offense. And you can't say that at a job interview. "Thanks for interviewing me; I don't want to touch your hands."

Something else you can't say at job interviews: "Occasionally I take an extra-long bathroom break because I can't breathe, but don't worry, I'll be fine in a few minutes." I mean, I guess I've never actually tried to say that, but I just assume it's a bad idea, given I live in a country that routinely mocks all manner of physical, mental, and psychological challenges.

When I got back to my apartment after discovering that my time with my job had come to an end I sat very still on my couch for a long time. It was that or make a cake and then eat the whole thing. I know it's a cliché for a person of average-but-more-than-television-girth to stress eat, but I've been stress eating since I was five and my kindergarten teacher, sympathetic to slow eaters, would let me sit in the corner to finish my lunch if I took too long eating. I'd stuff extra food in my lunch so I could take a really long time and thus spare myself over half of the "sustained silent reading" period.

Sustained silent reading is hell for kids who hate (and/or are shitty at) silent reading. I got my extended lunch down to a science until I was just packed up and pulling out a book when it was time to move on to the next subject.

So, cliché or not, it's ingrained in me to spend my time eating when I am in a state of fear or anxiety. Losing my job induced both.

I did manage to text Ronnie, because it's what my former therapist, who moved and was never replaced, would have told me to do. Ronnie was my emotional contact person in times of trouble, if you will, and when she had times of trouble I was hers, though now she and Mia were married so I guess I'd been replaced in the old emotional support human role.

The system we had worked out was that I would text with whatever was happening and a green/yellow/red light for how welcoming I was to the idea of being contacted back. I sent: Laid off. Mostly numb. Hate job hunting. Yellow. Which basically indicated that she could reply but shouldn't worry if I didn't engage in a conversation.

She sent back: Fuck those fucking fuckers and a heart emoji.

You know your friends love you when they have a million questions they want to ask and they're super worried about you and they distill all of those things down to one non-demanding, high-curse-word-load sentence.

And a heart emoji.

As a rule I hate emojis because they're overused and I don't always know what they mean. But the heart emoji was…well, even I knew how to interpret a heart from my oldest friend.

After sending my text—doing my "self-care due diligence," my old therapist used to say before she moved to Portland and abandoned me—I resumed staring into space until my phone vibrated sometime later.

Dec: Throwing you a pity party. Making pizzas. Tomorrow at six.

The advantage to my particular friend group—the Motherfuckers—was that I wouldn't need to tell anyone else; now they all knew I'd been laid off. The disadvantage was they'd now try to show their love in different ways, and Declan's was food and parties. On the other hand, he made great pizza, I had nothing better to do, and I would be safe with my people. Better to be at his place than out in the world somewhere.

Still, it was a bit presumptuous that he just assumed I wanted to be part of a social gathering, so I punished him by not responding.

Within twenty minutes I got See you tomorrow! heart emoji messages from both Mason and Mia. That was the entire OG Motherfuckers crew reporting for duty. And yeah, okay, I was pretty numb from the low buzz of looming fucked-upedness, but it wasn't a bad thing, knowing my friends were thinking about me.

At least, that's what I thought until I was up all night imagining horrific job interview scenarios, trying to figure out what I'd do if I couldn't find work, and picturing what it would be like living in the guest bedroom at Ronnie's. The way my friends would eventually turn against me because I couldn't support myself, how I'd become this embarrassing hanger-on at drinks whom they couldn't disinvite, but who also couldn't pay his own way...

I woke up (that's a fancy phrase for what was essentially just regaining a muggy sense of consciousness without any accompanying alertness) around ten the next morning feeling unable to see anyone, including my friends. Possibly ever again.

Anxiety has different faces for everyone, and this is probably the most messed-up feature of mine: telling me again and again, persuasively, that the Motherfuckers—the first people who ever accepted and loved me for who I was—are on the verge of disowning me. No matter how much I know it's not true, it still seems real.

Since my friends had been at war with that voice for years, all of them checked in throughout the day, even when I didn't respond. Which led to a whole other round of "I'm not good enough to have wonderful friends like these," so by the time I was forcing myself to drive over for the Oscar's Laid Off Gathering, I'd been yo-yoing between extremes of "they're too good for me and I should be thankful" and "they secretly hate me and I should move to another country and change my name" all day long.

But then I got to Declan's and couldn't make eye contact with anyone and they sat me in a corner with a bottle of sparkling water, making noise around but not at me. I really, really didn't deserve them.

I'd never had friends until college. And even then, I wouldn't have had friends except that Ronnie and I were freshman year roommates (before she transitioned, obviously), and she was friends with Dec and Mase and Mia, and they came around a lot and just sort of looped me in. It happened slowly over that first year and suddenly I had...friends.

What's that thing with snake poison, where you take it in small doses every day to grow your immunity to it? That's what happened with the Motherfuckers. Eventually I built up a tolerance to their, like, happiness and friendliness and optimism. Now my brain just recognizes them as a part of me. The same thing probably happened to them: eventually they built up a tolerance to my moods and freak-outs.

The most important thing you need to know about my friends is that they're all way better people than I am. You can tell because they threw me a pity party. There's the aforementioned Declan and Sidney, who got together during the commission of a video series called *The Love Study* on Sidney's YouTube channel. Then there's Mia and Ronnie, disgustingly married to each other. And the last of the official Motherfuckers is Mason, who once tried to get married (to Dec) and was left at the altar (by Dec). Which was awkward for a while, but now it's fine. Though of all of us Mase is the one who wants a white picket fence and 2.5 kids.

Sounds fucking awful to me, but to each his own, I don't judge, whatever floats your life raft, et cetera.

Since I didn't want to get my impotent rage-slash-panic germs on anyone, I took up a seat in the corner and didn't leave it except to use the bathroom and acquire victuals. By which I mean vegan, gluten-free, cauliflower-based pizza that turned out to be delicious. It used to be that my friends had an informal rotation for who'd sit with me, trading off for the duration of the social event, but that was before Jack. Jack was new to the group. Dec had collected him from work, and for reasons I didn't understand (I would have suspected sexual favors if I didn't know better), he kept mostly showing up to drinks with the Motherfuckers. And was now also on the invite list for ad hoc gatherings to celebrate catastrophic job loss.

Jack and I had no other setting with each other than arguing. Since neither of us was all that nice (and everyone else in the Motherfuckers was very nice), it worked out. He thinks he knows everything, I definitely know everything, and even though for the most part we would arrive at the same point from different angles, we spent most of our fights poking at each other's angles to prove they were incorrect.

I probably shouldn't have been surprised when it turned out bickering was actually foreplay.

Since the party was in my honor I was obligated to stay through dinner, and I did. In my corner. Weathering the well-intended reassurances of my friends was hard enough, but when Dec brought out one of those quirky adult card games where kittens exploded I had to get the hell out of there. Too much goodness on a bad day.

Jack apparently had a similar thought. It wasn't the first time we'd made our escape at the same moment. This time, instead of parting ways on the sidewalk with a lukewarm *we know each other through friends* wave, both of us stopped.

He stopped a second before I did, which I immediately decided made him more desperate. It wasn't charitable, but I believe in keeping track of who has the advantage in any encounter. Even a one-off.

"I live ten minutes away," he said.

"Good for you."

His lips twisted a little, from not-smile to not-impressed. "This is a pity fuck, Oscar. Take it or leave it." With that he turned and made for a black two-door something-something on the other side of the street.

I hesitated. For about five seconds. But following up a pity party with a pity fuck sounded about right. "Just to clarify," I called as I caught up with him, "I don't do relationships."

He hit a button that unlocked his car. "Just to clarify, I'm not offering one."

Don't miss The Hate Project *by Kris Ripper,*
available wherever Carina Adores books are sold.

www.CarinaPress.com

Also available from Hudson Lin
Three Months to Forever

Ben is looking for an adventure when he accepts a temporary assignment in Hong Kong, but he never anticipated how his life might change when he meets a sophisticated older man named Sai. Their initial attraction is sizzling and soon grows into more as Sai takes Ben on a tour of the city's famous landmarks and introduces him to the local cuisine. Sai stimulates Ben's intellect and curiosity, and for jaded corporate lawyer Sai, Ben's innocent eagerness is a breath of fresh air. It would be so easy to fall in love…

But nothing is that simple. Sai's job forces him to do things that violate his morals, and his relationship with his family is a major obstacle to any lasting relationship with Ben. For Ben, he misses his family back in Toronto, and can he really leave behind his home for a man he's only known for a short time? With the clock ticking, they must decide whether to risk it all and turn three months into forever.

To purchase this and other books by Hudson Lin, please visit www.hudsonlin.com/books.

Discover another great contemporary romance from Carina Adores.

Oscar is a grouch.

That's a well-established fact among his tight-knit friend group, and they love him anyway.

Jack is an ass.

Jack, who's always ready with a sly insult, who can't have a conversation without arguing, and whom Oscar may or may not have hooked up with on a strict no-commitment, one-time-only basis. Even if it was extremely hot.

Together, they're a bickering, combative mess.

But maybe while working together to clean out the house of Jack's grandmother, they can stop fighting long enough to turn that one-night stand into a frenemies-with-benefits situation…

The Hate Project by Kris Ripper is available now!

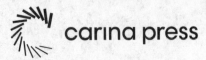

CarinaPress.com

CARKR0621TR